RECLAMATION

From Darkness   Book 3

Roxanne Ward

Idaho, USA

Copyright © 2025 by Roxanne Ward

December 2025

Cover image by Ashleigh Ward

Cover design by Vivian Ward

ISBN paperback   Bowker: 979-8-9880010-4-1 KDP: 979-8278284420

Genres: Science fiction, dystopian fiction, speculative fiction, post-apocalyptic fiction, military fiction, romantic fiction, mystery fiction, suspense fiction

NOTICE: This novel contains adult sexual content, unethical behavior, offensive language, and military violence.

File 3

Other Books by Roxanne Ward

Both series trilogies take place in the same setting of post-apocalyptic Colorado with crossover characters and events, but their stories and perspectives are unique. Visit me at <u>Roxannewardauthor.com</u>

The ***From Darkness*** series. Set in the wilderness of Colorado, it is an action-packed, page-turner with romance, espionage, escapes, rescues, battles, humor, and so much more.

1: ***Sins of Survival***   2: ***Lion's Creed***   3: ***Reclamation***

The ***Highmind*** series tells Connor's story, a genetically enhanced child, tasked with decoding the rebel secrets in his memories. This is a clean story with a Christian backstory and is appropriate for all readers. Flesch-Kincaid reading level: middle school and above.

1: ***Somewhere Else***   2: ***New Haven***   3: ***Journey to Cali Bantu***

Dedication

to Ashleigh

"Every noble work is at first impossible." ~ Thomas Carlyle

Prologue

I t was a fluke that the tyrannical Corporate Elites discovered the secret town of New Haven. The Corporates were unaware that a town existed within the old Eisenhower tunnels. All their reports confirmed it was a poison bunker based on the radioactive material that leaked from it. But that story was a careful ruse manufactured to hide a democratic community from the oppressive Corporate government.

It began when a team of mercenaries went to investigate suspicious activity surrounding an anomaly their drones detected. The off-site base was where the first time the Corporate's Garrison Army and New Haven's Defenders fought. The Defenders won, taking out every Dranger soldier and abandoning their off-site offices. When no report was received from the mercenary team, the enemy sent a larger force to both sides of the tunnel to uncover the mystery.

The New Haven Defenders had no chance of winning a fight against the Corporates. Outnumbered and outgunned, their small town's professional soldiers topped out at sixty-three. But they fought bravely until fate handed them a miracle, or two, more like three.

The enemy soldiers marched the last ten miles to the tunnel on foot, trying to stay under the radar of the Fringers, named because they lived on the fringes of the territories. The Corporates made an unprecedented non-interference contract with them when the Fringers threatened to release one of their nasty secrets. If published, it would collapse the fearful hold they had over their enslaved citizens and send them into a fevered insurrection. That prevented the Garrison's from bringing their more formidable weapons and a bigger army. That was the first miracle.

Through careful manipulation by the Corporate rule, they believed the Fringers were marauders who robbed Dailys and kidnapped their families. That belief continued with the citizens of New Haven until recently. Fate threw the two armies together, and New Haven was spared. They let go of their destructive prejudice and fought together through the tragedy of battle to victory. That was the second miracle.

The third was the storm. An angry wall of wind and snow blocked the Corporates from sending more troops. But this blessing came at a price. New Haven was discovered, and the Fringers had exposed their organized militia. They both had poked the Corporate bear, and every man, woman, and child was now the primary target of a formidable enemy.

It had been a week since the battle at the tunnel, and the death of his ten soldiers still ached through the Fringer Guard's commander. Will was raw and wounded by the bullets of emotion ripping through his heart. The pain of second-guessing and visions of death festered inside him. Still echoing in him were the soft and gripping funeral cries from loved ones. The loss left everyone with conflicting viewpoints, of being both tragically proud and rightfully angry. Though each soldier volunteered to go, it was Will's stubbornness that led and pushed the council into the untenable scenario while hiding facts they deserved to know.

A year ago, Will helped broker a repugnant deal with the Corporates to keep the overloads from wiping them out. They enjoyed many months of peace, but its guarantee was unraveling more each day. It was only a matter of time before the Corporates eradicated the Fringers and eliminated the threatening information they held.

With this certainty, Will convinced the council that Fringers needed to be ready to defend themselves, and with their approval, his army grew. When they grew too large, he sought a place to house and train his troops. Establishing a military base was greatly debated because if the Corporates discovered they were forming an army, it would change the status quo. But in the end, he got permission to look for an old warehouse in an abandoned town.

After weeks of searching for the right home for his soldiers, he stumbled upon a wounded Dranger. Will, who was an ex-Dranger, showed the mercenary soldier his Dranger tattoos. Knowing he was dying and needing to report his findings, the man told Will the location of the rebel facility they had found. He gave him the key card he had stolen during the assault, and his last gesture pointed Will toward the rebel stronghold.

The buildings were heavily camouflaged and extremely modern. As described by the dead soldier, it showed signs of a battle. It was a risky place to be because despite the dying soldier believing he was the last man alive, it might still have been reported. It seemed too good to be true, but it was too ideal to leave. They occupied the stronghold for months, and no one came back, not the Corporates or the previous inhabitants.

After his tech man broke into the computer files, they gathered evidence that the previous tenants may have fled to the tunnel. It was Will's goal to make these well-supplied people their allies. Their first attempts at contact were unsuccessful. But when Will received reports that the Corporate Garrisons were heading toward the area, Will asked to send their soldiers to assist the tunnel dwellers.

The council denied Will's request. It was his Guard soldiers who solved his problem. They resigned so they could take up arms as citizens and join the Avalanche Strike mission. In the meeting after the battle, the council reinstated them at their previous ranks, conceding they had the right to go "hunting" as well as defend themselves. They also conceded that Commander William Alexander had not broken the rules directly, but he willfully ignored the intent of the rule and seized upon a loophole. The council had been deceived, and they were justifiably angry.

The leaders of both free communities had been examining their new alliance, and it was time to discuss how to proceed for the mutual benefit of the Fringer Township, New Haven, and their armies, the Guard and the Defenders.

Will had talked with Gray and Bannon several times using the secure hardline between New Haven and the Hold, which had been renamed Fort Sentry. When a temporary break in the weather presented itself, Taylor, Relic, and Will were invited to the tunnel town of New Haven.

The council was vehemently against any Fringer attending the post-battle meeting being held at New Haven, let alone the leader of their army. They wanted to back away from their part in the battle, believing they could return to a peaceful truce with the Corporates. Hundreds of Fringers from all over the Township stormed the Council House and demanded that Will be sent to the meeting. They knew they were at the mercy of William and his Guards because there was no other person who could lead this unavoidable army in these uncertain times.

Will expected the meeting to be held in a tent outside the town, as he did before, but he was told they would be shown around as guests of honor and return to Fort Sentry the next day. As they stepped into the vehicle Commander Gray had sent for them, they were stunned by its newness and high-tech instruments. Their new allies were obviously well-funded. With their unified armies and their new friends' formidable technology, hope may have a fighting chance.

Chapter One

Will over thought his attire for the meeting of his career. He didn't want to appear overly militant or inappropriately casual. He wanted to show respect and strength. He landed on black jeans and a collarless white button-up shirt. Leita said he looked more delicious than scary. He laughed and told her he'd remember that.

Looking out of the large utility vehicle, his post-battle penitent mood returned. It was why he liked to drive rather than ride. He set his mind on imagining what a tunnel town would look like. He wondered if it would be dark and dank because underground places were like that. He thought about Hunter, one of his soldiers, who was too badly injured to return to the fort. He was being cared for at their hospital, where he was reported to be in good health and ready to go home. *How could he heal in a place like that?*

Still staring through the window and lost in his thoughts, he didn't notice they arrived until the vehicle pulled up to the entrance at the barrier. He briefly opened his window to take a deep breath of clean air. The driver went through several layers of security before being allowed into a small underground corridor. They traveled down the dimly lit passageway, and again they had to pass through more layers of security. Will was impressed.

But when the driver pulled into the town, Will was astonished. It was bright and beautiful, and when he propped open his window, the air smelled fresh, and the oxygen level seemed higher than the air outside. *Interesting.* They drove past windowed enclosures where people tended livestock. Then the corridor opened up to a bustling little city. It took him a minute to notice that every structure utilized shipping containers for its construction, but the final product was stunning.

The homes and offices featured colorful and creative designs with windows, porches, and balconies, and they were decorated with attractive foliage and other décor. The ceiling did not fool one into thinking it was the sky, but it provided a cheerful ambiance. People were bustling about, working and strolling together. It was like a scene from a forgotten time.

They were met by the Defender, Gabe. Will remembered his name as the one who reported the status of his troops at the east entrance. Gabe explained that they would eat lunch and then see Hunter before attending the meeting at Town Hall.

The organizers decided to allow the visitors to walk through the town and understand its scope. It was a notable show of trust. They walked the streets, passing municipal buildings regularly interrupted by blocks of housing, while attracting the stares of the citizens, unaccustomed to outsiders. Arriving at the dining area, they were inundated by school children weaving past them, stealing glances, and giggling as they were herded to the park next door.

The dining area was nicely decorated with slate flooring and separated from the street by a faux weathered fence laced with green ivy. Scattered within the dining space were dozens of tables, charmingly accented with jars of wildflowers that looked stunningly realistic. A lattice wall woven with delicate vines gave privacy to the tables where they were seated.

The server arrived with water, and the day's lunch choices flashed on the electronic unit she set before them. The main course options included chicken, sausage, or a peanut butter and jam sandwich. The sides were raw carrots and reconstituted pears. Before Will could ask, Gabe assured them that Corporate additives were not used at New Haven. Gabe said something about hating it as a Daily, but he didn't give any hint that he knew how nefarious it really was.

Will, Taylor, and Relic asked as many questions as the time for lunch would allow before they were back walking down the street. As they passed the Rapid Aid Center, which seemed small for a hospital, Will wondered where Hunter was being kept. His concerns were soon answered when they turned down a side street corridor, and he saw a mint green and blue building that extended beyond his view. It was labeled the Asilo Hospital of Goodwill.

When they were completely out of the corridor, Will was stunned by its impressive size. While most of the structures were two shipping containers wide and two high, this one had multiple sections on either side that were three wide and higher than the neighboring roofs. Though it encroached on the street, it didn't block the traffic in any significant way. In between the two sections was an alcove where an emergency cart was parked at one end, leaving the front double doors easily accessible. Two potted plants flanked a bed of pink flowers dividing the alcove and the street.

Inside the lobby, Gabe talked to the receptionist, who buzzed them through the door to where the admitted patients were housed. They took a short walk to the elevator and rode it to the second floor. Down another hallway, they were led into a room where Hunter was being fussed over by two nurses.

"Slacker," Will said, crossing the room in two large strides. "All this pampering and flirting is going to ruin you. I might have to go back to calling you Softheart." Will smiled and joked, but he could see Hunter's bandaged neck, and his leg was heavily wrapped up from ankle to mid-thigh. Concerned about his wounds, Will shook his hand gently. The nurses left, and the four talked about the battle, the comrades they lost, and the town of New Haven.

"They have treated me well, sir. Yesterday, they took me out in a wheelchair, and I saw just how incredible this place is. I was taken to a place they call the Rec Room, with all kinds of games. Then we went to a charming diner for lunch. I even heard they have a bar! This place is beyond belief!" Hunter exclaimed enthusiastically. He was in good spirits, which relieved Will considerably.

Dr. Maya came in, and Gabe, Relic, and Taylor left to check out the Rec Room that Hunter said was at the other end of the corridor.

"So, how is he doing? His leg still looks like it needs extensive care."

Maya looked at Hunter and Will. "He has healed much quicker than I expected, but his wounds need to be kept clean, and when they're completely closed up, he should start physical therapy. The Hold has a place for that equipment. Is there anyone there who has medical training?"

"We have healers, but they don't have access to modern medicine like you practice here. They use herbal and home remedies, and they don't reside at Fort Sentry," Will answered honestly.

Maya nodded without judgment. "Fort Sentry, I like that name better than the Hold." Will smiled. "I'm sure I could get clearance to send someone with you. In fact, I have an excellent nurse here who has just passed her residency and been promoted from practitioner to doctor. We don't have a position available for her, and she asked me about transferring to the Hold, I mean Fort Sentry."

"That would be amazing. Can she do that? Can she leave New Haven to go to Fort Sentry?" Will added.

Maya gave Will an apprehensive grin. "Well, I haven't brought this to the town officials, so don't repeat this. When we agreed to move here, we all signed a contract not to leave because our location was a secret, but that has changed. Give me some time to work it out, but I'm sure we could at least loan you a P.T. for a bit."

"P.T.?" Will questioned.

"Physical therapist, sorry," Maya smiled.

Will told Hunter goodbye, and he thanked Maya for helping him and went to join his friends at the Rec Room. He was surprised they allowed him to walk unescorted until he saw the cameras following him. He smiled and gave a casual salute.

As Will walked through the mid corridor, he noticed a glass door on the left. Arching above it was an unlit electric sign with the word Derecho. He cupped his hands to peer inside. The room inside was dark, but small accent lights gave shadowed outlines of a stage and an open floor area, surrounded by chairs and tables. *That must be the bar*, he thought. He walked onward.

Down on the right, he saw two large wooden doors propped open like welcoming arms. The beautiful, well-lit room housed rows of benches, and a glowing, colorful glass pane shone behind a podium. He stepped inside and examined the stand decorated with a silhouette of a man in a long robe, continuing the welcoming gesture of open arms. It reminded him of the woman standing in the courtyard at the Dranger jail.

"Wow, this is a church," he whispered. "New Haven not only allows its citizens to practice religion. They support it." He knew nothing about religion or God. It seemed like magic mumbo-jumbo because no God would let people suffer so or send them to accomplish impossible tasks.

As he continued his walk, his attention was drawn to the plaques where their dead were immortalized on the walls. They had lost many people in their endeavor to live free, and they honored and remembered them, which also reminded him of his days as a Dranger.

He arrived at the Rec Room, filled with game tables and sports equipment to check out. He missed playing pool and the team sports that he and Rival enjoyed at the Neighwah Academy. Will was astounded at how many amenities the citizens were provided with for fun and happiness. Maybe it was the only way to keep them locked up. Gabe came through the door and told them it was time to go.

The building right next to the Rec Room was large but not as large as the hospital. It had a domed roof which was higher than the other roofs, and it was also three shipping containers deep. Six fancy columns supported a section of the building that hung over the entrance. The sign in the front read New Haven Town Hall. As Gabe held the door for them, it was plain to see he was proud of his town and this place especially.

They were given a quick tour of the interior that started with a beautiful lobby decorated with incredible works of art. Gabe took them through the double doors on the left into an ornate oval meeting room with a backlit domed ceiling. Numerous cushioned seats in a semicircle faced the podium and the two desks that flanked it.

They went back through the lobby to the other side of the building, where the office doors labeled with legislators' names lined the hallway. As they walked toward the stairs on the other end, Will saw the old and new portraits of notable people and documents that covered the walls. They were led upstairs to a sitting area where Gabe left them to announce their arrival.

Bannon Vogel sat in his office, trying to decide how much he should trust these outsiders. He and many others had worked relentlessly and died courageously to create New Haven. How could he just divulge its secrets to strangers? He remembered the long journey of six hundred people from the Denver Territory following an impossible dream of hope.

Step by step, they toiled to plan it, build it, supply it, and fill it with five hundred fortunate, like-minded residents. They sacrificed everything to belong, and they traveled through dangerous lands to get here. Some gave their lives to keep it safe, and the wall near the church holds the proof of too many names.

Gray and Haru came into the conference room through the hallway door while Bannon motioned for Gabe to bring in the guests. A round of greetings and introductions preceded the settling into chairs around the table.

When Bannon called the meeting to order, he recognized Gray first, who was anxious to get to the numerous matters they needed to discuss. He activated the screens that slid up from the center of the table and began.

"We discussed our need to protect our communities from the Corporates, who are now fully aware of our locations and our alliance. The roadblock strategy was is our strongest defence, and here is where we are on that. Highway 6 across Loveland Pass is so locked up in snow that we did not address it in our plan.

"We disabled I-70 on the east side of the tunnel here and here." As he spoke, red dots appeared on the displayed map. "We also collapsed this section of Highway 91 south of Breckenridge. And this morning, we completed setting mines along both of those thoroughfares. There is little chance they can repair the roads or breach these barriers with the number of troops they will need to attack us now that winter is settling in. And though our winters are long, I do not doubt that as soon as they are able, they will make quick repairs. And that doesn't even touch on the surface-to-air weapons they probably have."

Will piped in to give information they may not be aware of. "The combined defensive personnel under the Elites are called the Garrison. They do report they have ballistic weapons, but they have not been deployed since the Poststrike Wars. The treaty between the states declares that launching even one missile would allow the neighboring territories, like Utah and Kansas, to target us regardless of its trajectory. That makes me doubt they'd play that card. But our neighboring territories are weak, so the treaty may not deter them. Or they don't have any, and they just use the concept of them to hold the other territories at bay."

Gray looked at Will and said, "Thanks, I didn't consider the other state territories, nor was I aware of that treaty. It will help decipher intercepted messages."

There was a long pause, and Will knew he had revealed he had extensive knowledge about the inner workings of the Corporate's defensive branch. They may guess he had connections to the Garrison Army, but this was no time to hold that kind of information back.

Bannon broke the long pause with the obvious question, "I agree that for now, we can consider the ballistic threat to be low, and New Haven and the Fringer Alliance are relatively inaccessible. But we have been discovered by the Colorado Territory Garrison. What's our next move?"

Haru, the town counselor and spiritual leader, was pretty good at reading faces and body language. He had spent the last two-plus years studying people who were drenched in secrets. He was seeing those same looks on everyone at this table. They were dancing around the problem before them, and he was tired of the game that they didn't have time to play.

"Our clock is ticking down," Haru said. "It's time to talk about the elephant in the room."

"That being," asked Will.

"Nitu Cabal," Haru said matter-of-factly.

Will was confused, but he saw Relic stiffen, and Bannon put his head in his hand.

"We may have some information on that," said Relic matter-of-factly, "if you're willing to share what you have."

Will stood up, "What is going on here?"

Haru jumped in. "I think sharing what we have is an excellent idea."

"Relic, what is Nitu Cabal?" asked Taylor.

"It means beautiful rebellion. Some attribute the saying to the Templar Knights, but others say it came much later." Will gave Relic a get on with it gesture. "It is the military plan for reclaiming the nation, and a reference to the location of Cali Bantu, which is just a word scramble of Nitu Cabal."

This was all moving too fast, and Bannon stood, and so did Will. The tension was like a static charge sparking across the room. Gray remained seated, Relic calmly waited, and Taylor started sniggering. Haru just leaned back in his chair and smiled.

"Gentlemen," Haru said, "It would have been nice to ease into these topics after a week or so of discussions. It's true, we don't know each other well, but we have few choices and less time. We can end it here and now, and hope things stay peaceful. Let's see a show of hands of everyone at this table who believes that we could go back to how we lived a month ago?"

Will was visibly upset and got up and walked to the counter at the back of the room, grabbing a beverage and a small selection of the treats provided. "This is too fast. You know nothing of us nor we of you," Will said with his back to the group.

Gray calmly looked at Will and said, "Actually, we know you hacked into our computers and learned a lot about us. Plus, we have mutual friends who told us a lot about you, William Noland/Alexander, ex-Dranger, Dirk, and a previous member of the Neighwah Command. I know these things, and I still respect the hell out of you. And trust me, you're not the only one who has secrets to hide, but we both just sacrificed the lives of our precious people because everyone here wants the same thing: freedom and peace."

Gray saw Will turn to sit back down, so he continued. "I agree with Relic and Haru. We don't have time to hide our cards. We have a very small window before hell descends on both of us. Let's see what we have, so we can work on finding this Cali Bantu before they do."

"So, you're with the RH, the Robinhooders? I see they told you about us. Why didn't we get the intel on you?" Will stewed over it a little, but one thing was clear. Though the RH had not told the Guard about the tunnel, they hadn't shared with New Haven what the Fringer Township held over the Corporates.

"We used to have a constant connection with RH, but since the breach at the Hold, I mean Fort Sentry," Gray corrected himself, "it's been sporadic. We didn't know enemy soldiers were coming to the tunnel or that you were coming to defend us."

Will shook his head. "There were warnings from hunters and Loners, and they told the RH who live among us. The rebels who know how to contact you may not have gotten the intel. We were warned that Garrison soldiers were coming over a pass in the south. The tunnel was not mentioned, but we were already suspicious of the activity surrounding it."

The room was still and silent.

"So," Haru said, coming back to the previous question, "we are stuck with the other choices. Find Cali Bantu on our own or work together."

All in favor of working together," interjected Bannon. All hands went up, albeit reluctantly. "Is it okay if I bring my top tech guy in here? He has been studying Cali Bantu and knows more about it than I do."

Within five minutes, a lanky man with dark, curly hair and wire-rimmed glasses came lumbering in with a small laptop in his hand. Uneasy introductions circled the table with Rand reaching over to shake hands before he took his seat.

"Wow, the tension in this room is thick. Did something else happen?"

"We're about to share what we know about Cali Bantu," said Bannon.

"Okay," Rand stumbled over the word with uncertainty. "That was quick,"

Taylor decided to propose a trade to relieve the maddening tension. "Okay, how about we give a secret, then you give one."

Bannon nodded, "We'll go first. We have the dragon statue of Vadina with the symbols on the base."

Relic smiled. "Ahh, so that's what was meant by the fire keeper's clue. I've spent months trying to muddle it out. Well, we have the song."

"Song? I hadn't heard of that one," said Rand.

Haru jumped in, "We have the castle puzzle, and it's been solved."

Will gave in to the crazy and said, "I have the Sanguine Blade." That raised Rand and Bannon's eyebrows and left their mouths agape.

"Wow, that was like a rapid fire of secrets. I can't wait to examine these things. Oh, wait, do I get to see them?" said Rand.

"Yes, Rand," conceded Relic, "I think you and I will be working long hours together on this because we have more." Relic sighed and paused before he gave the last clue. "We have Miranda's book and her apprentice."

"Who is Miranda, and who is her apprentice?" Rand and Gray said together, leaning forward with eager interest.

"She was Will's step-mother, and here is her apprentice," Relic gestured his hands toward Will. "She was the daughter of Dr. Logan, a Highmind technologist, who worked with Dr. Petroff on bio-technology. He was killed trying to escape, but his daughter got away. She educated Will and gave him the Sanguine Blade before she and Will's father were killed."

"She was Tianna to me, and I didn't find out who she was until a couple of years ago." Will had his head in his hands, shaking it back and forth. *Here we go again. Every time my secrets are revealed, things go terribly wrong. How many people will suffer this time, and how many times will I have to learn this lesson?*

While most people were filing out into the hall, Gray sat down next to his new friend and put his hand on the broad back of the Commander, who saved his town. "I know you think the world is on your shoulders, but you're not alone anymore. None of us are." Will looked up and nodded. "Just stay here for a second. I'll be right back."

Everyone had left the office when Gray returned, shaking a set of keys in his hand. "We need a drink, my friend. Or at least I do."

Will smiled. "I passed that bar. It's near the church."

"No, that's the teen hangout. Come on."

Gabe drove the two to the east end of town to the Shangri-La Bar. Walking through the outer patio, Gray pulled out his keys and let them into a bar straight out of the history books. Will settled on a stool, looking at his reflection in the mirror behind the bar. Gray saw he was still in overthink mode while he made two old-fashions with Bannon's top-shelf whiskey.

"This ought to do the trick," Gray said as he presented the tumbler full of deep amber gold, topped with a maraschino cherry. Will looked at the glass with awe. Not even the Neighwah Rec Room made drinks that looked this good. Then he sipped it.

"Damn, that's good. It's got a sassy flavor with a nice bite, like a greedy kiss."

Gray laughed out loud. "I like that. You challenge me to create a drink worthy of that name."

They sat for several hours telling the stories of their conquests and hard-lived lives until Gabe drove up and took Gray home and Will to his dorm room.

Relic and Rand had followed Bannon through a side door that led to his office. The décor was rich with darkly stained woods and priceless artwork. Behind a commanding desk with a large leather chair was a wall shelf dedicated to renowned literature, many were first editions. Two comfortable chairs faced him, and a water pitcher with glasses was perched between them on a small but elegant table.

Relic had questions about this immense project that was put into play right under the Corporates' noses. "Bannon, how in the world did you accomplish all this?" he blurted before they took their seats.

Bannon told the story of his family's patriotism and his parents' and wife's deaths. He explained how they purchased the tunnel and added to their vast supplies from the inventories of crashed business-es and abandoned warehouses.

"We undertook a massive renovation project to repair and enlarge it. Soon after we completed that phase, a nuclear waste accident was staged, allowing the whole tunnel to be closed off. I feigned insanity due to the death of my father and the ruin of his legacy. I had overspent on the project, and rumors flew about my monetary downfall. My company was considered risky, and my friendship awkward. I was left alone to work on securing my toxic mess unencumbered."

"Shakespeare has so many life lessons. But I've always wondered, at what point does acting crazy manifest itself into reality?" Relic interjected.

Bannon smiled at his quickness and wit while recognizing Relic had tweaked a tender nerve. Every plan he had put in place was not to succumb to the bloody fate of Shakespeare's Hamlet, but the ghosts of failure still haunted him. He brushed the issue aside.

"The next step was the hardest," he continued with a steely resolve. "We selected citizens based on health, ability, and loyalty to the movement. We acclimated them, trained them, and eventually moved them inside. It was a long, complex symphony of elements that needed to be harmonized perfectly. Though all manner of talents were required to run the town, the key factor was the ability to keep it secret. The information was so intensely layered that anyone questioned would have few answers to give.

"Thousands of shipping containers were loaded into the tunnel under the guise of a radiation barrier. It appeared to Elites and the Upper oligarchs that Vogel Enterprises was bankrupt, and I had gone mad. It gave Dana, my sister, a good reason to sell off everything we weren't taking with us. We used those credits to run our off-site teams and barter for necessities. Then, we just disappeared.

"Teaching once-enslaved citizens the organization and responsibilities of freedom and how to protect it continues to be a challenging task. The parameters of a democratic society are messy enough, but add imprisonment, and you have one hell of an irreconcilable paradox. Though every step has been fraught with challenges, the experiment was working. That is until now."

Chapter Two

Jillian Takota curled up in her big, comfy chair with her cheek resting on her hands. So many evenings she had sunk into the softness of these cushions to read and sip on the herbal teas she got from her best friend. Billie's herbal blends were as delightful as they were soothing, especially after her days being on her feet all day working at the Rapid Aid Station, or the RAS as it was called.

But tonight was anything but relaxing. The past week had swept up her peaceful life like a tornado and plopped her back down into the tempest-torn existence she thought she escaped. The pleasant, safe life in the New Haven sanctuary was now exposed, and its future foreshadowed by annihilation. Everyone acknowledged the threat the Corporates posed. It wasn't a matter of whether their sanctuary would be discovered. It was a matter of when. But that thought lived in the ether and was not said out loud. Well, the matter was pounding at their doors now.

She recalled the day she discovered she was pregnant. She noticed a change in her cycle, but she attributed it to a very busy week of pulling extra shifts, finishing her final paper, and studying for her exams for her trauma medicine degree. Having a child was in their plans, but not yet. However, bodies do not follow plans, and her condition was confirmed by the two tests she secretly took at the RAS.

The only person she told was her sister, Ari, who helped her plan a quiet, romantic evening to tell Gray the happy news. It had been a year, almost to the day, since Gray and Jilly made love for the first time in the Harold Seger Observatory. They got married in July, and here they were pregnant in October, but she was beyond happy about it.

Jilly brought the subject up months ago, and they decided to begin trying after the winter holidays. Gray figured Jilly's clock was nudged by her involvement with Billie's baby and her sister's pregnancy. He agreed because he believed he had time, and maybe a chance to discuss it further before they committed. New Haven was safe for now, but he knew it wouldn't last, and she should too. Jilly realized the news would surprise Gray, and he was rarely fond of surprises. Yet, she believed that underneath his masculine banter, he'd be happy.

Jilly and Gray both had Wednesdays and Thursdays off, so she planned the reveal for Wednesday night. She told Bannon she wanted to have a special evening with her husband, and he promised to keep Gray busy with his favorite task, checking the instruments outside the tunnel. It would take him several hours, allowing Jilly and Ari to set the scene. Though Jilly did most of the work, she looked lovingly at her nine-month pregnant sister, who was comfortably snoring on her big overstuffed chair.

Candles and silk flowers decorated the table, and soft music played. Though everyone ate their meals at one of the four dining halls, special meals could be ordered and delivered to one's residence for credits. On Sunday, Jilly put in her order for the special of the day, roasted elk with burgundy sauce, baby potatoes, salad, and peach brandied preserves for dessert. The finishing touch was a set of two knitted baby booties, one pink and one blue, incorporated into the candle and silk flower centerpiece.

She and her sister put bets on how long it would take for Gray to notice them and make the connection. Ari said thirty minutes, but Jilly disagreed. Her husband was extremely observant, and she guessed he would see it within minutes of sitting down. She closed her eyes, bathing in the bliss of their happy future when suddenly, her cerebral paradise was replaced with a terrifying reality.

Alarms rang, and red lights pulsed through the tunnel in the late afternoon. Announcements instructed everyone to report to their assigned locations. This was no drill—the tunnel was being attacked. Jilly called a bus to get her sister to Town Hall to be with her husband, Bannon, and she ran to the RAS to prepare for casualties. The sprinkler system kicked in as a fire prevention measure before she could duck inside.

She shook off the water under the porch before walking in. Her boss, Andie, PA Ann Drea Channing, asked her to gather suture kits and extra triage equipment. Andie gave the two intern students a quick review of their duties and the serious symptoms that require urgent attention. They rushed to get as ready as they could be, and then the waiting began.

They looked out at the still-pulsing red lights reflecting in the water that pooled on the street. It cast an eerie pink glow on the iridescent paint used on the tunnel walls. The anticipation and dread of combat made their minds spin them into what-ifs and maybes.

"Maybe it's a good sign that there aren't any wounded," the male medical student said, trying not to show the tension rising in him.

"Maybe it's a false alarm," Jilly said, though she didn't believe it.

"What if they can't get the wounded inside?" said the male intern.

"What if the *enemy* gets inside?" the med-assistant said, with fearful brows straining her young face.

"Let's not work up problems we don't have. We may only have a few patients with ambulatory injuries. All the serious injuries will be brought to the hospital. Or we may get slammed with minor as well as serious ones. We are as ready as we can be," said Andie in her commanding tone.

"They might still be approaching the tunnel, and the fighting hasn't begun yet," added Jilly. "Maybe they'll turn around when they hear the screaming siren drones or detect radiation. Perhaps it will all—."

Just then, a bus pulled up, and the whole staff went out to assist the patient through the doors. The soldier had a deep shrapnel gash on his outer left thigh, but it didn't appear to have cut an artery. The driver sped off as the medical staff buzzed around the injured young man.

Before his leg was cleaned and stitched, another patient was dropped off with a severe burn on her arm. A strip of cloth was seared into her burned skin and needed to be painstakingly removed. After being sprayed with a numbing agent, Jilly began the arduous task. They had a ten-minute lull before the real rush started. The adjacent dentist's office waiting room was opened to accommodate the overflow of patients waiting for treatment. The two interns worked as fast as possible to triage the wounded in both offices. Most had bleeding issues, and when they were resolved, they returned to the battle.

The music videos usually playing in the waiting room above the nurse's counter were replaced with a bulleted statement of protocols. Jilly had no time to read the information, but thoughts of their Defenders fighting, especially one, swirled in her head.

Good news finally came. The battle was over. The Corporate's Garrison army had retreated, and all the injured soldiers who required medical attention were secure in the RAS or the hospital. The strange news was the victory was attributed to a Fringer army joining the fight. The worst news was that several soldiers were in grave condition. As busy as they were, they had no time to think or listen to any of it.

Jilly had been ignoring her wrist phone, but when Gray called, she immediately excused herself and took the call.

"Gray, I've been worried about you, about the Defenders. We've been so busy. How's it going on your end?" Jilly asked.

"It could have been worse, but it's bad enough. Can you come to the hospital for a few?"

"Why?" asked Jilly, "Or should I say for whom?"

"It's Axle. It's not good."

Jilly ran to ask Andie for a short break. She granted her request. All the most urgent patients had been treated and released or transferred to the hospital. She rushed through the mid-corridor to the hospital and found Axle's room. Gray was holding his brother's unconscious hand. She remembered waking up to that very connection when she had been poisoned on her way to the Hold. No words were spoken between them. None were needed. She bowed her head and prayed over Axle, asking for comfort and healing for Axle and those who worried over him.

She slowly walked back to the RAS, feeling the full extent of the day's exhausting events settling in her bones. She placed her hands on her womb where her child lay, soaking in her anxiety and fatigue.

"Don't worry, little one. I'm going to take good care of you," she whispered.

When she walked into the nurse's station, Andie rushed over to her.

"How's Axle?" She was always short and to the point.

"It's a waiting game. He's unconscious, but not comatose, and he has some serious injuries. Maya says it's fifty-fifty."

"You need to eat something, Jilly," as she pointed to a plate of sandwiches and dried fruits brought by the NorthEast diner. It was a sensible suggestion since the staff's pace had slowed. Her stomach felt anything but hungry, but she remembered her promise to her unborn babe and forced down half a peanut butter and strawberry jam sandwich, which tasted uncommonly good to her. She refilled her water cup, grabbed a handful of dried fruit, and got back to work.

It was nine-thirty at night before the RAS officially released the last patient to go home. They both needed sleep, but Jilly offered to stay for any straggling issues until 2:30 a.m., when Andie would relieve her. While covering her shift, she called Town Hall to check on her sister. Bannon said she was tucked in at home. He added he was praying for Axle as well as the other brave Defenders fighting through their injuries.

How differently this day had gone from the one she had planned. She was supposed to share her cheerful news with the man she loved. Instead, she had spent the afternoon and evening patching the brave men and women that her husband had to send into battle. She worried about him, knowing this day would affect him greatly.

She said another silent prayer for Axle, Gray, Ari, her secret child, and the whole town. She seemed to be doing that quite often today. It made her think of all of Haru's persuasive conversations. He was right, prayer helped. If nothing else, it gave her courage and hope. Putting her words to her pain and praise helped occupy her mind during the agonizing waiting stage.

Now wasn't the time to share her news. Though it wasn't right to keep it from him, the last thing Gray needed was more stress and responsibility right now. She had looked forward to the delight in his eyes when she told him he was a dad to be, but it would evoke a different set of emotions now. She thought of the telltale decoration sitting on the table at home, and she hoped she would beat him home. He may not notice the flower arrangement after a day like today, but it wouldn't be right for him to find out that way.

She sat at the RAS desk, staggering through the last of the paperwork and wearily filing it. After fielding one call, she was relieved to discover there was little left to do. The interns had restocked the treatment kits, cleaned and put away the equipment, tidied up the patient rooms, and disposed of the biohazard trash. Her eyes were heavy as she lay her head on the desk. The next thing she felt was Andie gently shaking her shoulder.

"Jilly, wake up. I'll take over from here."

"Okay, thanks. It's been quiet. I only got one call," she said through a yawn. "It was at 11:15, from the female burn patient. She had been taking only half of her pain medication in case there was more fighting, and she was needed. I convinced her to take the full dose and get some sleep. I made a note for one of us to call her tomorrow to see how she was doing. I also finished the paperwork and filed it. Everything is done. You could get some sleep, too."

"I got enough sleep, and I have the final opinions regarding my dissertation to review." Andie had just completed her general MD doctorate. Jilly had recently finished her Physician's Assistant degree with a focus on trauma medicine. The techniques she learned were beneficial during this whirlwind day. Though there weren't any new positions open, they would both be better caretakers, and their credits would increase. And now that the tunnel was discovered, a large trained medical staff could be tragically necessary.

Jilly collapsed into bed next to her restlessly sleeping husband. He stirred and wrapped her into a welcome cuddle, and they both fell quickly into sound sleep. Jilly didn't wake up until 9:00 a.m., discovering Gray had already left. She woke up to a churning stomach and made a frantic dash for the toilet. She was fortunate that she only had the occasional mild bout of morning sickness, but she hadn't eaten much yesterday, and her baby was scolding her.

The screen in her front room was on with a new report waiting. She quickly grabbed one of the protein bars meant for emergency lockdowns from a cabinet above the long side table. Slowly, she nibbled her way back to feeling marginal and got herself ready for the day. Hitting the power symbol embedded on the side table, she watched their large screen come to life. One of the high school teachers came on to give the latest report.

Marcus Miller here with New Haven News,

The leaders worked through the night to negotiate an alliance with William of the Guard, from the Fringer Township. That we needed to ally with each other was not in question. The purpose of the discussion was to decide the parameters.

An impending storm required the Guard army to return to their base, which used to be the Hold, but is now called Fort Sentry. The lengthy process of gathering the citizens' opinions was not possible. Our emergency protocol, initiated when the battle began, gave the New Haven Legislators the power to sign the agreement. The approved accord is summarized below.

An Alliance is officially approved between New Haven and the Guard and includes the following agreements:

New Haven will provide the Guard with the following:

• Continued access and residency to all four Hold buildings

• Agreed-upon resources

Both will maintain:

• Continued peaceful interactions

• Continued communication, negotiations, and full disclosure of further alliances

• Reciprocal military assistance as required

We are fortunate to be a part of a powerful alliance that stands for free self-governance. A complete copy of the bill will be available on your tablets later today.

The dining halls, schools, and most municipalities will resume their regular schedules tomorrow. Until then, meals will be delivered on carts. The recreation facilities, which are manned by Defenders, will also be closed until further notice.

This is New Haven News signing out.

This was the first she had heard that this army was made up of Fringers, so she went back to the previous messages to check what she had missed while working. It was true. A Fringer army did assist the Defenders. They were much more organized than the rumors suggested. She had gotten to know Aniya, a Fringer rescued by Jax and Axle while on a mission, but she never said anything about the tribes being united.

Conversations about the alliance flowed through her head, but she couldn't think about a treaty now. The whole day and its fallout felt out of her hands, and she had more pressing matters on her mind. She sat at the table, twirling the dangling booties around her finger while obsessing on the issue dominating her thoughts. After taking a moment to push aside impossible wishes, she dialed Gray still woefully fingering the tiny booties hanging from the vase.

"Hello," Jilly said to the receptionist at Town Hall. "Is Gray there? Can I talk with him?"

"Hi, Jilly," she answered in her friendly tone, "How are you?"

"I'm fine. It was a crazy night at the RAS, and we're all on pins and needles hoping Axle will improve. But somehow I was able to get some sleep. How about you?"

"I'm good, but I mean, man, that was something last night. Can you believe it? A Fringer army coming to our rescue. Wow. Never would have guessed that one. Okay, I'm connecting you now."

"Hey, honey," Gray said kindly. "I just couldn't wake you. I'm sure you had a long night."

"Looks like yours is still going. You couldn't have had much sleep. You doing okay?" she asked.

"I got a good four hours. I can't talk long, Jilly. The people are erupting in angry flare-ups all over the town."

"I know I saw signs being walked down the street. They should be thankful they're not in Corporate chains. Any news on Axle?" she asked. She would have called herself, but the nurses didn't need to tag-team the information to both of them.

"Yeah, they upgraded him to stable. He woke up in the middle of the night, and they removed his breathing tube and a bunch of other junk." Jilly smiled at his name for the very devices that had brought his brother back to them. "Maya says he's got some healing to do, but he should make a full recovery."

"Oh, thank God. That's amazing news." Relief flooded her with emotion. She reeled in her reaction and changed the subject. "Is it true, the Fringers came to defend the tunnel?"

"Yeah, wild, huh? I met the leader. His name is William. He's a huge wall of dark muscle. He was dripping blood through a torn material he had ripped from his shirt to bandage his arm. He's like some kind of Rambo. I'm waiting for his call from the Hold. They've taken it over and renamed it Fort Sentry. Oh, hun, gotta go."

Jilly hung up the phone, not wanting to hear the click from his end. She was an emotional mess, which she quickly dismissed as hormones. She walked next door to check on Billie and little Katie. They had both gotten up late, so they walked to the diner to get some breakfast. The Defenders were standing around the diner cart, and they told them there had been some trouble that morning. Billie and Jilly said they shared their frustration and thanked them.

"So, Fringers," Billie said when their meals were delivered. "I mean, I've been working closely with Aniya for almost two months now. I gotta admit, if I'd have known they were peaceful people living free, I might have tried to join up. But she never gave me any indication they were organized enough to have such a formidable army."

"I'm not sure why they would help us or how they found out about us, but I'm glad they did. That's got to put them on the Corporate radar, though," Jilly said with a distressed expression.

"And us too," Billie replied, returning a concerned look.

"I guess we should be thankful," Jilly said. "I wonder how their soldiers fared. We didn't get any at the RAS, but I'm not sure we'd have let them in. It's all very confusing." Jilly grabbed the provided breakfast from the cart and added a side order of yogurt and a plate of pears. It got Billie's attention, but they walked in silence back to their shared yard. When Jilly began to plow through her food, Billie had to ask.

"Wow, how long did you go without a meal?" Billie asked while putting more tidbits of food on little Katie's highchair tray. The simple scene had Jilly taking a breath to reel in a sudden surge of powerful emotions.

"Gosh, I don't remember when I ate last, and it was nonstop work till late last night." Jilly hated lying to her, but this wasn't the time or place to reveal her secret.

"Yeah, I'm sure it was grueling," she said with a curious look at her friend, whom she usually teased about her small meals. "Gabe caught a couple of hours of sleep, and he's back on duty to quell the locals. I imagine Gray is too." Jilly nodded, and Billie sighed. "Why can't the residents give them a break? I mean, I know they have freedom of speech, but do they have to complain about everything?" Billie sighed in frustration. "Our soldiers have been hard at it with very little sleep, and they don't even appreciate what they did for them."

"It reminds me of something my dad said," Jilly replied as she stabbed at the last chunks of pear. "The more government does for people, the more they expect and the less they do for themselves."

"That's messed up," her friend responded.

Jilly waved goodbye to Billie and headed to the hospital to visit Axle. He was awake, but she could see he was in considerable pain. She checked his chart and called for the nurse.

"I think he needs his pain medication. I see it's about twenty minutes early, but he's showing signs of distress. I can take care of it for you," Jilly said to the on-duty nurse.

"No problem, Jilly. I saw his vitals at the station and grabbed his meds on the way in." Jilly smiled at her friend, letting her attend to Axle. "Let me take a look at your stitches. You're lucky they are still intact. You know, Captain, you should stop trying to stand up. We have you on a video feed, so don't deny it." She added the medication to Axle's I.V. and winked at Jilly.

"She's right," Jilly said in agreement. "If you tear those stitches, it will set your healing process back a couple of weeks. I have a feeling since Gray promoted you, and congratulations by the way, he needs you to help him sort out the whole being discovered problem."

"I hate this lying in bed all day," his voice was getting slower. "Where's Jax?"

"She's getting discharged. She said she'd come before she headed home."

His eyes were fluttering, and Jilly knew he wouldn't be awake much longer. "I know Gray is working on securing the roads that lead to the tunnel. You've been out there and know the roads as well as anyone. How about I have him send some maps, and you can work on a plan?"

He smiled and gave a thumbs-up before closing his eyes and surrendering to the drugs leaching through his veins.

Chapter Three

S oon after the battle, Ari and Bannon welcomed their son, Sebastian Thomas, into the world; a new mission statement had been approved; and the residents were warming up to the idea of befriending the Fringers. The town returned to its familiar schedule, but an undeniable dread crackled through the streets.

The Corporates knew where they were now. And though they had retreated, it was only because they had not prepared for the level of combat they encountered. They were on a reconnaissance mission and wound up facing two armies. But the Corporate Garrisons would return, and they would come with a fully prepared and utterly ruthless battalion of men.

Bannon watched from his office, which hung over the street below. People went about their business, detached from the impending peril. They shelved their dreadful problem with the same lemming mentality that was seen when the meteorite threat was publicized years before it was due. The normalcy with which they approached their daily tasks was more than peculiar.

It's not that they didn't care. It's that they abdicated the responsibility to their leaders. They would patiently wait for the legislature's decision and then slam it down without redress. Bannon shook off his self-serving victimhood and returned to his responsibilities. His duty was to keep the town safe. Their duty was to keep the town going. He conceded that despite the rabble of discontent, no one was derelict in their duty.

Though winters at their location were fraught with mechanical issues, they also provided an effective barrier between them and their adversaries. The latest weather report confirmed that Corporate armies would not be able to reach them due to the considerable amount of snow that had fallen in the last storm. It would give them more than protection. It would give them time.

To further protect them from an invasion, a crew was currently deconstructing all the roads leading to the tunnel, the fort, and the Fringer Township. However, this was a temporary solution. They would use the time given to devise and implement a defense plan. Keeping in mind, the Corporates also had this time to decide how to destroy them.

Jilly still hadn't told Gray about her pregnancy. He came home late every evening, piled into bed, and left in the morning before she got up for work. It was a relief that he wasn't there to see her morning wretch routine. She still envisioned a reveal that involved her telling him, not him guessing.

Since she had worked through her days off, and the RAS had slowed down, Andie was giving her nurses time off in split shifts. Jilly said she preferred mornings off, so for the next two days, she didn't start work until after lunch. She was pleased it allowed her to keep her secret for a little longer, but Gray promised he would take the next day off.

Tonight, she would tell him no matter what. She took an extended warm shower and dressed for the day. Knowing the importance of checking on her unborn child's development, she had to get to a sonogram. But Gray had ears everywhere, and she didn't want the news to slip out from anyone but her.

Ari had been bothering her to stop putting it off, but, as Jilly reminded her, Ari had taken her time to tell Bannon about her pregnancy. Since the sonogram equipment was at the hospital, she would have to sneak her way into the room to accomplish her task. She would use her visit with Axle as cover for her objective.

Jilly sat with Axle while keeping an eye on the activity in the halls. By 10:30, the morning bustle had died down considerably. She said goodbye to Axle, entered the hall, and surveyed the path toward the internal exam room. Before she could plan her next move, she heard someone call her name.

"Jilly," said the nurse manning the counter. She gestured for her to come over to the counter. "Did you know we have a Fringer soldier in here?"

"Really? No, I didn't," Jilly said, but she thought, *if he was hurt, why wouldn't we take care of him?* Jilly knew none were sent to the RAS, and it made her wonder if other injured Fringers had been turned away.

"We have him in the quarantine ward."

"What's wrong with him?" Jilly asked.

"He has a compound fracture in the leg from a gunshot wound, and he caught shrapnel in his neck from a sticky bomb. Maya had to perform several operations to save him. It was bad, but he's recovering. It's sad, though. No one knows he's here, and he isn't allowed visitors."

"Poor guy. Will his leg heal?" Jilly felt bad for this man who had sacrificed so much only to be left alone in a strange hospital with an injury that may leave him crippled.

"Maya isn't sure, but she says he's improving every day. It's a secret, though."

"I won't tell a soul," Jilly promised.

She slowly walked toward the exit and dodged into the maternity room when no one was looking. Closing the door, she strapped on a pair of gloves, warmed up the sonogram machine, and quickly squirted some gel onto her abdomen. It was much harder to operate the probe on herself, but she just wanted a quick verification of the baby's vitals. She was relieved to see the normal development of crucial organs. It was a hasty examination, but she was satisfied with the information. As soon as she could tell Gray, she'd let Andie do a more thorough inspection. She cleaned the probe, set everything back in its rightful place, erased the sonogram file, and tossed the gloves in the bin.

Her heart was pounding when she slipped out into the hall. She froze as she heard Maya's voice heading her way. She had no business being in this wing of the hospital. She ran toward the first room she saw and closed the door.

"You don't look like a nurse," said the heavily bandaged stranger, with his leg slightly elevated.

Crap, that's right, the Fringer soldier is in here.

"No, well, yes," she stammered. "Actually, I am, a nurse, I mean, but I'm not supposed to be here." She peeked out the door and quickly shut it again.

"Well, that's clear as mud. I knew something was up when you weren't wearing a mask. You're the first face I've seen. I'm Hunter," he said.

"I'm guessing you're the Fringer warrior we are secretly treating."

"Some secret. You just walked in. Do you regularly go around breaking into hospital rooms?" he asked.

Watching out the door, Jilly saw her chance. "Sorry, got to go." She made it out and sighed with relief when she escaped through the front doors.

Walking up to her home, Jilly was greeted by a lively dog and her happy owner, Connor. "Hello, Libby." She bent down and petted the dog, who wagged her whole body in response.

"Are you up for a walk? I don't have school today because I'm in a tutoring program with Rand now. I guess I outgrew high school," Connor shrugged.

"Wow, I mean, I knew you were smart, but I guess that makes you a genius." Connor's face flushed slightly, being more self-conscious than proud.

She was going to decline his offer, but a walk sounded like a good idea. Though it was supposed to be a day off for Gray, he was still fully occupied with the aftermath of the battle and the town's reaction to it. "You know what, Connor? I think a walk is an excellent idea."

"You sent for me, sir," Easton said as he stood before Gray's desk at attention.

"At ease, Private Mundy. Have a seat," Gray said as he sorted through his various piles of in-progress paperwork to find what he was looking for. "Ah," he said while pulling it to the top.

Gray rocked back in his seat and smiled at the young man who had become one of his most reliable soldiers. He hadn't started that way. He was an angry, rebellious boy in constant trouble. Gray recruited him into the Defenders more to reel in the boy's behavior than to give him a career.

"I couldn't be prouder of all that you've accomplished. Your team received the highest marks allowed on your primary training mission and excellent marks on the other two. Excellent in marksmanship, top of your class for test scores, and you tackle every assignment with diligence and professionalism."

"Thank you, sir," he said, tipping his head downward. Like many youths, he felt uncomfortable accepting compliments.

"E," Gray said, using the nickname he had given him over a year ago, "What I'm about to tell you is top secret." Easton nodded, acknowledging the privilege of being trusted. "We are about to go on a critical mission. It could have us gone for weeks, or it could be months." Easton sat on pins and needles, wondering if he had extra duties while his commander was away, or was it possible he was on the go list? "I'd like you to be on this team—"

"Yes, yes, I'd love to go," he said, letting his excitement interrupt his commander. "Sorry, sir. I didn't mean to cut you off." Gray tried to hide his amusement at E's enthusiasm.

"Please hear me out because this mission is very dangerous. We are taking on the Corporation."

Easton sat for a minute. "I trust you have some kind of weapon or intel that gives you confidence it is possible. No matter what, sir, it would be an honor to serve on this mission."

Gray explained the mission basics and told him when the next meeting would be held. He felt good about securing the last team member. Although he didn't look forward to his overbearing mother's reaction, Easton was an adult, and he had the right to make his own decisions. He returned to reviewing the supply list Gabe had worked on. Axle was going over the maps, and Andie was compiling the medical supplies.

Without satellites to predict the weather, a new storm had moved in quicker than anticipated, and their Fringer visitors were still on the road after their one-night stay. It was in full force now, and Gray was waiting for the phone call to confirm Will, Relic, and Taylor had made it safely back to Fort Sentry. His fingers tapped out a rhythm on his desk as he attempted to organize the numerous issues demanding his attention. It was then that Gabe came into his office and shut the door behind him. Bad sign.

"Now what? I really don't need anything else being piled on my desk today." Gray leaned back in his chair and folded his arms across his chest.

"Yeah, well, I figured you'd want to deal with this personally, sir," Gabe said with apprehension.

Gray sat up, shaking his head, "Just tell me."

"I think I'd rather show you." Gabe clicked the digital file into Gray's computer and hit play.

The screen showed the Fringer soldier in bed at the hospital. The patient, Hunter, was speaking to someone who had come into his room. Though the camera stayed trained on Hunter, Gray recognized the voice that answered back. The interaction was extremely brief, but what in the hell was his wife doing there?

Before he could give it more thought, the call from Will came in. He would have to deal with Jilly later.

Jilly came home from work, surprised to see Gray already there. He was sitting on the couch with his domineering look of disapproval. She rolled her eyes, ready to soothe his frustration from a bellwether week.

"Hi, I didn't expect you to get out of work so early. That means we can go to dinner together," she settled her small tote on the table and walked over to plant a much-neglected kiss on her husband. She expected him to extend the kiss, but he pulled back ever so slightly. She dismissed it, still assuming his agitation was work-related. It was obvious he had something on his mind, which was an understatement considering the havoc he was dealing with.

"How was your day?" he asked as nonchalantly as he could muster.

"I visited Axle. He seems to be healing up nicely. He has been behaving and staying in bed, poring over the maps you sent him. He should be released in a few days," she was about to ask about his day when she noted him cross his arms across his chest and direct his anger at her. Not good.

"Yeah, heard you had a visit with our Fringer patient today. See, we have his monitors turned on temporarily. Do you know why we have the cameras turned on right now?"

"I can guess," but before she could explain, he began interrogating her like a criminal.

She knew she wouldn't be able to get a word in edge-wise, so she just shouted, "I'm pregnant!"

That was not what he expected. "What?" He thought for a minute and said, "I... we... okay, we'll get to that in a minute. Why would that make you visit a stranger under guard in the hospital?"

"Did your cameras follow me into the internal imaging room? Because that's where I gave myself a screening to check the baby. I knew if I went to Maya, she would tell you because we're, no doubt, deep into some military protocol right now. I wanted to tell you myself."

"Again, why did you go in there?"

Her resolve was wavering as she tried to hold back the sobs, straining inside. Her emotions had been much less manageable lately.

"I heard Maya coming down the hall, and I ducked into the first room I came to. It happened to be his." Her wall suddenly broke, and she collapsed on the couch in a sobbing heap. "This is not the way I imagined telling you would go. Did you even notice the table?"

He looked over at the flowers in the center of the table and saw the little booties dangling against the sides of the vase. His shoulders drooped when he realized he had been too engrossed in his job and too angry to pay attention to the clues right in front of him. He had vented the last few days all over her. He sat down next to her and took her in his arms.

"I'm sorry. I'll be honest, I was worried you were caught up in something having to do with your father and those searching for you. I feared the Corporates discovered your death was a ruse, and they learned you were living here. I started wondering if that's why they attacked. Or maybe you were being blackmailed, and this guy was the contact. I asked about your day, and when you didn't immediately confess, I thought the worst. I'm sorry, honey. But back to what's most important, pregnant? Really? When did you find out? How? Is it for sure?"

She sat up, attempting to regain her self-control, though her sniffles still betrayed her. "Well, first, I need to say this. I get your concerns, and I can even understand your thought pattern, but you went from curiosity to a full-on conspiracy. You should have asked me, and let me talk, rather than rant at me as if your worst fears were facts."

"You're right. I should trust you, and I do, but I don't trust this world. I will try not to 'rant', but don't ask me to stop protecting you. I can't. Okay, seriously, tell me about the baby already."

She proceeded to describe how the turmoil of the past week had kept her from sharing the news. She let him know the baby appeared healthy, but she needed to have a doctor confirm her findings since her exam had been rushed. She concluded by saying she didn't know how far along she was.

"Okay, now that you've told me, please make an appointment with Maya."

"I'll message her now. By the way, does the whole hospital and Defender unit know ... I, umm, went into the Fringer room?"

"No, just Maya and Gabe."

"I'm sorry," Jilly replied quietly. "I'm sure that was embarrassing. And just to let you know, the only other person who knows about the baby is Ari."

"Yeah, I figured that," he answered with a crooked grin.

The meetings at the security office had been brutal and weighed heavily on him. Gray had heard of the Cali Bantu myth. It was believed to be a place where a weapon or a cache of weapons was stored. No one knew the nature of the weapon, whether it was a weapon, or if it was even true. But whatever it was, it was rumored to be extensive enough to overthrow the Colorado Corporates and maybe beyond.

William, Relic, and his advisor visited yesterday. They all knew a more thorough investigation was needed, but they were chased by more than their Corporate foes. The season was also nipping at their heels, and if they wanted to have a chance to defeat their enemy, they needed to get going. Because of the research done by Rand and the Highmind child, Connor, they had narrowed its location down to a searchable area. The final plan to leave in a week was set in motion. It was the most challenging mission they had ever led, and by far the most dangerous.

Gray's intention to send Axle as his second was an obvious one, but his injuries left that position undecided. Connor was another concern. There was no question that he was a necessary member of the team, but he was twelve. Children have no business in combat situations, but Connor was the only person they knew who was trained by one of the founders of the elusive site to locate and access it. This kid wasn't just smart, he was crazy, Highmind smart. And his recall abilities were off the charts.

And there was more. The Fringer leader, William, had also been trained as a child by the daughter of another one of the mysterious Highmind Robinhooders. Neither Connor nor Will had been old enough to receive adequate training before their mentors were murdered, but the hope was that they had enough knowledge to muddle through.

Sending young Connor on one of the most dangerous missions to date was unthinkable. But worse was sending him with a warrior along with his soldiers, none of whom he had been able to vet properly, left alarm bells screaming in Gray's ears. He knew he had to take charge of the mission and ensure this child's safety. But before that, he had the fearsome task of breaking the news to the child's parents.

The departure date was less than a week away. It was late one night when Gray called Jilly to sit at the table. She could tell she was going to hate this news before he spoke one word. She placed two glasses of water before them, struggling to hide her unruly emotions. It was alarming how many possible issues came to mind, but leaving was a prominent theme. She took a breath and waited for him to reveal his news.

"I know this is a bad time, but I have to go on an excursion, and I don't know when I'll return. It could be a couple of weeks, or it could be a couple of months. There's no way to know. Jilly, I'm so sorry."

She had expected more of a lead-in, allowing her to formulate her rebuttal, but his abrupt statement caught her off guard. It was the same move she used on him the day before. He was cunning that way. If she weren't so riled, she'd call it smart.

"Where?" She did her best to hide the panic in her voice.

"It's a survey, and it's top secret. I can't get into it."

"A survey? That sounds like something you could send one of your captains on. Why does it have to be you?"

"If I told you, I know you'd agree that I'm the only choice, but I can't."

She hated his job... again, still. Why couldn't she get her emotions in check? He was the military leader of their town. The only response she should have given him was something along the lines of *I understand,* but she didn't. She loved him.

She even believed he was making the best choice, the responsible choice, the choice the universe demanded. But she needed him to be here. She needed to be first; the universe be damned.

Chapter Four

I t was one a.m., and it wasn't the first time Gray had checked the clock. Stressful thoughts repeatedly wrestled his brain from sleep. Gray appreciated Jillian's support regarding his secretive job, but in the spirit of quid pro quo, it meant he had to be sympathetic to the somber moods it evoked. She would never ask him to disclose guarded information. And yet he knew she was concocting her own answers just as he had.

He wished she could let it go and trust him, but why should she? He had lied to her in the name of duty many times over the years, and she always listened to his explanations. But today, he cornered her like a wolf after its prey, tearing into the details of the hospital visit. Sure, it was his duty to know why she had visited a patient in restrictive custody, and he had a right to an explanation, but not to attack her. He tried to justify it as instinctive masculinity, his protective nature. But he had turned his beast on her to control *her*, instead of the threat. In a moment of clarity, he saw the possessive fiend within him.

He thought about the secrets he had been compelled to keep about who she was and the danger she was in. Every time he had confided in her about town business, she had proved her loyalty. So why did he feel the need to leave her out now? If it were about protecting her, it might be better if she knew. And yet, she was kind and helpful, two things that made her vulnerable to trouble, and she has a terrible habit of trying to handle things by herself.

That was why he taught her self-defense moves and how to shoot. She was a good student, but it did little to relieve his concerns about her open-hearted nature. The truth was, he trusted her with protecting everything and everyone but herself. It made him overly protective and controlling. Yet, looking at it from her perspective, those forceful tactics were what caused her to withhold her problems. He often worried that if this rift between them grew too large, she might leave him.

He was sitting up now, shaking his head adamantly. The thought of losing this woman, this companion, this perfectly imperfect love, was unbearable. He had to tell her. He wanted to.

"Jilly," he shook her gently. "Are you awake?"

"Uh, yeah, yeah. I am," she yawned. "I am now because you woke me up." She was rubbing her eyes and yawning again.

"I don't want to keep secrets from you anymore. It's exhausting and painful. You deserve to know."

She turned to the clock on her nightstand. It read 2:07 in the morning. "Oh, well, huh. What? I what? You mean the secret town stuff?" she yawned again, "Sounds like stuff I am not supposed to know. I mean, I get it, I just—"

He put his finger over her lips and started spewing his truths. There was no stopping him. When he finished, she looked at him with a stunned and fully awake expression.

"You mean you're taking Connor, our little neighbor, baseball-loving, dog-smuggling, fast-talking kid, who at eleven fell in love with a deaf sixteen-year-old who broke his heart? That Connor?" She transitioned quickly from one mad to a whole new one. "Who decided he should be endangered on such a mission? I don't care how smart he is, or what he knows about this Cali, whatever. He's just a kid."

He shouldn't have been surprised that her one takeaway was that a child may be put in danger. Maybe it was the hormones, or more than likely, it was just her nature. They talked for a bit longer before tangling in a loving embrace. His honesty, no matter how illicit, invigorated the tether that linked them, entwining them ever tighter. She knew he had betrayed his oath as the security officer, but she would protect the information with her life because *his* life depended on it.

"I love you so much. I know you shouldn't have told me, but thank you. Thank you for trusting me." She was charged with warm loving desire. She couldn't hold him close enough or kiss him sweetly enough. Their passion stormed into the next hour with torturous touching, leaving climaxes deliciously out of reach until finally they reached that blissful summit only true love can find.

He meant to top the event off with something heartfelt that shared how precious she was to him, but he felt his mind falling, gently tumbling into a tranquil sleep, the kind he hadn't had in a long time, the kind he desperately needed.

Jilly lay awake, swimming in the afterglow of revitalized affection. She couldn't deny that she had been flaunting her melancholy mood enough to make her point. She didn't want him to betray his duty, but the news he was leaving had sent her hormone-hell into overdrive. She needed the why, the honest reason, because deep down, she knew he would not abandon her for a minor excursion. It was some-thing dangerous. His confession revealed the gravity of his mission as well as the impending peril of the tunnel residents. He would protect her, but she would also protect him and the information he shared.

The next morning, Gray was still floating in happiness. He didn't see his reveal as a betrayal. It was a benefit to his marriage and his leadership. He needed her understanding to carry him through whatever he was tasked to do, but more importantly, it deepened their connection and filled the chasm that had started to grow once again.

However, exposing Cali Bantu and Connor's status as the key to accessing it added one more person who may be compelled, against their will, to divulge it. The thought of how such information might be extracted from his wife or Connor made his blood boil. But he took comfort that she would be safely secured here in the tunnel, allowing him to focus on protecting Connor.

He left Jilly sleeping soundly. It was her day off, and he whispered in her ear sweet wishes for a good day. The next day, he got a call from Jilly asking him to come home as soon as possible. She never did that. He knew it was something serious, and he sprinted to their house. She met him at the door, looking pale, with puffy, red-rimmed eyes.

"I lost the baby," was all she could get out before her sobs regained their tragic rhythm.

"Did we...," he couldn't finish his thought. His throat was thick with emotion.

She kissed him. "No, my love. Our union did not cause this. Having sex does not cause the miscarriage of a stable fetus. It was a beautiful connection, and I'm happy our child got to be a part of the love between us."

The thought was both moving and disturbing to Gray, so he changed directions. "You should be at the hospital. Let me take you," he was as sad as he was terrified about her state, and he regretted she had gone through this alone.

"I'm not in danger, Gray. I'll go, but right now I need you. I want to be held by you. For right now, I need this grief to be ours alone."

She had settled herself back into clean clothes. He walked her to their bedroom upstairs, quickly made up the stripped bed, and settled her next to him. When she fell asleep, he went downstairs to the bathroom and found a coiled ball of sheets. He saw the remnants of blood on the floor and her attempt to wipe it up.

A mournful sigh escaped him as he imagined her struggling through this alone. He wanted to be strong and surround her in his protective embrace, but he, too, was overcome. Sorrow for this dream that had begun to take shape in his mind, sorrow for the tiny human that was cheated of their love. He had imagined seeing her cradle their child in her arms. It broke him that he wasn't there for her as the tragedy unfolded. And the guilt that, within a week, he would have to leave her was drowning him.

He walked back upstairs and lay down beside her. She stirred, and he rocked her back to sleep in his arms. It would be hard to leave her alone, and he wished he had a choice. Waking up first, he headed to the bathroom to take care of the blood-stained sheets. He wasn't squeamish about blood. He'd seen plenty as a soldier. He'd held dear friends and enemies alike while their lives flowed out of them. He picked up the sheets and put them in the washer. He added the detergents and turned the dial to the stain setting, but then he froze.

This wasn't a stain. It was his child. The reality, as well as what they had lost, hit him. He felt his chest squeeze as dread dug its claws deep inside him. He collapsed in front of the washer, his head in his hands, while doleful, primal sobs escaped from the abyss where his soul now resided. His vision blurred from the tears that fell like a steady rain. He should push the start button for Jilly, but he couldn't. It was a task he had done hundreds of times, but this was different. He was washing his child down the drain, and into the digestive juices of the sewer.

He was still sitting there contemplating the solemnness of the moment when Jilly came into the laundry room. He stood up and leaned his hand on the lid. They shared more than a look. They shared understanding. This wasn't a simple household chore. It was a funeral. They both looked at the washer, wondering if this memory would return every time they washed clothes. Jilly quietly put her arm around her husband and said a simple prayer.

"Lord, we give to You our child. Bless him or her, and wrap us all in your healing arms."

"Amen," Gray followed.

Jilly took his hand in hers and they pressed the start button together.

The next day, Jilly went to the RAS. Andie called her to her office. Jilly explained the delay in confirming her pregnancy. She said she knew that she had miscarried because she had seen the tissue, which she believed was the fetus. To her, it was conclusive proof. She was also sure her body had successfully purged her womb, and she didn't require further medical aid. Jilly reported to Andie that she had taken her vitals and made a promise to keep her in the loop until she resumed her regular cycle. Jilly knew Andie was busy getting ready for the mission, and she was comfortable letting Jilly manage her medical treatment.

Grateful that Andie gave her the day off to recover, she called her big sister. Ari was on maternity leave and told her she was coming over. When she shared her loss, they cried, holding little Sebastian between them. Ari promised not to share this with anyone else but Bannon. Jilly thought back to the night Gray bared his soul to her, and she agreed Ari shouldn't keep this from her husband.

On the way home, Jilly stopped at the church and talked to Haru. He had kind words and good advice for moving forward. He was also going to be on the first part of the mission. He wouldn't be gone as long as Gray, but she would miss his kind counsel and wisdom.

It was four days before the mission was scheduled to leave. Gray parked at the Deegan Chance Maintenance building and walked into the machine shop. He had requisitioned weapons and armor upgrades for the mission, and they were ready for pickup. He was especially excited about the state-of-the-art compound bows he ordered. He watched William wield one in battle, silent, stealthy, lethal. He wanted one.

He had four bows made, and one was a surprise for Will. It was an upgrade to the homemade one he built from abandoned town scraps. He held the weapon and examined its quality craftsmanship. It was elegant, sleek, lightweight, and so foreign. Though it would be some time before he matched Will's skill, he was excited to learn. Gray couldn't wait to surprise him.

The next few days were filled with numerous meetings and checking off tasks. Time was slipping by too quickly. Soon, he would be leaving his wife. She needed him, now more than ever, but he could not stay. He walked into Bannon's office expecting to hear more of the same. The same schedule, the same people assigned to the same vehicles, the same protocols for travel. It felt like these had been on repeat at every meeting. He knew them, he presented them, and he didn't need the rerun. He slumped into the chair in front of Bannon, wondering why he had called him here instead of the conference room.

"I asked you here to give you a team member update," Bannon said, watching Gray. He knew there was no way this was going to go well.

"I know it isn't one of the soldiers. So, I'm assuming this is one of the people hitching a ride on the Friendship Tour."

"No, this is a mission changer."

"We're a day away, Bannon! It's kind of late to make critical changes. Is this new person trained and vaccinated? Who is this person, and what job is being filled? Why all this subterfuge?"

"Dr. Channing has received her doctorate. She wants to work at Sentry as the Fringer Medical Director for the Fort and the Township."

"And who is going in her place?" Gray was positive it would not be Maya, and he was pretty sure he was not going to like Bannon's choice. Connor and his soldiers deserved a professional medic, not a newbie out of college.

"It's Jilly," he said apprehensively.

"The hell it is!" yelled Gray as he stood up, kicking his roller chair forcefully across the room and pounding the table.

"She contacted me when she found out Andie opted out," Bannon said defensively. "She made a good case. She really is the best choice. Maybe the only choice."

"Why can't you make Andie go? Jilly just lost a baby for fuck's sake!" his voice was full of panicked emotion.

"This mission may not be voluntary for the soldiers, but I can't make a civilian go against her will. Andie is terrified to go. She confided in me that she doesn't have what it takes. You and I worried about her assignment from the get-go."

"Yeah, but what the fuck, Bannon!" Gray was pacing now. "Your solution is to replace her with my wife?" He paced some more and threw out another rebuttal. "It's too late to train her."

"She told me you have been giving her self-defense lessons for months. And she knows how to shoot and handle a gun. That's *more* training than Andie got. She is also a field and trauma specialist. She's up to date on her vaccines, and Connor trusts her. And most importantly, you told her what's going on and what's at stake. You unwittingly made her my only choice."

"I don't trust her not to sacrifice herself if something goes south."

"That sounds like what you expect of *everyone* on the team, including yourself."

It did not escape Bannon's attention that he was sending his wife's sister, who had become very dear to him, on a dangerous mission on the heels of a devastating loss. He also knew he was asking too much of his brother-in-law, his friend, to accept it. But Jilly was truly his only option. The conversation with Jilly that morning echoed in Bannon's head.

"Gray is going to worry about me whether I'm here or by his side," Jilly stated, rolling her eyes.

"It may alter his priorities, which could compromise the mission," Bannon retorted.

"It won't. He knows, as do I, that if this mission fails, we all die. Besides, protecting Connor creates the same scenario. But if I'm there, I can help protect Connor, because he trusts me, and I won't be tangled up in combat. I'll be next to him in whatever place Gray has planned for attack scenarios. He always has a plan," Jilly argued. Bannon chuckled.

"You don't think Connor will gravitate to Gray in a dangerous situation?" Bannon asked.

"You know Gray will stuff him in a hole before he drags him into combat. At least I'd be in that hole with him. Connor loves Gray, but he's a child talking to a man he admires, so he tends to guy-share. Saying the things that make him look mature and brave. He doesn't try to impress me. He shares his crazy ideas, his inner thoughts, and his fears. Fears like failing and letting people down. He needs someone he can confide in while he's going through this mission.

He'll self-implode if he locks others out, trying to be brave and not worry them. In other words, he's a child who needs a mother.

"But more than that, I am well-trained in trauma and field medicine as well as self-defense. Hanging out with Gray, Gabe, and Axle has exposed me to countless battle terms and strategies. I'm healthy and vaccination-ready. You don't have anyone else who's close to my qualifications that the town can spare."

Bannon looked at Gray, who was standing with his hands splayed on the sill of the large picture window that looked over South Street. The man behind the mayor's chair had a duty to the whole town, not just his family. He could see the undeniable logic of the choice, but so was his desire to protect his wife.

Mayor Bannon Vogel popped his anxiety medicine into his mouth and took a long drink of water.

"Gray, please come back and take a seat," he said, and inhaled deeply. "You're family, and I love you both, but you know this mission is our only shot, and she is more than our best choice. It has to be her, and she wants to go. She needs to go. In your heart, you know it's true."

"Don't ask my heart that question," he said as he slumped into the chair, "but the dispassionate officer in me agrees."

Gray sat in the conference room where the rest of the meeting would commence. He knew he had lost this battle, but he wasn't ready to give up. If he could get Jilly to change her mind, Bannon couldn't make her go. Maybe they needed to convince Andie to postpone her Fort Sentry job until after the mission. Before he could add anything to their conversation, the rest of the team began to filter in.

Gray stewed in his mood during the meeting, and Connor watched him closely, trying to tease out the reasons. The leader side of him was in abject conflict with the husband side, and there was no win for either. The agenda focused on last-minute reviews and updates. Connor watched Gray's reaction when he heard Jilly was going.

Gray was only slightly surprised when Connor blurted out his disapproval because she was, and he paused, troubled. Jilly must have shared on their recent walk that she had been pregnant but miscarried. It only proved how close Jilly was to this child. More evidence of her being the one for the job.

Gray sadly shared the news of the pregnancy, and then reported that they had lost the baby in the same sentence. The news was as brief as his child's life, and he fought back the tears.

Chapter Five

B annon ended the meeting and watched as Gray quickly headed for the door. He didn't engage with those involved in after-meeting chatter, nor did he offer his usual witty banter as he exited. He just left, forgetting his tablet on the table. Bannon knew he was making a straight line to Jilly.

It was a conversation that had to happen, but he wished Gray would take a moment to cool down his simmering mood, which was not known for conjuring wisdom.

Gray briskly marched to the RAS, where Jilly was working. He opened the door with charged authority and searched for his quarry. Those in the waiting room eyed him with interest as the receptionist explained she was with a patient. Holding back a grumble, he sat in the chair furthest away from everyone.

He ran through his speech—or, if he was being honest with himself, his lecture. He reviewed his "damn good reasons" why this was a bad idea, and again, if he was honest, the reasons it was bad for him. He tallied the reasons she thought it was a sound idea—for her, for everyone.

He ran his hand through his hair, which he was sure was turning greyer by the minute. Why did this woman work so hard to make his job difficult? She was a high-value target who insisted on being among the people. Crazy. Impossible.

He was calming down because this was not the place for his caustic energy. Looking past his wrath, he noticed the other people waiting. He overheard two of them mention they came for follow-up care from treatments that originated at the hospital. And another man had just walked in carrying a tiny infant. He checked in, saying he was here for her first wellness check.

The tiny wail and the clenched fists waving above the carrier stabbed through Gray like a hot blade. What was left of his snarling anger was overcome with profound sadness. He thought of Jilly having to see this child, full of life. She would check the little body and discuss the newborn's upcoming milestones. And she would smile sweetly, burying the grief of losing her own child just days earlier.

It was killing him to watch this baby full of life when, less than a week ago, they washed theirs away. People rarely brought infants to the security building where he worked, but her job was full of children of all ages. She had no place to escape the heartbreaking reminder. He didn't know how she did it.

Winning a fight suddenly lost its appeal. He got up and left. He had to relinquish his stubbornness. Connor needed a mother's care as much as Jilly needed to provide it.

Gray returned to Bannon's office to retrieve his tablet. Bannon was amid a phone conversation on speaker with Will at Fort Sentry. He waved Gray in and gestured for him to sit in one of the chairs in front of his desk.

"I think we can help you with that," Bannon answered. "We have several civil engineers who can evaluate the roads and help you repair them. Let me contact my maintenance department and get back to you on that."

"Thanks, I'd feel a lot better knowing the fort and the villages won't be easy targets in my absence." Will's confident strength and intensity flowed through the small speaker located on Bannon's desk.

Bannon ended the call and turned to Gray. "I assume you got the gist of that conversation." Gray nodded. "I have an idea. Henry is all but done with his civil engineering degree. I say we send him as one of the passengers on the Friendship Tour."

Gray thought about the reasons it would make sense. Plus, Henry could spend some quality time with his son. The man's concentration on his schooling made it easy for Connor to maintain his secretive life. Now that Henry was informed, the hours of driving would provide the perfect environment for the conversation they needed to have.

"How many passengers does that make?" asked Gray.

"Well, there's Tanya, who is moving to Fort Sentry permanently, and Haru, who's going to help her set up the ministry outreach program. Dr. Channing, Andie, is also moving there to head up the medical department. Aniya is going to be in charge of their food production and livestock program. That's four, and Henry would be five. All but Aniya will go with you to the towns on the Friendship Tour stage of the mission and be introduced to the Fringers.

"It is a logical step for us to take since we have joined forces with them. Tanya and Andie will return to the Fort, and Henry and Haru will return to New Haven. We have to work out the final drop-off plans with the Guard, but we're sending one of our trucks to pull the trailer and accommodate the extra people and provisions. When they head back, they will bring everything but what you need for Operation Reclamation. The rest of the team will head to Aspen."

"I know the plan. We'll pick up our tracker there and search Pyramid Mountain for Cali Bantu, and from there," Gray said with his palms up, "it's a mystery."

"Okay, I'll talk with Baker in maintenance to clear Henry for temporary duty outside the tunnel. Was there something else?"

"No," Gray said, still sorting out his conflicting moods.

"Please, tell me you didn't berate your wife when you left here," Bannon added, expecting Gray to explode. His normal grumbles and snips had been transformed by personal tragedy, untenable responsibilities, and an eruption was imminent, and that was before Bannon dropped the big bomb on him. The man deserved a temper tantrum and a target for his blistering rage. Bannon preferred it to be on him rather than his fragile sister-in-law.

"I thought about it," Gray said with a sneering look at the man he unjustly blamed for the debacle, "but I decided I needed a better approach."

"A wise choice. Shall we go to the gym for a round of boxing then?"

Gray puffed out a dismissive, "If only there was time," response and even managed a weak smile. But in truth, his anger had been smothered by grief and sleep deprivation.

Bannon was not fooled. Gray was his closest friend and his brother by marriage. "I'll let you know the final decision regarding Henry. And Gray, go home, get some sleep. Let Axle handle the sit work."

"If only there was time," Gray repeated as he grabbed his tablet and walked toward the door.

Gray walked into the Security Building and saw Axle sitting in his office. No doubt Bannon had messaged him. His brother had been seriously injured in the battle a week and a half ago and had recently been released from the hospital.

"Gray, let me work on these logistics for you. I've tuned in on every meeting, and I'm up to date. You can peruse my work tomorrow."

"So, are you going to rework the security protocols for Jilly?" Gray said, his tone biting like a towel snap. Axle knew he wasn't the target, but, as it sometimes happens, their roles reverted to the big and little brother.

"Yes, and I think my perspective would generate a more logical plan. You are too close and emotional about this, Gray." Axle didn't want to poke the cornered bear, but the truth had to be said out loud.

"She's your sister-in-law! How are you not close to the issue? And besides that, you might not even go!" Gray said, incensed.

"Of course, I love her, and I am compelled to create a good, safe plan. But I am not being sucked down the whirlpool like you are. Desperate people make desperate mistakes. That's what you've told me numerous times. And just so you know, I'm working out, and I'm almost back to my previous routine. So, I *will* be ready. So don't you dare pull my slot out from under me, *brother*."

Gray took a breath. Axle was making sense, and he wasn't. Maybe he should go home. "It's not up to me, Ax. If you want to convince someone, that person is Maya. I'm glad you're recovering, and I don't want to replace you. You have an extra four days after we leave to heal up while we're at Sentry. But if you're not cleared when we head to Eagle, I can't let you run sweep for the mission," Gray said.

Axle sighed. Could his brother drag him on the mission without Maya's okay? Probably, but he wouldn't, and Axle knew he shouldn't. Gray ousted Axle from his office chair and called Gabe to take Axle home. Gabe was just under Axle in rank, and he was also the one who would take Axle's place. Though they were close friends, it was a quiet ride to the small home Axle shared with Dewy.

Gray's sleepless nights were filled with heartache, worry, and anger, and they had left their mark on him. His grief journey skipped bargaining and landed flatly on grumpy melancholy. It was a frightening state. It was like existing outside of himself, while avoiding looking into his own eyes. He plodded up to his door and used his band to open it.

Seeing Jilly's tote on the counter, he knew she was off early. He strode upstairs, skipping steps. He felt that familiar lump form in his throat as he passed the empty would-be nursery that had lost its purpose. Further down the hall, he found Jilly on their bed. Her tear-streaked face was gentled by sleep. He sat down and leaned in to kiss her cheek. She stirred.

"What time is it?" she asked, propping herself on her elbow to check the time display. "Oh, you're off early."

"So are you. Are you okay?"

"Yeah, I just," she paused. "I just…" a sob fought for release, but she restrained it. "I needed to come home. I'm glad you're here. I need to tell you something."

"Bannon told me you took Andie's place on the mission." Gray eyed his wife with a calm but serious intent.

"There are a number of reasons I'm the perfect replacement. For one—"

"Save your breath. I was force-fed a litany of arguments in favor of you filling the position," his tone was a mix of irritation and fatigue. "I just want to know why. Why would you volunteer for such a dangerous mission? It will expose you to the very people who murdered your father, erased your identity, hurt you, poisoned you, hell, I had to kill you to save you. I'm going to have a devil of a time protecting Connor and his identity. You double that responsibility," he sighed. "I can't lose you, Jilly."

"Well, I can't lose you either. I'd rather be with you and face whatever comes beside you than wait here alone, wondering if I'll ever see you again. I need to be near you now more than ever, and

Connor needs me to be with him, too." Gray lay back on the bed with a heavy sigh.

Jilly leaned up on her elbow and rolled on her side to look at him as he stared at the ceiling. "Look, Gray, the Corporates aren't stupid. They're not going to believe we're on a winter meet-and-greet with the neighbors. That means everyone on this mission is on their list. They aren't focused on my father's innovations right now. They want whatever it is we're going after because it's unknown, and that threatens their reign. I know I'll be under your orders. I promise," she said, putting her hand up to pledge, "to listen and do as you say."

"Yes, you will," he responded in a calm but authoritative voice, while still fixated on the ceiling.

He sighed and rolled over, placing his finger on her lips, signaling the conversation was done. Nothing would change her mind or Bannon's, and he hated to admit it, but he agreed. On his way home, he checked with Maya. The only other replacement was a nineteen-year-old who wasn't defense-trained or vaccinated, and barely out of nursing school.

This wasn't what he wanted, but it was past the discussion stage. He took her into his strong arms, and she sank into his broad-chested comfort.

Gray didn't see himself as a hero, but he knew he was well snarled in the calling. He thought about something Will said to him. "Destiny is a cunning bitch who enslaves the honorable to achieve her goals, and there is no avoiding the path she sets you on." He felt the truth and weight of it fully on his shoulders.

It was the morning of their departure, and the final meeting was held in the Legislative Room with all the mission team members and the support team. Gray and Jilly sat with Connor between them. Connor looked up at Jilly with eyes that longed to say the right words. He squeezed her hand and gazed at her sympathetically. She squeezed in response and gave him a sad smile of understanding. She directed her attention to the final review and the last-minute changes. The meeting ended, and they gathered onto several buses to the garage and vehicle exit on the west side.

All along the street, residents lined up to cheer on the brave team, venturing out to meet their Fringer allies. They sported homemade signs and threw streamers and paper flowers. It was a heartwarming display of support. Though few details were disclosed to the public, the people had a sense that the mission's goal was intimately tied to their survival.

The crowds ended at the security barrier near the Defender's west garage, where the bus carts disappeared from the townspeople. The buses emptied quickly, and most were ushered into the Brute. Lana would ride with Jax in one of the mini Brutes with Beckett and Mack in the other. The five vehicles and the trailer were bursting with mission gear and supplies to present and trade with the towns.

When they arrived at the final barrier on the far side of town, the convoy paused as the gates opened. Ohs and ahs escaped the passengers, who rarely got the see the light of day. It didn't take long before Henry and Gray were deep into civil engineering conversations, Haru and Tanya reviewed their plans, and Jilly and Andie spoke quietly in the back.

The road wasn't smooth like the New Haven streets, but it was passable and much better than the roads ahead, according to the warnings given in the briefing. A pee break at a spot called Maryland Creek was a welcome reprieve from the bumpy ride. Stepping out into the cold air brought back more memories and comparisons to their well-ordered town.

Connor sought out Gray on their way back to the Brute. "Hey, O.G., my dad wants to talk with me, 'spend some time,'" he said with air quotes.

"He is fully aware there are limits to what you can share, and more than that, he understands it. Remember, our 'purpose' of this trip," Gray followed with his own air quote notation. "We are visiting the Fringer towns to introduce ourselves. Truth be told, we will be doing that. We thought about introducing you as our school spokesperson, but we decided it was too risky. The Corporates are very aware of the prophecy saying a Highmind offspring will be trained to locate Cali Bantu. They will be highly suspicious of a child traveling with soldiers."

Connor looked alarmed. "So, how is that going to work? Will you lock me away every time we hit a town?" his squeaking voice exposed irritation.

Gray laughed, "Is your voice starting to change?"

"You're deflecting, O.G.," Connor replied with his arms crossed in front of him.

"We have a plan that will be put into play at Fort Sentry, but before I get into it, I want to ensure the pieces are in place."

"So, no hint about how you plan to mess with my life?" Sarcasm radiated from the child with a man's job before him.

"Nope," he said with a sly grin. "But you'll only be locked away for the first night. Tomorrow morning, we'll leave and go on an adventure," he paused before adding with a gleam in his eye, "to the lake!" Connor smiled at that.

Back at the vehicles, bag lunches were handed out. People got a good start on them before they were told to load back up. Jilly wasn't very hungry until she began to nibble off a corner of the peanut butter and jelly sandwich she had requested. It quickly disappeared, and she wished she had another one. During her pregnancy, she had developed a hankering for them, and losing the baby hadn't diminished that craving.

The passengers were roughly bounced down the road like tempest-tossed sailors on a deep-sea voyage. The briefing had described that the roads would be rough and full of unknown hazards, but the reality and time spent enduring it was abusive. When the Brute stopped in front of a fallen tree blocking the way, the thankful riders exited the cab. They knew the reprieve would be short as they watched the Defenders revving up their chainsaws and making quick work of the problem.

Jilly's head was pounding, and she could taste the acidic spit forming in her mouth. She walked away from the vehicles, and when she was out of sight, she heaved while hanging onto a tree. Deep breathing her way back to stability, she took a sip from her water bottle. She closed her eyes and felt her head beginning to clear. She justified her illness to the roughness of the road, but a concerning doubt pecked at the back of her brain. She wanted to dismiss it, but something was going on with her. Looking at the pathway back to the group, she saw Connor watching her with visible worry.

"Jilly, are you okay?" he asked softly as he approached her.

"Yeah, it's just motion sickness. The road has been rough, and I'm not used to riding for this long."

"You're probably still weak from ..." He stopped mid-sentence, and she could see he felt bad about breaching the unmentionable topic.

"It's okay, Conner. And you're right. My body is a bit out of whack, but I'm fine, honest. I'll be right behind you. I just need a minute. But Connor, please keep this between us. Gray is already worried about me." He gave her a thumbs-up and walked toward the Brute to give her some privacy.

A second round of seat changes took place with Easton and Tanya riding in the mini Brutes while Lana sat with Haru in the Brute. Jilly curled up in the back corner to try and get some rest.

At the abandoned town of Silverton, they turned onto Highway 9. It was a semi-paved road, meaning it had considerable potholes and patches that needed patching. Cracks that created rises and falls, as well as chunks of the old asphalt, were strewn about, requiring careful navigation. It was a hard ride with constant rocking from side to side.

The passengers endured their treatment without complaint. It was similar to the trip they had taken in the transports to New Haven, but these smaller utility vehicles doled out a much harsher ride. Jilly was asleep next to Dr. Channing with no sign of distress. Connor and his dad talked quietly, and Haru and Lana looked out the windows, making occasional comments along the way.

The road wandered along the Blue River, which once fed the Green Mountain Reservoir before the dam broke. The old water level left a stark line of barren ground and struggling vegetation where the mountain lake water once lapped gently onto the sloping shores.

They parked by the road next to a thick wall of vegetation. The passengers watched as Jax, Gray, and Beckett got out. Gray reached his hand into the bushes and spoke, and then three of them swung open the bush-covered gates. The entourage filed through and re-closed the gates. They were now on a dirt road, which was categorized as poor. This one was lined with gravel, but it was piled up on the sides from the recent snowplow activity.

If they thought the roads were rough before, they were now treated to a dirt trail full of ruts, sloppy puddles, and places where it was completely washed away. The brutal seasons and frequent use had left the route looking better suited for walking than driving. Gray was ahead in a mini, enjoying the sport of four-wheeling a bit too much.

Jax wasn't trying to keep up with Gray, but she was still running the Brute quickly on the rutted roads. She turned to check on her moaning passengers and saw the seats were full of pale riders. She pulled over and said, "I think we need a break."

They slowly poured themselves out into the fresh air and clear blue sky. Performing various stretches and deep yawns, a crisp breeze wafted around the battered crew, refreshing their lungs and bringing smiles to their faces once again. Between the chilly air and the still ground beneath their feet, they readied themselves for their imminent arrival.

Jilly was taking a little longer to regain her composure. She and Andie decided to walk ahead for a bit. Gray traded vehicles with Defender Jax, and after picking up the walkers, they pulled onward to Fort Sentry.

Black Creek Reservoir came into view. It was a pretty lake whose dam, they were told, had been rebuilt. Jax said it was small as lakes go, but most of the passengers had never seen one beyond the dried-up formation they just passed. To them, it was massive.

"Can we swim in that water?" Connor asked her, thinking of the refreshing pool back at New Haven.

Jax turned her head slightly from the road and answered him. "I imagine it would be very cold, even in the summer months."

The next and last leg of their journey was another earthen road that headed up a rise. When they got to the top, Jax stopped to let the travelers see the view. It was breathtaking. They could see the lake they had just passed as well as another, a much larger lake, further up the Black Creek Road. From their perch, the world offered a miniature version of the landscape they had traveled through. Sounds of awe expressed the appreciation of the view from the high ground.

Before they climbed back into the vehicles, they saw a man coming up the trail on a horse, followed by a reddish-brown dog. They recognized him. It was William of the Guard.

"Welcome to Fort Sentry," he said. "It's hard to see because it's camouflaged, but," he pointed, "it's right over there."

The tired travelers strained to see it, but it was like their eyes couldn't focus correctly. It looked thick and blurry, like an abstract impressionistic painting. As they drove closer to the buildings, they could see the paint shimmer and react to its environment.

Few had noticed the effect close up when they were led out to go to New Haven. It created an ingenious deception. They parked in the central area of the buildings and exited the rigs. William jumped down from his horse to shake hands with everyone in the group, and they followed him inside. His well-trained dog shadowed him, calmly accepting the head rubs and pets from the crowd while a soldier came and led the horse away.

They were led inside the Alpha building, which looked very different to the previous residents. The fences around the activity area had been removed, and four new buildings sat against the wall. The area was mostly open space. The army they expected to see was absent, but two men were coming toward them. Both were dressed in civilian clothes.

"Hi," the civilian with a tablet tucked under his arm said. "My name is Relic." A chorus of "Hi" was returned.

The other man had a kind smile and reached out his hand, saying, "I'm Taylor, Will's adopted father." A series of handshakes was exchanged.

Before any introductions could be offered by the group, a soldier approached.

"Commander," the man said to William, "the briefing room has been prepared."

"Thank you, Nash. This way," the leader of the Guard instructed, and the travelers followed without question.

They were led into what used to be the DOR, where the Defender operations were conducted. It was now labeled the GOR (Guard Operation Room). They walked past the desks with various computers, view screens, and communication devices to a small elevator that barely held four people. The second floor opened into a short hall lined with several closed doors. Will's loyal dog lay next to the door they entered. It was a sizable conference room with a large table and a dozen chairs.

All eight passengers, plus Gray, William, Relic, and Taylor, filed in, filling every chair and leaving two Guard soldiers standing to the side. William sat at the head of the table, Relic to his left, Gray at his right, and Taylor at the other end of the table. The standing soldiers Rival and Nash were introduced, and the visitors, in turn, gave their introductions.

William began. "This will be a short briefing. The topic is our youngest team member." Everyone looked at Connor, who nervously shifted positions. "You were told at New Haven that Connor was chosen for his 'unique abilities'. That description was an embellishment by the reporter. Although he meant no harm, making that assumption could have dire consequences if repeated beyond this room. If this impression is associated with Connor, the Corporates will believe he is a Highmind. He would be a target, and as a child, a soft target.

"It is unlikely that information will escape the secure town of New Haven, but out here, anyone could fall prey to bribes or torture. We believe the best way to protect him is to change his identity. As far as any of you know, this boy is the son of a Lone Fringer who was brought here for medical treatment with our new doctor. He will be kept in a secure location until tomorrow morning. At that time, a healer, Tura of McCoy, will arrive and walk him in front of the Guards present and into the Infirmary. Since he is a stranger, do not interact with him. Are there any questions?"

Jax raised her hand. "Are you worried you have dissidents in your army?"

"I have no reason to doubt my people, but only a fool would dismiss the possibility," he said with a tinge of annoyance. "Traitors have more opportunities outside of a locked-up town to make connections and compromise our people. We keep much from our troops until they have a need to know."

Haru was next. "What is a Lone Fringer?"

"A Lone Fringer does not belong to a tribe. We have people from every Fringer tribe in the area. Every child would be known by someone here. But very few would know a Lone Fringer's child."

Dr. Channing raised her hand. "Can I assume more information will be coming my way since he will be my patient?"

"Your patient will arrive with his paperwork completed for you, and you will review it like you would any new patient. For tomorrow, all you need to say is that you heard his condition is not contagious."

Connor was hearing this information for the first time, like the rest of the people in the room. He reluctantly raised his hand, gazing apprehensively at the powerful man sitting at the head of the table. In a low voice, he asked, "What's my name?"

It wasn't meant as a joke, but everyone began laughing. The child gave a hesitant smile and sat up straighter, trying to summon his courage. His dad saw he was feeling insecure and grabbed his hand under the table. Gray raised his hand, and the room became quiet.

Gray looked at Connor thoughtfully. "I'd stay with Connor. It's what you're used to," he said honestly. "No one needs to know your last name, if Lone Fringers even use them. Fewer mistakes will be made that way."

Haru whispered something to Gray, and he nodded.

"You don't have to decide right now," said William, seeing that Haru was concerned about Connor. "But we will need to know soon." When no one raised any more questions, he signaled the soldier, Nash, who bent down to receive his instructions. Then he turned back to the group. "Okay, everyone, except the military team members, please follow Taylor, who will give you a short tour and get you settled into your quarters. Your gear has already been taken to your rooms."

Gray looked at Connor and added, "Connor, you will wait downstairs with Haru. He will go over the details of your assignment for tomorrow's ruse." Although those not joining us on the mission didn't know the real goal, Connor doubted they were naive enough to believe all this secrecy surrounding him was about the Friendship Tour.

As they left, Nash and Rival sat down, and four more soldiers filed in. Their make-shift uniforms had been carefully crafted by the soldiers themselves, which gave proof of their dedication, but it did little to portray an organized force. In other words, it screamed they were under-funded and undervalued by their benefactors. Gray thought about it and pondered the advantage of being underestimated.

Gray considered the gifts they brought for the Guard army. He couldn't wait to present them to William, and it made him feel like a kid waiting for a holiday.

There was only one Guard on duty in the room when the New Haven crew came downstairs. His crutches leaned on the desk beside him. He winked at Jilly, signaling her unplanned visit with him in the hospital was still a secret. She just smiled.

As the rest of the group was walking out the door behind Taylor, Haru and Connor stayed.

"Hi, I'm Hunter," the soldier said to Connor and Haru. "I was told to keep you two here for a couple. You can sit anywhere you want. It shouldn't be too long."

"Are you the soldier who was treated at New Haven?" Connor asked.

"Yes," he answered. "I guess it caused a lot of issues."

"Everyone understood you deserved good medical care, especially since without you guys, we would have lost the battle. New Haven citizens are terrified of two things: being discovered and disease, and you represented both of those, but not now. I hear you will make a full recovery. That's what matters."

He smiled with gratitude. Hunter didn't know why they were dragging a kid on a mission about introductions. But he was loyal to William, and he would keep this to himself whether Will explained it or not. He noticed the child was fidgeting and brimming with nervous energy.

"Hey, come with me," Hunter said as he grabbed his crutches. "I know rocking down those roads all day can be brutal. I think I know just what you need. We have a workout room close by."

He led them out of the command center and down the hall, smoothly moving his body in sync with the props as if they were part of him. They passed the infirmary, Haru's old office, and stopped at the door to the storage room. Connor froze. His nervousness turned into a full-blown panic attack. The last time he followed a soldier down this hall, she was a Corporate infiltrator. She kidnapped him and locked him in this same dark storage room, where he thought he'd be killed.

"Is he okay?" asked Hunter.

Haru nodded kindly and gestured to the soldier to give them some privacy. He reluctantly crutched back to his post.

Chapter Six

"Connor," Haru was holding the child's shoulders, "I understand you associate this with a bad memory, but I think it's one you're ready to face."

"What if I can't face it? What if I'm not ready for any of this? What if I can't find this Cali Bantu? Or say I find it, but I can't access it, and do whatever it is that I'm supposed to do once we're inside? Everyone is counting on me, and I don't even know what I'm supposed to do. What will happen if I fail? People could die, and it would be my fault." Connor was shaking, and Haru steadied him.

"You are not alone in this, Connor. We are all responsible for the success of this mission, and everyone has these fears. Everyone I've spoken to is honored to work with you. Look at all you've done. Keeping your grandad's information safe, starting a baseball league, and decoding the location of Cali Bantu. You are a phenomenon.

"You are one of the bravest people I know. And I know, this is more than anyone, let alone a child, should have to shoulder, but you've accomplished every step and every duty put before you. I believe in you. But you're not in charge, and therefore, the only job you have to focus on is following orders.

"Now, take a breath," Haru said, and Connor did. "It's just a room. How about we start with a look inside? Then we'll walk in there like we own the place. Ready?" Connor thought of Gray and how courage radiated from him. He would walk into this room and laugh. Connor nodded, straightened his posture, breathed in deeply, and grabbed the door handle.

The room was well-lit and full of exercise equipment that surrounded a central floor mat. Shelves lined one wall, filled with bands, weights, balls, and jump ropes. The creepy, dark storage room, once crowded with stacks of boxes, shelves, and the threat of death, was transformed into a place he was familiar with—the New Haven gym. For several weeks, he had been enrolled in self-defense and strength training classes to prepare for the mission.

Connor walked in hesitantly. *It's just like training classes*, he mouthed silently and climbed on one of the stationary bikes. He began to peddle, but like the New Haven Gym, the tension was set too high, so he loosened it. He began slowly but quickly stood up on the peddles and surged into a furious pace. Haru was impressed with this prodigy child who was impervious to failure. He prayed silently that he would be guided through this difficult part of his life and delivered into a peaceful future.

"Oorah!" Connor yelled triumphantly while pumping his fist like the Defenders in his training classes.

The conference room upstairs was filled with all the military personnel who were on the mission, except the sweep team. They were still in New Haven. This was the first time both teams had gathered together. Will and Gray restated the duty regarding their youngest charge.

"This is no ordinary child. He is incredibly bright and specifically trained for this mission. He is the key to finding, accessing, and utilizing the objective of our mission," Gray said. Nash, one of Will's men, put up his hand, and Gray gestured for him to speak.

"Why can't he train Relic, so he doesn't have to go? I mean, even without the threat of the Corporate thugs, this isn't going to be a simple grab and go. It's gonna get brutal."

Will spoke, "He cannot train him to deal with the unknown, and more importantly, he can't teach Relic to think like him. He may be short and vulnerable, but he's indispensable," They laughed at the irony more than the humor.

"Not only do we have to protect his person, we need to protect his identity. If the Corporates get wind of us traveling with a child, they'll know we are after Cali Bantu, and that he is one of the prophesied Highmind children," Gray answered.

"They are going to assume we are after Cali Bantu regardless of any cover story we could conceive," Will said. 'They will be tailing us wherever we go to confiscate what we are after. But our agreement with them will cause them to hesitate and send minimal troops. That time is what we are counting on."

Will continued, "As you know, he will be posing as a Lone Fringer child who came to the Fort for medical treatment. He is traveling with us because we are bringing him back to his family. There will be a guard assigned to him at all times, and it is a high-priority assignment. Whenever possible, that duty will fall on Gray or me." He paused and turned a steely gaze upon the soldiers gathered around the table. "Be alert and mindful of your conversations. If anything happens to this child due to reckless or traitorous actions, I will gut that person myself."

The Guard soldiers straightened their posture, looked their commander in the eye, and placed their palms on the center of their chest in unison. Their hardened expressions said they vowed to follow his order and that his warning was not hyperbole. The Defender soldiers observed the response.

Gray noted Will's style, too. It was more authoritarian than his, but the Defenders lived in a hidden sanctuary. The Guard lived in the world of Drangers, Neighwah, and other predators. He thought about his soldiers. Though they were physically ready and recently battle-tested, this would be weeks of travel under the constant threat of combat. He hoped they were ready for the mental anguish of warfare, of hunting humans and being hunted by them in return.

"Okay, we're going to bring Connor in here," said Gray. "He needs to meet all of you before we head out. We've trained him and explained the structured routines we'll follow on the road. But remember, he's twelve, so let's chill out a bit."

Connor walked in and took the one open seat remaining. It was on the corner between William and Gray. Introductions circled the table, including a few details they felt would help Connor connect with them. The meeting continued reviewing the protocols for various situations.

Will began, "There is one more person who will join us further down our route. He is a Lone Fringer, a tracker, who is familiar with the area we will be traveling through. We've never met him, but he comes highly recommended by the RH." William turned and spoke to Connor, "On this mission, Connor, your protection is paramount to our objective. We discussed your cover story. You must follow the safeguards and orders that let us protect you." Connor nodded. "Have you decided on a name?"

Connor looked around the room and saw the people charged with his safety. They were real people with personalities, memories, families, and lives they treasured. The thought of even one of them being harmed or lost defending him was unbearable.

"I ... I'm not sure yet." Choosing another name felt like a childish game, and he didn't believe it would fool anyone. He was tired and undone by the long day and heavy task before him, before all of them. "Not to sound like a kid, but when's dinner?"

The room erupted in laughter, the kind that comes when a moment of brevity releases the tension of an unsettling future. Gray knew Connor enough to see what he had done. He smiled at him and mouthed the word *touché*.

"I agree. It's late, and this day has dragged on long enough," Gray said before another issue could be launched.

The New Haven mission team members were happy the day was finally over. Everyone but Connor, Gray, and Will were dismissed. The visiting soldiers were led to the area where the curtain homes of the Hold used to stand. In their place against the far back wall stood four shipping container structures, each with two doors accessing the visitor barracks. Blocking them from the soldiers' arena were three restroom trailers.

Haru and Henry had settled into their rooms hours ago. Andie was settled into what used to be the counselor's office, and Aniya was housed in the Delta building, where the animal husbandry and farms were managed. Unlike her colleagues, who had rooms without bathrooms or kitchens, Aniya was issued a full apartment. Lana, Jax, Mack, and Beckett followed the Guard soldier to their rooms.

While her husband attended the meeting, Jilly had been able to settle into their room. She opened the door and found it sparsely adorned but clean. The size was similar to their bedroom back home. She recognized the furniture was from the curtain home collection. A desk was parked against the wall adjacent to the door, a tall locker on the opposite wall, and a queen bed was centered on the back wall, flanked by small nightstands. She smiled at the memory of Gray describing the curtain home to her while she was hospitalized in the Hold.

She unpacked the totes she had packed for herself and Gray into the locker. Stowing the tote, she lay on the bed. She hadn't even closed her eyes before she heard a knock on the door. It was Andie.

She came in, shut the door, and got right to the point. "Okay, something more than road sickness is bothering you. Before Gray gets back, I need you to come to the infirmary with me. We're doing a full workup on you."

"I think I know what it is," Jilly answered. "But it can't be true."

"I think you may be right, and it can be true. Come on, Jilly. We have to find out."

It was like she was living through her first days here all over again. She followed Andie across the yard and into the clinic.

After the meeting adjourned, Gray asked Will to follow him. While everyone was busy heading to dinner, it would be the perfect time to share the treasures he brought. Will brought him to the storage area where the boxes of supplies Gray brought had been stored.

"I called Taylor and got the sizes of the people on your team," Gray said as he opened the first box and took out one of the warm-weather gear with bulletproof armor.

"Oh damn!" Will gasped. "Gray, you have no idea. Thanks!"

"That's not all," Gray was gleaming with child-like excitement as he opened up more boxes with hi-tech weapons, precision gun sights, surveillance equipment, and various stealth apparatuses. Will was overwhelmed. These were more than gifts; they were lifesavers.

"I've saved the best for last," Gray said with a big grin. Will smiled, his eyes sparkling with anticipation.

Gray carefully and proudly opened a hard case. Inside was a new state-of-the-art compound bow. The bow Will used had been hand-made by him, and he had mastered it, but he told Gray it required constant tweaking, repairs, and adjustments. Will inhaled deeply while his eyes widened.

"Get out! Holy shit!" It wasn't a proper thank you, but it was completely genuine.

Gray showed him another hard case. "There are two more for your best archers. But this one's mine," Gray said, pulling the weapon out of its case. "I could figure it out on my own. I've shot a traditional bow before, but I was hoping you could give me some pointers."

"Gray, I'm speechless. I can't wait to show Tommie and Nash. They're my best archers, and they're gonna freak. Let's get dinner, then I need to check in on Connor and talk with him myself. I need to get him to trust me if I am to watch him. After that, we'll go to my office and set the sights. I'm hoping we have a bit of a connection before we go to the lake tomorrow. You're going to love this weapon. So quiet and so lethal."

Normally, Connor would have been put in one of the guest buildings, but because his ruse had him arriving tomorrow, he was taken to the Guard Operations Room. The old commander's room was now the bunk room, and it was where he was quartered. An oversized bunk bed was set against the wall with a locker at each end. Next to the door stood a square table without chairs.

Will's office was upstairs by the conference room, and the old Defender barracks that was the DOR had been remodeled into a small studio apartment. It was simply furnished, but he didn't need much. He liked to think of it as spartan chic, but when he described it to Leita, his girlfriend, she called it military bleak.

Haru was there when William and Taylor walked in. Haru stood, so Connor stood.

"Sit, sit," Will said. Then the three men sat on the edge of the lower bunk, Connor sat on the floor next to his dinner. Though there was a generous distance between the lower and upper bunks, Will still had to lean forward.

Connor spoke first. "I don't know what to call you. Your troops call you Commander, but you introduced yourself as William of the Guard. Which is your preference?"

"What do you think, Haru?" Will asked. "I need his trust, but I also need his respect."

Haru answered thoughtfully, "Connor is not like any child I have ever known. He thinks very deeply and intellectually. I believe if he respects you, it will be because he trusts you. What he calls you will have little effect on him," answered Haru.

"I see. In that case, when it's just us, you can call me Will, but when we are with the team, call me sir."

"Yes, sir," Connor said respectfully. "Sir, would it be possible to get me a chair for that desk over there?"

Will smiled. "I like you. You're quick and funny. We have a lot in common, you and I," Will said thoughtfully.

"How so?" Connor asked between bites.

"For one thing, our trust is hard-won. We have seen and learned things that inspire great caution." Connor could see he was very direct and to the point, like Gray. He sounded confident, honest, and maybe even sincere. Sincerity has a vulnerable connotation, and to assign such a soft trait to this warrior man conjured up a strange combination.

"For another," Will continued, "we were trained to carry sensitive information for the rebellion at a young age. That makes for a unique childhood. You experienced the loss of your grandad, and I witnessed...," he looked down before he continued. "I... I lost both my parents when I was around your age." Connor could tell it was a difficult memory, and the details were probably more gruesome than he was willing to share with a child.

"Do you think I should change my name?" Connor asked. He wasn't sure why, but suddenly the opinion of this man, who oozed power, mattered to him. "I mean, we are already giving me a new identity of a sick Fringer kid. Is there any reason to believe the Corporates know of me?"

"We can't know," Haru cut in. "It's likely they knew your grandparents participated in the Highmind experiment. Deegan was never identified, but you disappeared before you could be tested. It's possible they've been looking for you."

Connor contemplated that with a few more bites of dinner. Then he turned to Taylor. "You adopted Will?"

"Yes, and I changed his last name to mine to protect him. It's hard to say if it helped." Taylor replied honestly.

Will added, "The person who trained me was the daughter of a known rebel who had infiltrated their intelligence agency. After they killed her, they even sent a manufactured family to watch me. I was just a kid, and it's a miracle the Sanguine Blade was not discovered."

"Yeah, I didn't know the castle that GD, that was my nickname for my grandad, held so many important clues. I showed it to my friend, and I carried it in my tote when we moved to Fairplay." Connor shared.

"I, too, confided in childhood friends," Will said, "and could have easily compromised this mission before it even began. But destiny doesn't let go of its players so easily," everyone chuckled, but Will and Connor. They knew firsthand, it was more ominous than humorous.

"You know, Connor, you don't have to change your name," Haru offered. "It's your age that will make the enemy think you're a Highmind. Why else would you accompany us? That's why we created this story. But changing your name could keep them from connecting you to Deegan. And a new name can redefine you like a costume."

Will chimed in, "Sometimes people come up with a new name to invoke power and respect. It helps them achieve a difficult goal. Take Relic. It wasn't the name he was born with, and I still don't know his real name. It is the person he chooses to be, an expert in history and philosophy. Reframing yourself from a civilian to a soldier is a tough task when you see yourself as Connor, the one who hides. Drangers choose a name of power after they graduate from training. Mine was Dirk, an assassin's blade."

Connor's shock was evident. "You were a Dranger?" he asked before he could stop himself.

"Yes, I was, and then I became a Neighwah soldier, and now I am a Fringer Commander," he answered proudly.

Connor was stunned. He reviewed his preconceptions and preju-dices, which he reminded himself were not without reason. He again spoke without thinking. "Why should I trust you? Why should any of us? The Drangers and Neighwah threatened us, beat us, and killed innocent people, and you say you were one of them!"

"I like your honesty, Connor," said Taylor. "Will doesn't tell the story very well. Allow me to add some more details. He came to live with me after his parents were killed in front of him. He was only eleven. We changed his last name to keep him safe. And yes, he joined the Drangers, but it was the only way to save the life of his friend, who was sold to them by his toxer father.

"Then Corporates blackmailed him into joining the Neighwah when they figured out that he was Miranda's stepson. And again, he served to keep his family and friends from being arrested, which we all know is just a prelude to torture and execution. He also used his position to gather important information while doing his best to maintain his values."

"He does tell a better story, Will," Connor said, pointing his thumb at Taylor. Will smiled. "But you are right about trust. It's hard-won." Turning back to Taylor he asked, "Did you know Will's parents?"

"When I met Will's parents, I already knew who they were, because the Robinhooders had arranged their escape. Not knowing I was the RH contact, they introduced themselves as Dailys wanting better jobs. They said Will was an orphan whom they offered to bring to his family. When we reached the town, I changed the story to say he was my stepson and his mother had died, so I was adopting him. But it didn't take the Corporates long to figure out he was Tianna's stepson," Taylor said. "They had his image recorded. If they have your image recorded, no name change is going to help. That's why we're keeping you hidden."

"So," Will said, moving on from his dreary story, "while you are at Sentry, you will have to stay here. When Tura arrives, she'll bring you in, and I'll spread the word about who you are. But tomorrow we have a fun day planned."

"Who is included in *we?*" Connor asked, remembering he was planning on spending the day at the lake with Gray.

"You, Gray, and I are going fishing."

"I'm jealous," said Haru. "I have a meeting, and then Tanya and I are unpacking all our materials."

"I can't go either, but I'll see you on the drone camera," added Taylor.

Chapter Seven

G ray woke up early, excited to meet Will for bow practice. He was enjoying his friendship with the like-minded military man whose rank equaled his own. He dragged Jilly's willful hair away from her face and kissed her sleeping head. The showers were in a trailer across from their row of rooms. Though he had rinsed off yesterday, he was rushed and exhausted. This shower was soothing, and he took the time to notice the handmade forest-scented cleansers.

Closing his eyes, visions and memories were called to the watery surface of his mind. The fragrance brought forth memories of a canopy of pines towering over fresh-smelling ferns and precious little wildflowers. He stepped out of the shower and toweled off.

The Fringers' self-reliant approach to life limited them to the resources naturally provided by their environment. Though they lacked a variety of supplies, they excelled in creativity. The soaps he just used proved that. He couldn't wait to see more of their delightful amenities and see both worlds improve with trade agreements.

It was a stark difference from life under Corporate rule, where they were punished for sharing, speaking, and trying to be self-sufficient, where hope itself was forbidden. He was thankful every day that he met Bannon, who risked everything to create a better way of life.

Gray put his toiletries back into the shower room locker assigned to him and messaged Will. He responded, saying to meet him in the conference room, where they would set up their bows. Rushing up the stairs, Gray saw the two bow cases sitting on the table. He also noticed two golf bags leaning against the wall. Will had no doubt found them in one of the building's storage rooms. Gray smiled.

"Bannon said when they were building the Hold, he used to take practice swings off the roof," Gray said as he pulled one of the clubs out for inspection. "I messed around swinging a golf club a couple of times, but it's been years."

"Well, don't feel bad," Will smiled mischievously. "I won't expect much of a contest then. It's not your fault you weren't properly trained."

Gray smiled. "Maybe not, but I'm a quick learner, especially when I've been so neatly challenged."

Will directed Gray to the armory room door at the end of the hall. Though most personnel were unfamiliar with this room, Gray knew it well. It was the armory, and it was full of the gear and weapons he had brought for them.

What immediately caught Gray's eye was the addition of a door that led to the outside. He looked at it curiously. They were on the second story. Had Will added a balcony? That would interfere with the camouflage. Gray gestured toward it.

"Wait till you see this. Relic engineered it, and my maintenance crew knocked it out." He was giddy to share his addon. Opening the door caused a grated ledge to extend ten feet beyond the building. When it stopped moving, a cable railing unfolded.

"Wow, that is a nice design, and the view is inspirational," Gray said, as he cautiously stepped onto the platform, relieved that it felt solid beneath him.

"This is where I gaze at the view, hit golf balls, and scan the approaching road. It's a great place to destress. It allows me to focus on something that doesn't involve the struggles of being in charge."

Will threw down a thick grassy mat with several holes lined up near the edge. He unhooked the cable rail and inserted several golf tees into the holes, balancing a ball on each. Swinging a 3-wood club, he sent the first golf ball soaring into the distance until it dropped in the ample forest. He hit two more times and set Gray up.

Gray ran through the lessons given by Bannon so long ago. Grip the club, set your stance, keep your head down, elbow straight, and swing through. He took a few practice swings until he felt ready. *Ping.* He didn't hit the ball nearly as far as Will, but it flew straight and sailed a good distance. The next two were less satisfying, but he enjoyed the feel of it.

"It makes me wish we had a course to play," Will said, stepping up to take another turn.

"So many wonderful things were lost. We probably don't even know half of them," Gray added.

"There was a nine-hole course on the base where I was stationed during my stint with the Neighwah. It was only for high-ranking offi-cers. Rival, my roommate and now my second, liked to watch them from behind the surrounding vegetation. Before my last mission, Captain Garriset let me caddy for him and try out the putting green. "

"I don't think I've ever seen a golf course," Gray said. "Do you ever shoot your bow from here?"

"Sometimes, but I usually shoot at ground level. I've lost a lot of arrows from here."

"Well, the good thing about these arrows is they have a chip that allows us to find them."

"Do you worry they'll be tracked?" asked Will.

"No, the signal has to be activated from the bow that shot it. Their range is limited to a thousand yards. Not that this will shoot a thousand yards, but ..."

"It allows you to follow your prey," they said at the same time.

They continued to vie, shot for shot, before going in to set up their bows. Gray's bow was set up at NH, but he watched as Will adjusted the length and draw strength and set the pins.

The torque and feel of the weapon created a connection that went beyond simply aiming and pulling a trigger. Sending the arrow silently slicing through the air was exhilarating. Gray loved this weapon, and he was happy to add it to his arsenal for the mission.

It was still early when Gray ushered Connor into a mini, while Will climbed on his horse. Connor watched Will trail them on his mount with his dog, Copper, trotting beside them. It was a short drive, and Connor stepped out feeling the cold breeze blowing off the water. He was surprised to see that a swath of snow had been melted off the beach, just for their activity.

A spreading ribbon of sunlight sparkled and shimmered across the lake with the rays of the rising sun. The ripples made a soothing rhythmic sound as they lapped against the shore. It was majestic and mesmerizing, and the prettiest sight Connor had ever seen.

Gray surprised him when he handed him a fishing pole. Will was securing his horse while Copper ran to the water and busied himself with amusing antics. Gray went over the basics of casting a line as Will walked over to join them. It took Connor quite a few tries to get his line to go where he wanted. Will was the first to hook a fish, and he let Connor reel it in. While Connor was transfixed with this new skill, he was happy to interrupt his new pastime to throw a stick for Copper. Gray took the opportunity to walk over to Will.

"Did I ever tell you that Connor over there is excellent at lip-reading?" Gray said to Will with his eyebrows raised.

"Of course he is. That kid is something. I look forward to getting to know him," Will answered. "I hear he has quite the story."

Gray turned away from Connor and said, "As do you. I've often wondered what you could leverage against the Corporates that allowed you to bring the Fringers to permanent towns. And for over a year, they have let you be, knowing where you are. What was that deal about?"

Will nodded with acknowledgment and also turned away from the boy to speak. "You don't want to know," Will sighed, remembering the moment he discovered the hideous secret that still haunted him.

"Actually, I do. We are co-leading this mission, and I need to know what you have over them."

"Well, there are numerous evil deeds done by them that no one would be shocked by, but there is one that would cause the people to rise up in such anger that it would override their threat of death. At least, I think they still have that much spirit left in them."

"Okay, even more interested."

"The basic necessities of life, particularly food, are the biggest reasons the Dailys are complicit. One of the constant warnings being thrown around by our supervisors was that we had to be frugal with the food supplies issued to the Dailys. But the Uppers had all they wanted.

I worked picking up and hauling the dead bodies to the crematorium. Hit every drop-off station in all three territories every week. As you know, bodies are immediately collected and taken to the freezing stations. I always thought it was for the people's protection, but I learned that diseases are much more threatening in living bodies. Dead ones aren't usually that dangerous."

"I still don't get why that knowledge would cause a stir among the people."

"It's what they use the bodies for that threatens their hold on the Dailys. The crematorium also serves as a jail, and no one sent there is ever released. At a building not far from there, is where the protein powder supplement provided to Dailys is processed." Will said no more and let the fact sink into his friend.

It didn't take long. "Are you suggesting those mother-fuckers were feeding us dead people?" Gray said, trying to keep his outraged voice beyond Connor's hearing. "How do you know for sure?"

"Because they buckled when we threatened to expose them."

"Why the hell didn't you? How can you let something that gruesome continue?'

"Warren, Relic, and I realized the response would be chaotic. Thousands of unarmed rebelling Dailys would die horrifically, and then the broken people would starve or be forced to return to their oppressive lives, which would be even bleaker. We decided to wait until we could make a stand. It was a decision I battle with every day. And here we are, making a stand and preparing our armies to take them down." Will cast his line and gazed wistfully across the lake as if he imagined a place where life was simple. Where he was free of command and the tragedies of evil.

Gray gripped Will's shoulder in an attempt at comfort, but nothing could quell this ache but a victorious battle. His anger grew. When he got to the Elites, he could rip them to pieces. *What kind of sick, inhuman fucks feed families dead people?*

The two men fished quietly for the rest of the outing. Before their adventure was over, they had five fish. Gray showed Connor how to clean them and let him do the last one by himself. Setting them in a grated basket, they cooked them over a campfire. There is something extra delicious about a meal one worked for and ate fresh.

It was time to go, and everything was packed in the mini for the short ride back. Connor had enjoyed himself thoroughly, but he could tell something had changed since Will and Gray's conversation. They were sending an unspoken message that he shouldn't ask.

Will secured Copper in the mini with Gray and called Connor over to his horse. "Connor, meet Little Bet." It was the biggest animal Connor had ever faced so closely, but he trusted Will, so he petted the horse's neck like Will demonstrated. Will climbed up on his horse and reached his hand down to Connor. "Gray, we'll see you back at the fort. Come on, Connor, let's ride."

He took Will's hand not because he wasn't afraid but because he didn't want to look afraid. Seated in the saddle in front of him, he became aware of how high off the ground he was.

"I gather there's a story behind Little Bet's name," Connor said to deflect from his nervous demeanor.

Will was not fooled by Connor's deception, but he was impressed with his courage. "Yes, and it's an excellent story. It will make a good tale for the road." He started slowly and taught Connor how to move with the horse. Then he urged the animal faster. Connor gripped the saddle horn while Will held the reins with one hand and Connor with the other. Then he stood up in the stirrups ever so slightly above the saddle, elevating Connor, too.

Connor would have been terrified, but Will was so strong and so in control, the act seemed effortless. The boy relaxed into the experience, feeling the horse lifting off the ground and landing as if, between leaps, they were flying. Little Bet heaved powerful breaths as Will focused on the path. Connor felt their bond as if tethered by an unseen force, and the three of them galloped as one. The powerful synergy between man and horse was extraordinary, and the ride was pure exhilaration.

They traveled past the turn to Sentry, and Will halted his horse beside an old truck. Nash and a woman got out of the cab. The soldier helped Connor down from Little Bet. Will quickly landed on the ground after him and dashed to Leita. Without regard to the child or the soldier, he took her in his arms and kissed her hungrily. Leita welcomed his appetite with greedy enthusiasm.

"I thought Tura was going to bring him in," Will whispered into the fiery ringlets exploding around her head. "Not that I'm disappointed, but I should have been consulted. Do you understand the plan?"

"Tura was getting ready to leave when Kory fell violently ill. She told me I was to escort a Lone Fringer child into the Fort to be treated in the medical facility. I am also to hand this to the new doctor," she held out a paper with the details of Kory's symptoms. "She was hoping the new doctor could send some medicine for him."

Will was relieved to hear she seemed unaware of the entire plan, but he was sure she would pepper him with questions about why she had to come all the way out here to parade some kid into the fort. Will read the information briefly, noting the high fever, rash, and loss of appetite. It concerned him that his friend was so ill.

"Ventura must be beside herself with worry," Will said, referring to Kory's wife.

"She and the kids are worried they'll lose him, and Tura won't let them near in case he's contagious. She is hoping to prevent an outbreak."

"I'm sure the doctor has something that will help him. We'll send it out today. Did she explain the details of this plan?" Will asked while wondering what illness Leita may have brought with her. It was the last thing they needed before the mission, but hopefully, this doctor will manage it.

"No, she had quarantined herself in Kory's home to treat him. She sent me a brief note and said you'd fill me in." She wondered what crazy scheme Will had gotten into.

"I see, "Will said. "Well, it's all about keeping the rumors at bay. We have reason to believe the Corporates are buzzing around not buying that a Friendship Tour is the reason."

"Corporates? I thought they couldn't come here."

"Well, the battle may have altered those rules," Will suggested. "But, don't worry. We aren't going to cause trouble in the townships," Will said smoothly and gave her a wink for good measure. Will turned toward Connor, "Leita, meet Miles, Miles, this is Leita."

Will looked at Connor, who didn't flinch at the sudden name change. This kid was quick, and he respected him more every day. When Connor held his hand out to Leita, she noted his soft hands. Will cursed himself for his negligence. A Fringer's hands would be callused from a hard life living off the land. Connor figured out the misstep too having labored as a Daily.

"Well, let's get this little charade going," Will said. "I'll ride back while you three wait here for thirty minutes. Nash, when you get to Sentry, pull up to the front entrance of Alpha. Escort them to the infirmary in front of the troops, who will be there for their briefing on the Friendship Tour. I'll give a short explanation." Will knew this would only fuel Leita's curiosity.

"Got it," Nash replied. Leita's mind was listing off a series of questions she would ask Will. *Why the cover-up? What was going on here?* She intended to get some answers as soon as they were alone, well, soon after anyway.

Connor wasn't confused about why Will decided to change his name, but he was skeptical about the loyalty of the woman beside him. It could be a long thirty minutes before they leave. After answering a few casual questions, he decided to use up some of the time for a bathroom break.

Jilly sat on the edge of the gurney and looked at the results of the tests Andie performed. She was speechless.

"This is why you can't make assumptions, Jilly. You would have never jumped to these conclusions regarding another patient. You wouldn't have guessed about someone's condition, you'd have done tests, made sure you knew." Andie's tone was marked with admonishment as well as concern.

"I know, I know. I would have, but I didn't want to deal with the news getting out. Confidentiality aside, our town is small and full of well-meaning busybodies," Jilly said in an uncertain voice.

"You're not the first woman to have to deal with this kind of loss, and as a health provider, you should know you can't skip facing the emotional part of this. Did you really think that if no one knew, you could push it away? You would have counseled a patient that trauma doesn't evaporate. It keeps swirling back around until you deal with it," Andie blew out a long breath and put her hand on Jilly's shoulder. She spoke softly and said, "But here we are."

The positive pregnancy test and, even more compelling, the ultrasound printout she held in her hand were proof she had not lost the baby. Andie checked her over thoroughly and told her what she already knew. Blood loss happens sometimes, and in this case, it was not detrimental to the fetus."

"There was tissue in there. It wasn't just clotted blood. I saw something solid."

"Well, perhaps there were two fetuses, and one was not developing or attached outside of the womb. Without a bio-sample, we'll never know, but that evidence is long gone. We've got different problems now. For one, I'm going to have to take your place." Andie knew Jilly was in denial, but the tests were indisputable.

"No," Jilly shook her head. "I can't make you do that. Just keep this between us for now. Let me think."

"You have to tell Gray," Andie said with her hands on her hips.

"I just... dear God. I should be jumping for joy, but I'm frozen between... Ahhh, this is crazy." It always amazed her that her flight-or-flee moments resulted in a different response, freezing. She was paralyzed, unsure how to navigate the opposing obligations. She believed with all her heart that Gray needed her on this mission. His life depended on it. If she told him, he'd make her stay. She couldn't lose him. But this could tear them apart. He'd be alive, but they'd be back to living on different plains. She knew what it was like to be on the other side of this kind of betrayal. It's what had led her to break up with Gray.

She should talk this out with someone, like Haru, but just thinking of another person knowing before Gray caused more fear. She was frustrated. This problem, no, not a problem. It was unexpected and even inconvenient, but her child was not a problem. Every part of her was embroiled in the battle, trying to see the correct path.

Jilly instinctively wrapped her arms around herself. She missed Ari. She needed Ari, and she pulled on memories, desperately trying to elicit the comfort of her older sister. If she imagined hard enough, it might calm her restlessness. But it wasn't a memory of Ari she flashed on. It was her mother.

She was no more than three or four, and her mother was cuddling her and drying her tears. Jilly pulled hard at the vision, willing it to come out of the shadows and into full view. She could almost feel her mother's arms holding and patting her back like a comforting heartbeat. Jilly relaxed, losing herself in the kind smile and sweet voice as she sang to her.

The whole mental journey took mere seconds, but it settled her, gave her the resolve she needed. She pulled herself together and returned her focus to her own child. This vulnerable, tiny being was listening to the drum of her heartbeat and counting on its promise of protection and love.

"Thank you, Andie. You are a true friend and the Fringers are lucky to have you as their doctor, as am I."

"Here," Andie said warmly, and she handed her a bottle of prenatal vitamins. "It's been a long day, and you've had quite a shock. Take some time to process this. Don't worry. I won't betray your confidence, but you have to tell Gray. He is your commanding officer, and he needs to know."

"Yes, he does, as my husband and father to this child more than my boss. And I will tell him. And I promise to take care of myself," Jilly said with conviction.

"The baby's somewhere around nine to ten weeks. I need more time to examine the ultrasound to be exact, but I'd say your due date is roughly late April to early May. I'll be able to check in on you during the Friendship Tour, but if your health is in jeopardy, or he commands it, I will take your place."

Jilly bristled at that but thanked her friend. Tucking her little picture in her daypack, she went to her room. She was relieved that Gray wasn't back from his outing with Will and Connor, and she hid the evidence in her tote. It felt good to lie down, though she doubted it would result in sleep while her situation pounded through her head.

She had tough questions to ponder, and the answers had to be logical and selfless. *Should she stay on this mission? Would going on this mission hurt the baby? Was it selfish that she still wanted to go? When, how should she tell Gray? How is he going to react? Would he let her choose, or would he force her to return to New Haven? What about Connor?* The honest answers evaded her.

She grabbed a cold pack, shook it, and laid it across her forehead. The relief slowly worked to calm her throbbing head. She did some meditative breathing and focused on the small being growing inside her. She felt herself sink into the soft blanket spread across the bed. Soon, she fell into a deep sleep with her hands cradling her womb.

The soldiers were lined up in the yard when Connor and Leita were buzzed through the front access door. Connor felt self-conscious when all eyes were on them as they walked behind Will while he addressed his troops.

"Now that we have our own doctor, we will be granting clearance to civilian patients requiring advanced medical attention. Be assured that no contagious issues will be brought here. The doctor will also be making trips to the Fringer townships to administer medical help and preventative care." Will got his soldiers' attention back on him, and the two disappeared through the infirmary door.

Dr. Andie brought Connor back to the exam room while Leita waited in the tiny lobby. Just for good measure, she took his vitals. On his New Haven physical, he was reported to be a healthy child, and she didn't find anything to the contrary.

"So," Connor asked, "what's wrong with me?"

"You have a suspicious lump under your arm, *Miles*," Andie said, emphasizing she knew his pseudonym.

Connor rolled his eyes in acknowledgment, "I know that. What is it from, and what are you going to do to me?"

"Well, if I were actually going to do something, I would take an MRI and a biopsy. Then, depending on what it was, I'd treat you with medicine or a scalpel. Whatever I decide on, your body will have to reflect the treatment," Andie said with a straight face.

Connor was leaning away, thinking this ruse had gone far enough, when Andie started laughing.

"You should have seen your face," Andie said.

"That was a rotten joke," Connor replied with a look of retaliatory mischief in his eyes.

"The good news is that I am diagnosing it as an infection, so a round of antibiotics will suffice. It will also allow you to travel immediately without worrying about the complications of a wound. I printed an MRI film this morning from a textbook example, which will go into the file under your new name."

"Do I have a last name?"

"Good question, I'll have to ask William," she said, looking at the incomplete chart.

Chapter Eight

Will called the full team in for a quick briefing to address Connor's name change. Gray said Jilly was sleeping, and he'd fill her in later. Will expressed the visible concerns regarding Connor's story. They decided Connor would have to wear a sling to validate the seriousness of his problem, and Andie suggested he wear gloves because the antibiotic had caused an irritating rash on his hands. This sort of drug was unknown to the tribes, so they would have no reason to discount it.

The Guard soldiers, joined by the Defenders, were pouring in from every door and area. He worried that adding more details as they went was a sure way to expose him. Connor needed a Fringer chaperone who would help him navigate the culture and pull off the labyrinth of lies.

Arriving at his room, Gray found Jilly tossing and turning in a bad dream. "Jilly, Jilly, wake up. You're dreaming." She looked up at him with the most woeful eyes. He knew she was reliving the miscarriage. "You're okay," he said as he rocked her.

"Sorry," she said with a slight smile, "still recovering from the long day we had yesterday. I'm glad I got some shut-eye, but I had the craziest dream."

"What was your dream about?" he asked, hoping he could open up a needed conversation.

"Well, we were at the cave, and a huge, winged lizard was guarding it." It was actually a dream she had the night before, after Connor had told her the story of the Vadina myth. This more recent dream involved her running through the forest trying to save the infant in her arms, but she left that part out.

"It was probably because of what Connor told you about that dragon statue," Gray grinned at Jilly, who nodded with a smile. "Speaking of Connor, Will had to give him a new name. A different person came to escort him into the infirmary without notifying us."

"Does Will trust her?" Jilly asked with fear.

"I don't think it's that he doesn't trust her. It's just one more person who didn't need to know. It's hard to control a narrative when people outside the mission know too much. They may say something that seems harmless, but it gives away another piece of the puzzle. If they get enough..." his brows raised.

"I can see that," she said with understanding due to all the military briefings she had attended lately. She ran through her own secret reasoning, which was no different than the reasoning Gray had used to protect her. She was controlling the narrative to keep her spot on the mission, so she could protect the people she loved. She was needed as the medic, as Connor's parent en locus, and to protect Gray. Call it crazy intuition, but she knew if she wasn't with him, something horrible was going to happen.

"So," she asked, "what's his new name?"

"Miles," Gray said with a grin.

"Miles? Why Miles?" Jilly asked.

"I thought it was a take on the long journey we have before us, but Will said it meant lion-hearted soldier."

"Well, that seems like Will. It's done, so we'll have to get used to it," she said.

"Remember, when we go to dinner tonight, he will be introduced to us. Don't act too familiar."

She nodded while biting her lip. "It will be hard not to hug him when I see him, but I can pull this off."

Will entered his private quarters, and Leita was there. Her hair was free of its hair ties and combs, and it sizzled and burned with the color of flame. She smiled, and it enchanted him.

"You have been very busy, and access to Sentry has been difficult since the battle. I've missed you," she said in her delicious, warm voice.

"I have thought of you often. It's good to see you."

She was already in his arms, and he was running his hands along her waist. He kissed her neck where her pulse throbbed gently under his lips, taking in the smell of wildflowers and rosemary. His hands traced their way over her shoulders and gathered her ringlets of copper fire. With heat in his eyes, he was a ravenous man sitting before a banquet, deciding what to start with.

He kissed her lips tenderly, and she returned his gentleness with a hunger, plunging her tongue into his mouth to play with his. They matched moan for moan, touching and searching for the next area to send the other higher. He closed his eyes to drown in every bit of the sensation as he pulled her onto the bed.

Sitting behind her, he focused on the buttons that trailed down her back. They didn't need to be undone. Lifting her shirt over her head would have sufficed, but he took pleasure in undoing them one by one, slowly working his way down her back while planting kisses to her exposed skin. When his job was complete, he pulled the blouse from her. Although she had worn a breast wrap when he held her earlier, she had since removed it.

He admired her toned body and the graceful curve of her slender back. She was tall but slight, and he could have wrapped his arms around her with length to spare. There was a time he was apprehensive about overpowering her, but she was stronger than she appeared.

She arched her back toward him as his hands cupped her perfect mounds. With little need for encouragement, she turned around and straddled him. He began to lower his head to taste her delicate breasts, but she blocked him as she busily removed his encumbering uniform. Tugging off his shirt, she pulled him to her, skin to skin.

His hands reached up to cup her swells and teased each nipple between his fingertips. More moans of indulgence escaped her, and he felt his desire rise higher. She turned and sighed against the strong arms that embraced her.

It was a sexy sigh that ate at his iron control and called to his neglected needs. He stood and shed his trousers, and she dropped her winter slip and her tiered skirt. Viewing the new places to tease and torment, he knew he should continue his slow assault, but his patience was losing out to his body, which had been alone for too long.

She, too, skipped the leisure journey across his body and settled her hands on his cock. It was steel hard, and the veins feeding it were pulsing in anticipation. His lust surged through him like an animal obeying an instinct.

"I'm in need, Will," she panted. "We'll take more time on round two."

He flashed a big grin at her, took her hips in his hands, and guided himself inside her. She was so slick and ready, he groaned out loud. She too let out a sound of pleasure as she moved up and down, forward and backward, undulating her hips like a wild dancer.

She arched above him, losing herself in the heat of pleasure. She was so beautiful when in the throes of climax, her face filled with passion while gripping his shoulders and crying out. The more she moved and fed her desires, the stronger the fire in him burned. When he burst into a climax, it fired off every nerve like a bursting star. Breathless and hearts pounding, they lay glistening in each other's arms until they settled into the peaceful glow of sleep.

They awoke to Connor walking into his room next door. Will knew he was at the infirmary while they were making love, but he felt sorry for the lonely child imprisoned in this little cell.

"What did you think of Miles?" Will asked. He was searching for the cracks in his story, and he knew she'd be happy to point them out.

"Well, I'll be honest. I think there's more going on than a medical issue."

"Why do you say that?" Will said nonchalantly.

"He's got pampered hands for one. That boy does not toil in the forest or live off the land. And he doesn't talk like a Fringer, let alone a Loner. He's educated, very educated," she said, tilting her head and drawing her brows together. "If you're trying to hide him, the performance needs work."

"Yes, you are right. It does need work. I have a favor. While you're traveling with us, I need you to chaperone him. Teach him to be a Fringer, and don't let him reveal himself."

"What's going on, Will? Does this have to do with the blackmail evidence you have on the Corporates? I never asked you to tell me, but if I'm to protect him, I need more about him and what we're doing."

"No, this isn't about that. We need him to help us access something. None of us knows exactly how he'll be able to help us until we arrive at our destination. He's the reason we have a direction to follow. We can't find what we're looking for without him. It's complicated."

"Oh, I think it's pretty simple. You are using this twelve-year-old child, probably a Highmind, for your military operation," she said with a dash of disapproval.

"I wish you were wrong, and I wish it wasn't necessary, but yeah, that's the gist of it," he said firmly, then sighed. "Will you help him? His life may depend on it."

"As well as my own, I'm guessing. But yes, I will help him. However," she negotiated, "you must tell me enough for the three of us to understand and trust each other. I don't want to get mired in the Corporate shit, but don't leave me vulnerable, so I unwittingly stray into unknown danger. I mean, if I'm to be tied up with him, toss me a bone for gods' sake."

Leita hoped she wouldn't regret her commitment. She knew it was a serious request, and she would rather remain uninformed. Looking back at him, she saw he was grinning. Not the, I won the argument kind of grinning. It was the kind that meant he had taken her "bone" metaphor as a suggestion for round two of their reunion.

She rolled her eyes with annoyance at his singularity of thought. They were in the middle of a critical discussion. He pulled her back down, and she started to resist until she felt a familiar warmth tingling low in her core, giving his idea momentum.

"We'll have to be a bit quieter this time," he growled in her ear.

"We can try," she teased.

Leita learned that Connor was an undocumented Highmind who was trained by a member of the rebellion. He had absolute recall, and he could read lips. The reason he was on the mission was his ability to solve puzzles, which they hoped would gain them access to a resource they needed to secure. He did not tell her they believed it was a powerful weapon, but he did warn her that the Corporates were also hunting for it.

Gray, Will, and Conner met before lunch in Connor's room to discuss the amendments to his story.

"When you are in public," Will explained, "you will wear these thin gloves. Leita read through our ruse in seconds, starting with your hands not being those of a hard-working Fringer."

"I noticed," said Connor. "She and Nash kept looking at me curiously when I answered their questions. I knew I bombed my cover, so I just turned on my shy mode. I should have prepared better, sorry."

"That is our fault," Gray sighed. "We didn't prepare you to be a Fringer because this plan was a last-minute change."

"Well, the good news is," Will answered, "Leita is someone I trust completely, and she has been a Fringer for almost twenty years. She has agreed to work with you and escort you in public."

"Though Will trusts her, don't share the details of our mission. Try to stick with getting through the Friendship Tour," Gray added.

"I've been thinking about this. It seems to me that Lone Fringers would be frightened to seek fancy medical care," Connor explained. "Fancy means expensive, and everything expensive comes from the Corporates. However, a mother who is worried about her child would push past all that. She might even smuggle him into one of the Fringer towns to find a cure."

Will and Gray looked at each other and smiled.

"He's right. That story sounds more likely and may keep the watchers, we know are here, from paying too much attention to him," said Gray.

Will agreed, "I follow you. If we can pass him off as a Fringer, they won't pay much attention to him. They're looking for a Highmind because they assume we are after Cali Bantu. To stop us and attain it themselves, they must capture our Highmind. That puts Relic at risk, too."

"True, he needs better security," Gray affirmed. "But doesn't the Neighwah have images of everyone from the territories. Aren't they able to match Connor and Relic's faces?"

"Yes, but their satellites were destroyed too, and according to our deal, they aren't allowed to bring or gather electronic information on Fringers. They can relay information, like we do, but it takes time. And, the database they could smuggle in here would be limited. They would need a clear and current photo of him to use face recognition, or they'd have to look him up specifically. It's doubtful Connor is on their radar. But it's also doubtful he'll stay that way."

"Used to be my fantasy to be a kid spy," said Gray.

"That's because you weren't faced with it," groaned Will. Connor nodded emphatically.

Will and Gray began to reminisce about the trouble they caused their parents with unashamed glee. Gray wanted to try coffee, so he stole an Upper's cup, which had moonshine in it. Gray's dad had a devil of a time managing a drunk eleven-year-old and sneaking the cup back to the site. Will shared the time he snuck past the barriers after curfew to go hiking and spend the night in the woods alone when he was thirteen, causing Taylor considerable anxiety. Gray began a memory of a time he snuck off, but he decided he would finish it when Connor wasn't present.

"Okay, it's agreed," Gray interjected. "We'll leak the worried mom story, and say we don't have the time to take him back, so his dad will meet us at one of our stops."

"I like it," agreed Will. "Well done, Connor."

"With that settled, who's hungry?" asked Gray. Connor jumped up, and Gray laughed, saying, "Well, I guess you are."

"He's a twelve-year-old boy. Of course, he's hungry. Let's go," Will added, uncurling himself from the bottom bunk.

After having lunch in the conference room, Leita decided to begin Connor's training, starting with those who already knew him. The old animal section in the Alpha building was being remodeled into the ministry office. While Haru and Tanya unpacked the supplies and set up the office, they would ask Connor questions, and Leita could help him answer them. The person who was the most familiar with the Fringer lifestyle was Haru due to his counseling of Aniya. As they pummeled Connor with questions, the team focused on organizing the items they would distribute to the Fringer towns.

Next, they went to the new animal area. It had been moved to the Gama building, where it had been greatly expanded to house large livestock. It included a new stable and an access door to an outdoor corral. The hours passed quickly and ended when the dinner announcement was made.

The soldiers going on the mission, as well as those helping pack the supplies, sat at the cafeteria tables as Will introduced "Miles" to the group. He quickly told them the fabricated story and went straight into the preparation for the morning departure. It was a good attempt to deflect unneeded questions coming Connor's way, but it didn't work. Even Fringers were curious about the Loners in the wild places.

Will bristled ever so slightly, but he watched in amazement as Connor navigated every inquiry with practiced skill. He smiled at Leita, who beamed proudly at her student. They both congratulated themselves, but they knew it was classic Connor. He consumed complex material at a furious rate, and with such a complete grasp, he could spit it back out with remarkable proficiency.

Will suddenly realized the grave responsibility before him. This ill-fated child was a priceless asset to this mission, and who knows what else. And on a more serious note, he was equally important to the Corporates. He knew firsthand that they viewed people of all ages as resources to be used, and they would kill to attain this resource. All that on the shoulders of a boy, who was taken from his family, his dog, his home, and his friends. He wasn't even allowed to keep his name or his past. He was set adrift in a lie and utterly alone.

Later, when their dinner had settled, a vigorous basketball game was played by two teams of men. Connor watched the discussion to decide who was "skins" and who was "shirts". The meaning was instantly clear as one team removed their grey-green T-shirts to distinguish the teams. They were powerfully built and in their prime. He watched in amazement as the men battled to sink the orange ball into the chained sleeves.

Relic was the referee, the only boundary between an all-out brawl and a fierce but orderly game. They were warriors. Connor had never seen such determination toward a singular goal. When they ran, jumped, and slammed back onto the floor, it reverberated beneath his feet. It was impressive. Connor realized that if they were this resolute about a game, they would be more so about the mission and the safety of its members.

Early the next morning, they would repeat the rough ride back to I-70. It was there they would meet up with the soldiers who were tasked with following at a distance on sweep duty. The Friendship Tour stops included Eagle and Glenwood Springs. That's when the ruse ended and the Reclamation mission began.

"It's not a ruse," Haru explained. "We will be meeting and inform-ing the townships of the services and supplies we have to offer in the hopes of saving souls, improving health, and establishing trade agreements. All of that will strengthen our alliance. Although we will only make two stops, representatives from every tribe will come, so they can bring our message back to their communities."

As the evening waned, the final items were loaded, and last-minute preparations were made. Tensions ran high as the teams prepared for the hazards ahead. Gray knew it was killing Connor and Henry to act like strangers, so he arranged to bring Henry to his son's quarters for some private father-and-son time.

The rigs were lined up like railway cars parked inside the fort's courtyard, bordered by the four buildings. A gentle snow was falling as they gathered outside. The diverse group of eighteen people climbed into their respective rigs with choreographed efficiency. Since Leita was seen as Connor's guardian, it was logical for her to ride in the truck with him. Also in the truck were Haru, Tanya, Henry, and Will. The best news was that they all knew the real Connor, so on the first leg of the journey, they could engage naturally.

The rigs slowly made their way down the sloped, mud-slicked road. The flakes were gaining in number, and soon the trees were speckled with snow. It blocked the far side of the lake with a wall of white as the benign snowfall grew into a storm.

"It's nothing to worry about," assured Will. "We can get through this. We have snowplow crews along the road. It's actually good cover because the snooping drones don't tend to be flown in this stuff."

It took longer to navigate the snow-covered roads on their way out, but it was a quieter drive. Will watched Haru and Leita laugh and talk with an ease he didn't have with her. They had promised an uncomplicated relationship. It was what they both wanted. *Damn.* He remembered her words at the river when they made love for the first time.

"I am not looking for a public camp date or a future husband. When I do, it will probably be someone more settled. You are like a wild stallion, strong and dangerous. Although that intrigues me, I have no intention of beating myself up trying to tame you. And for now, I like my independence, too."

Will used his commanding presence to express himself; Haru used soft words. Will was resolute and aggressive regarding his goals; Haru was wise and tempered. Will had a turbulent history; Haru had been raised to be a man of God since boyhood. Will was a wild spirit with a violent destiny; Haru was a calming force with a divine future. *Damn.*

Did he love her? He cared for her deeply, but did he love her? He had no answer. Could he make her a commitment? That he could answer—Not now, maybe never. *Damn.* His territorial nature kicked in. Haru may be perfect for her, but he sure as hell wasn't going to give her up without a fight. And if he won, would she be happy? *Damn.*

Chapter Nine

The gate at the end of Black Creek Road had already been plowed and opened by the lead team, and the caravan pulled through. Jax and Jedi slid the camouflaged gates back into place. The passengers had been prepared for the drive, which would be a bit less grueling but twice as long as the journey that brought them to Fort Sentry. They would travel back down Highway 9 to the I-70 junction, where they would meet up with Axle, who would oversee the sweep team.

I-70 was used regularly by the Fringer towns and colonies that tucked themselves near the vital artery. It was in decent condition because, until recently, it had been maintained by the Corporates. However, it had taken a couple of years of heavy traffic abuse, first from the tunnel repairs, followed by the transport of supplies disguised as containment material.

So, it was again riddled with the issues of age and primitive maintenance. The Guard lacked the personnel or resources to repair it, and keeping it in poor condition gave the impression that it wasn't used much. It helped hide the Fort and kept the Corporates believing the Fringers were unorganized isolationists. Since the battle, the façade was no longer effective. It was why Henry had joined the mission. He would help evaluate the road conditions and develop plans for their repair.

As they bounded along, they passed the sagging flotsam on the perimeter of the ghost town. Just two years ago, it was a bustling city, but the radioactive rumors sent its residents back to the eastern side of the tunnel.

Within months, all those living north of Cripple Creek and west of the mountainous Continental Divide were relocated to the eastern side. It wasn't that radiation was detected this far out, or that the Corporates were concerned for the immediate health of their charges. They just couldn't risk their laborers living beyond their sphere of control, where the free Fringer philosophy would corrupt them.

When they were within a couple of miles of I-70, Gray's instruments detected the movement of several Corporate drones hovering over the junction. They did little to conceal their presence to observe the large group. Numerous messages sent over unsecured lines ensured the "Friendship Tour" news would leak out naturally, demonstrating they weren't hiding anything.

Their direction and activities over the next few days would reinforce their cover story. No one believed the Corporates would buy it completely, but while they continued to investigate, the allied freedom fighters would get further down the road without involving civilians in aggressive issues. The food protein secret was still ready for release, but neither side was prepared to deal with that debacle yet.

Colorado Springs Command

General Dermit sat before the blank screen that connected him directly to the five Elite rulers of the three Colorado Territories. Ena, Dio, and, Tria were the supreme directors, named after the Greek words for one, two, and three. No one knew their real names or where they broadcast from. Nor did anyone know why four and five were conspicuously missing. Almost everything about them was top secret. Though Dermit was one of the highest-ranking military officials, even he had never met them in person. The four boxed faces displayed on his screen were supposedly transmitted from their covert mansions, which, he was sure, were luxurious beyond imagination.

Ena, head of security and a military genius, was a woman of absolute perfection. Her warm cocoa skin and strict, short haircut of midnight black were utter perfection. Her double-breasted, wine colored jacket was collarless and simple, but it radiated power. She was a paragon of control, of herself and those under her, which was everyone.

Dio, manager of health services, was a typical aristocrat. His light brown hair was parted on the side of his youthful, handsome face. Though his style reflected cashmere casual, and he looked as if he had been called off from some leisure activity, he had a stalwart demeanor.

Tria's severe style reflected her mean streak. Her razor-sharp, short red hair with black tips contrasted her porcelain skin, and she always wore black attire with no hint of feminine appeal. Her specialty was resource logistics.

Dermit thought they were cold and lazy and used to wonder why they wasn't replaced. They never advocated for the people. They saw the citizens as tools to use. The people need more protein—grind up the dead. The managers need entertainment—traffic more women to the brothels. Keeping the status quo was more important than anything, and there seemed to be no laws to stop them.

"General, "asked the one called Dio.

"Yes, Director Dio," Dermit submitted.

"What have you learned about the tunnels and the Fringers since the battle?"

"We have established that the tunnels are being used to house a city named New Haven. We assume that the radiation accident was a ruse to secure it. We are unsure of its population or purpose. Though its weapon capabilities are high-tech, its military force is small.

"They have been inactive for over a year and never showed signs of aggression beyond defending their town. If they had not received assistance, I believe our small force would have overtaken them. That assistance came from the Fringers, who learned of our approach and intervened. They have an organized, but poorly funded, army they call the Guard. Their highly camouflaged base is assumed to be somewhere up Highway 9."

Tria interrupted, "Who are the leaders of these armies?"

"We have yet to discover the name of the one Bannon Vogel employed for New Haven's security. But we are familiar with the Fringer leader. He is called William of the Guard. He is the same William Alexander, whom we found in a Dranger pack and recruited into the Neighwah. He is the stepson of Miranda Logan, whose Highmind father betrayed us. We believed her father had the Sanguine Blade and gave it to her before she died. We suspected it was passed on to William, but we never found any evidence he had it, or that it even exists."

"We were told William Alexander was dead, but your report says he was seen at the battle. If he is alive, why doesn't he show up on our locator?" asked Ena.

Dermit had already been punished for losing their favorite asset. It was during the fabricated prisoner exchange to trap the Robinhooders that ended in disaster. Denter would have been tortured in front of Will until he disclosed everything he had gleaned from his stepmother, who used the alias Tianna. Though they all knew the story, he recited it in his report again. "His locator went dead soon after he was shot. We saw he was wounded from our surveillance drone as they whisked him off in a med-van. It stopped transmitting, but we continued to follow the van."

"Yes, we've all heard the story about him being taken to a Robinhood hideout and blown up along with a top RH rebel. Why didn't his biomites control him properly? Whose job was it to manage him?" asked Dio.

"The procedure was done several times, but it didn't take, so he was never assigned a manager. We started the process five months before he "died". It usually sets in within a couple of weeks, and we detected them in his bloodstream. But they never attached to his nervous system. Some bodies reject the first round, so we began a second attempt, but that didn't work either. We tried a third round, but we didn't have a chance to check its progress before we lost him." The four Elites stared at him with no sign of frustration, and he hoped it was because it was old news.

Ena took back the forum. "Tell me about the caravan. What is its objective?"

He expected a punishment to follow the previous discussion, but they changed the subject. Interesting. He did his best to maintain an unemotional expression as he searched the faces before him for signs of frustration or concern. But as usual, their poker face skills were exceptional.

"The only intel we have discovered," Dermit continued, "is that New Haven is sending representatives to meet with the Fringer leaders to establish relations and trade. They have nineteen people traveling in their group.

"The informant reported the band consists of spiritual leaders, medical personnel, those utilizing the transport, and a small military detail. It is being sold as a goodwill mission. However, it is logical to assume they seek to strengthen their military alliance, and it's also safe to assume they are all soldiers and well-armed.

"One curiosity is that a child is joining their team. Our sources said he was a Lone Fringer, brought to the fort for medical care. As advised, we used high-altitude drones to monitor each side of the tunnel. When three UTV vehicles exited the west gate four days ago, we followed them. Our distance drones were unable to penetrate their window shields, so the images were not definitive enough to ID the occupants. The child didn't show up until the next day. And he came in a truck from one of the Fringer towns."

"Where were our hi-tech surveillance drones?" Ena asked.

"Our best camera drones were focused on locating the Fringer army base. We are trying to confirm the location. We are investigating an anomaly above Blue Lake off Black Creek Road," answered Dermit.

"Continue to gather that critical information. What have you observed regarding the Guard's interactions?" Ena asked.

"They have been sabotaging the surrounding roads to obstruct our access, but they have made no aggressive moves toward us since defending the tunnel. Blocking the roads has been effective in preventing us from sending an army large enough to defeat them. It would be problematic to clear the roadblocks or repair the roads until spring. With that and the blackmail material, they believe their safety is secured.

"Every action we have detected supports what one would expect between two newly allied forces. Though this isn't a favorable outcome, the combined potential of these two forces poses little threat to our troops and armaments. We are still observing them to discover alternative objectives.

"We have a source whose husband trains as a backup soldier in one of the towns. Though she has never been to the Fort, she reports that the only information she has received confirms the Friendship Tour's goals and procedures. She has communicated with others in several Fringer towns and found no signs of combat readiness or military build-up. We are still monitoring the caravan closely, and we have our people and informants who will infiltrate the towns where they stop."

"Acknowledged," Ena said, and the screens went blank.

"Not even a goodbye," Dermit said with an aggravated whisper, "cold-hearted bastards."

Suddenly, the screen flashed on again, and the singular face of Ena was displayed. "Within the three days, I want to know who this child is, the names of the individuals on this Friendship Tour, the person in charge of the New Haven army, and their capabilities."

"Understood, Director," Dermit said and bowed slightly from his desk chair.

"Goodbye," Ena said, no doubt to mock his insolence.

Hard fear froze Dermit in place, dreading the pain of his disrespectful comment. It came, hitting him hard, and sending him tumbling out of his chair and twisting into a contorted ball. It was quickly followed by intense, humiliating pleasure that had him bucking and panting on the floor.

He lay still for several minutes, trying to recover from the conflicting sensations of pulled muscles and the flush of sexual release. How could he have been so stupid? Of course, they were listening. They were always listening and, unfortunately, watching. Lesson learned. He worked to tamp down the impotent anger that always followed their assaults and staggered to the closet where he kept his extra clothing.

The Allied Army Team

Jilly had been too ill to pay attention to the scenery on the first leg of the journey, where she huddled in the back seat of the Brute. She had moved to the seat directly behind Gray and was staring out the window. As they passed through Silverthorn, she imagined that as soon as the radiation rumor was dispelled, this town would repopulate.

It would be an important trade hub due to its proximity to New Haven and Sentry. She shared her vision with Gray, but her optimism was dashed when he said the Corporates had booby-trapped the place to keep neighboring territories from occupying it. Seeing her disappointment, he added that it was possible and likely they would decommission them, but it wasn't high on the priority list. She hoped it was true because most of the town's structures were quite nice and in good repair.

When they reached I-70, they proceeded to the meeting place where Axle and Easton were hidden and waiting to join the caravan as the sweep. Jax ran over to Axle and dragged him behind a bush for a quick hug and a rushed kiss.

"I see you made it," she said with a smile. "How are you feeling? And be honest. I won't rat you out. I promise."

"I feel good. Honestly, I'm ridiculously rested, and I've been work-ing out. I'm more ready and prepared than I was on our last mission." He winked at her, and they kissed again until calls from their com-rades rallied them to take their places.

It was time for lunch, so pee breaks were taken, and lunch sacks were handed out for the passengers to eat en route. The road issues would be minor compared to the drive behind them. It was silent as they got back on the road, except for the sounds of lunch bags rustling.

The plowed road stretched before them. Jilly was mesmerized by the world that sped by her window. Numerous ponds of various sizes were reduced to flat open spaces of pure winter white. Broken remnants of abandoned towns were scattered beside the road while the snow piled up around them. The further away they went from the tunnel, signs of life began to emerge. Hand-built sleds and wagons used for hauling leaned against recently patched houses and smoking chimneys. As they passed the smaller communities, people stood waving excitedly.

It was a picturesque drive. The evergreen forest and rugged canyon walls were impressively contrasted by the newly fallen snow. The candlelit windows and smoking chimneys in the distance proved many had settled outside of the city centers. One scene passed, making way for the next as the beefy tracks of the Brute rattled endlessly over the snow-packed pavement.

The New Haven passengers had never ventured outside of their small communities without being shielded inside a transport. Jilly knew she lived well in the sealed town of New Haven, but this was raw and real. She had heard Gray speak of how he missed the outside world and how he looked forward to the reconnaissance tasks that carried him beyond the tunnel. Looking out her window, she understood.

They were almost to Eagle, their first destination on the Friendship Tour. The sweep team of two Mini-Brutes and three soldiers had pulled off to set up a camp in the woods outside of Eagle. These vehicles were covered in high-tech camouflage, so they wouldn't be tracked by the drones that flew overhead. Staying behind to give assistance as needed was their job. The night before they were to move out, they would park just past the town, wait for them to pass, and continue their sweep.

Eagle wasn't as large as Silverthorn, but it was busy with people who had come for the celebration. An old electric truck led the train of vehicles to an open lot where they parked. When they came to a stop, the townspeople descended upon the visitors with excited enthusiasm. Connor wore a face mask to protect against the cold weather, but mostly to protect his identity.

"Welcome to Eagle," said the mayor. "This is our Town Center. It used to be a middle school, but now it's our everything place. It's also where we'll have our Harfest celebration."

Jilly thought back to the training file on Fringers. Harfest was the yearly festival where all the nomadic tribes got together to trade information and goods on their way to their winter places. It was also when all the young men and women over nineteen gathered together to meet each other. Some would make pledges and join different tribes for a courting period. Then on the next Harfest, they could get married in the joining ceremony.

Now that the Fringers are settled into permanent towns, Harfest is held at Eagle in the fall and Glenwood Springs in the spring. The annual party used to be the only time the tribes got together, but being in permanent homes allowed them to send letters and visit each other as they wished.

A crew got together, unpacking the items New Haven sent as gifts and those they brought to trade with Eagle. The City Center utilized the numerous classrooms for shops and offices, and the cafeteria was their dining hall. The gym was big enough for the whole town to gather and have celebrations. One wing of the school was used for visitor boarding, which was where they were led with their gear in tow.

After the radiation accident was reported, the Corporates hastily abandoned the towns, leaving all the larger items like furniture behind. It gave the Fringer residents ample furnishings to fill every home, business, service, and even guest accommodations.

Gray met with the town officials to secure their supplies while Jilly unpacked their items in their room. The lead minis were locked up and under guard at an uninhabited shop and used to secure the weapons and mission gear. It was also where they stored the goods for the next event at Glenwood Springs. The items and gifts intended for Eagle were loaded into the various classrooms assigned for their exchanges.

It was still early in the afternoon, so after a tour of the City Center, the team set to work getting ready for the gathering tomorrow. One long hallway of classrooms in the school served as stores where the townspeople had permanent shops. In the next hall of rooms, the team began setting up their displays. One room had children's toys, books, and games. In another room were clothing, sewing items, recipe books and cooking equipment, and decorations. A third trade room offered tools and other hardware supplies.

Tanya and Haru set up their mini church, and in the room next to them was where Jilly and Dr. Andie set up their clinic. While Jilly and Andie began the fury of unpacking and organizing, Andie was approached by a woman from McCoy. She reported that the medicine she sent had cured Kory and prevented any further spread of the disease.

Jilly was both happy and worried. Now that this crisis was resolved, what if Andie felt it was her duty to join the team? She was relieved when Andie expressed her concern that this was exactly the reason she should remain.

Finally, the trade rooms were settled enough to lock up their store doors in anticipation of the evening's events. That night, the whole town would gather in the gym to officially launch the Harfest with the evening meal.

At dinner, the mayor of the town raised a glass, "We welcome our valued allies from the town of New Haven. We look forward to fine friendships and tempting trades."

"Salute," came the loud response.

Jilly sat next to Connor, who was unusually quiet. "So, Miles," she said, addressing him by his pseudonym, "how has your journey been so far? And how is your arm doing?"

Connor moved his arm with the fake ailment, adding a slight wince for show. "The swelling is gone down, and my motion is better," Connor answered in the vernacular a Fringer would use. "My mom will be happy it wasn't like what my grandma had. Her lump got bigger and bigger, and she got sicker and sicker."

"How was it riding in a vehicle?" one of the people at the table asked.

"It's faster riding in a vehicle, and I like that, but sitting so long makes me sore and restless."

"I know what you mean," said Will on his other side. "I'd rather be on my horse."

Connor smiled, "I like horses. We have one."

Gray smirked at his improvisation, "I didn't know that," he said with a slight warning look.

"It's my dad's, but sometimes I get to ride with him. He said he'd teach me when my arm works better," Connor said to correct the liberty he'd taken. He was tired of being managed with lie upon lie. Even though he understood, he enjoyed grabbing back a little control over his story and seeing his watchers squirm.

Will grinned at Connor, puffing up at the fatherly reference. It was a genuine smile that glowed with honor. Will admired Connor's courage and his dedication to their cause. He knew what it meant to lie and hide year after year, and he wished he could carry the burden for him. But the youth showed no need for coddling. Not only was he carrying his own, he still had his sense of humor.

Leita sat on the other side of Will, but her attention was devoted to Haru, who sat opposite her at the long table. Will was not a jealous man by nature, and he had to remind himself that he and Leita were not pledged. In fact, Leita had told him she could never settle down with him. He was too wild, and taming him was not in her plans any more than being tamed by him. But he felt like she had crossed a line that, though ambiguous, was nevertheless there. Haru was no match for Will, and he was quite bold to push himself into his territory in front of him.

Haru, being astute at interpreting human behavior, turned to Will and began talking to him to calm the ripples he had caused. Will responded as kindly as he could but then turned to Leita with a curious stare. Was she simply engaged in conversation? Or was she making a play? Was Haru? Their conversation centered around information regarding their different lives. It never crossed a line or got personal, but she was laser-focused on Haru and not him. He fought the urge to rebuke her, control her, but he focused on restraining his childish emotions instead.

Will did not know this man, but his reputation would suggest he would be interested in learning about the Fringer lifestyle. Maybe that was all he was seeking. Yet, he was the very description of the sort of man she told him she *could* settle down with, sensitive, safe, and stable. Will could never be that man. Perhaps it was selfish of him to hold her back.

And what exactly was the nature of his hold? They had never exchanged promises or expressed their love. He cared for her, but did he love her? Will thought back to the feeling he shared with Molly. No, he didn't feel that way, but first loves were often imprinted with fictional memories. In most cases, when people returned to their first loves, it obliterated the memory with the discovery that it was no more than the myth and mirrors of youth.

Chapter Ten

The evening ended early since the next day's schedule was full. The shops would be open, the joining ceremonies would be celebrated in the afternoon, the new pledges would be announced, and they would end with a dance and a live band. Gray snuck Henry into his son's quarters to spend time together and instructed Nash to slip him back to their room in an hour or two. Jedi was assigned to guard Connor in his room, but while Henry was there, he listened to music on his headphones.

Will took Leita to a balcony overlooking a garden with a small pond. The clear, cold night made the stars especially bright. It would either be a prelude to a steamy evening or a heart-to-heart about their unclear relationship.

"I know you are questioning my interaction with Haru. Did you want to get that settled? We've been intimate for almost a year, but we've neatly avoided the issue of us." Leita's eyes were focused on the stars, not Will.

"We set our boundaries early on. We agreed a commitment was… how shall I say, ill-advised," Will said softly with his eyes trained on her profile. The gentle moonlight highlighted her stray strands and outlined her high cheekbones and subtle nose. She was beautiful and he desired her greedily, but when he tried to summon the feelings of love, they eluded him.

"I care so much for you, Will. I love the wild danger of you, but I can't pledge to it, and I'm not playing games to get you to ask me for one. That being said, I have no other man in mind, and I am happy to continue as we are." Leita felt the sting of her words in her heart because her honesty could end her closeness to this extraordinary man. She turned, looking for the evidence of hurt in Will's eyes. It was he who now looked skyward. His look was introspective and stoic, which could imply hurt, but that was the problem. He held his world apart from her. Even the parts he could share, he held back.

Finally, the two turned to each other, staring with unrevealing faces. It was a metaphor for their fundamental issue. Their physical connection was intense, throwing sparks of lustful desires around for all to see, but they lacked the core emotions that bind two souls. They weren't in love, and it wasn't foreseeable that they would be.

"So, my dear Leita, would you like to pursue a pledge? If children are in your future, it may be time to explore other possibilities. People are beginning to see us as a couple, and worthy men would not try to meddle with an involved woman," Will spoke softly and sincerely.

"And only a man with a death wish would challenge you," she snickered.

Will tilted his head and gave her a smirking nod, "True that. But I will do as you wish. I am not pledgeable. Not now, or in the foreseeable future. If you ask me, I will stand aside," Will answered, gripping the rail of the balcony with a whisper of woefulness in his voice.

"Well, tonight I feel the same. We may be reaching the end of our tryst, but I am not so eager to put this novel down yet. Let's be grateful for this honest moment, and enjoy more of our story," and she tiptoed up and kissed him gently.

He smiled down at her lips, poised for more. "Perhaps our tale has not climaxed yet," he said, continuing the metaphor as well as the kiss.

The honesty between them fueled their connection and their hearts. Perhaps, if they reached further, they might feel that which eluded them. The heady ache deep in their cores overshadowed the love search, and they stumbled back to his room. She leaned against the door as he worked his way down her neck and fumbled with the key. Pouring inside the room, he lifted her in his arms and onto the bed.

Clothing flew off while the persistent ache building deep in their centers grew. Her satiny skin and brazen nakedness called to him. She faced him on the bed with her arms reaching for him. He went to her, cradling himself between her legs. Slowly, he cupped a breast with one hand, twirling and rolling her responding nipple. With the other, he traced her graceful collarbone down, down, down, to the place she yearned for him to touch while maneuvering his hardness against her side. Round and round his finger moved, teasing her nub into a hardened knob of want. She moved and undulated with his skillful pressure. He knew what she liked, and he enjoyed how she wriggled against him. She began to gasp, and he rolled her over and positioned himself between her thighs.

Slow and strong, he slid into her center. She felt heavenly, and he found more pleasure as she squirmed and moaned, signaling him to release her and give her over to the climax she craved. Picking up the pace, she cried out, and he lost himself in the gentle spasms of sweet surrender.

The warm freshness of post-lovemaking serenity flowed through his veins. He felt that elusive peace, wishing it would last. She lay well pleased in his arms as her hand drew swirls across his abdomen. He wished he could lie here forever. He wished he had been born to a simple life where destiny didn't endanger everyone he dared to care for. He wished he believed it was possible to do this thing Tianna asked of him. To conquer an army with a single blade.

Leita was already asleep, and he kissed her temple and closed his eyes, hoping he too would fall into slumber.

With breakfast and clean-up out of the way, everyone went to their stations within their classroom shops. Over a hundred Fringers from all the towns around Eagle came. Gray stood by Will, surveying the unsafe circumstances.

"Relax, Gray," Will said. "We know every Fringer in all the established towns around here. We have spent months going into each one to recruit soldiers. If unknown people come into Eagle, we will know. Even the residents of this and other towns would report a new face."

"Just the same, let's keep Miles," he said with emphasis, "close to us. No one has a reason to talk with any of them."

"Agreed," Will said.

Gray took the first watch as Will caught up with the many friends he had here. Gray stopped in the church room and saw Haru, Tanya, and Leita handing out gifts and speaking about the ministry. He knew Haru enjoyed connecting with new people, but he wondered if the attention he had given Leita last night at dinner had upset Will. Will had a connection to Leita, but their relationship was unclear. He hoped it wouldn't be an issue when they went one way, and the team went another. It wasn't any of his business, but he needed Will focused.

Gray and Connor stopped in on Dr. Andie and Jilly, giving check-ups. They had assembled quite a crowd, so they invited the local medicine woman to sit in with them. They were exchanging knowledge as they performed their ministrations. Gray escorted Connor to the next room when they finished.

Jilly watched her husband protectively escort Connor through the festival. She placed a hand on her abdomen to assure herself she was doing the right thing. He tossed in his sleep, worrying about his charges. She didn't want to give him another one. She would be their child's protector, and let Gray concentrate on being hers and Connor's.

There was no other choice for a medic on this trip, and they couldn't travel without one. Dr. Andie had already found a couple of urgent concerns among the Fringers that may require New Haven's hospital to provide support. These issues required a doctor, and Jilly wasn't ready for that.

Connor wanted to visit the Fringer candle and soap store to get something for his mom. The room was bathed in fragrances of vanilla, honey, sandalwood, and all manner of scents. He found a candle with rosemary, which he couldn't stop inhaling, and suddenly realized his credits wouldn't work here. Gray pulled a couple of trade coins out of his pocket and paid for Connor's purchase.

"What are those?" Connor asked quietly as they made their way to the door.

"They are New Haven trade coins," Gray said, and then bent down and whispered in his ear. "Something a Lone Fringer wouldn't have."

"Hey, Miles, Gray," Henry said, coming up behind his son. "Did you buy someone a present?" he was pointing to the item weighing down Connor's bag.

"It's soap for my mom," Connor answered and pulled it out for his inspection.

He smelled it and nodded with approval. "I'm getting this for my daughter," letting Connor know he didn't need to buy Mishka a present.

Will came and relieved Gray, saying Wurden needed to talk with him outside the building. Connor's next wish was to visit the library, so Will escorted him. When a call came in from Nash, Will stepped away from Connor to talk privately with Nash and guard the only door.

"We've got three strangers, a man, a woman, and a young girl about twelve or thirteen. They claim to be Loners, but they're far too curious and bold for off-grid types, let alone Fringers. They keep the girl tightly between them, and she doesn't look like she's comfortable with them. Wurden and Gray are checking them out. They have a bad feeling about them," Nash said.

Will's eyebrows knitted together at the thought of using a girl to get close to Connor. It would probably work. He was smart, not savvy. He pressed his tongue against his teeth as if it would help him work through a decision. "I'm calling it," he said with conviction, "Parading him around is a bad idea. I'm getting him out of here. Tell Gray and Wurden to stall them."

"Yes sir," Nash answered and went to deliver the message.

Connor was busy at the librarian's counter, checking out some books. He didn't know what Nash said, but he could see Will, and his look meant trouble.

Will decided to initiate the emergency protocol before either of the strangers saw Connor. He knew Gray would be upset that he wasn't consulted, but he was talking with Wurden, and time had just run out.

Gray approached Wurden, the elected official from Will's hometown of McCoy. Together, they walked over to the three suspicious visitors.

"Welcome to Eagle, strangers. Nice day for a festival," Wurden said with a smile.

"Yes, we've missed going to these. Haven't been in several years. We were excited to hear a new community has joined forces with us, but we'd like to learn more about them," the man said. They didn't talk, dress, or act like Loners, except for the girl. The more they talked, the less Wurden trusted them.

They engaged in several minutes of small talk before Wurden introduced Gray. "This is Gray. He's from the town of New Haven."

They exchanged nods while the strangers kept their hands in their pockets, which wasn't unusual in the freezing wind.

"What do you do in New Haven?" the woman asked Gray.

"Mostly I shuffle papers and settle petty disputes," the Commander of the Defender army lied and laughed nonchalantly. "How about you? Where are you from?"

"We live off the grid, but we heard you were having a festival, and we needed supplies," said the man. "I'm Quinn, my wife Fran, and our daughter Bri. We heard other Lone Fringers were coming, so we decided it must be okay. Have you encountered any?" Wurden narrowed his eyes. Lone Fringers called themselves Loners, and he never heard any Fringer except Relic use the word "encounter".

"Well, they rarely introduce themselves, but I know most of the ones who'd come to a gathering. I've lived among the Fringers for well over a decade and officiated half a dozen festivals and trade deals with outsiders. I am pretty good at remembering faces, but I don't remember either of you," said Wurden. "How far did you travel to get here?"

Wurden got right to the point, which is exactly what the town official would do, but Wurden wasn't this town's official. He was a ranking member of the Fringer Coalition council. It was a test to see what they knew, and they didn't seem to know much. Loners were skittish. They would have found out about the town before they entered it. Their untorn clothing and perfect English were not those of off-grid inhabitants. They knew little of Fringer ways. They were Neighwah.

The girl watched her boot as she dug at the muddy snow. At least that behavior resembled Loners, Wurden thought. "Must have been a tough trek through this cold, wet snow. I'm guessing you're camped outside of town near the river," Wurden said as he pounded out the cracks in their story.

Quinn smiled, pulling Wurden aside by his jacket, astutely watching for reactions that would clue him into the location of his protection detail. Gray's eyes followed them with predatory focus. He was ready to respond, but Wurden signaled for him to stand down, at least for now. No one else flinched, not even the man with the cap and vest sporting the words, "Crowd Control". Quinn tucked that information away and gave Wurden an imposing stare.

Quietly but firmly, Quinn addressed his quarry, "Look, you're right, we're from Denver. We don't fully buy this *Friendship Tour* excuse for dragging all these people, most of whom are of soldier age, down the I-70. We have a right to know what you're after."

Wurden didn't shrink at his puffed-up plumage, and he hammered right back inches from the slightly shorter man's face.

"Your rights ended at the divide. *That's the deal.*" Wurden said it with such intent that Quinn wondered if his statement referred to an actual deal they had with the Corporates. It would explain the stand-down approach order he was given. "As far as the age of the people they brought," Wurden continued, "well, maybe you haven't noticed, but there aren't many elderly people anywhere. Which, by the way, is the result of your policies, not ours."

Quinn wanted to argue that he knew they had just left a military outpost, but he didn't want to give that up specifically. "You and I both know what you're doing here," Quinn said as a stab in the dark move. But in truth, he hadn't been told what the Corporates believed these Fringers were up to.

Composed and unruffled, Wurden stomped at the timid, annoying man and answered him with confidence. "It's simple logic. Introduce the tunnel residents to our communities as soon as possible to assure them they aren't you," he added with a mocking smile, and continued. "It's true, our harvest celebration is a little late, but invasions have a way of complicating schedules. Now, you can believe me or not, but as long as you're peaceful and don't cause problems, you have permission to check out our Harfest in that building," Wurden said as he pointed to the school. He spoke with practiced sincerity, but behind his cool exterior, he was poised in an uncompromising stance, ready to act.

They still stood face to face, and Wurden waited for his counter-move. "Just in case you think you can overpower or outwit us, Fran and I are Neighwah, but the girl isn't. She *is* a Loner from a family we *found* along the way. As long as you keep *your* cool, she won't be hurt. Now, let's see if we can be a little more candid with each other. Our objective is to investigate what's going on with this sudden party of yours. You seem to have organized and weaponized yourselves, and then you attacked us at the tunnel. You killed a lot of our soldiers. That wasn't in the deal."

"You brought an army into our territory, and that went well outside the deal. We assumed you were going after our women again, and maybe you were," Quinn was unaware the Corporates had kidnapped their women. It could be a lie, but Quinn could feel the man's emotional rage, so he kept his defensiveness in check.

"We ran you off in self-defense. We were just as surprised as you that people were living in the tunnel." Wurden could weave truths and lies with the best of them. "You should have warned us."

"Well, you certainly got prepared in a hurry," he said with a smirk. "And what exactly is going on here? Why the convoy in the lead of winter?" Quinn had his hands on his hips now.

"We brokered a deal with the high-ranking Corporates, so of course, we're prepared. I doubt you, on the other hand, are important enough to know what the *deal* entails, but I'll simplify it. The Corporates don't want war, and neither do we. However, don't mistake us for submissive Dailys who raise their hands in defeat at your command. I'm sure you were told to *cooperate* and not threaten us," Wurden growled under his breath. "Those are orders I'd heed if I were you, or things will go horribly wrong for a very long time."

What Wurden disclosed, whether knowingly or not, was that there was a *deal* and it had teeth, possibly fangs. Quinn wasn't sure it was true, but he was suddenly unsure how to navigate his orders. He had been told not to engage in violence that could be traced back to Corporate forces, but he thought that was to maintain their cover. Now, he wasn't sure, but he was tasked with documenting the people on the tour and tagging William and the child. He hoped he didn't stumble on any political trip wires, but he had to complete his mission.

"I need to meet with William of the Guard before I go. We know he is William Alexander, a deserter from the Neighwah Command. I'm sure there is no deal to harbor criminals. We have suspicions about the child you brought and want that meeting arranged too," Quinn said through his tweaked jaw.

"Will is off somewhere. I'm not his keeper, but I'll let his people know. The child came for medical treatment and was picked up this morning by his Loner father. They're gone."

The couple stood indignant at the news they didn't believe. After a few huffs, Quinn and Fran stomped away, dragging the frightened girl between them until they entered the building. Wurden returned to Gray as their detail followed the enemy. Wurden was filling Gray in when Relic came up behind them, his face wrapped in a winter scarf. He gestured for them to follow him quietly into one of the school's storage barns.

Chapter Eleven

Relic approached them with a thick scarf drawn across his face. It was cold, but that had nothing to do with his fashion choice. As he was filled in, Gray saw the worry build in his eyes. Relic thought about all the intel samples that were easily gathered, like photographs, fingerprints, and DNA. As a Highmind camp escapee, he couldn't be captured, not with what he knows. But he couldn't talk about any of that now. Gray got the message, if not the information.

"Our first order of business is to secure anyone they may be looking for," said Wurden.

"Already in progress," Relic said through the muffle of his scarf. But he offered no details, leaving both Gray and Wurden curious.

Relic pulled Gray aside and whispered, "Gray, we need to make sure they don't touch anyone. Who knows what devices they could plant on someone? I have no doubt that they have developed biological robomites by now. They may try to infect one of us," Relic said with a grave timbre in his voice.

"Shit, they grabbed Wurden's arm," Gray gasped while still keeping his voice hushed. Alarm bells were clanging in his head as he worked out the reality of computer robomites and the implications of biological robomites.

"I saw. We need to check him out, now!" Relic mumbled while pointing a hidden finger toward Wurden. Wurden had been respectful of the need for the military team to have private conversations, but he was getting an uneasy feeling that he was the topic of this one.

Gray walked back to Wurden. "Come with me." Wurden glared at him. "Please, it's important."

Wurden was led away, alarmed by the abrupt seriousness that filled the storage barn. The leader was in the unfamiliar zone of following the orders of others. He felt woefully uninformed, and that was untenable.

Gray had just met Wurden, and though Will said he trusted him implicitly, Relic was acting like he didn't. As far as Gray was concerned, the jury was still out on all three of them. Everything about this mission was moving too fast. It felt like they had a hold of the proverbial tiger's tail, and letting go was not an option.

They admitted to kidnapping a child whom they would kill to complete their mission, and who knows what happened to her parents. The continual stream of paradoxical conundrums was taking its toll, and his fists balled up reflexively at the thought of his wife and Connor being targeted in Corporate Elite espionage.

They proceeded to the Eagle City Center. Gray was almost at the door with Wurden. Nash joined them and directed them to a small first aid room where Andie, dressed in hospital scrubs, stood by a long metal table. Wurden figured out the reason no one was talking. It was the result of his interaction with the enemy. He removed his jacket as instructed, which was immediately bagged and taken out of the room by Nash. Andie searched Wurden's arm for a small hole by rubbing a blood reactive agent on his skin, but she found no bubbles to indicate a puncture.

Relic pulled Gray out into the hall to explain the threats of contact with Corporate thugs. The list was long, including sunset drugs, bio-mites, as well as tracking and monitoring devices. Bio-mites were an invention still on the table when he escaped as a Highmind. There were two different goals. One was for continual healing, extending the lives of soldiers and high-level executives, like the Elites.

The other type included a transmitter and receiver used to control those infested with the pain and pleasure centers in the brain. If they were using the controlling kind, they would need to be delivered by injection, and mental training would have to follow, but they would be able to track him.

"I believe Wurden's jacket is too thick for penetration from needle wounds that wouldn't be felt and noticed. I don't fully understand this kind of bio-weapon, but," Relic added, "I'm not sure Wurden would be a valuable enough target. But if they did inject him, he would have a reaction of some kind within a few hours."

Gray and Relic went to the small office next door, where Nash sat at a table in front of the bagged jacket. Relic took out a bug-detecting device, which Gray recognized as an obsolete model used at the Hold.

Gray silently held up his hand and took off his pack. He unzipped several pockets before a satisfied smile warmed his face. Removing the newer, more sensitive device, he handed it to Relic.

"We *all* feel protective of the kidnapped Loner child," Relic said, still wearing his scarf, as he made a thorough sweep of the item. Gray assumed Relic worried the Corporates could ID him with his voice, but if they were listening, he wanted to send a message. "They broke the treaty by sending troops into our area. All we did was defend ourselves. Hopefully, when they see we have nothing to hide, they will release her to us and leave us alone."

The passive message irritated Gray and made him want to smash his fist into something, or better yet, the smug jerk holding the child, but he stayed still and quiet. He knew they wouldn't buy Relic's performance or care what happened to the young girl. And to keep the peace, they'd kill her and dump her where no one would find her. Gray tamped down his anger and focused on the issue.

These same Neighwah soldiers were after Will, Relic, Connor, and, if they figured out who she was, Jilly. Through them, they hoped to discover what their mission was truly about. He decided to play Relic's game of downplaying their operation.

"I guess you're right. There's nothing they're going to find here, and the sooner they see we just want to do a meet and greet, they'll return home. But they better not hurt that kid. I hate kid killers. I really do, and I'm going to make sure she's safe." Gray said the last part more aggressively.

"Yes, we should work on a way to secure the girl before they leave. But we have our own power over the Corporates, and murdering a child may cause us to unleash it," Relic answered, still muffling his voice as he bagged up the jacket.

Relic held the tiny micro listening device he found clinging to the sleeve where Wurden had been grabbed. He held it up and, with a gesture, asked Gray what he should do with it. Gray held up a baggie, and Relic dropped it inside. He handed it to Nash, standing guard outside, suggesting with his walking fingers and shovel movements to take it away and bury it. With the inside and outside of the jacket cleared, they stepped into another office, and Gray fired off his questions to Relic in rapid succession.

"Where are Connor and Will at this minute? Exactly what the hell is a bio-mite? And how do we check for them before a reaction sets in? Do we have to quarantine the whole team?"

"We have more immediate issues. You can be sure they have planted cameras around town, and they will capture the photo IDs of our team, fugitives, and everyone they can for their archives,"

Relic said. "We need to deal with this immediately before they have time to transmit the data. Then I'll tell you everything I know about bio-mites."

Gray stepped out into the hall and called the closest Allied soldier over. "I need a sweep for monitoring devices inside and out of the town center. Then we need to find the drones they are transmitting to and stop them before they can relay any information," Gray said. "Get everyone available. No one is off duty until this is done."

Gray returned to the office where he had left Relic. They ran through various maneuvers to protect the high-level targets, as well as finding a way to rescue the child hostage. He swore to himself that their plans would have a tragic end if they used a sunset drug on her. Without the antidote, the girl may already be dead. Gray discussed with Nash the need to keep Relic and Will safe. He smiled at the idea of telling Will that he was under protective custody. He'd probably punch him. Still worth it.

"I'll start with Connor. We had an escape plan in place that only Will and Nash knew about. All I know is it included a survival pack and an escape plan to get out of the city. What I don't know is how they'd get out, where they would go, or what Will would do after he got the boy out. He is the best survivalist I know. We need to trust him."

"Are you saying this plan has been put into action?" Gray stood frozen in disbelief as his fury boiled. "He was my charge! I could have followed the escape plan. I, too, have excellent survival skills. You didn't even inform me! I don't know Will or any of you well enough to trust you with Connor. Is this how you treat your new allies? My confidence in your people just dropped to rock bottom!" He said, pointing his finger to emphasize his frustration.

Relic kept his cool. "Well, let me tell you a little history about Will. He has fought his whole life to save this world from its current state. He has never once asked for anything for himself. As a key target, he has suffered being orphaned, conscripted, kidnapped, blackmailed, tortured, and every other horror that the Corporates could throw at him since he was ten. But no matter what they did to him, it never deterred him, and every action he took was to save someone besides himself.

"I understand your concerns, and I see how you could misjudge our actions, but you were not available for all the drills and protocols we put in place. Just as I'm sure we missed the ones you devised. Besides, they both needed to escape, and all this happened while you were right next to the enemy. Trust is elusive these days. Situations arise that alter the moral codes of the most virtuous people.

"Our two very different societies have been thrown into an arranged marriage and an impending war. Granted, we don't understand each other very well, but we can't afford to disassociate ourselves from one another. Both you and Will painstakingly chose the best people to join the mission, as well as those you left in charge. Everything you two have done has built confidence in you with all the Allied team members. I know the trust between us is untested and shaky, but I encourage you to offer your support without knowing exactly how it will turn out."

"I could do that in most situations, but he took Connor! My wife is also a high-level Corporate target. Is she next? Will isn't immune to these mite things. He was in the Neighwah!" Gray said, poised in a commanding stance.

Relic took a breath, "You are more correct than you know. Just before Will left the Neighwah, they tried numerous times to biomite him. Only the most valuable assets are targeted because the technology is expensive, and it requires a long training period. According to the Robinhooders who sent Will to us, Will's body rejected every attempt."

"Do we know what their capabilities are?" Gray took a breath and sat down, understanding he needed this information. He pushed his temper aside.

"Once injected, they take a couple of weeks to infiltrate one's nervous system. They control an infected person by attaching themselves to the prefrontal region of the brain at the pain and pleasure receptors. They cause discomfort until one follows the suggestions programmed into them, and when one complies, he or she is rewarded with pleasure. Some fall in line easily, others get ill and die, and some take their own lives, thinking they've slipped into insanity."

"And how did Will react?" Gray asked.

"He had little or no reaction. But I know he isn't infected with the controlling biomites," Relic assured him.

"How do you know? Can you tell if someone is infected?" Gray challenged.

"If I have access to a good microscope, I can detect the mites, but the trouble is. I need a brain sample. It's the only place to find them because they don't travel through the body. That's the surest method. I can also test disobedience and compliance to detect whether the patient is being artificially stimulated. Not knowing what kind of training the person received makes that a lengthy process."

"Are you saying you took a sample of Will's brain?" Gray's voice rose several octaves with disbelief.

"There are places in that part of the brain that can spare a small biopsy without harm," Relic said, knowing Gray was appalled.

"Just for the record," Gray said cynically, "I don't want pieces of my brain under a microscope unless I'm dead."

"Noted. Back to my account. Before I escaped the Highmind camp, we had just developed computer robomites, and we were well on our way to finding a way to use them on people. The original experiment was to increase intelligence and improve health, but the Elites ended those projects in favor of one that allowed them to control behavior. I left long before it was ready for use, but I know the basic premise."

Gray tucked Relic's confession away and asked his next question. "So, what made you go searching for these mites, and how do you know Will is immune?"

"I did a routine check on Will to rule out infectious diseases he may be carrying when he first joined us. That's when I discovered active biomites in Will's blood sample, and I concluded the Corporates had solved the biotic problems."

"I thought you said he didn't have them!"

"Let me finish. I was shocked and worried he was a spy, so I observed his actions. Biomites are not sophisticated enough to think. They just attach themselves to certain kinds of brain cells and manipulate the person to act, or not act, on whatever thoughts are planted by behavioral conditioning. I deduced Will had not finished the programming, or they hadn't attached. Whatever the reason, they weren't working.

"I witnessed actions that defied the biomites' functions, like hiding important objects, killing Drangers, training Fringers to fight, and revealing seditious information about the Corporates. Never once did he display episodes of pain or pleasure. He went back to where he had hidden his blade and killed Neighwahs, and nothing.

"So, I questioned him about his inoculations. He admitted he was given many vaccines, and there were three that gave him severe headaches. The second of those left him unconscious for almost a day. But each time, he recovered by the next day. We shared a tent, and one night I drugged him and took a brain sample by going through his nose. I discovered he did have biomites, but instead of clinging to pain and pleasure receptors, they were free-roaming in his blood. I put—"

Gray interrupted. "Let me get this straight. He's infected, *and* he has Connor?"

"Gray, you need to listen. As I was saying, I put his brain tissue in the cultivator, and there were some mixed in with it. I wanted to see if they would attach or, if not, why they couldn't. When I checked the sample the next morning, the mites had repaired a portion of the biopsy's severed edges. Will's biomites are not programmed to control, they're programmed to heal."

"How is that possible?" Gray asked. His interest was so intense that he was momentarily distracted from his concern for Connor.

"I can't say, but I'm guessing a Robinhooder in the Highmind camp secretly continued to develop them using our research. They enhance the body's own healing systems to speed up the process. It must take an enormous amount of energy, so—" Relic saw Gray motion him to move on. "On his first injection, Will was given the healing mites instead of the controlling ones. When he didn't react, they gave him a second and third injection of the controlling bio-mites, but his healing bio-mites attacked them." Relic speculated.

"Does he know?" Gray asked, wondering if Will, the loyal and honorable person Relic described, was aware of these things and didn't tell him.

"He constantly questions his fate and whether he is worthy. Knowing this would kill him, and possibly our mission if he decides he should bow out."

"So, no. He doesn't know," Gray gave Relic a sideways glance.

Relic shook his head slightly. "Gray, I believe in Will. Every step he's made has been selfless and honorable, and he's delivered the Corporates serious damage. What I do know is, the controlling mites aren't sophisticated enough to decipher thoughts, only physical responses to planted memories. If he were infected, his actions would have betrayed him by now."

"I agree, for one man taking on an army, he's done an amazing job of holding them at bay, but let's face it, they aren't damaged. I believe in him, too, but these things are beyond his control. It's good that you held it back. Good for him, and good for us. Does anyone else know?"

Relic shook his head and looked at the man before him. They had just agreed to spy on Will. It was ironic because he had even fewer reasons to trust Gray.

He must devise a reason to keep Gray under surveillance and divulge it to Will. Then both would be watched, and both would bring him the information. His head ached. Although it was woefully dishonest, he felt confident it was the right thing to do. He would be searching for disloyalty in them while being disloyal. The paradox was that of a Greek tragedy. And in such tales, the mastermind always loses.

Will and Connor

Connor was disoriented and scared. Will had received a message, and he swiftly grabbed Connor, pulling him down a hall to a room where Jedi, a Guard soldier in civilian clothes, stood waiting to let them in. Connor heard the door lock behind them. Visions of his kidnapping at the Hold began to run the terrifying memory through his mind. Like that room, this one was also lined with shelves. On these shelves was the ready-to-go gear he had trained with in New Haven. It included backpacks, thick coats, and weapons. It was a one-stop get-out-of-town quick room, and everyone had a set of pre-packed supplies at the ready.

Connor watched, frozen in fear. *Where was Will taking him? What were they running from?* Will bolted over to a section of the shelf marked with the number 12. It held the smallest pack, a child-sized coat, and a small pistol with an ankle holster. He pulled the tight bundle off the shelf and removed the shoulder straps that bound it, causing it to bloom on the table.

"This is the Go Room," Will said sternly, but it did little to explain what was happening. He handed Connor the pack and coat, saying, "Put this on."

"But I already have a coat on," Connor answered in a half-whimper. He could see the intensity of Will's manner, and the boy's hackles were fully raised.

"Remove it quickly, Connor. We need to move." It was then that Will saw the terror growing in Connor's eyes. Taking his shoulders, he squared the boy in front of him. "Unsafe people are in town. I can protect you, Connor, but you have to trust me and do exactly as I say."

The boy tried to tuck his doubts away and nodded his head. He took off his lightweight jacket to don the oddly heavy coat and sad-dled the backpack over the bulky outer layer. Will was also gearing up. He had a large caliber handgun strapped to his waist and a compound bow that he slung over his shoulder.

He turned to Connor and put a straw hat over a warm scarf, which he tied below his chin. Conner watched the efficiency he demonstrat-ed during this whole ram-rod preparation for what he didn't know. He could see the plan had been fine-tuned and practiced, which was as organized as this room.

When they left the Go Room, two Guard soldiers, Jedi and Mack, escorted them through the halls, sporting serious weapons and lethal attitudes. When they reached the shop, they stopped and let them in through the guarded entrance.

Inside, Connor saw a well-used buckboard wagon with tall side-boards, a passenger bench, and an area for a modest amount of storage. It was already harnessed to two large horses. Flanked by old school buses and the remnants of a mechanic shop, the wagon and horses were parked in front of the large shop door. Three Fringers joined them with a load of supplies, ready to move out. They would look like all the other Fringer carts traveling in and out of the Harfest celebration.

Will secured their packs behind them while Connor climbed up to sit in the middle seat of the passenger bench. He stopped when he noticed the odd structure of the seat next to his. The seat and floor were lower than the rest of the bench. He thought about Will's height, such a seat would make him appear shorter. He smiled at their attention to detail. Will sat in the height-shortening seat and proceeded to smear his face with light-skinned makeup. Wiping his hands on a towel, he handed the jar and towel to someone standing by, pulled on a pair of work gloves, and tucked his hair under a forest green beanie.

The garage door was pulled open, and the driver grabbed the reins, clicking at the horses to move. They joined the innocuous traffic of Harfest goers on a rural street leading to Highway 6. Though I-70 would have been faster, it was designated for motorized traffic during the festival. They were headed west as Relic adjusted his hat, heading over to talk with Gray, who was watching the strangers head for the school building.

Though everyone else in the cart engaged in conversations about the festival, Connor was afraid to speak, let alone ask questions, but he had plenty. He wondered if Gray or his father knew where he was or what was happening. He hated worrying them. Though Connor assumed the other people in the cart were trustworthy, none of them were speaking candidly about their hasty retreat. Maybe hasty was an overstatement since the horses were barely trotting. Where they were slow-trotting to, he did not know, but he looked up at Will, hoping at some point, he would share the plan with him.

Connor was so in his head that he had ignored his surroundings. Being aware and what to watch for had been part of his training at New Haven. Being scared and confused wasn't an excuse to tune out. They were the signals to be extra vigilant. He wasn't aware he had been looking down until he looked up and saw Will studying him.

The strong protector gave him a slight smile and nodded at the approaching sign marking a town called Gypsum. Connor snapped out of his thoughts and began surveying his surroundings. Connor searched the trees and abandoned buildings, watching and listening for movement, flashes of surveillance gear, or startled movements by wildlife.

The ride in vehicles down the old, poorly patched roads was bumpy at best, but a horse-pulled cart with solid wheels gave him a new experience in rough riding. Every deviation in the road was met with the bouncing and noisy cart springs.

Several hours outside of town, the driver stopped at a building with a collapsed sign. The only discernible word left on it was Church. The passengers got up and stretched their legs, arms, and the abused parts of their bodies. They scattered to find privacy to relieve themselves before they got back in the wagon.

Will walked Connor to a grove of trees where they were met by two people hidden beneath a camouflaged tarp. Connor could see a small woman and a man hiding who were similar in appearance to them. They traded coats and headgear, and Will and Connor took their place under the tarp. The Will and Connor imitations left the shelter of the trees and got in the wagon. Connor watched it leave.

"Will ..." the child said in an anxious whisper, but he was cut off by a single gesture. Connor didn't know how long they waited under the tarp sheltered by that group of trees, but his limbs were stiff and cold before Will snuck them into the church building. Connor was shocked to see a horse standing in the lobby and munching on hay.

"Connor," Will said, "meet Ranger, your ride."

Connor looked at the huge creature with intense hesitation.

Chapter Twelve

"We can talk now. I don't detect any drones," Will spoke quietly as he looked at the device in his hands.

"Then why are you still whispering, and what's with the tarps?" Connor whispered back.

"The tarps shield us from infrared detectors. And though I can detect drones that are actively flying, I cannot determine if they've landed to observe and listen. We'll wait until it gets dark before we move out. I suggest you get some sleep since we'll be traveling through the night."

"So, what was the reason for the sudden escape?" Connor was as far from sleep as he could be.

"Strangers were spotted in town, and they turned out to be Neigh-wah agents with a hostage," he said a little too matter-of-factly.

"A hostage?!" Connor loudly whispered. "Who?"

"A girl about your age," he said with a worried look.

"Why? Why would they kidnap a girl?"

"If they hadn't been discovered, I'm sure they would have used her to get to you, maybe lure you out, so they could grab you."

"That wouldn't have worked," the boy said with confidence.

"Gray said she was beautiful and very scared," Will replied, tilting his head.

That might have worked, Connor said to himself. "Did they save her?"

Will shrugged his shoulders and said, "I'm sure they will try. It depends on the kidnappers' insurance plan."

"Like hurting someone else if they didn't do what they said?" Connor remembered his defensive training. "We were told not to give in to blackmail."

"That's easier said than done," he said. "Three times I gave up my freedom to keep people I care about safe."

"I know about the time you were forced to join the Drangers and then the time with Neighwah, but when was the third time?" Connor asked.

Will told Connor about his family. It started with his father finding an abused and starving woman while in the woods. She was painfully timid, but Will formed a special bond with his woman, who became his stepmother. She taught him the forbidden subjects of math, science, history, and literature, and she told him many stories.

Will explained that he discovered she was teaching him things that held clues to the rebellion. Though his family was poor, like all Dailys, he enjoyed a wonderful childhood until the Neighwah began harassing them. His father heard that a group of workers had been killed in an avalanche in Colorado Springs, and they were looking for replacements. They joined up with others escaping Pueblo and made a run to the border.

The boy listened intently as Will continued saying they were caught at the border because the whole worker trade thing was an elaborate plan to capture Tianna. Will said he had to listen without saying a word as the group made a deal to trade his stepmother for everyone else's safe passage. She was to sit in the field until the group made it to the border, and then they'd take her. They only let the workers through because the Colorado Springs officials, who were not involved in the plan, had paid good money for them, and their soldiers were poised to fight for them.

"I grabbed my dad's binoculars from our gear and snuck back to watch. I believed they had a plan to rescue her because she was so calm and willing," Will said while staring at a religious depiction of Jesus. "I watched her blowing dandelion seeds into the wind like it was just another day, and she was enjoying a simple moment. I knew she was in mortal danger, and I cared deeply, but I did nothing because I believed someone would save her.

"The next thing I knew, a shot rang out, and it came from where my father was hiding. I saw the red mist spray from her head, and I still thought it was part of the plan, even when she crumpled in the field. Then an explosion roared from where my father was sheltered." Will's voice was eerily calm, mimicking his shocked state of mind and the moment that still eluded him.

"I was still frozen with disbelief when Taylor's son, Pierce, drugged me with a dart, threw me over his shoulder, and ran to catch up with the cart as it crossed the border."

"That must be a terrifying memory," Connor said.

He tilted his head for a moment and moved on unceremoniously. "My dad and my stepmom were fair-skinned. I got my dark coloring from my real mom. And since they made sure no one knew they were my parents, Taylor registered me as his adopted son. By the time I woke up. I was no longer William Alexander. I was Will Nolan.

"I don't know Pierce, but I like Taylor. I'm glad you had him," Connor noted.

"I gave him a rough time. I was an angry, messed-up teen, but he and Pierce kept me safe and allowed me to grow up. It wasn't until I was rescued from the Neighwah that I figured out who my stepmother really was. The Robinhooders had helped her escape and entrusted Tianna to my dad.

When she died, the Corporates looked everywhere for the Sanguine Blade they believed her father had passed on to her. But while I was a Dranger, we shared a job with the Neighwah. When they ran my DNA, they connected me to my real dad. They thought I had the blade, or that I could lead them to it. That's why they trapped me into joining them.

They tried to break me, befriend me, and control me. They even told me my dad had escaped the blast, and he was alive. I had built up the story to them that I wanted to kill him because he killed Tianna. They thought I would reveal something if they paraded a man who resembled my dad in front of me."

"Did you want to kill him?"

"No," Will said. "I just wanted to know what happened, why he did it."

"Did you ever find out?" Connor asked.

"He was saving her from the horrible life that awaited her. She made him promise when they married that he would never let her return, even if it meant taking her life. That day in the field, she was holding him to it."

"Wow, it's like a Greek tragedy. So, these Robinhooders are behind the rebel faction? Do you think my grandad knew them?" Connor asked.

"There is no doubt he knew them. I believe your grandad was pretty involved with them. They helped hide his participation in the Highmind experiment. He was given precious works of art to hide, and he knew about Cali Bantu enough to train you to access it," Will said.

"I was told to hide my abilities, so I wouldn't end up in the High-mind camp. GD, my grandad, taught me to act simple-minded. It's ironic that at two years old, I was intelligent enough to act unintelligent. Before I turned twelve, I would have been forced to take the brain scan for density, and they would have discovered me."

"If they had, they would have taken you and used you," Will said with authority.

"So, are you looking for your dad?" Connor was amazed that both of their storylines had so many similarities.

"No, the RH confirmed that he died. The whole mission was an elaborate lie to get me to cooperate. Before they could use their decoy dad on me, the RH ambushed the operation and kidnapped Rival and me. They got Rival to the Fringers and helped me escape into the woods. I was living on my own off the land for the better part of a year before I joined the Fringers."

The boy looked at this strong soldier confessing his vulnerabilities, wondering how to respond. He imagined young Will seeing his family being killed in front of him. He wanted to express his compassion, to take in his sorrow, and show him that the pain of the young boy he used to be mattered. But Connor let the moment go. William of the Guard wasn't that vulnerable young boy anymore. He was a warrior.

Connor had never been threatened and tested the way Will had. If he had not been invited to the tunnel, he would have experienced the cruelty of the Corporate world in the Highmind Camp. He was safely secured in New Haven, but now he was back out in the Corporate world, and they were running. He suddenly felt very afraid, afraid of the future, and afraid of the people after them.

Get some sleep, we leave at sunset." And just like that, Will was back to commander mode. As the tall man positioned his pack under his head and stretched out on a pew, Connor took a cleansing breath and smiled to himself. Despite the horrific theme, he valued the exchange. Connor thought back to just a few weeks ago, when he questioned traveling with this frightening Fringer. In a short time, respect and sincere trust had developed between them.

Will eased into sleep easily, but Connor was restless. He needed to reason out the events of the day. He wondered about the girl hostage back in Eagle, the abuse Will suffered as a Corporate soldier, and all the events that made Will into William of the Guard, warrior extraordinaire, but mostly what was to become of them.

Looking around the modest room, or nave, he evaluated the stability of the structure. Though it seemed to be intact, it had been gutted. He headed to one of the few pews still left at the front of the church. As he walked toward the sanctuary, something glistened in the ray of sunlight that spilled through the side window. Most of the floor was thick with dirt and dust, but it must have been uncovered by the gust of wind that followed them inside. Scooting across the bench, he picked it up and rubbed it clean.

It was a small silver cross on a broken chain. He also found a book left in the back pocket of the front bench. It was a songbook. It was old, but the pages were well-made and didn't crumble like some books. Connor could read musical notes, and he recognized some of the melodies from the times he attended Haru's services. At the back of the hymnal, he found scriptures arranged by topics and events.

He opened the book, and there at the top of the page was a verse from Deuteronomy 31:6: "Be strong and courageous. Do not be afraid or terrified because of them, for the Lord your God goes with you; he will never leave you nor forsake you." How the perfect words of encouragement found baffled him, but they had a powerful effect on him. He fully understood how dangerous faith and hope were to the Corporates.

Having these items was enough to get him severely punished by the Corporates, but the hope they gave him outweighed the threat. He put the book in his breast front pocket. He looked around at the bare dirty walls with skepticism. He though of movies where characters were saved by hiding in stick-built structures. But he learned that bullets could go through walls and words don't provide actual protection.

Yet the walls kept him out of sight and the words gave him comfort And the cross, well, it gave him something to hold on to. Though he didn't believe in luck, he felt lucky that he found them. he smiled at the irony. He put the cross with the broken chain in his left pocket, so he could hold it when he prayed. Lying his head on his pack, he was suddenly overwhelmed with fatigue and fell asleep quickly.

He was awakened by Will shaking him.

"Is it time to go?" Connor asked faintly.

"You're burning up, Connor. How do you feel?"

"Not so good. My head hurts, and I'm cold."

"Well, you're going to get colder," he said as he opened the boy's jacket. He dug into his pack and took out a med kit. Connor began to shiver as Will plowed through the kit. When he found what he was looking for, he sat Connor up. Nausea and dizziness rolled the boy's head.

"I think I'm sick, Will."

'I see that. Here," he said, handing Connor a small white pill, "swallow this. It will help reduce your fever. We're a good ride from Glenwood. But we can rest there. The rest of the team will show up tomorrow morning."

"I can make it. Don't worry," Connor mumbled.

Will ignored Connor's attempts at bravery and focused on checking Connor's breathing and pulse. "Don't worry, we have contingency plans in place. Just rest for a few, while that analgesic kicks in, and we'll head out."

Will felt the helplessness of a parent as he looked at the pale child. He was rethinking traveling in Glenwood, which would be infested with Corporates by now. A new destination that no one knew of was forming in his mind. While Connor slept, Will ate a quick dinner, readied the packs, and saddled the horse. He left out some banana chips and electro-light juice for Connor and felt his head. It was much cooler, so he woke him up. Connor struggled through the chips but drank the juice at Will's insistence.

He climbed up on the horse and effortlessly lifted Connor in front of him, draped the infra-blocker tarp over them, and put on a set of night goggles. The once fearful boy was too sick to worry about the high-ride. He trusted Will to take care of him because it was his only option. Will's new goal was to secure his charge in a warm, safe place where he could recover.

"Let's go, Ranger," he said, and he clicked his cheeks and pressed the horse forward.

They trotted down a side trail that paralleled the road. Soon, the boy slumped back against Will as he navigated the dark trail by the crescent moon, illuminating the shimmering snow.

Connor was in and out, and he desperately needed to lie down, but he was trying not to sound whiny in front of this warrior. He wanted to be brave, but all he felt was frail. He remembered the scarred slash across the knuckles of all the Guard soldiers. Hunter said it was from a blood brother ritual. It must have hurt, but it was a test of bravery as well as an enduring sign of loyalty. He wished he had a scar like that to look at and remember to be strong, as he held his cross in his clumsy, gloved hand.

"How much further?" Connor asked during a short break.

"About an hour to town, but we aren't going there. We're stopping by Bayley's. I'm looking for the hidden route to his cabin. He lives outside of town."

Connor started shivering again, and Will knew he had to find Bayley's place or some other shelter. It would be hard to keep Connor comfortable without building a fire. And a fire where no one was reported to live would be investigated, so finding the cabin was imperative. He took out the paper and flashed his dull light on the clues he had been given. Connor was leaning on him and eyed the handwritten document.

"What does emanon mean?" Connor asked weakly. "See the note at the bottom, ' find emanon'.

"It's written in some kind of code, I think," Will said deep in thought.

"Well, emanon is no name backwards. Not much of a—" Will interrupted Connor before he finished.

"Of course, No Name Creek. There's a trail called Jessie Weaver that follows it. I think we're close." With that, Will rode Ranger at a quicker pace.

Connor's fever was back when they got to Bayley's. He let them in, but relegated Connor to the spare bedroom where he could be quarantined. Will carried the boy who didn't stir and put another tablet under his tongue. Connor stirred.

"Will, am I going to die?"

'No, Bayley went to get a healer. I know you feel bad, but you'll feel better in the morning. I've seen this before.' Will didn't know what to do. He hadn't been sick since he was a young boy, nor had he dealt with people who were ill. Though he had no idea what was wrong with Connor, he gave him the needed reassurance that all would be well.

"Blood brother," Connor said weakly. "Hunter, he told me about the soldiers being blood brothers. Before I get worse, can I be a blood brother, so I can die with honor?"

Will could see he was scared, and not much seemed to scare this kid. "You know I had every intention of making you blood brother. I just wanted to wait until we were on the mission trail. We'll do it now." He knew he shouldn't, but he wasn't sure if Connor was going to be okay.

Connor watched Will go to his pack and get out a knife. Not just any knife, *the* knife.

"Is that—"

"Yes, this is the knife Tianna gave me on that day."

It was beautifully made with a handle of deep mahogany highlighted with a magnificent grain pattern. The grip had a finger-hold shape, with carved markings that Connor was too weak to analyze.

"I recognize this," he said, "means balance... of...," Connor moaned and rolled his head. "Can't think. Sorry."

Will pulled out the double-sided blade and held the sharp edge against his fist. As weak as Connor was, he was focused on the mysterious relic. The blade had a burnt reddish hue as if it were permanently stained by the violent prophecy it was destined to set in motion. A lightning bolt shot down the blade, flashing silver through the bloody pigment.

"Repeat after me. 'I pledge to fight at your side for the glory and allegiance that brings a better fate to all'. Say it and ball your fighting hand into a fist."

Connor repeated the pledge weakly, keeping an eye on the blade Will had in his hand. He knew it would hurt, wondering how much blood was required for the ritual, yet he remained silent. He didn't dare back out now. The weak child drew out his dominate left hand from the covers and complied.

Will grabbed his tiny wrist and small fist, doubt filling his heart. But when Will saw the boy's brave resolve and the desperation in his eyes, he took a cleansing breath and slashed across the existing scars on his own balled-up fist. Before Connor could overthink it, he sliced across the top of his four little fingers and smashed their bloody fists together.

It burned like nothing Connor had ever felt. His eyes widened as an intense sensation of pain spread from his arm, contracting every muscle in his body. He collapsed into an unconscious state. Will had never seen that kind of reaction, but he had never done the ritual on someone so ill. He assumed he had fainted, and he bandaged Connor's hand as well as his own and wondered how he would explain the wound to Bayley, the healer, Gray, and Henry. It was the boy's wish, perhaps his last. How could he refuse?

Will let Connor sleep while he stoked the fires in both the main room and Connor's. He rummaged through Bayley's kitchen, finding some dried veggies in a jar and a container labeled "stock" in Bayley's freezer. He threw it all in a pot, set it on the wood stove, and rifled through Bayley's herb selection. It was then he heard footsteps outside. He grabbed his gun and manned the door. He was expecting Bayley, but he prepared for trouble. Peeking out the window, he saw it was his friend and a bundled woman. Will opened the door, noticing the orange glow of sunrise rounding the ridge across from the cabin.

"Were you planning on shooting me as I walked up to my own home with help for my uninvited guest?" Bayley grumbled.

"It's always an option," Will gave a low chuckle as he returned his gun to lean against the door jam. "I raided your kitchen and started some soup," Bayley mumbled sarcastically as he walked to the stove to take over the process.

The woman was slowly unwrapping her layers, exposing her silver hair and weathered face. A veiny hand was extended to him. "I'm Freida. Where is the patient?" Will hoped her elderly appearance was equal to her experience.

"This way, Freida, and thank you for coming out at this hour. Did Bayley explain our need for secrecy?"

"Everyone who visits Bayley needs secrecy," she said in a gravelly voice.

Chapter Thirteen

Will watched as Freida examined the boy. Her gnarled hands scrutinized his body with gentle, experienced precision. He was awake but groggy as she felt around his throat, listened to his breathing, and looked in his ears. She unwrapped the bandage on his right hand and frowned at the suspicious wound she knew was common to Will's soldiers. She laid the boy back on the bed, and sleep began to take him again. Wanting him to be awake for the rest of her assessment, she gently shook him, and he responded after several attempts. Connor looked at the woman and then around the room with concern until he located Will leaning against the door jam.

"Are you a healer?" the boy mumbled with a roughness in his voice.

"Yes, I'm Freida. I was trained by my grandmother. Tell me what you are feeling, Miles."

Though his mind was foggy, Connor remembered the name Will gave him to protect his identity. "My throat hurts some, but my headache is gone. I feel better than I did when I got here. But I have this weird tingly sensation all over me. It isn't painful, but it's ... odd."

"Rest is what you need, and the short nap you got is the reason you feel better. The tingling is probably due to the rash you have. Open your mouth so I can see your throat."

"Hmm, it's red and swollen with some tonsil stones. That and your fever are common with strep throat. How did you hurt your hand?"

Will interrupted, "He was delirious and tried to swing at me while I had my knife out."

"Odd that your hand is also bandaged, and that it matches the wound so many in your charge have. Please tell me you don't believe in bloodletting," she said sarcastically.

"No, nothing like that," Will dismissed her insult. "It's a long story," he said and then quickly changed the subject. "I didn't know he had a rash. Maybe I didn't notice it because I kept him bundled up as we rode here. Can you make him well?"

"I believe so," she answered without looking at him.

Freida asked Will to leave the room. He stood outside the open door, keeping his eye on the old woman. Freida leaned near the boy's ear and whispered, "Do you feel safe with him?"

"I don't feel safe without him," Connor whispered back sincerely. "He has taken good care of me."

She sat back and gestured for Will to return. "He needs rest, liquids, and easy food. He seems to have improved already, if the description I got was accurate. Do you have any antibiotics in your med kit?" Will shook his head. "Well, I'm not certain whether his infection is bacterial or viral. Use these herbs in a tea to ease the skin rash and reduce the fever. Tomorrow, a doctor will arrive with the tour, and they'll have medicines, but he may need them sooner. There's a guy who grows the molds for bacterial infections. I'll talk with him. Let me know if he doesn't improve or if he gets any new or worsening symptoms," she said as she leaned heavily on the mattress to slowly rise.

Will took the herb bag and thanked her, and gave her some supplies from his first aid kit as compensation. He prepared the tea and brought it to Connor, saying he'd stay until he finished it.

"Let me see your arm," he said while sitting with him. Connor brought his arm out from under the blankets. It was covered in tiny red dots. Will hoped it wasn't from something in his blood that he caught from the ritual. He didn't remember anyone else getting a rash after the blood brother rite, but several of his soldiers said they felt a tingling sensation several hours after the ritual. It seemed unimportant until now.

Connor woke up a few hours later, drank some water, and worked his way through a bowl of soup and a piece of bread. His fever was down, but it kept spiking as the tea wore off. Will knew he wasn't out of the woods yet. After lunch, he tried to get up to help with the dishes, which had Bayley picking him up off the floor and depositing him back in his bed.

Baley was a crotchety character, complete with a grizzled beard and a big heart. Both Bayley and Will tried to be encouraged that Connor was holding his own, but they needed him to get well as quickly as possible. He could not stay here. It wasn't safe. The team would arrive in Glenwood the next day, and two days later, they were scheduled to be back on the road to Aspen. Though going to Aspen was not disclosed in the tour schedule, delaying the mission was problematic. It would give the Garrison time to increase their forces and entrench themselves along both the roads leading out of town.

"Do you have any books around here?" Connor asked weakly, though he wasn't sure he could focus while feeling so badly. "If I'm going to be grounded, at least give me something to do."

"Here is my box of library books. I get a new batch each month. They're probably too hard for you, but you can have at 'em, Miles," said Bayley, and he walked out, closing the door to Connor's room.

Connor stifled his inner comments about his abilities. There was no need to endanger Bayley by revealing his reading ability or what his real name was. He just said thank you and sat cross-legged on the bed rifling through Bayley's collection while holding his woozy head. What he wanted to do was decipher the code on the Sanguine Blade, but that was another thing Bayley had to be protected from.

Though he could hear Will and Bayley mumbling beyond the closed door, his curiosity was focused on an interesting book called *Dancing with the Lion* by Jeanne Reames. It was about Alexander the Great as a kid. He had noticed several books about this ancient king on a shelf in Will's studio room at the fort. Connor opened the book and settled in: *Chapter One, Runaway*.

"Your people are due in Glenwood tomorrow," Bayley told Will. "As soon as they arrive, Freida will get word to the man you call Gray and fill him in about where you are and Connor's condition. Do not worry, she is an X-Robinhooder. She knows how to be discreet. He and the doctor will be brought here to check on Miles's condition when it's safe."

"I don't imagine that's going to go very well for me," said Will.

"Yeah, he got sick on your watch. By the way, what happened to his hand while I was gone?" Bayley asked, already having heard from the reserve Guards about the soldier ritual.

Will got up and poured some stout tea into his cup. "Well, the truth is the kid asked me to make him a blood brother. He's met many of those serving in the Guard, and he wanted to be brave like a soldier. He was afraid he might die, and I wasn't sure he was wrong. How could I deny him that request?"

"So, you're going with the 'the kid was near death, so I slashed him with my knife' defense? Yep, wouldn't want to be you," Bayley laughed out loud. "I'll just listen from out here when that little scene goes down. Do want to listen, though."

Will let out a sigh and went outside to take in the fresh air his mood demanded. He reviewed the ritual request and the moment, and asked himself if he should have done something different. He came back to the fact that no one knew why Connor had a rash, and that worried Will. The most likely cause was the illness Connor was already fighting.

He was sure there was no rash on Connor's arm when he held it for the ritual. Though all Guard soldiers were initiated by becoming blood brothers, only the first few were done with the Sanguine Blade. He wasn't aware that any of them got a rash, including Will's first members, Calen and Nash, but it's unlikely they would have complained about such a minor ailment.

He was dreading Gray's visit as much as he eagerly awaited the medicine and the doctor's opinion of Connor's illness. He shivered from the morning chill, watching his smoky breath billow in front of him. If he had grabbed his coat, he could have stayed outside longer, maybe even scouted the area, but he was shivering now, and the last thing he needed was to weaken himself and catch Connor's illness. He headed back in.

The warmth enveloped him, causing a hum of relief to escape his lips. He quietly peeked inside Connor's room and found him fast asleep with a book threatening to spill from his hands. He walked over and eased the book away, causing the boy to stir and roll over. He felt his forehead, finding his fever was still there but much lower. He found a ribbon in the book box and marked Connor's page.

As he put the book on the nightstand, he saw the blurb at the top. It praised the author's portrayal of Alexander the Great's coming-of-age story. Tianna often referred to Will as being like Alexander the Great. He thought it was because his last name was the same, but even Relic had made connections between them. He wondered if Connor's choice was a coincidence or if he had heard him being compared to this ancient king. He chuckled at his question. Everything this kid did was calculated. Connor studied what intrigued him, and he was studying him.

It was high noon when Connor woke up, and his rash and fever were gone. He seemed to be fully restored, which was quite the change from his glimpse at death the day before. Will was as relieved as he was curious, since Freida said he would probably need antibiotics. Bayley had left for town to lead the team members back, which allowed Will and Connor the opportunity to speak privately. The first thing Connor did was inquire about the Sanguine Blade.

"Can I look at the symbols on your knife?"

"Well, good afternoon to you, too. Yes, you are welcome for the care you received, and I'm so glad you feel better."

Connor froze. He hoped he hadn't damaged the respect Will began to feel for him. "I'm sorry. I do appreciate how you took care of me. Thank you—"

Will laughed, "Stop. I was just poking at you. I know you are obsessing over your inability to decode the symbols on my knife. Your fever was pretty high. I wouldn't be too hard on yourself."

"Well, I've never had my brain betray me so completely, but I would like the opportunity to prove it was that and not my lack of skills. So, before Bayley comes back, can I take a look?" Will was already opening his pack and digging deeply into some hidden chamber to retrieve it.

Connor looked at the rich auburn mahogany and the symbols etched into it. He also analyzed the metal sheath, which was masterfully etched and highlighted in black. It displayed a rugged cliff edged by a river. Where the river fed into a lake, a wooden bridge gave access to the jagged terrain. He thought back to the bridge that led to the castle and the blade being the "key". It implied it was more than an artistic design.

"Well, I'll need to confer with Relic, but it could be a clue to the entrance. The only visual we have of the range after the meteorites is a painting, so I'm not sure how we can confirm it. But this side," he said as he turned the knife over, "looks like a Celtic cross, so the letters are probably Celtic too. The Celtic cross symbolizes health. The twisting serpents represent how physical and mental states are entwined and require balance for one to be healthy."

Will flinched, knowing how true the statement was and how far he was from attaining such a balance, but it didn't seem possible to achieve both while being the warrior destiny required. He watched Connor slide the knife out. It still had the remnants of their mingled blood. Will cursed himself for not cleaning it, but Connor did not startle at the sight. He considered the blade's name and symbolism as well as the honor of being among the few who were allowed to use it in the primal ritual.

"Thank you for making me a blood brother. I know I am not worthy, and I'm sure the tall people will harass you for it. Sorry about that, but thank you."

"Tall people? You mean adults?" Connor nodded, and Will laughed. It was a burst of true laughter that one shares with friends. He gestured for the blade, poured some water from Connor's glass onto his shirt, and wiped the blade clean. In earnest, he handed the blade back to Connor, telling him, "You are worthy. You are braver and more honorable than you take credit for."

Connor gave him a silent smile that reflected the difficult decisions he had endured during his young life, knowing Will understood. "This lightning bolt boldly striking down the business end of this weapon is a symbol common to most cultures. It symbolizes power, strength, and energy, and it has also been interpreted as a sign of divine intervention. Hmm," Connor turned the knife to and fro.

"What are you looking for?" asked Will.

"Divine intervention," answered the child, engrossed in his search. "Do you have a magnifying glass?"

Before Will could respond, he heard Bayley's voice entering the cabin.

It was early the next morning that Gray came to the cabin. He brought a med kit and instructions for treating Connor, but bringing a doctor would have brought a team of Garrison soldiers on his heels. As it was, he knew he'd be followed, so he had a plan to extract them.

"We've got spies everywhere in town," Gray said with an undercurrent of urgency. "I imagine they're in these woods, too. How's Connor? Can he travel?"

"Yeah," Connor said, coming out of the bedroom. Gray instantly noticed the bandage on his hand and looked at Will, whose hands were tucked in his pockets.

"How was his hand injured? Was his illness due to infection?" Gray questioned.

"The good news is, he's recovered," Will replied.

"Will, tell me that was not an inflicted wound." Gray knew all about the blood brother pact, and an alarmed expression bloomed on his face.

Will looked directly at Gray. Both men adopted a posture of fortitude, preparing to defend their actions. Will regretted injuring the child but not fulfilling his wishes at that moment. Gray second-guessed the decision he and Relic made to keep Will in the dark about being biomited. Both men were taking their arguments to their personal conclusions in their heads while staring each other down.

Will fumed that Gray would think him capable of endangering this child or any child, while Gray's mind began to whirl into worries of espionage. What if Will knew about his condition, and infecting Connor was the plan all along? But why wait? And why do it so blatantly? Will was too smart to be so careless. It brought Gray back to believing Will was loyal and unaware of what he carried.

The whole cerebral battle only lasted a few seconds before Connor stepped in to say his piece out loud.

"I asked him to make me a blood brother. I... I thought I might die," Connor said in defense of his new brother. But it didn't escape Connor that Gray didn't look as mad as he looked frightened.

"I say we stop bellyaching over things that are done," Will added to change the subject. "Let's get out of here before they block this road. Connor, go pack. Bayley, do you have another trail out of here?"

"Maybe on foot, but this ravine is pretty steep. Where do you want to go?" he asked.

"There's an access tunnel at the horseshoe turn near the end of Red Canyon Road," Gray said. "Warren told me that the tunnel accesses an old meteorite shelter beneath the Holy Cross Power Plant. He is pretty sure it is unknown to most of his people, so he assumes that includes the Corporates."

Bayley nodded, saying, "I can draw a map to that horseshoe turn that avoids town, but it will take a whole day to get there by horseback, more on foot. First problem is crossing the Colorado River, and—"

"I have another idea," Gray interrupted. "We put Connor in the mini's smuggler hold in the undercarriage, and you and I will drive there in plain sight. Will can hike up the ridge and cover us. I have soldiers all along this ridge to assist us as needed."

"It's risky," Will said, shaking his head. "But not as risky as traveling with him for the better part of a day through treacherous terrain. Are you afraid of tight spaces?" Will asked Connor. He said it softly with sensitivity to show Gray he possessed such skills.

Connor wasn't sure, but it felt like his warrior brother just mothered him in front of Gray and Bayley. "Did you just call me a wimp, *blood-brother*? Is this where I call you out? Rather unfair advantage, but if it's required to avenge my reputation as a soldier—" Will took a step back, shocked by the boy's bold response.

"Oh shit," Gray said. "I think he just became a teenager. That's the first symptom, reckless defiance." Everyone but Connor burst out laughing.

"Oh, you're funny, you are," Connor retorted, but his smirk revealed his amusement and relief that moment didn't turn punitive.

Still laughing, Gray motioned Will outside for a sidebar conversation. While outside, they took on the afternoon livestock chores.

"They're going to come up this road. And we'll likely meet them on the way. Is Bayley staying here, or riding his horse to town?" Gray asked.

"Neither," said Will. "I think you should take Bayley with you in the mini. When they get here, they're going to tear this place apart. They'd do worse to Bayley if they think he has the answers they're looking for. I'll hang back here and take care of the trespassers. Then I'll take the horse as far as I can go on the trail Bayley talked about. I know people here who will help me sneak across the bridge at night."

"We need to leave here quickly. RH intel says the Corporates called up the file on Deegan Chance and his family tree," Gray told Will.

"They know who Connor is." Will said, and suddenly added, "They'll go after Henry."

We were already taking actions to secure him. He has a sister in Breckenridge, and there is no reason to believe they know that. We'll send the truck back with a decoy, Henry. People are traveling back and forth on I-70 all the time because of the tour."

"They'll stop some of them," Will said.

"Yes, but if they get stopped, they won't be able to do anything except ask questions. But you can bet they'll have a warrant with Henry's photo on their devices. If they find him, they can take him for questioning," Gray replied.

"If they kidnapped Henry, we'd release the blackmail material," Will said with conviction.

"I don't think Henry has it in him to resist their questioning techniques, so they'd know this is about a military action, not introductions. Then, not even your extortion scheme will stop them," Gray said with a concerned look.

"Okay, who's going to take him there and how?"

"We'll get him out of town the same way we are transporting his son into it," Gray answered.

"We'll move Henry tonight when it's dark in one of the sweep minis hiding outside of town. Those vehicles have the best high-tech camo, so they're hard to detect. Even still, we'll hide him in the smuggler bin in the undercarriage. They should be in Breckenridge within four to five hours. We'll leak out the rumor that the return truck is scheduled to leave tomorrow morning. We were looking for someone who looks similar to Henry to hang around the return team and help with packing. They won't jump him in town. By the time they figure out they've been had, Henry will be tucked in Breckenridge with his sister's family."

"Hold on, Gray. How is it we got this intel before the Neighwah soldiers did? They are pretty good at messaging." Will had alarm bells ringing everywhere in his mind. As soon as he got back, he'd have to consult with Relic. Maybe there was something to his concerns about Gray.

"Even after the satellites went dark, they didn't see a need to upgrade after the tunnel was lost. The old lines have been sabotaged at a slow but steady pace. The hardest obstacle is the Continental Divide, especially in winter.

"But we can use the tunnel, while they have to go around and over. But, on this side of the divide, we both use a network of relay drones to deliver messages. RH gave us this intel two hours ago, and we doubt their spies will have it for several more hours. However, the Elites know we have the tunnel advantage for relaying information. We have to assume they have or are trying to find a way to counter it."

"Is Henry aware of everything that's happened?" Will furrowed his brows as he asked. "Because I can't believe with all that has happened, that he is okay with Connor continuing on this mission."

Gray looked at the sun already lying heavy on the horizon.

"Gray, answer me. Does his father know?"

"What would you have me do, Will? This speeding locomotive is set on its course, and we can't stop it. Either we take the day, or they do. We have a chance of winning, it's a sketchy chance, but it's a chance. Winning will mean freedom for all of Colorado. Losing will mean thousands die. In case you forgot, my wife is at risk too. Whatever happens, I'll have plenty of demons to live with."

"Those demons aren't yours alone. But no one is keeping you in the dark about what she faces, and no one has taken away your right to protect her." Both he and Gray knew it wasn't that Henry didn't have a right to know everything about his child, his only son.

The question was, did he have the right to take him off the mission? Though Gray was correct in his assessment of the situation, it fell in the face of the very thing they fought for.

"Don't you think I'd love to find a safe offramp? And no, Henry doesn't know Connor is a Corporate target. He thinks he's been successfully hidden. And no, he doesn't know he was seriously ill, and he isn't going to find out either.

"Look, if Henry is secured in the bomb shelter, we'll make sure he gets to see his son before he leaves. And while we've talked a lot about Henry's rights, what about Connor's? He not only knows the drill, he's devoted every one of his young years to it. Is it right to take that from him? How will he feel if it all falls apart, and he wasn't even allowed to try? I will tell the boy these events are top secret, and you know what he'll do? Protect his family.

"Henry loves his son deeply, and I don't doubt he'd die to save him, but you and I know that's exactly what would happen. He's not a soldier. You, I, and the whole team will do what is necessary to protect Connor, and unlike Henry, we are trained to do that." Gray paused, rubbing his forehead as if it might send his anxious worries back into their lair. "This whole mission is a do-or-die gamble, Will, and at the first sight of danger is no time to veer this way or that. We're betting everything and everyone we hold dear that we'll win. If I have to sin to win, I say so be it."

Gray was flushed with determination. His posture was resolute and self-assured, but Will knew better. It was the oath destiny demanded. A promise to accept whatever heartache and suffering she saw fit to attain her goal.

As many battles as Will had won and lost, this one worried him. They were trekking into an unknown place, hoping to find something, to fight an army that made theirs look like a pesky ant hill, one they could easily burn down. But long ago, when he was a child, he also made a vow to this destiny. He wouldn't have let anyone take it on for him, and neither will Connor.

He grabbed his friend's shoulder. He knew all too well how it felt to carry the fate of the world. "You're not alone, brother," Will said. "We are all in this. You are right. We cannot act in war the way we do in peace. We may not be proud of all our deeds, but I will fight by your side till victory or death."

Chapter Fourteen

Neighwah Head Quarters

General Dermit turned on the screen with great apprehension. He waited ten or so minutes before the Elites joined the meeting.

"General, please give your report," Ena stated.

The title made Dermit roil with hatred and fear. Generals were powerful leaders. He was nothing more than a chained puppet they used for their self-empowering deeds and disgusting amusement. It was cruel irony that even though he executed their commands without hesitation, it was his emotions about them that resulted in punishment. Feeling his pain churning up, he reeled in his emotions before the punishment took further hold of him.

"Director, when we got to Eagle, William Alexander had left, and the child was on his way to his family. There is a high probability that William took off with the child whose treatment was a ruse to bring him on this mission," he reported.

"Which you missed," added Tria.

"We have no intel to confirm it, but it is a prevalent theory now," he said with an expectation of some form of painful retort.

"Consider it more factual and less theoretical," Ena replied with an air of cruel authority. "We believe the child to be Connor Wayther, grandson of Deegan Chance. He and his wife participated in the first Highmind experiments decades ago. Neither he nor his wife showed signs of cognitive improvement, but he was tested before we developed the brain scan assessment. His wife died soon after the disaster, and Deegan was assigned a low-level job as an architectural assistant in Denver. When he died, his remains went directly to the crematorium, so his brain density was never assessed.

The Uppers monitor Dailys' transfers. We don't track them at this level of command, but since discovering the tunnel is inhabited, we have been reviewing the transfers that didn't check into their new assignments. Most were ordered by Vogel Incorporated. We believe Bannon Vogel is responsible for the creation and the inhabitation of the tunnel town. If Deegan Chance was a Highmind, he was likely the architect.

"I see," Dermit answered. "Would you like to hear the rest of my report or discuss our plans going forward?" He was sincere in his request for clarification, but a punitive sting came his way regardless.

"Complete your report," Ena answered.

"We have installed six undercover agents to infiltrate the town, but we expect they will be identified. The Fringers are a tight-knit group that has an intricate network, and they are quick to spot and report strangers. We also have a small contingency of snipers nested in the woods. I just received information that the night before last, two travelers were detected on a horse on the trail along No Name Creek. It is an uninhabited area east of Glenwood. It could be visitors traveling to the fair, but we are en route to investigate."

"I want you to find Will and the child, Connor," Ena demanded. "I am sending you our Daily file photo of our most current picture at nine years old. It was derived from a low-resolution image that was retrieved from drone footage at an unauthorized playground."

"I will inform my agents," Dermit answered.

"I expect a report tomorrow evening or sooner if the situation changes," Ena said.

The screen went blank, and he blew out a long breath of relief and let his tense shoulders fall. At least their timeline was feasible. Calling his secretary, he asked for the drone specialist to communicate the new orders. Using drone networking was a lengthy process, but he could easily make it happen within a day. Without satellites, the relay drones were his only form of communication in remote areas. The good news was that it was also the rebels' only option.

Bayley's Cabin

Will was already making his way through the woods along the road leading to Bayley's cabin. Pausing to ready his bow, he considered Gray's decision to keep Henry in the dark about his son. He knew Gray was right about not letting Henry know everything. If Connor were his son, he'd be livid. But he wasn't a father, and just as important, Henry was no soldier. He and his son were in danger, and nothing could put that fact back in its bottle. Henry didn't have the skills to protect himself or his son, but the Allied Army did, and they would.

He spotted a pair of his Guard soldiers, so he moved further down the slope. Back at the cabin, Gray helped Connor into the mini smuggler's hold. Suddenly, Connor sat back up. "There's plenty of room for two. Why can't Will come too?"

"Enemy soldiers are coming up this ravine. We need Will to clear the road. With his bow, he can eliminate trouble without a sound."

Though Connor was naïve about the horrific details of war, he was quite astute regarding the concept. He eyed the bandage across his hand, confirming his indoctrination into the world of soldiers, and he took a breath to summon his courage.

"How does Will get to the power plant then?" the child asked.

"He'll get there," Gray said, as Connor was secured in place.

Bayley was busy clearing away the remnants of Will and Connor's visit when the Allied team sent a small drone, signaling Gray that they were approaching. Gray went to sit with Bayley on the porch, waiting for their Corporate guests. He hoped Connor could maintain his composure in the small, unheated space where he was sequestered. They stood when the two strangers pulled up in their side-by-side and got out.

"Greetings," said a stocky man bundled in gear. Gray and Bayley stood poker-faced, watching their enemy stalk over toward the mini. "Nice ride you've got there," said the stranger while the other stood silently. "Mind if I check it out?"

"Actually, I do." Gray said calmly, "What are you here for?"

"I'm looking for a fugitive, William Alexander. Seems he has kidnapped a child in addition to his other crimes."

"What does he look like?" asked Bayley, leaning comfortably against the porch strut and chewing on a piece of straw.

"Dark skin, tall, with battle scars and tattoos on his forearms," came the answer from the voice.

"What other crimes?" asked Bayley.

"For starters, he deserted the Neighwah and sabotaged a Corporate operation. If we had known, he survived—" the man stopped and threw out his hands. He didn't come here to have a legal argument. "I know you know something, so is he here, and if not, where is he?" the man yelled.

Gray envisioned Will had his bow drawn and steadied on the annoying twit, waiting for him to make a dumb move.

"Relax," said Gray. "It's no secret. We know him, but he left days ago to return a kid to his family. Where he is now, who knows? Probably taking some God-awful long route back to his fort to enjoy nature. He's a bit of a loner."

"Is he in that cabin?" the frustrated man asked. Gray was losing his patience with this dullard.

"Come see for yourself, but leave your camera-infested jacket out here," said Bayley. "That's my house, and I don't have to let you inside. This is Fringer Territory, and your rights here are limited."

The man followed Bayley inside while Gray and the other man stayed outside, exchanging silent glares. It was a short tour inside the small cabin, and the two men came back outside.

The blustery man grumbled as he passed by Gray. "I will find him, and if I learn you've been helping him, I'll drag both your asses back to headquarters."

They got in their vehicle and started back down the trail. Will gave his men the signal that the targets were moving away from the cabin. Gray started the mini to let it warm up, tapping three times on the floor, and Connor tapped three back. Gray was impressed that the kid had maintained silence in his coffin hideaway, and even more impressed that he gave the okay signal instead of begging to get out.

Will traveled down the hill, keeping the cabin and the mini in his sights. As he and Will suspected, he saw two enemy soldiers making their way to the cabin, hiding in the heavy shadows as the sun set. He followed them using his binoculars on the heat-seeking setting, allowing them no cover. He also located two Guard soldiers, and he flashed his identity and his instructions in two words, "follow, Guard".

They knew that meant to protect the mini because the words for following the enemy were "stalk prey". Will turned back up the ravine and settled above with a clear view of the cabin's front door. The two men crept toward the porch, unsure if they were alone. *Thwack!* A man screamed in pain as an arrow suddenly protruded from his thigh. The other man raised his weapon, randomly shooting in the direction of the arrow's path.

"Wrong move, buddy," Will whispered to himself. *Thwack!* No wounding shot this time. One of Will's signature arrows hit him squarely in the chest. He fell, seized, and within seconds, he was still. The other man also lay still, knowing that going for his gun would be his last move. He was in agonizing pain, waiting for his invisible foe to decide his fate.

Quickly and quietly, Will approached the wounded prisoner with his handgun drawn and ready. The man had thick camo paint plastered on his delicate features, and while raising his hands, his over-sized helmet fell to the ground. It gave way to long, dark curls that cascaded around the terrified face. Will realized he was a she. Not that it mattered. She was a soldier. Her fate was that of all enemy soldiers.

"Live or die, which is it?" Will asked. It was the question he always asked his fallen prey. It was a pivotal moment. How they answered and the words they used counted.

"Live," she gasped in pain. "As long as that life has some point to it. But if I am to be tortured and toyed with, I choose death." She made the mistake of looking at the body of her comrade, surrounded by a crimson stain seeping into the white snow. She took in a breath and turned away. She had to look brave enough to mean what she said.

Will said nothing as he disarmed her. "My men will come. If you can be turned and trained, your life will hold honor and purpose, eventually," he said with a cold stare. She cried out as Will dragged her to the porch beam and began to tie her to it.

"How do I do that? Prove that I've turned?" the woman gasped as the pain of being moved still sang through her body.

"Well, I'd figure that out if I were you. I can't have a traitor in my ranks."

She watched him walk over to her dead partner, waiting for him to abuse his body, but he didn't. He approached the dead man and just stood over him. She imagined he was looking for something or some other unknown purpose. But Will was giving the man his customary send-off. Then he disappeared into the woods, leaving her tied up and wounded, as the shivers of shock set in. She wondered if anyone would come before her injury, and the chill of the night did her in.

Will traveled down the ravine to find a pair of Guards and instructed them to secure Bayley's cabin and the prisoner and retrieve his arrows. While making his way down, he discovered the mini had been stopped by the two men who had visited the cabin. Although he knew the mini could withstand some weaponry, he wasn't sure if the undercarriage where Connor was hidden could, so he decided to intervene. He quickly made his way down to secure an advantageous position, but when he began to draw his bow, his soldiers walked over to the two men who raised their hands.

Another pair of Guards joined the two holding the enemies. In the procedural briefing for this mission, at least three pairs of soldiers were scheduled to pull surveillance duty in areas where enemies were detected. With four here and two or more enemy soldiers looming on the trail, he knew the Guard Reserve soldiers in town had been activated.

Will watched the mini continue on its way while the enemy was detained. A signal flashed from across the ravine, and Will flashed back. It took twenty minutes for Will to reach his team. Jedi was excited to see his commander, having been in the dark regarding his whereabouts.

"Is the mini still being protected?" Will asked.

"Yes, I have set up teams to secure it to its destination," answered Jedi. Will gave the hand sign for Connor, meaning he was on board. Jedi nodded. "Understood."

"There's a team securing the cabin and our next recruit. There's also a river drop lying up there."

"I'll take care of it, sir. We've got another team up here besides us. The Reserves said they'd stall them until we are out of town."

"Sounds good. Their move failed this time, but there'll be more," Will said.

"Yes sir," Jedi said.

"Good hunting," Will smiled as they grasped each other's forearms, before heading their separate ways.

Will climbed up the west side of the ravine toward the meeting place where his ride to the next safe house would be waiting for him.

Bayley turned to Gray, "Did you know my road was crawling with soldiers?"

Gray smiled, "Arranged it, well, our troops anyway."

"Huh," Bayley huffed, both happy and unhappy about the plan. "Guess I'm grateful, but can't say I like that kind of company. Did the healer tell you Will and Miles were with me?"

"No, I came directly here. There were several places Will could go if we put the escape plan in play. He left clues letting us know your cabin was his objective."

"What is it about this kid that makes him so important? I mean the fact that you brought him is evidence enough, so don't deny it," Bayley said. Vigorous tapping came from below.

"You okay, Miles?" asked Gray. Three taps came in response.

Gray opened the small door to allow Connor to talk.

"How much longer?" came an anxious voice.

"Fifteen minutes. Can you do that?" asked Gray.

"Yeah, but I don't want to do this again. And Gray," Connor said with a pleading tone, "drive faster."

"You got it, bud," and Connor felt the motor rev up.

"So, back to—" Bayley started to say, but Gray interrupted.

"Hey, grab your gear, Bayley. Here's your stop." Gray reached over to shake Bayley's hand. "Enjoyed getting to know you. If I'm ever in Glenwood, I'd love to stop over," Gray said, dismissing the conversation Bayley wished to continue.

Bayley huffed a chuckle at the diversion from his question, and he waved as he got out, "Anytime."

Chapter Fifteen

J edi and Dom made it to the cabin after scanning the area for more combatants. Dom took the fold-away sled off his pack and tied the body of the dead man to it. Jedi set to work treating the woman with the arrow protruding from her thigh.

"This arrow needs to come out. It doesn't appear to have hit any main arteries, but it's hard to tell until I remove it." He began opening up a med kit and pulling out bandages and gauze. "Hold these," he said, then he grabbed the scissors and took his blade from his waistband.

"What are you going to do?" she asked as fear pooled in her brown eyes.

"Well, first," he started, "I'm going to cut your pants away." And he proceeded to cut the pant leg off above the injury. He unscrewed the arrowhead protruding from the other side of her leg, leaving the straight shaft free to be pulled through. Before he pulled it out, he cleaned his knife with an alcohol wipe. Every movement scorched her with pain that threatened to send her into unconsciousness. Though blacking out may spare her some pain, they would be free to do unthinkable things to her, so she fought against that inky world. She focused on the blade and quickly wiped away a tear.

"Relax, I promise not to cause you more pain than I have to," he said. "But if I nick an artery, I have to find it to clamp it."

"Pardon me if I am having trust issues here," she said. While she was talking, he carefully grasped the arrow and yanked it out in one fast move, as she released a piercing shriek. Blood immediately began to pool around the openings on both sides of her leg. Jedi sprayed both punctures with numbing wound foam that slowed the flow of blood, causing her to wince. He grabbed the gauze, pressing it onto the wound, bringing forth more screams.

The anger gave her a quick release of energy, and she fought against her restraints. She started to shiver, and her color went from pale to grey. She felt a sharp stab in her neck, and the world went dark. Jedi started an I.V., wrapped her in a shock blanket, and secured her to another sled.

"Here's Will's arrow," Dom said, handing it to Jedi. He walked over to the body still lying on the snow. "So, did you say this one goes in the river? Won't they see it?"

"It will be dark by the time we get there, so I doubt anyone would see him," Jedi suggested. "But even if they do see him floating by, they aren't going to jump into a raging ice-cold river at night to retrieve a dead body. The most they could do would be to drive down the road to some known catch point. By then, we're long gone," answered Jedi while they tied the dead man to another sled.

"And her?"

"We'll smuggle her to the medic in the garage, and then we'll bring her to the fort when the tour ends," Jedi answered. "It will be a rough ride in the smuggler hold of the supply trailer, but if she survives, she'll have the same opportunity all prisoners get." They began their trek down the trail to meet the team, with a transport waiting for them.

Connor was beyond relieved when they slid him out of the casket-like compartment that held him. He saw they were in a garage where four soldiers stood guard. He was shivering as Gray wrapped him in a warm blanket, and one of the soldiers led him to the office. They stopped at a bank of lockers where he tapped a code. Within seconds, a false door slid open, and he was led down a ladder to a dimly lit tunnel. The three-foot wide passageway seemed to snake on and on till it ended before a hatch with a dial in the center. Inside was a short hallway with three doors, one on each side and one at the end. They went to the end one, which led to a small medical facility.

"How are you doing, Connor? I heard you had a rough ride to town," Jilly said as she sat Connor on the exam table and took his vitals, which were understandably irregular.

"It wasn't bad until we were stopped, and I heard Gray arguing with the enemy soldiers. Then our troops came down, and we continued. I was trying to be so still and quiet, but it was hard to be trapped like that."

Jilly saw his bottom lip begin to quiver, and she brought him into a hug. Her safe embrace released his emotional dam, and he cried openly.

"You're okay now, Connor. We got you. They kept you safe, and we will do whatever it takes to keep you safe. It's alright now."

"Look," Connor said as he pulled off his bandages and showed her his slashed knuckles still raw from the trauma. "This says I'm a brave soldier, but I don't deserve to have it while I sit here crying like a baby," which brought on a fresh round of sobs.

"Seriously?" said Jilly. "I've seen lots of soldiers cry. I've seen Gray cry."

"Gray?" Connor said, heaving a sigh.

"I bet Will has cried, too. It's cathartic. It is an honest way to express grief and acknowledge pain. Being brave is about staying the course when choices are hard and times get difficult. It's about caring enough to go through hardship to do something remarkable. It's not about being an uncaring robot." The whole time she was examining the child, becoming more relieved with every healthy reading.

"She's right," came Gray's voice where he stood by the door. "Soldiers may keep their emotions in check during a battle, but it's normal to break down after. I would be worried if they didn't. Being brave doesn't mean you aren't afraid. On the contrary, facing fear is the essence of bravery. If Will were here, he'd agree." Gray winked at his wife, and she smiled in return. "And just to be clear, Connor. No one is questioning your bravery. In fact, I am more than impressed." Then he left.

Jilly was about to put antibiotics on Connor's knuckle wound when he jerked his hand back. "I want it to scar," Connor said. Jilly rolled her eyes as Relic came through the door.

He gestured for Jilly to come over to the next room. "I need a blood sample from him," he said.

"Why? Are you worried about the illness he had?"

"In a word, yes," said Relic.

"The kid's been through a lot. Will a finger stick be enough?" Jilly asked.

Relic looked up and left as if the answer was on the ceiling. "It's enough for now," he sighed.

Later, Relic and Gray sat on the lab stools looking at the screen with the three tiny squares darting in and out between the disc-shaped blood cells.

"What am I looking at?" asked Gray.

"Connor's blood sample," Relic answered.

"He's infected?" Gray stood shocked.

"Yes," Relic knew he had dropped a bomb on Gray, so he continued as Gray stood there with clenched fists.

"The healing kind can be transferred by bodily fluids, but the controlling ones don't roam free. They have to be injected. This blood pact ritual causes me to believe Will's whole army has these biomites. But the good news is they appear to be the healing type. Those who received his mites will probably benefit from the healing properties in them."

"Probably, but you're not certain."

"I did everything to try and get his biomites to react to things that go against the Corporate order, nothing about these mites work that way. He escaped and they couldn't find him, he killed their soldiers without physical consequences, and he hid the Sanguine Blade from them for over fifteen years, and nothing."

"Maybe he's not close enough. Didn't you say they can transmit? Maybe these are for location."

"As I said before, I can find no such signal being transmitted or received. Will has hidden right next to them numerous times, and if proximity activates them, why didn't they work then?" Relic saw Gray ease up a bit. "Look, I'm not sure how long these things last or if they can replicate, but bottom line, I think Connor will be fine. It was probably the mites that saved his life."

"You are not going to drug Connor to get a piece of his brain, Relic. Not an option," Gray stood with his hands at his side like a challenged gun-slinger. Then he dropped his hands when he asked, "So you think they can replicate themselves?"

"Honestly, I need to run more tests, but they are carbon-based, so the body could provide the materials. Perhaps there are different types, each serving a distinct purpose. I'll poke around and see if I can evoke any physical or emotional responses in Connor. We also need to test anyone who has exchanged blood with Will. That includes all the Guard members."

"Could that tell us if they can replicate?" Gray asked.

"Maybe," Relic said reluctantly.

"So, you are saying knowingly or unknowingly, Will could be making spies?" Gray asked again, though Relic had strongly suggested it was unlikely.

"No, I'm not saying that, not yet. But I *am* saying that the goal of this mission is critical enough that the Elites will do anything to take control of it and the weapon." Relic returned his attention to the screen and added something to his notes.

Gray worried that even if there was evidence, Relic wouldn't accept the possibility that Will might be a spy. It wasn't that Gray believed he was, but he wasn't ready to dismiss it either.

Jilly stood at the lab door, astonished at what she had just heard. It was not her nature to eavesdrop, but the more she heard, the harder it was to stop listening. She quietly returned to the little cafeteria where she had left Connor, draining a bowl of soup. She filled herself a large bowl of the steaming chicken noodle soup and grabbed a healthy handful of crackers and dried apples.

"Wow, Jilly," Connor mused, "this trip sure has roused your appetite. I used to wonder how you survived on the mouse-sized helpings you ate, but ..." Connor paused. When Jilly told him she was pregnant, he researched the symptoms and risks that his friend may endure. Learning was his way of managing the worries her condition generated. It also avoided having to ask questions about her private biology. He was adding the recent display of symptoms she displayed after her miscarriage, and they didn't add up to one recovering from a miscarriage. But they did indicate, quite plainly, she was still pregnant. Maybe she said that so she could go on the mission with Gray. He had a hard time believing she would tell such an egregious and painful lie.

"Jilly, is something going on with you?" Connor took a breath and then said, as carefully as one could, "Are you still pregnant?"

She almost choked on her soup. Letting out a deep sigh, she answered him honestly. "Leave it to a child to figure it out." She was snickering, now, but she sounded more troubled than amused.

"So, I have to ask. Does Gray know?"

Jilly got up and closed the door. It would be a perfect turnabout if Gray stumbled on their conversation.

"No, he doesn't, but I never meant to hide it from him or cause anyone grief. I did experience what I believed was a miscarriage, but now I don't know what happened. It could be that I lost a twin, but there is no way to know now. For a bit, I thought my body was just readjusting, so I dismissed it. It wasn't until I took a test at the fort that I was sure. By then, it was too late. The Fringers and the Guard hired Andie as their doctor, whom they desperately need, and I accepted this mission. I also thought to myself, do I want to sit home alone, worrying about Gray? Worrying whether the world we have fought for is at an end, and dying in the final battle without him. Or do I want to be with the man I love and fight for what I believe in?"

"Well, sounds like you have all your justifications in line," Connor said, knowing it was not the supportive response she was looking for.

"I know, I'm risking the baby, but I can't bear to raise him as a Daily. That is, if any of us are allowed to survive a Corporate victory."

"I get all those reasons for you wanting to come on the mission, but I think you should tell Gray. At some point, he's going to guess, like I did, and that won't go well either."

"I don't know if he'll notice. He's up to his neck in problems. Every time I think about telling him, some new nightmare gets dumped on him. I just heard the latest one, and no, I'm not telling you. You already have a secret on me."

Connor looked at her with a curious expression. It sounded like the secret she had just discovered was about him. It seems having secrets about fellow team members was the new norm, at least on this journey. But Connor didn't know if a truth-telling moment would make things better or worse.

They sat there looking at their empty bowls when Gray walked in with Relic. Jilly stiffened. She didn't know Will, Relic, or the Guard team at all, and she had no clue whether she could trust any of them.

Relic said all the Guard members had joined a blood pact, and that meant half the mission team was potentially infected. And the star of their plan, Connor, was too.

She sighed. As much as she hated this part of Gray's world, she was now a participant, trapped in the thick of it. She deemed that in the name of protection, she would not complicate things further. She would observe, but not reveal what she knew, at least not until she had to. She was so caught in it now that she was unable to stop the tumbling escalation of lies and secrets. But she knew that when all her secrets finally spilled out into the light of day, they would be seen for what they were: deception.

Chapter Sixteen

Gray and Relic walked into the cafeteria and were startled by how quickly Jilly bounced up and brought them both generous bowls of the soup. Connor watched as Jilly tried to give a convincing performance of normalcy, making him chuckle out loud. Jilly bristled.

Connor smiled at her. "I was just thinking about being worried that I wouldn't like being outside of the tunnel. But when I got outside, I loved it. I found the big sky and crisp air invigorating and realized how much I missed it. The next thing I know, I'm being smuggled in small, dark places and back to living underground. It's ironic."

They all laughed. "When we get on the road to our next destination, I'm hoping we will have lost our Corporate tails, and you won't be hiding anymore," said Gray.

"That would be nice, but unlikely. What's out here worries me, and now I'm afraid of the outdoors all over again. More irony," Connor added with an eye roll.

Gray gave a thoughtful look, nodded, and patted Connor on the back as he got up from the table. He was already done with his meal. He was a fast eater. Connor recalled him saying it was a military thing. Relic and Gray left while Connor and Jilly cleaned up the lunch dishes. Then Jilly led Connor to the staff bunkroom.

"You'll sleep here, but you can wander about. There's a small physical therapy room where you can work out and a screen room that offers lots of movies and old TV series," she said.

"Before you leave, could you give these books to someone who can bring them back to the Eagle Library? And if they have a library here, could I get a couple of new ones? Maybe some about an adventure or science fiction stories about space travel," Connor asked.

"I'll try, she said.

"But no more fantasy monsters. The real world is scary enough," Connor blurted.

"Yeah, your brief renditions gave me nightmares," she grinned and left.

Connor took out the book he had borrowed from Bayley. He was almost to the end. He had his tablet with all the downloaded stories, but he liked holding a real book in his hands. It reminded him of the time he spent with his grandad. He and his sister would sit on the floor next to him in his favorite chair, in front of their boarded-up window. Though books were illegal for Dailys, his grandad somehow secured a small collection, and they read them over and over until he was able to get different ones.

Jilly walked back down the tunnel and climbed the ladder up to access the garage. She walked over to Gray, who was talking to Axle. Jilly wondered what Axle had snuck into town to tell Gray. He was on sweep duty and supposedly camping outside town. She didn't want to know. She could barely juggle the issues she had.

"There's going to be a band for the joining ceremony tonight. I heard they were pretty good. I'm taking Jax. We could use a night off from the fray," he said. "Mack and Beckett can handle it."

Gray turned to Jilly as she approached. "We're in, right Jills?" She gave him a questioning look, and before she could speak, he said, "I've got lots of watchers roaming everywhere. We're secure."

Jilly smiled, "That sounds wonderful." She let her mind wander as Gray drove them back to their room. She knew Connor had one of Will's Guards watching him, which didn't sit well with her, but Relic would be there too. He, like Connor, couldn't be seen, but he wouldn't have attended anyway. He had plenty of problems to obsess over.

So many issues nagged at Jilly, but she didn't want to think about them tonight. She had brought her favorite sweater to wear to the festivals, and she didn't get a chance to wear it at the last town Harfest. There was so much confusion with Connor being whisked away that when the ceremony in Eagle began, she was still in her street clothes. But tonight, she would dress up and look her best. Tonight, she would make Gray notice her.

The Hotel Colorado served as the town center. It was once a lavish hotel, and it was quite large, so most of it was left unutilized. The lobby area had been turned into shops, supply distribution centers, and visitor lodging. One wing of the second story held the school, daycare, library, and medical facilities. The other second-story wing housed everyone who, for various reasons, did not live in houses. The main area of the second floor was where the team was boarded. The rooms above that were closed off from the heating ducts and access, except for the few that were used for storage.

None of the Fringer towns lived in luxury, but Glenwood had been hit hard by the meteorite strikes, and their supplies were in marginal shape. But they lived free, and it was hard to put a price tag on that.

She pulled on her favorite fleece-lined yoga pants and the sweater that Gray loved so much when she met him that memorable night in the observatory. Alarm showed across her face as she examined the pale blue sweater that used to fit her perfectly. Though she had fixed the loose buttonholes, it was severely puckering across her chest. Gaping holes between the buttons showed that her size had changed.

She grabbed a couple of safety pins from her med kit and contained her pregnant breasts.

With the front secure, she studied the busty gal staring back at her in the mirror. Jilly smiled to herself, knowing that would get his attention. Even though the full-length mirror had several cracks running across the top, which distorted everything above her shoulders, she felt good about her attire and spun around one more time before sitting on the floor to address her hair and face.

She was beaming with sun-kissed cheeks and a rosy nose. She had spent as much time outside as she could, and though it was cold, the snow was quite reflective. Even her eyes seemed brighter and bluer. But her hourglass figure was positively eye-catching. She wondered if it was too much. She grabbed the lavender scarf with blue forget-me-nots she had purchased from one of the stores and tied it around her neck, letting it dangle in front of her chest. It subdued her vixen shape, which she would expose later.

Gray had been distant physically since the miscarriage, or whatever it was. She used that reprieve to assess her situation, while he threw himself into his militant business. But she missed him and the closeness they shared. She longed for the joking and jesting that prefaced many intimate moments.

This sweater was the perfect icebreaker. She tugged on her fur-topped winter boots and joined Gray, who was waiting with Axle in the cafeteria.

Jax knocked on Jilly's door, and they went to meet their guys. Jax had tight jeans and a short pink sweatshirt decorated with numerous zippers and snaps. The tomboy-in-pink style looked good on her with her short, dark hair and mischievous eyes. The four of them gathered their dinner from the cafeteria line and sat down with their trays, sporting their choices of roasted chicken or elk stew, topped off with seasoned rice and a cabbage salad.

The conversation was cheerful, lively, and unfettered by problems. Jilly hadn't laughed so hard in weeks. It was the freedom to be herself that Jilly loved the most about sloughing her Daily status. She was openly engaging in liberties that Dailys were denied, such as telling jokes and laughing out loud in public, or sharing opinions, and engaging in analytical conversations.

The room echoed with the sounds of freedom. She looked down the long, bench-style table and waved at her colleague, Dr. Andie. She also saw Haru and Leita deeply engaged in conversation, with moments of playful teasing. She had assumed Will and Leita had a commitment of sorts, but now she wondered. She hoped Haru hadn't knowingly crossed a line with the fierce warrior.

"So, are those two an item now? I mean, what about—" though she asked softly, Gray squeezed her hand under the table. He smiled, knowing full well she meant no harm, but his sigh and expression told her she had crossed a line. She realized it was probably a loaded question or a forbidden subject. It involved a dear friend who was a fugitive, his woman, and their spiritual leader. Jilly doubted Leita was in touch with Will. In fact, it was doubtful that anyone knew where Will was, so maybe this was a planned decoy move.

Jax spoke first, effectively diverting the topic away from Will. "They spend a lot of time together because Leita is helping Haru and, um, what's the new minister's name?" Jilly was grateful that the conversation seemed back on track.

"Tanya," said Gray.

"Yeah, Tanya," Jax said. "They're setting up the little chapel. For now, it's here in one of the hotel rooms, but I heard they want to have outdoor services next summer and eventually find a permanent home in one of the churches. They're all in pretty bad shape, so it may be a while before that happens."

Gray gave Jilly a soft kiss on her cheek as the conversation relaxed back into happy chitchat, and they made their way to the ballroom.

Dyed rags with strings of white lights streamed across the walls and radiated out above the dance floor. Another swagged layer of dried flowers and handcrafted ivy was draped among the hanging lights. The townspeople had simply used what was available to them, but the old-world style décor transformed their guests into another time and place. It was romantic and magical, a Renaissance dreamland.

The band was still tuning up, so the foursome settled on the bleachers where their conversation turned to music. Gray already played the guitar regularly with a group they formed in the tunnel, and Axle had shown an interest in the electric keyboard. He took his interest further by studying music and joining the New Haven Musicians Guild.

"I hear the band plays Southern rock," Axle said with excitement. "Everyone says they're really good. They all grew up in the same tribe and have been playing together for years." Just then, the mayor's voice boomed over the gym.

"Good evening and welcome to Glenwood's Friendship and Harfest Celebration. The first of many, we hope. I do have some announcements, but I'll save them for when the band takes a break. So, let's get to it. Ladies and gentlemen, I present the *Bounders*.

The four looked at each other as the band opened up with an excellently performed cover of *ZZ Top's, La Grange*. Axle and Gray were charged with energy as they dragged Jilly and Jax on the floor. The live music from such an amazing band was thrilling. Jilly danced with joy, feeling the beat of the music move her body. It was glorious as though she were under a spell, and free like a shooting star charging across the sky. She thought to herself, it was one more freedom worth saving.

When the band took a break, Gray and Axle went to talk with the band members. Jax and Jilly went to speak with Lana, who was taking notes.

"I think she needs to be reminded that she can have fun too," said Jax.

"She's a dedicated journalist. I can't wait to read her article. I say when the music starts, we should drag her out on the dance floor," suggested Jilly.

When she stood up to follow Jax, she felt faint. She hid it well by sitting back down and telling Jax to go without her, pointing to Andie, who was coming her way. She left, and Andie sat down.

"I'm leaving in the morning, and I just wanted to see how you are doing," she said. "You look a little green."

"I overexerted myself. I just need to sit for a moment."

Andie went over to the refreshment table and got Jilly some juice. "Here, this should help." She handed Jilly the cup, and she drank it down gratefully. "I'm guessing you haven't told Gray yet, or I'd be staying, and you'd be on your way home."

Jilly bit her bottom lip. "I will tell him—"

"I know. You plan to wait until after it's too late to send you back home," Andie said with a discernible frown.

Jax came back with Lana in tow while the band made their way back on the stage, sending Gray and Axle their way. Which gave Jilly an idea. "Hey, Jax? I need to use the little girls' room. Tell Gray that Lana needs a dance or two while I'm gone."

Jax smiled, and Andie and Jilly left the gym. Andie led Jilly to the new Care Center they had set up for Glenwood. While Andie took her blood pressure and listened to the baby's heart, she asked her the same litany of health check questions that Jilly constantly asked herself. She used the adjoining restroom to provide Andie with a urine sample, which was normal.

"Well, you and your baby seem to be in perfect health. It won't be long, and you'll feel the flutter of movement." Andie filled a bag with supplies for Jilly. "Here, quickly take this to your room. It should be enough to carry you through a couple of months."

"Thank you, Andie. You are a true friend. I know you don't approve of me not telling Gray, or being here for that matter, but thank you." Jilly thought back to the first time she met Dr. Channing. She and Ari had just arrived at the Hold, and she needed medical attention after she and Ari were attacked. Andie seemed to be a cold, all-business nurse with no bedside manners, but guarded underneath her tough exterior was a kind and loyal heart. She had become one of Jilly's closest friends.

"Be careful, Jilly. And take care of that little one by taking care of yourself," Andie said as she hugged her friend.

When Jilly returned, Gray handed her a cup with clear, strong-smelling liquid—it was moonshine. Everyone clinked mugs and took a chug before she knew how to handle the situation. Jilly pretended to take a drink but kept her mouth closed around the lip of the cup.

"Hey, Jax, can you check something for me over there in the light?" asked Jilly as nonchalantly as she could. She thought about her friend Billie and her sister Ari. All of them had hidden their pregnancy conditions, waiting for the right time to share the news with the fathers. Jilly had assisted both of them in their deceptions, and now, here she was, needing the same favor.

"What am I looking for?" asked Jax.

"You have to help me," Jilly tried not to sound desperate, but the crack in her voice gave her away. "Pretend you're checking the back of my sweater.

Jax walked around and looked at her back. "What's going on?"

"I can't drink this."

"So don't. Why all the drama about it?"

"I'm pregnant."

"Already?!" Jax gasped.

"I did lose a child, well, at least I think I did. But evidently, there were two. Now there is one."

"And Gray doesn't know. Let me guess. You want to wait until he can't throw you in the going-home truck tomorrow. Look, Jills, I'm all for women being allowed to make decisions about their bodies, but this is not only your husband. He's your commanding officer, and mine." Jilly was about to jump into her litany of reasons, but Jax held up her hand. Then she pointed at the door and turned, which made Jilly follow her lead. Their backs were to their men. "Give me your cup." She poured the contents into the nearby trash can and filled Jilly's cup with water. "I'm not okay with deceiving my commanding officer."

"I know, Jax. I owe you. I won't let him find out, but if he does, I'll say it was all me," Jilly said as relief flowed through her.

"Yeah, well, the military doesn't work that way."

"True, but marriage does," Jilly smiled. The guys were looking over at them, and she raised her cup, clinked it with Jax's, and took a big swig.

Gray and Axle smiled back and raised their mugs in return.

"What in the hell are those two up to?" asked Axle.

"I don't know, but it's something. It's not enough that we have enemy spies with nefarious intentions, but now our women are plotting against us," Gray said, still smiling at them as they approached.

"I got you bro," Axle said, slapping his brother's back. "We'll sweat it out of them."

Gray gave a sly grin, "Yep, if Jilly drinks even half of that moonshine, she'll be spilling more than the plan."

Chapter Seventeen

C onnor was in the screen room, watching a Superman movie, when he heard his father's voice. He ran out and came in fast for a hug, almost knocking his dad over. His tears were threatening to pour down like rain, but he steeled himself against it.

"I've missed you so much," Henry said to his son while squeezing him close. "I can stay for a bit, but they're smuggling me out of here tonight. This mission is getting riskier by the day. Gray said if you wanted to go home with me, you could."

Connor stepped away from his dad. "You know I can't do that, Dad. There are clues and answers inside me that are needed for us to succeed and win our freedom. I don't even know what to expect, so I can't just tell someone how to do this."

"I know. If I drag you home, all of us could lose everything. If I leave you here, I may lose you. You can't know how impossible this is." Henry said, holding his head in his hands.

"I do know how hard it is. I risk losing you too."

Relic came in a few minutes later. "Henry, I'm glad you could come. I can't tell you how amazing this boy of yours is. You should be incredibly proud."

"Honestly, at this moment, I wish we were somewhere else, counting on a different someone to do this something."

Connor began to laugh. "Remember when I said that? We were hiding art, moving around, and leaving all our stuff at every place we landed. I was so frustrated that you wouldn't tell me why, I kind of lost it."

Henry chuckled, "Yeah, you said 'how will we get to somewhere else, sometime soon, to live in whatever they give us, for the work thing? I guess the answer to that is 'somehow'. I suppose now, we should add 'for someone to do something."

Father and son laughed with hard belly laughs, releasing some of their baggage of tension. It was a brief reprieve, and they clung to the moment until reality returned. They had no recourse but the path before them, a path that had death looming around every corner.

"Dad," Connor said, "can we talk about baseball instead?" Henry smiled, and Relic went back to his lab.

The crowded gym made it easy for Jilly and Jax to substitute the alcohol Gray attempted to add to Jilly's cup, but the party was winding down. Axle watched his brother lead his wife back to their room, stumbling several times on the way. When he was assured they were safely at their door, he turned to Jax.

"Did you know they have a hot springs here?" he asked with a suggestive whisper in her ear.

"What if I said I don't believe you?" she teased.

"Then I'd have to prove it to you," he said as he tipped her chin for a soft, slow kiss. She smiled.

Axle dragged her across the street to a large but empty man-made pool. She gave him a snarky look. Through the dim light, she could see the crack running across the bottom. But he pointed down at a second pool where steam was billowing into the night air. Numerous other couples were sitting on the benches lining the edges in their underclothes. They quickly discarded their outer clothing and slipped into the warmth.

"Ahhh," they both said as the warm water relaxed them.

Axle kissed her cheek and whispered, "I love you, Jax."

She lay her head on his shoulder. "I love you too." It wasn't a revelation. It was an affirmation that brought up visions of rings and futures, things that they had to deny themselves.

"If this tour thing goes down without a hitch," he murmured as she grimaced, "I'm going to marry you," Axle said, nuzzling her neck.

"If everything works out, I'll say yes," she gave him a smile that was both loving and haunting.

"I believe in this mission, and I hope it will work. I don't know what this prize is, or how it will help us succeed, but it has to," he said.

"There are so many weird aspects to this tour that are out of our control. Hell, I probably don't even know the really weird shit," she sighed and then looked at him sincerely. "But I do believe, Ax, in this and us."

They tipped their heads against the pool's edge and lay there soaking in the heat. He was happier than he had been since... Hell, this was as happy as he could remember being. The overhead light flashed, and couples started to pack up. Not familiar with the town rules, they were unsure if the light was the signal that the pool was closing, so they readied themselves to leave. They walked hand in hand, and Jax turned, walking backwards in front of him.

"So can I tell everyone we're pledged?" she grinned, teasing him.

"Hold up, let's keep this to ourselves for a bit. It's too early to get dressed up," he laughed and pulled her in for a kiss.

Jilly and Gray had had a long dry spell, and as much as Jilly looked forward to being intimate with her husband, she was exhausted. She was used to being sound asleep by ten, and now, it was past midnight.

She thought back to the chaos of the past three months. It started with Connor being commandeered for the investigation into Cali Bantu, of which she was aware but not included. Then she discovered she was pregnant, New Haven was attacked, and Fringers went from assumed terrorists to valued allies. She fought with Gray when he caught her in a captured patient's room, forcing her to blurt her precious news instead of the tender reveal she had planned.

She lost their child and volunteered for the mission to find Cali Bantu. And then she discovered she was still pregnant, and again waiting for the right moment to tell Gray. Based on the mission so far, which had been fraught with dodging the enemy, it was unlikely a right moment would present itself. Hiding her pregnancy from the one person who deserved to know was an emotionally exhausting task, and the longer she waited, the harder it was, and the angrier he would be.

They arrived at their room, and Gray pinned her against the door in a passionate kiss while fumbling with the key, which he dropped. She bent down to pick it up, and Gray moaned as her head became level with his aching manhood. "Excellent idea, baby, but we should get inside first." He was still laughing at his own joke when she stood up with her eyes rolling.

"You are well marinated, my love," she giggled and opened the door.

"That is true, but the real condumdrim—"

"Conundrum."

"Yes, the ... the question is, why aren't you?"

But the question left his thoughts as soon as he closed the door behind them. Again, he held her against it while he continued to capture her lips with his. His hand went to her breasts, and she gasped. They were so sensitive and full. He stepped back and grabbed her hand. He looked at her in that predatory way that made her melt and feel safe, wrapped in the heat of him. She could let go of the crazy world around them in those arms that would protect her from anything and anyone, except him. She was his to plunder. Their deprivation had been long, and their cravings were cresting.

He held her out, admiring her incredible figure. "You look so hot. I couldn't take my eyes off you tonight. This is officially my favorite outfit, and as I remember, this sweater can undo itself," he sighed into her neck, his heated breath sending shivers throughout her anxious body.

"Well, not anymore. I pinned it closed to avoid a wardrobe malfunction."

"That's unfair. I've been waiting for those buttons to slip all night," he murmured into the hollow of her neck. She laughed as she stepped back and pulled the sweater over her head. Gray watched her ample breasts pillowing over her lacy bra. His look was as hungry as it was curious.

"It's a leftover from pregnancy," she bristled at the compounding lie, but her body wasn't going to let her confess and halt the path to pleasure.

"Well, let's not waste it," he said, unhooking the front-clasp bra and unleashing the magnificent pair for his hands and lips. He didn't waver like a bachelor in search of the right seductive moves. He knew all her sensitive places and how to fondle them into a frenzy. Every moan she released affirmed his progress and drew evidence of his demanding urges.

She was beginning to pant and signal her heightened desire. "Hold on, sweety, this doesn't have to end so soon," he murmured hungrily in her ear.

"Yes, it does," she groaned. "It's been weeks. I don't want torture. I want now." And with that, she rolled him over. There was no need to waste time on arousing him, he was rock hard. She poised over him momentarily, looking into his smiling face, and plunged him into her mouth. He groaned loudly, and she giggled.

"Woman, don't laugh with my cock in your mouth. I might feel judged," he said as another moan escaped him. That only caused more giggling from his wife, but she quickly resumed her assault. It didn't take long before he pulled her up from her task and smiled at her. It was a greedy smile, but radiating with love. She was always beautiful, but tonight she looked more so. "I need to be inside you, love of my heart," he groaned.

Jilly kissed him softly and seated herself upon him. He almost came right then, but he held back, waiting for her to give her lusty cry of climaxing pleasure. He didn't have to wait long, and she was crying out his name. It sent him instantly into a torrent of rapture. They rocked through the extended moments of ecstasy and the slow fade of fire. Then the two gazed at each other, heavy-lidded and sated.

"I've missed you so," he said, bringing her in for a soft kiss. "I didn't know if making love to you would hurt you or make you sad."

"I guess we have to work on our communication because I was worried it might make you," she paused, "more melancholy."

"I was, I am, grieving our loss. But as bad as it was, is, it was harder to lose you. You went through it by yourself. I'm so sorry about that."

"I remember you coming home within minutes of me calling. And then you did everything right. You did everything I needed you to."

She snuggled at his side, enjoying the tenderness and warmth of their naked contact. If this wasn't the right moment, she thought, there was no such thing, but when she leaned up on her elbow, she saw he had fallen into a happy slumber. Another perfect excuse, she thought.

Will walked into the underground medical facility at midnight. Relic greeted him.

"It's good to see you safely here, my friend. Tell me about your trek."

Will gave a short version of the cabin stay and the battle, and ended with being smuggled from one house to the next to get here.

Relic nodded, "I was told to give this to you," he said as he handed Will a letter.

Will had seen this coming. He knew who it was from. He stuffed it in his jacket pocket and turned to leave the lab.

"Will, do you have a minute? I need to talk to you."

Will turned back toward the lab counter where Relic sat, silently implying he was ready to listen. Relic sighed as if he needed to prepare himself for the exchange.

"I'm worried about Gray," Relic said. "He has high standards for protecting the civilians, which is good. But the two he's in charge of now may be his undoing. One is a kid, his neighbor, and a former victim of a crime in the Hold under his watch. He promised Connor he wouldn't let anything happen to him, and now he's on our most dangerous mission to date. That would be enough to worry me about his ability to make hard decisions, but add to that his wife, who recently miscarried their child. I don't know how he will do, faced with the sacrifices this mission may entail."

"What exactly are you asking me to do, relieve him of command? I won't do that," Will answered.

"No, not that, or at least not now. Just keep an eye on him. He could be easily compromised by his numerous vulnerabilities."

"I will keep an eye on him because he is becoming a good friend, and I will help him as such." Will walked back out as Relic called after him.

"Just let me know what's going on, Will. I just want to help," he said.

He gave Relic a reluctant thumbs-up before he cleared the door.

"Does that guy ever sleep?" asked Connor, who met Will in the hall.

"Yeah, I've seen it once or twice," Will smiled. "How about you? What are you doing up?"

"I heard your voice. I've been worried."

"I can appreciate that, but that wasn't too troublesome. It went off perfectly. You can get some rest now. That's what I'm going to do," the exhausted man replied.

"Will, am I going to be hidden in one dungeon after the next? I know I can't be seen by the enemy, but I'm kind of done with being a mole and being moved from one vault to the next."

"I know, and I'm tired of hanging on the freezing ridges. But it's better than being captured or wounded, or worse."

Connor nodded. "Hey, I finished this book about Alexander the Great as a kid. You should read it."

"I long for the day I have that kind of time, and I'm living in a warm comfortable place. Maybe someday," Will said. He thought about all that had to be done before that was remotely possible. Finding Cali Bantu might give them the tools to win, but they still had to fight the war. That would take more blood and create more misery. Connor was smart and had been through a lot, but he didn't know the horrors of war, and Will hoped he wouldn't learn those lessons any time soon.

Colorado Springs Command

General Dermit braced his hands on the edge of his desk and let out a long breath. He was preparing for the pain that would be delivered when he gave his report.

"Do we have Henry and Connor Wayther in custody?" Ena asked without a greeting or other ceremonial drivel.

Dermit responded in kind. "No, they are being hidden, but their convoy is leaving in the morning to return some to the fort and others to the tunnel. We are setting up checkpoints and will stop every vehicle. Our agents are also searching Glenwood as thoroughly as we can within the parameters of the agreement."

"We may need to reassess this agreement," added Tria.

"Soon," Ena said dispassionately.

"We are ready to follow the team when they leave Glenwood. Their plans suggest they are heading back, but we believe they are going to Aspen. Though they were scheduled to leave this morning, our intel discovered they were delaying their departure. They didn't engage in any acts to ready their gear. It still sits ready to be loaded. We believe they are waiting for William to return before they leave. The group patrolling I-70 between here and the tunnel is turning around, but they are surveilling the surrounding rough country to make certain Henry wasn't stashed along the way, waiting for pick-up."

"How many of our Garrison are still in Glenwood?" Dio asked.

"Of the twenty-seven agents and five soldiers, eleven are still there, and four are missing," Dermit stated.

"If the convoy is heading for Aspen and starts moving early, do you have adequate coverage?" Tria questioned.

"The other team is ready to go. They are waiting for the signal that the Allied Army is loading their gear." Dermit was beginning to breathe a sigh of relief. Maybe his report wasn't as disappointing as he worried it was.

"I don't want this new convoy harassed," Ena said flatly. "Just follow them at a reasonable distance. We will make our move when they lead us to their destination."

"Do we have any information on where they are going or what we can expect to find there?" Dermit asked, knowing it was a risky question, but his people needed to know what to prepare for. "It will be difficult to contact my troops in that wilderness. Aspen is a wasteland. It took a direct hit by a large meteorite."

Dermit knew they wouldn't like him challenging them, and immediately felt the pain building in his body as it radiated through every inch of him. It was bearable, and it soon faded. *That wasn't so bad*, he thought. The Elites' pictures went black, and he let out a long sigh. Then his bowels loosened, and brown ooze rolled down his legs.

Chapter Eighteen

Glenwood Springs

Will lay on the bunk across from Connor and waited for the rhythmic breathing, saying he was asleep. He quietly reached for the letter he had stashed unopened under his pillow. He grabbed it now, wanting to get on with it.

Will,

I've missed you, and I pray you are well. [He rolled his eyes. She must be seeing Haru quite a bit to be praying.] *The closeness we have shared has been intense. I care deeply for you. If you respect me, never doubt that.*

I know you don't enjoy fluffy or break-the-news-gently talk, so I will be direct. [and here we go] *I need something more in a relationship than what exists between us. I have spent endless hours trying to define exactly what I want. It keeps coming back to love. I want to be __in__ love and be loved by someone who is __in__ love with me.* [She didn't need to underline it. He wasn't ignorant.]

No matter how I sort through our arrangement, it does not include love. I asked myself why it doesn't. Why can't it? I know you are capable of dedicating yourself because you are dedicated to this cause. You are dedicated to all of us. If I wait, will you be able to dedicate yourself to me?

I have come to know that it isn't me, it's your fate to save the people, and conquer the next crisis, which will probably take your lifetime, and your life. Destiny is your mistress.

He let the hand holding her letter fall beside him on the bed. His head fell back, and he closed his eyes. She wasn't wrong. He might have fallen in love with Leita, but he was already promised. He fought back the emotions that he was losing another person he was deeply connected to. Though he could not pledge his whole heart, she had a firm hold on the part that was his own, the part where the hope of happiness lived. The closeness they shared had been the balm that soothed his horrors away. Her visits and his anticipation of them sustained him. Having her in his life was more than a physical release. It was the thread that kept him connected to humanity. But it was a bridled love, and she deserved more. He read on.

You cannot give me what you do not own, and you do not own that part of yourself. There is someone I have met. I'm sure you are aware by now, it is Haru. Though you and I have no spoken promises between us, I want you to know I have honored the unspoken ones. What I need is your blessing for me to move on to explore this possibility.

With a loving heart, I wish you well,

Leita

Will sat up and took the letter with him into one of the offices. He wrote a short note to Leita on the same note and folded it up. He handed it to Jedi, whose guard duty shift was almost over. He assured Will that he would get it to the truck taking Leita back to McCoy.

Will vaguely awoke from a sound sleep as Connor grabbed what he needed to take a shower. He too needed to take advantage of this facility. There was no way to know when they would have another opportunity to take a hot shower. He was glad all their clothing had been laundered the night before. So, he threw on his sweats and went to the lunchroom to grab some breakfast.

He expected a power bar and dried fruit for breakfast, so he was delighted when he was greeted by Jilly cooking scrambled eggs and hash brown potatoes. He should have been steeped in the woes of Leita's letter last night, but it had always been on the horizon, stalking him. Having the threat finally settled left him solemn but also relieved. He felt lonely, but there few times in his life when he didn't.

He ate a large helping of breakfast because after this, it would be freeze-dried rations. Others arrived, and Will gave up his seat to retrieve his laundered clothes and grab a shower.

It was time, and Axle walked into the garage and headed to the office. He took in the scene of the unloaded gear visible through the office windows that peered into the garage. Piles of totes and other items stood ready near the Brutes while several soldiers stood around, not tackling the task in front of them. The Corporate agent, who was allowed in the garage to observe, stood confused by their lackadaisical attitude.

"Hey, Gray, is the *coffee on?*" Nash asked, using the new code for this part of the mission.

"Yeah, *get some,*" Gray answered, giving the response to move out.

Dom gave a thumbs-up through the window as he and Gray walked out of the office. Jedi walked toward a known enemy agent sent to observe their departure, while Tommie approached another suspected spy. They smiled, causing the two enemy agents to focus on them, as darts shot from the rafters, reducing them both to heaps on the floor.

Like mice, the Operation Reclamation team members came scurrying out from behind boxes, through storage locker doors, and popped up in the seats of the vehicles. Connor was rushed into place, joining Will under blankets on the floor of the Brute, and the whole team was in place when the quiet convoy left the garage.

Stunned enemy faces watched outside the garage as the team rolled out, catching them by surprise. It didn't take them long to realize that the gear bags sitting on the garage floor were decoys. The real gear had been slowly loaded into the hidden storage areas of the minis and the back section of the Brute. The visible storage areas were open and empty until they were slammed shut while the vehicles began moving out. Many of the civilian items the team had packed for the festivals had been loaded on the trailer that left that morning. There would be little use for casual clothing and non-essentials on the rest of the trip.

The deceived enemy soldiers dashed back to their cold vehicles. Unknown to them, the ones they had stashed down the road had already been dealt with, along with the soldiers. The Corporate Garrison team wouldn't be too far behind them, but Easton and Axle had some surprises planned to stall their progress.

"Those men lying on the garage," asked Jilly, "were they..."

"No, just drugged. Same with the ones waiting down the road. And while they were 'napping,'" Gray air quoted with a smile, "we messed with their vehicles a bit. We're not trying to start a war by killing Corporate soldiers. Not yet anyway."

As the convoy of Brutes started moving, Connor wondered how long he would have to huddle on the floor under a blanket. Though it was a vast improvement over the smuggler hold, he missed seeing the open landscape, even if it was from behind a window.

Within five minutes, Will and Connor were allowed to come out to enjoy the morning sun. They were greeted with dense woods and a double line of snowy tracks pointing down the quiet road. No one expected it would be a leisurely ride, and everyone had been assigned a window to watch for the enemy presence expected along the road.

"Are we going to run into trouble? Do the spies know where we are going?" Connor asked.

"They knew we were leaving today, but we are leaving well ahead of the time they expected. And somehow it was leaked out that we were heading to Aspen, but it doesn't matter much because that news would have broken the minute we took this turn. There are several roads leading away from this town. This way is the least maintained, but we don't know when they got the news, or whether they believed it, so we have to assume they are prepared and covering all the roads.

"We identified fifteen people that no one knew, so we assumed they were spies. The Fringers were our best eyes and ears because they are familiar with each other. Even the Loners have a contact. But the Corporates likely had some hanging around the edges, and then there are the people they've turned by compensation or blackmail. I believe that number is relatively few, but to answer your question, yes, we expect trouble," Gray answered.

Dom, who was in the lead, came on the radio when they were far enough out of town to talk. "We located two camps on the road this morning. One with three Garries, and one with four, but their camp was set up for more. I flagged the areas with beacons, but they're on foot. So—"

Suddenly, they heard gunfire up ahead. Gray stopped the Brute and flipped the monitor to heat detector and readied the G-Gun.

Gray handed out a gun to everyone and said, "Jilly and Connor, stay low. Jax, you work the Gatling gun, Lana up front, Relic guard the side door." Gray, Jedi, and Will hopped out with their bows in hand.

The silence made the passengers more edgy than the popping of weapons fire. Connor and Jilly were sitting on the floor holding their guns on the door, hoping that holding them was all they had to do. Connor went through his training with his eidetic mind. *Don't fire at bulletproof windows, hold the gun with two hands, breathe out when I pull the trigger*, but no one ever taught him to shoot from a huddled position. He'd have to struggle through that.

Jilly could tell Connor was holding his breath, and she tried to console him, though she was also quite frightened.

"Breathe, Connor. With Jax on the Gatling gun, bulletproof windows, and a dozen soldiers securing us, we're going to be fine."

"Unless they have drillmos. That was what killed Hannah. Those bullets can drill through just about anything," the boy said. He thought better of scaring his pregnant friend and added, "But you're right, they have a lot to get through, and it's doubtful there are very many of them."

Just then, something rocked the vehicle. Shocked yelps came from the passengers as a rock rolled against the side door. Jax steered the G-gun that way, but before she did, the other side of the Brute was struck with something softer than a rock. Connor and Jilly peeked up to see, but all that was left was a bloody smear.

Gunfire erupted, only this time it was all around them, not up the road. A bullet struck the side window, fusing itself in the clear panel. The men not fighting rushed to free the Brute of the large boulder with a winch from a mini. Stained voices yelled "GO!"

Jax floored the rig, and it lurched forward. It moved several hundred feet before it got stuck in a hole. She re-geared the vehicle, rolling it back and forth, and then punched it up and out. Jax wondered how far she should drive before she stopped to wait for them. Her question was answered quickly when two wounded men were being helped toward the rig. The men helping the wounded tried to open the crushed side door, but it didn't work.

"Holy Shit! What happened to the door?" asked the Guard named Nash.

He set his man down and climbed to the roof. Jax released the locking mechanism and removed the panel. It was instantly cold as Nash and Jedi lowered the wounded inside. Several seats in the passenger area were transformed into medical beds for the injured to lie on. The third column of seats was slid on tracks to the side, making an aisle for Relic and Jilly to move in.

Connor and Mack, having been ousted from their seats, found places to stay out of the medics' way. Connor sat on the console between Lana and Jax while Mack sat on the floor leaning against the console. Jedi and Nash went to their mini and signaled them to follow. They went at a slow pace to allow Jilly to treat the soldiers.

Jilly got to work with Relic, assisting her. The Brute's lights illuminated the red-stained snow, and three Garrison soldiers lay lifeless on the sides of the road with arrows protruding from them.

Inside the make-shift medic room, Dom lay on one table with a shoulder wound and a gash on his leg. Jilly asked for help holding the man down. He screamed as she inserted a thick syringe filled with spongy material into the hole left by an enemy bullet. He passed out, which would make suturing his minor leg wound less traumatic. However, it didn't allow Jilly to ask about Gray or the others. She turned over the task of stitching the laceration to Relic.

The other soldier was a woman named Tommie. She was groggy and pale. Jilly carefully removed her cracked helmet and checked her vitals. She didn't see any other wounds with a preliminary evaluation, but her pupils were unresponsive and uneven. She had sustained a hard blow to the head. It was safe to assume she had a concussion, so Jilly initiated the protocol. When her patients were stabilized, she made her way to the front of the vehicle.

"How will our guys get back?" Jilly asked Jax.

"There are four minis, two sweeps, and two leads. One of the leads is in front of us now. So, between the three left, there will be room for them. They will be along eventually, depending on how things went back there."

What if one of the minis is undrivable?" Jilly asked. "There won't be enough room for them then."

"I didn't see anything wrong with the mini we passed on the side of the road," said Jax. "But even if one of the rigs is damaged, they'll fix it or tow it with the other. If the battle was still ongoing or they needed assistance, I would have heard it on my headgear. They're just doing cleanup. When we get to Aspen, we'll assess our situation."

"Are there any medical facilities in Aspen?" Jilly asked.

"Hard to say. It isn't very inhabited that we know of. Aspen was struck pretty hard by a meteorite. Not much is left of the main town. We are picking up our tracker there, so I imagine there are others and inhabited dwellings there. How are our injured doing?" Jax asked.

"They should make it, if we don't have to travel too far. This road is rough and may reopen Dom's wounds, and the jostling won't help Tommie's head trauma," Jilly answered while adjusting the IVs that were swinging from the roof hooks.

"I'll take it as easy as I can, but we may have hostiles on our tail, and we aren't even halfway to Aspen yet," Jax sighed. "Keep me apprised of their conditions. There may be a place we could stop."

"No matter what, these two are out of the fight for some time," Jilly said while using straps to secure the soldiers from falling off their beds as the Brute rocked through the deep snow.

Jax kept the reality of a soldier's duty to herself. She reflected on her husband's words about wounded soldiers. "If they can shoot, and they're needed, they'll fight." She sighed internally. At least it was still daylight, so Jilly could see what she was doing. The tinted windows kept outsiders from seeing in, but in the darkness, it would be risky to turn on the overhead lights.

While traveling a straight part of the road, Jilly kept watching for the flash of movement behind them. She hoped as much as she worried that she would see an approaching vehicle. With the restricted radio protocols in place, no updates would come over the intercom unless the senders were very close or in trouble.

Gray and Will surveyed the incursion site to assess the carnage. Thankfully, they hadn't lost any lives, but two of their comrades were seriously injured. At this moment, he took solace that both were on the Brute and receiving medical aid. And as long as the reports that no vehicles, other than the two they dealt with, had taken this road were true, Connor and Jilly were safe.

Several Garrison soldiers had battle wounds, and the Corporate soldiers did not treat their wounded well. Normally, Will would treat and rehabilitate captured Garry soldiers to join his army, but there was no way to transport them from here. Plus, they had limited medical supplies, and more would be hard to come by. They couldn't take, treat, or leave them to be rescued, so they could join the fight against them later. Their own people had left them to die, slowly and maybe viciously, by predators. Only cold-hearted mercy remained, and they were dispatched quickly.

Of the six troops left, four worked on road sabotage, while Gray and Will tossed bodies into the woods and turned on their indicators to retrieve their arrows. Will didn't think about how many more lives he had dispensed, but he would later, and so would Gray. As always, with each body he took into the brush, he gave final rites. To honor and remember them, but instead of thanking them for their service, he asked for their forgiveness. It was some time before any words except orders and reports were spoken.

Will and Gray walked down the road, half a mile to the abandoned mini. It was turned sideways on the roadside and lodged in the snowbank. It was still functioning, so digging it out was a minor task. Soon, they were on their way with the heater warming their bones. Gray acknowledged the emotion of the moment, and a couple of hours from now, he would feel the shame of taking lives. He knew his dreams would echo with the pleading of enemy soldiers lying wounded and helpless.

It had been a while since he had been in heavy combat. He gave orders during the tunnel attack, and he was geared up and ready to join his troops. But he was held back when the Guard stepped in, requiring even more supervision. The leftover energy from hunting his fellow man was pumping through him, and he had felt a need to end the silence.

"I have to admit, I wasn't on board with such a primitive defense, but this is an excellent weapon," Gray said, holding his bow.

Will nodded solemnly, "Very quiet, very deadly."

It was then that Gray considered how many front lines Will had been on from both sides of the fray. He, no doubt, had countless scenes and specters plaguing him. That brought his melancholy mood to the fore. Gray still couldn't abide the silence, so he shared a couple of his tales, and Will eventually did the same.

A couple of miles down the road, Jax came upon the lead mini stopped in the road. Both Nash and Jedi were out of the vehicle, and Nash was pounding something into a tree. She slowed down, and Lana deployed the G-gun. The only signatures on the infrared radar were friendlies, so she waited for the team to call on their direct line.

"I thought I saw a flash of a runner, but he's gone now. I swept the road for electronic mechanisms or lit fuses, but I didn't find anything. The only tracks we found were elk. But Nash has marked the area with a beacon anyway, so the sweeps know we saw something," Jedi said on his shoulder mic.

"I doubt any of them could have hiked this far and had any time to plant anything. It probably was just an animal," Nash added.

"We'll keep a lookout," Jax responded. She took a breath, knowing most of their jumpiness was leftover from the battle. Experiences such as that tended to occupy a great deal of territory in one's mind and would for some time.

Rocking back down the snowy path, they followed the tracks of the lead team before them. Dom moaned, tried to sit up, and swooned, causing him to quickly lie back down. Jilly said something calming, and he relaxed into the makeshift bed. The mountains made for short days, and the night was rapidly closing in. She strapped a monitoring bracelet from each patient to her arms. It would be hard to see her patients soon, but these monitors would give her information. She hoped it would not require lights to administer aid.

When they got to a very long straight passage, she saw lights bouncing far behind them. It had to be the sweep team. Jilly hoped Gray was among them, but the vehicle was too far away, and breaking radio silence was too risky.

Jax slowed down and flashed her lights twice. The vehicle following flashed three.

"It's ours," Jax said. "I'm just not sure which one it is, but they would have flashed five times if they required assistance."

It gave Jilly some comfort because she didn't believe they would have caught up with them so soon if something bad had happened. Another hour went by without any enemy threats, but the condition of the road was grueling, and the injured soldiers were in danger of more than just suffering. Jilly herself was hungry and feeling nauseous. She pulled out a protein bar and took a cautious nibble.

"Jax, can we stop for a minute?" Jilly asked. "I really need to pee."

"Yeah, I think we all need a break," she said as she signaled Lana to contact the lead and sweep minis.

Lana grabbed the radio mic from the dash. "Lead, this is Main, come in Lead."

"Lead here, go ahead, Main."

"Need a short break. Copy?"

"Rodger that." The lead vehicle stopped while Lana repeated the message to the sweep.

Jilly wanted to wait for the reply from the sweep, but she needed to get out quickly. Her head was spinning, and she held onto the side of the Brute. The last sweep car pulled up behind the other two minis, and Gray quickly charged out upon seeing Jilly hanging on to the vehicle. Before he could reach her, Jax helped her stand up.

"She's a bit car sick. I'll walk her a bit," Jax said to Gray.

"I can take her," Gray said, holding his wife on the other side.

"Well, we both have to pee, so it makes more sense that I go with her."

"Okay, but stay on the road. You both can pee behind our rig," he pointed to the last mini parked behind the Brute.

As Jax walked Jilly to the back of the sweep rig, she began to heave. Seeing everyone looking away from them, she walked into the woods along the road.

"Jilly, he can't send you back now. When we stop for the night, you'd better tell him," Jax said while holding Jilly's bulky coat and hair out of the way.

"I know. But for the record, this road would make anyone sick. I'm not in danger, or sick because of that," Jilly answered.

The ride had been brutal, but no one else was puking. "Okay, but take your blood pressure when we get back to the Brute," suggested Jax.

"Will do," Jilly said while squirting a stream of water in her mouth, swishing it, and spitting it out. "Okay, I do have to pee, so let's get our butts behind that rig before someone sees us.

Climbing back to the road, they came upon Gray with his arms crossed and a *what-the-hell* look on his face.

Chapter Nineteen

J illy froze at the sight of Gray's challenging stance. Fear coursed through her. He couldn't have heard them. They were almost whispering. But it was entirely possible he heard her getting sick. She took a breath as her brain flooded her with defensive testimonials. After a ride like that, it was a wonder everyone wasn't heaving, but no one else was, only her. She took another breath. Before he could speak, she chimed in.

"I'm sorry I deviated from your suggestion, but I didn't want to leave ... that in the middle of the road."

Gray waved Jax back to the Brute and turned his glare back toward Jilly. "Uh-huh. We just came from a bloody battle where strong men lose their shit, literally, and you think we can't deal with a little puke? What the hell is going on? Are you still suffering from your miscarriage, or are you sick?"

More breaths. No one could accuse this man of beating around the bush. The only question was, how far did she want this lie to go? She had attained her goal of not being able to return, and so far, her lie was one of omission, she justified. But it was a lie nonetheless. But he was asking directly now, and if she answered his question without telling him she was pregnant, it would be a cold hearted lie.

They had worked through this secret-keeping issue before when he had her under protection surveillance. He had faked her death without her knowledge or permission. She remembered waking up in the hospital and hearing the whole shocking story, her story, for the first time after it had already gone down. They stopped seeing each other over it, and if she was honest, his reasons for secrecy outweighed hers.

A less introspective person may be able to say it was a quid pro quo, but she knew better. It mattered not who initiated the lesson. They learned it together and swore not to repeat it. Each time he stood before her, and she did not tell him she was carrying their child, it chipped away another piece of that trust they had worked so hard to reestablish.

Though her hesitation wasn't particularly long, Gray could see that her mind was working on an answer. His temper was rising. The truth is easy, but the consequences bring forth explanations and excuses. Perhaps he didn't know her as well as he thought. Perhaps she was involved with something treasonous. The last possibility darkened his mood considerably.

"Gray, there is something I have kept from you, but it's not bad. I'm not ill or in poor health. But I don't think we should discuss it here with everyone watching us. It's personal."

He directed his heated look at the Brute, causing everyone in the lighted cab to quickly turn their heads away. He clinched his jaw and waved her to the Brute. He knew bringing her on this mission was a mistake, and now it was too late to get her home. Funny, how she was ready to share her secret now.

He focused on the 'something I have kept from you' part of her answer. His temper flared hotter as he walked to the mini. No doubt, she kept whatever it was hidden because she didn't want to upset him and have him pull rank on her. Too late. He leaned against the door of the mini, stewing in his mood while Will drove. They took the position closest to the Brute while Gray's eyes bore a hole through their windshield, focused on the Brute, though he couldn't see into it.

Will didn't speak, lest he aim Gray's fury his way. Marriage, Will considered it when he was seeing Molly, but he soon learned that everyone close to him would be targeted. Jilly was the target that weakened Gray, and Relic's warning rang in his ear. He was drawn out of his thoughts when they caught up with the lead mini. He could see the mountain of trees lying across the road, frozen in snow.

Gray and Will got out and examined the obstruction. Nature had ripped the trees up at the roots and delivered them a formidable blockade. The passengers inside the vehicles watched as the four ranking officers discussed the situation with gestures and head shakes.

"Even if we could cut these beasts up, they're frozen solid into the road, so we won't be able to move them," said Axle.

"But we could build a road over it by filling it with more logs and packed snow," said Relic.

"I agree. Those trees are still firmly attached to the ground at their roots. They'll hold nicely," added Will.

"I'll get a crew working on it at first light," said Jedi.

"I believe the disabled vehicles, numerous roadblocks, and casualties we left the Garries should keep them at bay for at least a day," added Will.

"They'll catch up, and they won't have to look for us. Aspen is the only town of interest down this road. Wurden knew it was where we were going next, and he could have accidentally let it slip," said Will, and Gray nodded.

Gray looked at Will, saying, "We'll begin working on this at first light. It's biting cold and dark as hell. We don't need any more soldiers off the duty list."

"Yep," Will nodded and shouted into his shoulder mic, "Set up the shelters!"

Everyone poured out of the rigs, grabbing gear and performing their assigned camp tasks. The Brute door was pried open, and as soon as the shelter was constructed around the vehicle, two soldiers began preforming make-shift repairs on the door. It was quite cold, so they welcomed the work to hold the shivers at bay. Within ten minutes, the two sweep vehicles pulled up and joined the organized activities.

Soon, two large shelters were constructed. The structures were sturdy and versatile and allowed for various configurations. The other shelter was made by connecting shelter panels and floorboards between three of the four minis. Both shelters would be used as sleeping quarters, while the driver areas were used by the guards on duty to monitor the instruments and man the weapons. By linking all the instruments together, their observation zone provided a 360-degree view.

With the shelters up, the heaters began to satiate those gathered in the enclosed space. Soon, coats were unzipped, and hats were removed. The campers sat cross-legged on their bedrolls as stew began to bubble, and the bread was sliced.

Gray motioned for Jilly to follow him outside. She hoped the chilly air would help keep his temper to a minimum, but he seemed impervious to it. She, on the other hand, shivered intensely, and he drew her close to him.

"Tell me what's going on, Jilly, and don't waylay me with half-truths or lengthy justifications. Just be honest," he sighed. He felt he was keeping a calm tone and being quite civil.

"Okay, straight out then. I'm pregnant," she let out a huge breath of relief. No matter what came next, it was out.

"Okay, not funny. That worked once, but Jesus, honey, just tell—"

"Gray, I'm not kidding. Evidently, I lost one baby, but there were two. Andie thinks one didn't settle in the uterus, and my body rejected it. There is still a child inside of me."

Gray stood frozen with astonishment. He had a list of things he expected, but once again, this had not been among them. Irritations started adding up in his mind. "Andie knew? When did you know?" He was yelling now, and he saw Jilly look at the Brute windows to see if they were being watched. The structures were sound enough, but that did not mean they couldn't hear them fighting. But right now, Gray didn't care. "Damm it, Jillian! I never would have let you go if—"

"I know. You would have *told* me to stay. But, Gray, pregnant people work and serve all the time. And before you go into how dangerous this mission is, I just have one thing to say. If this mission fails, all the people of the tunnel and the Fringer towns are doomed. I had just lost a baby, and I needed to be with you. I found out I was still pregnant at the fort, but that feeling did not change. Andie has a lot to deal with in the Fringer towns, and the care they need is beyond my training. She is best suited for *that* mission. I, however, am specially trained in trauma medicine, so I'm a better fit for *this* mission."

"Pregnant persons are not allowed in combat. I would have disqualified you, or anyone in your condition," he seethed, "but now you are a liability."

"You said that when I wasn't pregnant." She was unaware of the cold, though her voice quivered and her body trembled. Her hands were balled up inside her mittens, and her arms flared at her sides as she stood her ground with determination. "You know what I know? I love you, and I will protect you as well as this child. And you will do the same for me. We are also here to care for Connor, who is the key to this mission's success. *Whatever it takes to help him succeed,* remember that mission statement?"

"I see where you are going with this, but Connor has to go. This child, our child, has no purpose on this mission," he said with his arms crossed and an angry pitch in his voice.

"Yes, Connor's contribution is critical. But if he's critical, so am I. Your soldiers will protect his body, but he's a child, and he needs a lot more than that. He needs the nurturing that only parents can provide. He needs that on his easiest day, but this is a terrifying and violent mission. In the absence of his parents, we, you *and* I, are tasked with this job.

"It's true, we had just lost a baby, and it was deemed unthinkable to send me into harm's way. But it's not my condition or logic that impeded your decision. I know this because sending Axle when he was barely healed from a grave injury was evidently a no-brainer. Well, sending me is a no-brainer too. You and Bannon couldn't bring yourselves to see that, so I volunteered. You are absolved, move on. Let's get this boy to that bloody mountain and set in motion whatever it holds."

She was breathing hard, and great, foggy breaths billowed from her as her body began to shiver violently. Gray looked at this fireball of temper standing before him. She was a force when she had her teeth in a cause. He was amused, but only for a moment.

"Those are dandy little arguments, but you are asking me to be okay with sending my wife and infant into battle. Well, I'm not, and nothing will make me be. You are correct, I would not have thrown in a yes vote, but I wasn't even invited to the discussion. And though I have no choice in you being here, I do have command," Gray assumed his military stance and a matching irate tone as he employed his gloved finger to lay down his point. "You *and* Connor will be under intense guard at *all* times. You will report your health status to me daily. And Jillian Takota, don't you dare step out of line, or..." he was shaking his head as if he didn't dare finish his thought.

Jilly held back further comments. He was in full military mode, and she *was* under his command. The heated moods they radiated could have melted their path as they returned to the shelter. Everyone feigned the business of eating. Though they couldn't hear the particulars of the fight, most of them guessed it was where marriage and duty crossed swords. Jilly wormed through the cramped quarters to sit on a bedroll next to Jax.

Gray eyed the way she and Jax exchanged whispers and bristled. She knew too, he deduced, and he gave her a look that said he'd deal with her later. He needed to get this over with, so he called for everyone to listen.

"It has come to my attention, Jilly has a medical condition, you all need to be aware of. She is pregnant." His disciplined troops listened, restraining the reaction such news demanded. "She and Connor require around-the-clock protection. Jax set up a schedule and send it to me. Lana, you have first watch. Everyone else, don't forget to check for the updated duty roster, which will soon be sent to your wristbands. I'll start the first watch as soon as I brief the other shelter." He left without kissing her, but that could be because he was in the company of his soldiers. But not sending her a smile and a wink, that was all about being pissed off.

Jilly felt all eyes on her as Gray stormed out of the shelter. She went into passenger area of the Brute to check on her patients, hoping to busy herself through the uncomfortable hush, holding the cramped space hostage. She was fussing over them without needing to. They were awake and responding nicely to the treatment.

She was drawn out of her busyness when a round of congratulations broke the awkward silence from the shelter section. She half laughed that they knew better than to offer Gray the same salutations. Jax led her back and handed her a full bowl of stew and two slices of bread. She ate hungrily while she gave a shortened version of her story. Then they cleaned up quickly for lights out. It would be an up-at-dawn kind of morning.

Jilly lay on her bedroll. It wasn't like the beds she was used to, but the heavily insulated, self-inflating mats were warm and comfortable and offered needed relief from a stressful day. The road had been dreadful. Though she needed sleep, her mind was determined to replay their fight. Guilt and exhaustion made her well up with tears, but she refused to cry. These men and women's jobs had just become more complicated and burdened with extra duties, and it was all because of her. She wasn't going to interrupt their sleep, too, by whimpering.

She ticked off her viewpoints, hoping to be able to put them down and rest. She agreed that she had responsibilities to the baby tucked inside her, but it irked her that he didn't think she took them seriously. She knew at some point she would be compromised, but she believed they would secure the object and be home before then. However, looking at the current road hazard made her wonder, what if they had to find a place to hold up until spring? Traveling with the threat of enemy attacks through rough winter terrain with a newborn would be unbearable. No doubt that thought was foremost in his mind.

But what Gray had completely dismissed was her responsibility to protect the freedom they both had sacrificed to achieve. And along with those freedoms came rights. There was a time, many centuries ago, when women were all but imprisoned, especially during pregnancy. They even called it confinement. He thought he could control her because she carried his child, but until that child was separated from her, he would have to leave the child's care to her.

Having to thoroughly work the whole mess out before she could get any sleep at all, she continued down her rabbit hole. It's as if he thought she was thrill-seeking or something. She would never have volunteered for a non-essential mission, but this mission was more than essential. Her family would be executed if it failed. It was her fight as much as it was Gray's, and even more so since their baby's life was on the line, it was ... she stopped.

Did she carry a he or a she? It was the first time she thought about the person she was carrying as more than secret cargo. She had made promises to protect and care for it, but she hadn't thought of him or her as a unique individual.

Who are you, Little One? Who will you look like? Who will you take after? Well, right now, I suggest I would be the logical choice. Your father is going to lose his mind trying to control everything and everyone. Sleep tight, Little One. It had been a rough evening, and she expected a few more, but she was glad he knew. She held her tummy and drifted off.

It was still dark when she woke up. Gray had her cuddled into his sleepy embrace. Again, her tears welled up, causing her to roll her eyes. Was pregnancy making her an emotional wreck, or was her moodiness warranted after their rough, and all but public, fight? She closed her eyes and sank into his warmth. She was content and almost fell back into a slumber when she felt something odd. Like bubbles moving, *no*, it was the baby moving. She was almost seventeen weeks, and it was a common time for quickening to occur. It would be several weeks, if not a month, before Gray could feel it, but she would be happy to add it to her "*report*" today.

Chapter Twenty

Reclamation Team

Gray was focusing on the job at hand. He could not afford to let his festering mood distract him as he operated a chainsaw. Will and he had consulted with Relic about the plan to fill in the space between the fallen trees rather than remove them. Relic showed them his tablet, where he had worked up a blueprint of the plan. Last night, the group was too weary, and the temperatures were too low to begin working, but they used the vehicle lights to study the blockade and calculate the construction required.

"What is your projected timeline?" Will asked.

"It will take most of the morning to implement the plan as long as we don't have many issues," said Relic.

Will and Gray gave each other knowing glances. Planners deal in the constructs of science and math. Builders deal with making science and math happen. But one thing is true of both. There are always issues, especially on repair jobs.

"But if all goes well," Relic emphasized with a grimacing look, "we'll be back on the road in about four hours. I believe the Garries may catch up with us, so we should prepare for that."

"We sent a small demo crew to bog them down with more time busters. We will break camp down after breakfast is done, and I'll brief everyone on a defensive/evacuation plan if it comes to that," Gray said. "This is quite the undertaking. I just hope we don't need to add a shootout to our troubles."

Relic walked around the worksite to continue assessing the progress and conformity to the plan. It was not as simple as many assumed. The engineering involved in constructing a strong and stable overpass was critical because the vehicles were heavy. If they didn't build it sturdy enough, the vehicles could get stuck, places could cave in, or even collapse. They could not afford to lose their vehicles or their gear and be forced to travel on foot. The bridge had to function correctly the first time.

He estimated they were still over fifteen miles from Aspen. There, they would stop and rest to pick up their tracker, who knew the area. Their goal, located somewhere near Pyramid Peak, was where their meticulous planning ended, and traveling blind began.

The road to the mountain was another ten miles from Aspen, but its condition was unknown. It could need extensive work, that is, if they could locate it under the snow. Then the search for the hidden entrance to Cali Bantu would begin, along with avoiding the expected traps. Once inside, they had to find and comprehend what had been left there and retrieve and/or deliver it. All while under the aggressive actions of the Garrison soldiers pounding on their heels in treacherous terrain and brutal weather.

Will and Gray were running the chainsaws and helping secure the logs to the winch they had rigged into a crane. Gray was delighted with the cool contraptions New Haven's chief engineer had devised for every contingency they might encounter. A drone was used to attach rollers to a massive healthy tree that had grown on the steep bank. It leaned over the road, giving the perfect angle for lifting the logs into place.

Will stood, taking a much-needed break, watching the hard labor being performed. He was thinking about the problem of what to do with the bridge after they crossed it. They couldn't let the Garries follow them. The only viable solution was to destroy it once they were safely on the other side. That was the logical choice, but it was a magnificent feat of engineering, a tribute to their power to command their circumstances. But that wasn't what made the decision heartbreaking. It was the realization that they would be trapped. There were no other passable roads. It was their only way home, barring driving through Corporate towns.

Jilly woke up to all manner of loud noises. It startled her to her core, thinking a new battle was being waged. Taking a moment, she realized it was the sound of chainsaws, barking orders, and beeping machines at work. She imagined Gray had given the order to let her sleep in while everyone else was working. She felt better than she did most mornings, so she stretched and grabbed her heavy gear to go outside. She looked at the industrious team trimming brush, securing logs to the winch, and setting them in place. She knew the Defenders well enough, but she had not spent much time getting to know the Guard soldiers. She observed the working crew and listed the names to memorize them.

"Let's see," she said quietly to herself as she mentally pointed them out. "Jedi and Beckett are down the road on demo duty. Will, Gray, and Axle are working with the chainsaws. Relic is making sure the plan is followed. Nash and Easton are guiding the filler logs into place. Mack and Jax are measuring and marking out the slope required, so the vehicles can climb it. The patients, Tommie and Dom, are serving breakfast in the other shelter, so that leaves Lana."

She was walking toward Gray while Axle was approaching her. Gray had probably sent him to see what she wanted, so he wouldn't have to talk to her. Jilly sighed. He had to face her sometime, but this was not the place. She raised her voice above the production, "Hey, Axle. Where is Lana?"

"She's in the other shelter," he yelled. "Better hurry and get some breakfast."

Breakfast sounded good. The smell of dandelion and chicory coffee met her as she walked in. She took this time to check in with her patients. Dom reported his stitches were sound, so she took him at his word and didn't disturb his bandage. Her quick assessment of Tommie's cognitive state confirmed she was recovering from her head trauma. She told Jilly that last night's rest and this morning's break from the bouncing down roads had alleviated her dizziness and headaches, but Jilly wasn't ready to clear her for driving or using heavy machinery.

Lana waved for her to sit with her inside one of the connected minis. Jilly dished up a bowl of oatmeal and added the dried fruit and brown sugar. Grabbing her coffee, she sat down in the passenger seat.

"Comfortable bed, hot meal, and coffee. This isn't camping, it's high living," grinned Lana as she held up her cup.

Jilly smiled as she cupped her mug to warm her fingers and balanced her bowl on her lap.

"How's the writing going?"

"Well, there's certainly a lot to say. It's hard to find time to keep up. I can't possibly write on the road, so I've been recording our trip vocally. With all the noise in the rig, it tends to require a lot of editing. With the secrecy of this mission, I've left out many details, but I have coded most of the secrets, with 'Tour' substitutes.

"This morning, I was sketching the blockade and explaining the plan to deal with it. I'll be able to fill in the specifics when we get home and we're safe." It was a loaded statement, "get home safe." It was what soldiers said out loud to declare their fate. She accompanied it with a soldier's hard smile, contrasting the chorus of harsh realities.

They sat together silently, eating their warm, gooey meal and drinking their coffee substitute. Lana left to join the work crew outside, and Jilly went back to the open area of the shelter to fully enjoy her beverage. She wondered what real coffee would taste like after hearing Will describe it.

It seemed everyone had issues with the turbulence of the road conditions. Setting aside her morning sickness, she had to admit this trip had been as expected until yesterday morning. The I-70 was bumpy, but it was maintained for the most part. This road, Highway 82, was in bad shape and laden with the hazards of snow-hidden depressions and obstacles.

The battle was the kicker, though it too was expected. But no one was talking about it, or perhaps not in front of her. It was the first time Jilly had been in one, a real one. She didn't include an attack on her way to the transport or the setup battle to fake her death, but in all honesty they were traumatic. She was going over the pinging bullets that were stopped in their paths by technology. She felt the panic rising inside her.

She tried to remind herself that the windows protected them, but her brain twisted the positive into what-ifs and could-have-beens. What if the windows didn't work, or they used drillmos? They could be burying their dead instead of evaluating injuries. She could be burying Gray. They could be prisoners.

She felt her heart beating wildly, and it was hard to breathe. She recognized the symptoms of Post Traumatic Stress Disorder. The words didn't do justice to the fear that was overpowering her. It was unbearable, inescapable, and on a repeating loop in her head. She was too lost to remember what she told others. The advice seemed hollow now. She pounded her pillow, lay down, but nothing worked. She shivered with fear and cried silently.

She thought back to the Defender wounded in the tunnel battle. She didn't want to take her meds to help her sleep through the pain of her burn. She was ready to work. Jilly was instantly aware of why no one was discussing this battle or the tunnel one. It was too hard to think about.

They tamped it down and focused on the problem in front of them, the obstacle. They were still in danger, and this was the best way to save their lives and complete the mission. This obstacle was the worst one so far, and they were on a time crunch.

She watched her teammates wielding chainsaws and positioning logs. They had fought the battle while she huddled in the Brute. And there they were pounding out a job with everything they had. She had a job to do too, pack up the Brute, so she got her mind on tackling it. The sounds and blood of battle still swam through her head. But if setting their mind on work allowed them to function, then she had to try to do the same.

"Hey," Will said at a bit of a distance from his friend. "Congrats on the news."

Gray sent daggers toward Will, who couldn't help but smirk. "She has no idea how this complicates things."

"I think you forget she was a Daily before she became a citizen of New Haven. Only Upper women and Corporates were treated differently during pregnancy." Will thought for a moment and tried to recall if he had ever heard about the top Corporates, called Elites, having families, but he quickly shrugged it off as a well-guarded secret.

"She grew up watching women toiling right up until birth," Will added. "And later, as a nurse in training, she secretly treated the

Dailys around her without proper medicine or equipment. I agree this mission has more hard duty days ahead, but she's not sick or weak. Be honest, Gray, would you stay home because your abilities were slightly compromised? Would you stay back because she forbade you to go?"

"What if she has another miscarriage and needs medical treatment? What if we get stuck out here until spring? What if she is killed in a battle?"

"We will likely face tragedies while we attempt to do this great thing, but to do nothing is worse," Will spoke with a sadness hinting at the many stories he held in his heart. "And knowing that, we charge on because if we fail, our deaths are assured, whether our bodies live on or not."

"I looked in on her a few minutes ago," Gray agonized. "I could tell she was reliving the battle. I wanted to help her, but the next thing I knew, she was packing up the Brute. I didn't want to pull her back under, so I got back to work."

"PTSD is tough for sure," Will agreed, "but we're not off the battlefield yet. This is just a break. I know it's hard to see her in pain, but maybe this reality check is what she needs to stay alive. Everyone here struggles with it to some degree. If anyone knows how to deal with PTSD, it's her. It's part of her specialty, and why she was the best person for the job."

Gray scowled at Will. He was tired of hearing why his wife and unborn child were needed on this difficult mission. Will spoke philosophically like Relic did, but well-formed words couldn't protect his family, and every one of them was on this mission. That's what he stood to lose.

Gray pondered his friend and the fate he was handed, the one Gray feared. Will had seen many battles and lost more than loved ones.

Chained to a destiny at a young age, he was denied a childhood. He was even denied love. He heard about the letter from Leita telling Will she was moving on. This man had given everything, and still, he continued to sacrifice as fate continued to rob him of every joy that came his way.

It set Gray on his heels. His compass was readjusting. He had women soldiers, and some had lost their lives. Everyone here was lying on the altar of war. And everyone would suffer if they lost, so they fought. They stood ready to sweat, bleed, kill, and die for this intangible thing. These ideas, called inalienable rights, were the essence of being alive, as well as the concept of how to live together, self-determined and united.

Freedom is precious and therefore the responsibility of all people. Wasn't it everyone's duty to defeat those hungry to crush it? He could not imagine standing safely by while others fought *his* battles, regardless of his physical condition. Why should his wife be an exception? She was more than a woman; she was a person. He should be proud of her courage. But his head still rang with a resounding *NO!*

He *was* proud of her courage and Connor's too, but they both had something in common: a child. And as long as he took a breath, he would do everything in his power to keep them safe. They may be among warriors, but he could never let them be frontliners. He'd protect the shit out of them.

He had been working while his mind played out his impassioned mental drama, not wise while running a chainsaw. But now the chainsaw work was completed, and snow was being shoveled up on the overpass on both sides of the hill. The minis with the plow attachments kept plowing up and backing down, plugging the holes as the crew used logs to stomp the snow down into the cracks. Slowly, the evidence of logs disappeared completely under a blanket of packed snow.

The shelters were torn down, and the camp was fully packed up. The hill was ready for the test run. Axle and Easton won the honor. Everyone watched as the mini tugged over the hill. A little sinking here and there, but the stability was better than expected. Several more trips with the minis were scheduled to pack the sagging spots before the Brute was scheduled to cross, but the job was deemed a success. Just as their cheers of triumph broke out, the demo crew came barreling in as fast as their tracks would allow.

"Take cover!" yelled Jedi. "They're coming on foot!"

With the camp completely broken down, Gray sent Mack driving the Brute while Jilly, Relic, Dom, Tommie, and Connor ran over the ramp using the large vehicle for cover. It held up to the heavy-duty Brute, so Will sent Beckett, still in a mini, to go next. Before the next mini could approach the ramp, shots came from the wooded roadsides. Two of the vehicles and eight of the fifteen team members had made it to the other side, and Will and Gray hiked up the wooded hill. While the Brute was sent down the road, the rest of the soldiers had positioned themselves on top of the ramp, laying down cover fire for Jax, Lana, Jedi, Easton, Axle, and Nash.

Jedi worked the gun from one of the two minis left on the frontline side. It allowed Axle and Easton time to dive behind a battered mini, which had been damaged when it rolled during the ramp construction. It was parked sideways against the hill with the functioning door facing the enemy. Easton and Axle were trying to open the damaged door to access its rotary weapon. Axle was able to smash the latch with his hatchet, opening it, and both men climbed in.

Easton quickly activated the rooftop machine gun and began laying down heavy fire. Jax's mini was faced the wrong way on the hill, but she expertly drove over the ramp backwards while Lana continued to fire the roof weapon. Axle opened the side turret to lay down more fire. Now nine were over with Will and Gray in the woods searching for Garries, who were trying to use the steep hillside to take their team from behind.

Gray and Will took the opportunity of the intense cover fire to signal to each other their strategic intentions. While the rest of the hostiles were focused on the direction of the minis, they would deliver their silent retribution.

The enemy was sending a barrage of bullets, which splintered tree trunks and pinged off the remaining mini. The Defenders and Guard matched the attack with their high-power weapons and the mobile grenade bombs that stalk the enemy. Screams echoed in the woods, but the pelting continued. Will and Gray took out several unaware Garries. From their vantage point, they saw a sticky bomb launcher being wheeled up the road.

Will and Gray worked on skewering the men manning the machine. The other team members scattered as a walking grenade crawled near the damaged mini, shattering the window and damaging the other door. Easton had crawled on the floor, but glass and shrapnel sliced through his outer gear. Somehow, Axle was spared the worst of it as he was not by the window.

Those lying atop the ramp were firing rifles backed by a row of grenade launchers. Easton saw his chance and drove the battered mini up the ramp. Though it was well peppered with enemy fire, the bulletproof shell on the back held. The line of soldiers lying on the crest of the hill cleared the way as the vehicle crossed over the hill. That left Gray, Will, and Jedi on the enemy's side of the ramp.

The returning gunfire from the road was silent. Will spotted a couple of Garries running, or at least limping, back down the road.

He also noticed Gray was no longer raining arrows at the hostiles. He made his way over to Gray's last known position and found him pale and slumped against a tree with a tourniquet around his thigh.

Will called for assistance on his shoulder mic, and Jedi, who was tucked behind a tree, rushed to his aid, as a solitary shooter scattered a row of bullets. One grazed Jedi's arm before he quickly made it to the cover of the trees.

"Damn it! Where is that rat?" Will asked.

"Northwest of you and about twenty yards up that ridge," Jedi answered.

A barrage of shots came from the team to keep the sniper crouched and give their men cover. Will and Jedi shoulder locked Gray between them, dragging his feet as they went. An Allied soldier bearing two handheld shields came along to offer more cover fire as the single shooter continued to target them.

Jilly demanded that Mack stop the mini to help the team members fighting behind them. As soon as the vehicle slowed down, she pushed through the rickety door and ran back to the ramp. Mack was busy making sure the mini was in a ready line with the others. When he stopped, he had lost sight of her. She lay on her belly in the snow at the very edge of the manmade hill. She was an excellent shot, and her comrades needed her and Gray was among them. He had been teaching her for the better part of a year now. She saw no reason to let people die, so she could hide away in the Brute.

She gasped upon seeing her husband being dragged to the edge of the road. A lump formed in her throat, not knowing if he was dead or alive. She moved away from the other soldiers, who were laying down cover. Then she saw it, a flash of movement creeping above them. She had the best line of sight, but she couldn't see a soldier. It could be a tree limb shedding snow, or a loosened rock tumbling down. Gray had taught her not to shoot at shadows. Know your target.

Then her target came into view through her scope. He looked wounded as he crawled along the steep crag, stopping each time he gained ground. Just as he was aiming his rifle toward her husband and his rescuers, she pulled her trigger. Staying with the image in the scope, she saw him slump and unmoving. The sound of her report was mixed in with others, but she had the only clear shot. She knew it was her bullet that killed him. She was glad. Maybe someday, she would mourn her actions, but she would never be sorry that she saved Gray. That is, if he was still alive.

The Allied soldiers noticed the shots quieted. *Was he down? Did someone get him?* The whispered question permeated through the team.

Axle looked over and saw Jilly holding up her long gun in triumph. "Gray is going to kill me," he muttered along with a prayer that his brother would have the chance to pummel him.

Will put Gray in the tattered mini that Axle drove back over, and Jilly rushed down the hill rifle in hand and hopped on the open door jam of the rig. Will grabbed her gun while she kneeled across Gray and took his vitals. Though battered and breezy, the rugged little rig tracked up the mound with little effort.

Over the hill, they carried Gray to the Brute and set up a medic bed to lay him down. She started an I.V. of plasma and put a warm blanket over him, all but his leg. She was a whirlwind of hustle, not noticing the passengers piling in to sit where they would not be in her way. Relic evaluated Easton, but his wounds were easily plugged with foam until he could be stitched properly. Relic was favoring his hand, but he joined Jilly as she worked frantically on her husband's artery, pumping his life onto the Brute floor.

Will stepped out of the rig, hoping his friend would recover. The enemy was still quiet. *Did they retreat? They must have realized the battle was unwinnable.* It was dangerous to assume so, but two things were clear. The Reclamation Mission team still had five vehicles, though one mini was badly damaged, and though the Brute's door had been Gerry-rigged to function, all were drivable. Their enemy, however, was on foot. They were beaten and wounded and could do nothing further but soak more of their blood in the snow. But it was a temporary ceasefire. They would return, and probably with a larger army.

He looked up at the feat of engineering and hard work that created the bridge before him. It had to go. Their enemies would regroup and clear the roads that the demo crew had damaged. They would repair their trapped vehicles and come at them with vengeance.

He sighed as he looked at the mound. It was their only road back home. If it were destroyed, it would be hard to untangle before spring, meaning they'd have to stay through winter. But leaving it for them to catch up could mean the mission would fail.

"Blow it up!" he said and returned to the Brute. Four vehicles rolled down the snowy trail, leaving one mini for Mack and Beckett assigned to the demo crew.

Chapter Twenty-One

Demolition Crew

Beckett and Mack were gathering the needed supplies from the storage area of the mini when Mack stopped Beckett from reaching for the sealed box of C-4.

"I think three sticks of dynamite will take this thing down. There's no reason to break the seal on the C-4," said Mack. "Besides, we need to get this done quickly. They may have guessed this move, and they're going to come back to secure it."

"You're probably right, but let's use four. We have one good shot at this. They are going to do everything they can to save this bridge. We also have to consider the chance of an avalanche. We don't want to trap or bury ourselves before we get passed that slide," Beckett added, pointing to the areas Relic had warned him about while they discussed this scenario.

They were the most trained and experienced explosive ordnance technicians on the team. They had been on the road demo crew that recently secured the Fringer towns and New Haven from a Corporate invasion.

Quickly, they went about the work of attaching the blasting caps to each stick along a fuse. They stuffed the prepared sticks in plastic pipes, which they filled with the gravel they carried for road traction and other issues. Then they buried them in the ramp at strategic areas. They had tied those leads into a singular spool of wire when the buzzing came.

"Drones!" shouted Beckett as he ran, laying out the fuse line as fast as he could.

Mack manned the machine gun, taking out two of the three drones that hovered and fired on them from above. Beckett made it to the mini, but he had been hit. Blood was seeping quickly from his side where his vest had a gap, and the straps hung in shreds. But Beckett focused on hanging onto the fuse reel while Mack drove slowly away, with his partner leaning out of the vehicle to lay down the wire. As they stopped so he could attach the detonator, more drones showed up. Mack manned the roof gun with the panel monitor, taking down another drone.

The other two drones turned back, so Mack popped open the compartment on the roof and launched one of their drones. Beckett was looking rough, but he sat holding the box, ready to push the detonator button.

On their drone's footage, Mack saw Garries beginning to crest the ramp, and he shouted, "NOW!"

Mack squeezed the button, and the screen flashed white, while they drove off at best speed. The drone caught up, and it could be heard securing itself in the compartment above. Beckett was conscious but moaning in his seat when the rumbling came from behind. A crash of trees and billowing snow filled the road behind them. Mack floored the accelerator pedal, slipping and sliding down the road to stay ahead of the avalanche.

When they were at a safe distance, Mack stopped, grabbed the med kit, and ran to the other side of the mini. He helped Beckett out onto the snowy road to assess his wound. He swore with each movement but cooperated as well as he could. The wind was picking up, and large flakes began to fly about. Mack hated exposing his injured friend to the cold, but he needed to get a look at his injury out of the cramped seat and his bulky gear.

Removing his vest and coat, Mack saw the bullet had ripped into his side, between the straps of his gear. He assumed it must have hit a rib because it turned and exited out his back. He didn't smell any hint of bowel, but it could have nicked his kidney or some other organ. Whatever it did, it was still pumping out a steady stream of blood. He grabbed the wound foam and squirted a liberal amount into the wound on both sides. Beckett let out a stifled cry. The oozing stopped, but he could still be bleeding internally. He needed to get him to the team where Jilly could treat him. As he was loading Beckett back into his seat, another drone rounded the bend, and then another.

Mack imagined the wounded Garries left for dead as the survivors spent their time manning drones. *Bastards.* Bullets pinged off the mini, but Mack didn't stop to engage. He just kept going. He was praying the bulletproof shielding would hold when a bigger drone passed by and a noisy projectile drilled its way through the back compartment. It missed them. Then another went through the roof and hit their dashboard. It took out some of their instruments, but the men were untouched.

The flakes of snow were increasing, and a gust of wind began whipping around, throwing them every which way. The drones must have struggled to fly in the tough weather because no more shots could be detected. Only one of their four headlights still functioned; their DEV (Driver Vision Enhancement) equipment was out, along with interior lights. The snow blew in through the three-inch hole in the roof; the heater fan was making a clanging noise; and the battery was getting low.

All Mack could do was drive as fast as he could on the blanketed road through the thick veil of wild snow. It would get darker soon, which would slow him down further. He tried to call in, but all he got was static. He wasn't even sure if the radio still worked.

Reclamation Team

Jilly had finally stopped Gray's bleeding, and she was pumping plasma through his veins, but it wasn't enough. He needed blood. Only one person had the same O-negative blood as her husband. It was Will.

"Can we pull over? I need to..." letting out a soft sob. "Will, please stop the Brute." She had an unbearable choice. Save Gray by filling him full of Will's Corporate mites or let him die. It wasn't that she hadn't made up her mind. None of the infected individuals had shown any signs of disloyalty. It was that Gray may never forgive her.

Will stopped without telling her they were within twenty minutes of their next destination. He looked at her, waiting for the bad news about his friend.

"He needs a blood transfusion. The plasma gives him fluid, but without red blood cells, he can't oxygenate. I know you're injured too, but..."

"My wound is minor," he answered.

Will, come outside for a few," Relic spoke to his friend. Will noticed Relic's hand was wrapped in a bandage, "I have something to tell you."

"Now?" Will asked, incensed. What could be more important than Gray's ebbing life?

"Yes, now." Will looked at him suspiciously as they exited the Brute.

"When you first joined our tribe, I took a blood sample from you," Relic said.

"I remember. You said I was clear of contagions and whatever else you were worried about. Has that changed?" Will asked.

"No, maybe. Let me go back to the first sample. This is a delicate reveal, but I plan to get straight to the point without bedside gentleness."

"Good, because my friend is dying in there," he said, pointing to the Brute. "Get to the point, he needs my help now. Besides that, I'm exhausted, edgy, and cold." His arms were folded, and he was leaning against the Brute.

Relic proceeded to tell Will about the Highmind Camp developments in mite technology and that he was infected. And with every blood ritual, he infected more people, and that included Connor. He ended with every test he had run and how he had been dedicating all his time to investigating this. He reported that the biomites in his system and others infected by him only showed evidence of enhanced healing properties.

"Not happy about the brain slice," Will finally said. "Why wouldn't they try to infect me with the other kind? That would better serve their purpose."

"I believe they tried on several occasions, but it didn't work on you. I can only speculate that an RH spy substituted their controlling mites for this kind instead. It acts like an antibody against the controlling kind," Relic answered honestly.

"So, am I going to live for a hundred years or something?"

"No, cells have a limited number of times they will duplicate, but you might live a bit healthier," Relic said, knowing that may not be Will's desire. He was a troubled man. "I'm not sure how long these things last, but I have established they can replicate." Relic let out a long breath, causing smoky steam to flow around him and quickly dissipate. "Look, I'm telling you this so you can make an informed decision about helping Gray. It could be the only way to save his life, but I can't promise it doesn't have unknown side effects."

"Does Jilly know?" Will asked. Relic nodded his head. "She confessed to overhearing me tell Gray. She wanted to help me study them."

"It seems odd that you would tell me you suspect Gray of being compromised when I had this going on," Will looked at Relic as he tipped his head and glowered at a man he thought he could trust. "Oh, I see. You had us watching each other." Will shook his head. It was evident that Relic didn't fully trust him or Gray.

"It seemed wise at the time. Look, if it were me knowing everything I know so far, I'd help him," Relic said, deflecting the conversation back to the immediate problem.

It was a lot to process, and he had no time to think it through. The thought of infecting another person with his robotic blood angered him, but death, that, was a whole other extreme. Will came back into the Brute and looked at Jilly. "Relic filled me in. What do you want to do?" he asked her.

She began to strip his arm. "As his doctor, I get to make decisions for him when he isn't able to. The thing is, we have no choice, but he's going to be fighting mad when we tell him."

"Well, I'll fight that battle when he recovers. Jax, get us back on the road as soon as we are hooked up. I don't want to get stuck out here in this snowstorm," Will said. Jax was already making her way to the driver's seat.

Blood transfusions were always risky, but patient-to-patient transfusions ran the additional risk of not being able to know how much blood was being transferred. But she was not set up for anything else.

She took Will's blood pressure and used her tablet to estimate how much time she should allow the transfer to go on before checking Gray's levels. Will sat back in the seat close to Gray, and Jilly opened the valve, allowing Will's heart to feed his blood into Gray's limp body.

The Brute rolled forward, moving at a slow speed. Jilly monitored Gray for fever and signs of rejection. The one risk Will's blood did not carry was disease. She prayed his little robots would get to work repairing her husband. Letting out a long breath, she remembered Jax and Relic had been working on several other patients she had completely neglected while Will drove. Though she knew her assistants would have alerted her if her expertise was needed, she needed to know about her other patients.

"Tell me about the injuries you've treated, Jax," Jilly said, collapsing onto a small jump seat she had folded out from the wall. She was spinning with exhaustion, and she let her head fall back against a cushion she propped on the window.

Jax began to list off the minor wounds that were being treated. "Connor was kept safe in the Brute. Jedi was grazed by a bullet on his left thigh, requiring eight stitches. Tommie is fine, and she's driving for Jedi. Dom's leg is stable enough, so he's driving Easton, who had several shrapnel wounds, requiring numerous stitches, none of which are threatening. Nash is uninjured and riding lead. And Lana is driving us with no injuries.

"Relic tripped while diving for cover and landed on his wrist. I secured it, and I think it's just sprained. Axle took a round in the butt. It's deep, but it's not bleeding anymore. I believe it's all muscle damage, no bones or spinal issues, but it will have to be surgically removed. I started him on oral antibiotics. That's everyone but Mack and Beckett demoing the ramp."

That's when she noticed Connor. He was quiet and tucked into a ball on the floor by the driver's cab. She went to him and put him in the jump seat beside Will. It caught Will's attention, and he nodded at Jilly. They were soon immersed in conversation while Jilly worked to stabilize her patients.

Demolition Team

Mack was focusing on driving as fast as the conditions allowed. He knew it was Beckett's only hope. Mack could not make out what he heard on the com panel, but he recognized Jedi's voice. Jedi was giving his report from the damaged rig running sweep. With what Mack could make out, he assumed they were waiting for his check-in. Mack sent a second message, hoping his team would hear him.

Garbled static crackled on the intercom. Jedi slowed down and held the headphones closer, trying to decipher the message.

"...pha Gho... It's Delta G... - Mack – urge... ..om in Al..."

"Delta Ghost, this is Alpha Ghost, please repeat."

"Beckett... help..."

"Lana, what's going on?" asked Will, hearing the chatter between minis. Jilly stopped the flow of blood and checked Gray's counts. She signaled a little more with her thumb and pointing finger. Will gave a thumbs up.

"It's Delta, sir. I think they're in trouble," said Lana.

"Okay, let's stop. They can't be that far back."

They picked up another call from Delta, which came in better and clarified the situation. Jilly began getting ready for another mortally wounded soldier. Axle was painfully moved to the passenger seat, leaning on his good side.

By the time they brought Beckett in, she had untethered Will from Gray. She put out the other bed and lay Beckett on his right side.

His vitals were sketchy, but no more than expected with a traumatic injury. He was in a lot of pain, so she administered a painkiller. As it was kicking in, she examined his wound with the mini ultrasound device. It was not the ideal tool, but it was good enough to show the pool of blood around his kidney, indicating the organ had been hit. With further inspection, she believed most of the blood was from a minor artery, but it had stopped bleeding. She decided to wait until they arrived at Aspen before she made her call regarding surgery. It may heal on its own, which would be a blessing since she had two other surgeries to perform. She started him on antibiotics and let him rest.

Gray was stable but still unconscious. Axle curled up on his side in the front seat, in severe pain, so she gave him additional pain relief. Beckett was resting comfortably. She leaned back and watched the snow blow toward them in the headlights. It was thick and growing thicker, making the trip slow. She closed her eyes, but she woke up fifteen minutes later when they stopped in front of a large building with a sign that read Aspen/Pitkin County Airport.

In the headlights, they were met by four heavily cloaked residents who waved them over. The Brute and the four minis stopped facing the large structure with a faded label, *Hangar 3*, painted on the hangar door. All eyes were watching the four strangers exert a great amount of energy to slide open the tall door of the metal building.

As soon as they were ushered inside, the doors were rolled back to their closed position. Jilly hoped beyond reason that there were medical facilities here, but it was unlikely. She was emotionally and physically drained, but she had much to do before she could rest.

She got out of the Brute and surveyed the huge open area. They were out of the wind, but the below-freezing temperature proved that their stay would require them to set up their shelters. She watched as one of the bundled strangers led Jedi and Will into an enclosed section that spanned one whole side of the building. Soft lights shone through several of the windows, but they did little to expose the dark expanse of the hangar.

The orange glow of a wood stove caught her eye as the door opened, and she longed to follow the others inside, but she had to stay with her patients in the Brute. She could have stayed in the warmth of the vehicle, but she wanted to have a say in where and how her patients would be housed. She still needed to extract a bullet from Axle, Beckett's injury could take a turn, Gray was still in critical condition and needed an artery repair, and infection threatened all those suffering wounds.

Returning from her thoughts, she noticed three people were standing on the far side of the hangar. They were holding their hands over a small glowing window that she assumed, in the dim light, was another wood stove. Another assumption was that Will knew and trusted these people who had yet to show their faces. She was suddenly distracted by four people who left the enclosed space and were approaching the convoy with large items in tow. They were silhouetted by the low light from the windows behind them, and the only one she could identify, by his height, was Will.

The shadowed items were three gurneys and a cart, rolling toward her with a sense of urgency. Maybe there was a place inside the long office for her patients. Jilly hoped it would be suitable for critical patients, but she presumed it was a better place than in a shelter on a cold cement floor.

The faceless stranger, who appeared to be in charge, called the others who were hovering around the wood stove on the far edge of the hangar to help. Will helped load the required gear in the cart while Jilly helped the others carefully transfer her patients onto the gurneys. Axle was able to limp out and lie on his side on one of them. Beckett moaned as he was moved onto the rolling bed, and Gray lay silent and motionless.

Gear was loaded, and the patients rolled toward the door with Jilly following. Jedi and Mack stayed to secure the vehicles as everyone else made their way to the warmth of the office. The heat of the fire checked off one of Jilly's requirements for her patients. If she were able to tap into their electricity, she could keep the oxygen machines flowing and portable monitors running and charged up. It was too much to hope for, but she prayed for a well-lit room that could be reasonably sterilized. Then she could operate on Axle as well as Gray or Beckett, if it came to that.

The three patients were rolled into a large room with four areas partitioned by short walls. The semi-private sections created three patient rooms, a treatment room, and a fifth section with full walls had an office with a bed. The building was run-down, but these rooms were surprisingly clean. Jilly was informed that they used it for medical matters, so it was scrubbed regularly.

Theo introduced himself as one of the inhabitants. He was of medium height with auburn hair and greenish-grey eyes. He had a ready smile that warmed the room. Jilly guessed he was in his late teens. He helped her settle her patient and told her that the availability of electricity was sporadic and strictly for critical purposes. Thankfully, her patients were deemed critical, so she was allowed the necessary medical equipment and low lights as needed. They also had a portable bright overhead lamp for surgeries. There was one outlet in each section where she could plug in the low-voltage monitors.

Jedi brought in her gear as well as the med kit. Jilly claimed the office area as her lodging and quickly arranged her belongings and her medical station. While in the lounge area where most had gathered, she gave the injured team members a medical once-over. Many had some kind of bandage or support binding for various wounds and injuries. None were serious, but the whole team needed a rest. She didn't have much hope that she would be able to join them.

Please give everyone a good night's sleep and a full day of staying put, she prayed silently.

Relic and Will came into the treatment room to help Jilly repair Gray's artery. She was worried he was still bleeding internally because he was still unconscious. She had been rushed and working in poor lighting when she stitched his artery and needed to ensure the repair was sound. Relic understood the biomites better than anyone else, but he had a badly sprained arm and would be able to do little more than position the light and give her the tools she needed.

She would need Will to clamp vessels and hold the wound open for her to stitch up the artery. Jax would have been a better choice, but she couldn't let her know about the biomites. When she got to Gray's torn artery, her hasty sutures were covered in a delicate layer of gray film.

"What the hell," she stared at the unfamiliar membrane.

"Those must be the mites," said Relic with fascination. "They have sealed the artery to repair it. Astonishing."

"This answers some questions about the injuries I've had. When I escaped the Neighwah, I fell into a creek and slammed my arm against a rock. I swear I heard it break, but by morning, it felt better."

"But if his artery is repairing, he isn't bleeding, and his blood levels are good, why is he unconscious?" asked Jilly.

"Connor was unconscious after I did the ritual with him. I thought he was sleepy, but he was out solid for quite a while," added Will.

"It may be part of the healing process. The mites put their host under to keep them still while they work on delicate repairs." Relic was in full science intrigue.

"That wouldn't be helpful in a crisis," Will quipped.

"Well, they can sense body chemicals, so perhaps a large rush of adrenaline would prevent that response. See how they have sealed the wound with their bodies? That is a temporary bandage. Underneath, they are stimulating the body to accelerate the repair of the blood vessel. This is incredible. I suggest we close and let them do their job."

"I agree," said Jilly with apprehension about the foreign bodies infesting her husband, and began the closure process.

Relic and Will settled Gray back into his little cubicle, while Jilly checked Beckett. She assumed the mites he received as a new soldier were also repairing his kidney. His vitals were stable, but he too was unconscious. She sent for Jax to help her with Axle, who did not have robotic surgeons racing through his veins.

When she and Jax got back to the medical room, Axle was propped up on his elbow. "This looks like my crew coming for their pound of flesh," he laughed with a hint of nervousness.

"Well, the good news is we're after your ass, not your ticker," Jax gave him a sassy laugh, surprising him that she understood the classic Shakespearean reference.

"Two women after my ass. That conjures up so many possibilities," he said, trying to defuse the inevitable field surgery jitters.

"Well, this one has a scalpel," Jilly smirked, flashing the sharp tool at him. "Can you remove those pants, or should we cut them off?".

"I'll get them off. We don't have many extra uniforms," he said as he stood wincing from the object biting at his flesh. He was down to his boxers. "These you can cut away."

Jilly and Jax laughed at his bashfulness and instructed him to lie down on the metal table they had just sterilized. It was draped with a sheet, but there was little they could do to reduce the chill of the metal.

Jax had cut away the boxers, and Jilly cleaned and examined the wound. It looked very swollen and painful. She mentally prepared for the added bleeding the swelling could cause, but before she began, she needed to locate the bullet. She took out a syringe and filled it with benzocaine.

"This will only sting for a minute or so," and Jilly stuck him with the needle.

"Ouch!" Axle said. "Jeez, if that's the painkiller, I can't wait for the slice and dice part."

"You should begin to lose feeling pretty quickly, then I'm going to take an ultrasound to find the bullet. No use slicing and dicing more than necessary."

When she was sure the initial shot had kicked in, she added a couple more cc's. The bullet was deep, and pressing down on his wound was going to cause a lot of pressure and pain.

"Can you feel this?" she asked as she poked him with a sharp tool.

"No."

Okay, this may still be uncomfortable because I have to press on the wound to find this bullet, so take a breath," Jilly advised.

He groaned through the procedure with the sheet between his teeth.

"There it is. You were right, it's deep, probably three inches, I'd say. The best news is it's in one piece," said Jilly, setting the transducer aside.

Jax got ready with gauze, and Jilly carefully made an incision near the entry wound. Taking the long forceps, she pulled out the mushroomed object. Jax wiped away the blood, and Jilly injected more numbing meds, which would help with pain and bleeding. Within minutes, he was stitched up, and the wound was dressed. Axle relaxed upon hearing that the procedure was complete.

Nash helped them move him onto the gurney, rolled him back to his cubicle, and into his bed, where a sheet and a warm blanket were draped over him. Soon, he was sleeping heavily.

Chapter Twenty-Two

Aspen

Jax left the room and returned with two plates on a tray, containing carrots and potatoes, along with a sizable venison steak. Jilly's mouth watered.

"Here, I thought you could use a dinner break," Jax said, handing Jilly one of the plates. "When you're done with your dinner, you should go to the lounge and meet our hosts. I'm going to sit with Axle for a few."

Jilly smiled as the plate was put before her. She had a protein bar for lunch and a polite piece of the quiche that was set out in the lounge when they arrived. With all that had happened and all her critically injured patients, she almost forgot about dinner.

She dug into the steak first, thinking it was more than she could eat, but her plate was soon empty. Jilly went to the lounge, carrying her empty tray, laying on the counter by the others. Everyone was relaxing on the couches, and she searched for an open spot. A round of introductions was fired her way. She tried to pay attention, but she was distracted by the scent of herbs with a delicate hint of something. Maybe oranges, she thought.

Lana scooted over, creating a space for Jilly to sit down. She sank into the soft, cushioned seat. It felt good after riding on the seats in the Brute. A young woman with an old soul quality approached her. She wore a loose-knit cap, which failed to control her unruly head of dark curly hair. She was dressed in clothing that was unfeminine. Though sensible in her remote environment, it did little to hide her beauty. And when she smiled, she was stunning.

"Do you like tea?" she asked and looked at Jilly with captivating, steel-grey eyes. They reminded Jilly of her father's eyes, intense with interest, but kind.

"Yes, thank you. It smells heavenly. I'm Jilly," she said, reaching out her hand, which was reciprocated with a smile.

"I'm Gretchen, but everyone calls me Etcher. Do you want a drop of honey?"

"Wow, honey. Extravagant," Jilly said and nodded with a gleeful expression.

Jilly clutched the warm mug between her cupped hands and inhaled the herbal blend. She took a careful sip of the steaming liquid, and her eyes rolled in delight.

"This is excellent tea. Is it blended here?"

"Yes, it's my favorite. I use wild syringa flowers, giving it an orange blossom scent. I have traveled all over this side of the divide, and I know all the places where the best herbs grow. I've gathered seeds for years and planted them in our greenhouse."

"Oh, are you our guide?" Jilly asked, wondering how someone so young could know enough to lead them on such a critical hunt.

"Yeah, I know the area you are going to, inside and out. My father took me all over this region while he hunted and scouted for our town, as his father did." Etcher gestured to a man with a cane leaning on his chair, and he raised his mug in acknowledgment. "He broke his leg last year, and it never healed quite right.

"She'll take you there, alright. No one knows the Elk Mountains better than my Gretchen," said her father from across the room.

"I'm glad we have an expert because though I've done some wandering myself, these wilds are unknown to me," said Jedi. "That said, I'm off to bed. Not sure what is on the docket tomorrow, but I'm sure it'll be something I wanna be rested up for." Everyone agreed as they set a row of empty mugs on the counter, already filled with dishes needing attention.

Etcher started rounding them up, and Jilly went to help. "Jilly, I was told you were pregnant, and I heard you've had one long day after another. You might not even get to sleep tonight, caring for your husband and the other injured. Please, have a seat, finish your tea, and then turn in. It's been awfully slow around here, so I'm good and rested and glad for the task. Please," Etcher smiled and gestured to Jilly, who was still standing. She piled the tray full of cups and plates.

"Thank you, Etcher. It has been a long day," Jilly sighed into her cup.

It was then that Jilly noticed Relic getting up and taking the tray of dishes from Etcher, balancing one side on his wrapped hand. He smiled at her. It was different than his usual smile. This smile filled his face, and his eyes flickered with affection.

She didn't embarrass him by resisting his chivalry. She smiled back. She was so young and pretty in the soft light. She couldn't be more than nineteen or twenty. And though Relic was around twenty-nine, if she remembered correctly, it was no more of a difference than the years between Gray and her.

She couldn't blame Relic. These times made even the most stalwart heart lonely. And Relic was a man after all, but she had never seen this side of him. He never even hinted that he was looking for companionship. But visible sparks were flying, and Etcher was not discouraging him. She smiled behind the mug she cradled in front of her. *About time, Relic*, Jilly thought to herself.

Etcher and Relic left the lounge. Jilly sat by herself and looked around. It had several couches that didn't match. One was blue, another had a rust weave, and the third was brown leather. The end tables and lamps continued the eclectic variety, but she recognized, due to Bannon's influence, that the pieces were high quality. A couple of warped paintings and old airport décor broke up the grey walls, but the overall effect was relaxing and unpretentious.

It was then she realized she had only seen this room and the clinic. She made a mental note to take a tour of the facilities tomorrow morning. She finished her tea and was about to add her cup to the rest of the dishes on the counter when Relic came in and set the empty tray on his one good hand. Jilly helped him load the tray and offered to carry it to the kitchen, but Relic declined.

"I've got it. I'm giving Etcher a hand, literally one," he laughed and beamed a grin so bright, she just smiled, knowing better than to interfere. As she walked back, she breathed a sigh of relief that Relic's injury was not one she had to worry about.

She was performing a check on her patients before she went to bed, and she saw that Axle's temperature was slightly elevated. She wasn't surprised that he was fighting an infection. The bullet was left in far longer than she would have liked. The Garries left out here with few medical supplies were riddled with disease, so it stood to reason the bullets they handled were too. And though the operating room was clean, it was far from sterile.

It wasn't too high, but she began an I.V. drip with stronger antibiotics than the oral ones she had given him earlier. She set all the monitors to buzz her med band to alert her if any of her patient's vitals became unstable. Sitting on the chair by her husband's bedside, she whispered to him. "I love you, Gray. Please keep fighting." Then she kissed his forehead.

She felt a deep ache of loneliness in the little clinic room that was hers. She stared at the ceiling in a bed without Gray. She smiled, remembering the story Dr. Maya told her about Jax climbing into Axle's hospital bed with him after the tunnel battle. She knew how medically unsound that was, but the idea tugged at her heart.

She forced her way onto this mission because she knew if she wasn't with Gray, some deadly moment would take him from her, and she had been right. She was the only one who saw the enemy approaching him, and she saved him. He was mortally wounded, so she sealed his leg as well as she could and performed the mite-tainted blood transfusion he required. His vitals were steadily returning to normal, but he had yet to regain consciousness.

What more did fate want from her? She was plagued with thoughts that she had made the wrong decision when it came to infecting him with Will's mites. She had no idea what ramifications the mites would have on his health, but he was in a desperate state, and she grabbed at the only possible answer. She prayed this unconscious state was part of its healing process. All she could do now was take solace that he was resting comfortably.

She was startled out of her sleep by something grabbing her arm. Panic seized her. Her breath came in fast, shallow pants, and she was back in the battle. As she broke free of the nightmare, she felt the hum of the band on her wrist. It was Gray! His readings were flatlined!

She bounced out of bed and ran to his room. Her tears already making trails on her face. He was sitting up ripping what was left of his monitoring leads off and pulling the tape off his IV lines.

"Stop! Gray stop!" she cried and tried to catch her breath. "It's okay, honey. We're in Aspen."

"I'm sorry. I didn't know where I was. I thought I'd been captured," he said as he lay back down rubbing his forehead.

"You were shot yesterday. I thought..." she wiped away a tear. "Just please let me make the medical evaluations and decisions. How do you feel?"

"I'm dizzy and tingly," he said as he felt for his leg, relieved to find it was still attached. "I know I was hit badly in the leg. Thanks for saving it. Is it going to be okay?"

"So far, it seems to be healing, but you have a long recovery ahead of you." She kissed him, saying a silent thanks for the answer to her prayers.

She wasn't lying about the recovery process. It could be months, well normally, and on a mission like this, she expected him to fight her every step of the way. She laughed to herself as the axiom, "Be careful what you wish for," came to mind. But in this moment, she would fight any demon she had to get him healthy, even if that demon was him.

"Gray, my love, I'm glad you're conscious and feeling better, but it's 12:30 at night. You need rest," she said as she checked him over and lay her head on his chest.

He pulled her head up to him for a gentle kiss. "Thank you. I'm sure I owe you my life. You should be the one in bed. I feel great, but you look beyond tired." He suddenly remembered she was pregnant. "Please, Jilly, I'll be good. Go back to bed."

"Thank you," she said as she reattached his leads, checked his I.V., and added a mild sedative to it. She could not have him ripping his sutures or the seal the mites formed on his femoral artery. "Well, I might as well check on Beckett and Axle," she yawned. "You stay."

"What happened to Axle and Beckett?" she heard him ask.

"Gunshot wounds, but they'll be fine," she had no idea if they were out of the woods yet, but he must have fallen asleep because he didn't continue questioning her.

Axle's fever had risen again, so she woke up Jax.

"I've already upped his antibiotics and fever reducers. I don't dare give him more and cause a reaction. Gray woke up. He's doing better, surprisingly well, actually. But he was pulling off his monitors because he thought he was captured. I put him out. If Axle's fever keeps spiking, we'll have to reduce it by putting him in a tub of cool water, and we'll need help."

Jax said, "I'll stay with him. In fact, give me the med band. You get some sleep. I'll wake you if anything changes."

Jax woke Jilly up around 4:30 am. Will and Jedi were helping load a delirious Axle into a metal trough tub with a tarp lining. It was full of snow water. It was so cold, it could create more issues, but they had no choice. His fever had to come down now. Jilly found the kitchen and began heating several pans of water.

He moaned loudly, weakly fighting his well-meaning captors as they lowered him into the frigid water. He began shivering. Jilly ran back to the kitchen and came back with a large pot of warmed water.

"Why are we warming the water up?" asked Jedi.

"It's too cold, which can cause more harm and send the body into shock. There is another one heating up. Could you go get it?" He was gone and back quickly, pouring the steaming pan into the tub.

Axle was trying to crawl out of the torturous cold, but within a minute, Jilly looked relieved, saying, "Look, his fever is coming down. Leave him in until he reaches 101°F, but monitor his vitals for shock. I'm going to check on Gray and Beckett."

She was so mentally and physically spent, it was a miracle she was standing. She felt nauseous and chilled as she sat in the chair by Gray with her head on his bed. That's where Will found her. He shook Gray.

"Shhh," he whispered, pointing to Jilly, wrapped in a blanket and sleeping soundly. "We have to talk while Beckett is out on a wheelchair ride." Gray nodded. "This wife of yours saved your life, twice. She crept along the ramp, trying to get a visual of you. What she saw was a wounded sniper creeping up behind us. She took him out with one shot.

"That was impressive enough, but when we brought you to her, she worked to clamp and suture your artery, then performed a direct blood transfer while we were on the run. Then she worked on Axle and Beckett. She's a force."

"She is," Gray said his hand gently stroking her head. She said he needed protection too, but he didn't think he'd need assistance from his pregnant wife. But he was wrong. She had saved at least five team members. They needed her. "Who donated their blood?"

"That would be me," Will said, and Gray almost came off the bed. "Is your reaction because Relic told you about my... condition?" Will felt the hackles on his neck standing on end. Will fumed at the thought of Relic telling Gray without telling him.

"Don't blame Relic. Think about the implications of Corporate mites infecting our team members. But evidently, all his tests have shown your brand of tiny creepy crawlers is beneficial. If it is the reason I am here, I should show gratitude. So, thank you for donating blood to me. Don't be offended that I've got mixed feelings about this," he said, and he paused. "How much did it take? Are you weakened?"

"The mites will accelerate my blood production. Relic and Jilly estimate I will be fully recuperated within a day. It is highly probable you will be well, long before this woman lets you do anything."

"You have no idea. The worst of it is, she has the power to do it," Gray huffed. "How are the rest of the troops?"

Will ran down the list of injuries, ending with his brother's condition, which was touch-and-go. Gray sighed, and then he saw Will's look. It didn't take words to know what he asked.

"Are you asking me to let you infect Axle with these mites?" Gray hissed in an angry whisper.

"I'm asking you if you want me to try and save your brother's life. I'm asking because we don't understand the risks. This is the same dilemma your wife had to decide about you. I'm sorry you didn't have a choice. And now here we are again."

"You don't owe me an apology," Gray sighed, realizing how complicated the issue was. "Having the same choice before me gives the unique perspective of both sides. And even with that, I'm inclined to say yes, hell yes, save my brother."

"Not so quick. I want you to have all the information. You know the only properties my mites have demonstrated are healing properties, but Relic says there is a possibility the Corporates could discover a way to reprogram or cause them to malfunction. Will Axle recover without them? Anything is possible, but it's not looking good right now, and time is running out.

"The mites need time, and lots of it, because I can't give him a transfusion like I did for you. He doesn't have our blood type, but I can perform a blood rite. When Connor was ill, it took about a day, and he recovered. But Axle has both trauma and an infection. We don't know how long it will take them to build up enough of them to fight both issues. We'd have to act quickly."

Jilly began to stir, and Gray rubbed her back gently until she fell back to sleep. He was still woozy from the sedative, but he was sober enough to understand what was at stake. He let out a long breath.

"Is there a reason we are not consulting our medic here?" Gray spoke while running a finger along her cheek to pull her hair away from her face.

"You can if you want, but do you think she'll allow it? She'll say he may come through, but she okayed it for you, despite it going against her oath. Which she explained to me, in depth, anticipating this very scenario every time someone became ill," Will said, rolling his eyes, and Gray chuckled.

Jax came in, and her eyes were red-rimmed. She was asking Will for the ritual to honor Axle before he slipped into death. She didn't know about the mites, and without a marriage document, she had no right to know. Gray knew there was a chance Axle would recover on his own, but he wasn't willing to take the chance that he wouldn't. This decision was accelerated because the mites needed time to replicate and get to work.

Axle had barely healed from his last injuries. He cursed himself for clearing him for this mission. Axle wanted to go so badly that Maya gave in. Gray wanted his best and most trusted soldier with him on this mission, so he allowed it. It was a selfish move, and now, here they were.

"Do it," Gray sighed, and Jax mouthed the words *thank you*. Will carried Jilly to her room, and she barely stirred. She was beyond tired.

Chapter Twenty-Three

Colorado Springs Command

General Dermit stood before his screen, terrified by the request he had just received. After reporting the latest failures of his team, another officer was invited to join the meeting. Dutifully, he complied with the order and called Colonel Garriset into the office. He wasn't tortured by what would happen to him. He knew. It was the manner of his impending death that scared him. He wasn't obsessing on escape routes because there was no escape.

He remembered a year and a half ago when his supervisor called him in to participate in an Elite meeting. It was the highest level of power and influence. To work directly with the Elites was the object of every ambitious officer. The rumors were that after a year or two, the general and his or her family were rewarded. They would spend the rest of their life in a beautiful, luxurious place away from the stress and ugliness of Corporate command and rebel headaches. He had been well rewarded as an Upper officer, but being the voice of the Elites was promoted as having all life's pleasures at one's fingertips.

What he believed would be the first of several introductions and briefings before his supervisor was whisked off to an endless vacation turned out to be a brutal murder. All the excitement of being promoted died when he walked into that room, as he watched his predecessor tortured to death before him. Since no top general's family was ever seen again after the "reward", it was tragically obvious they were killed too.

After the people on the screen coldly congratulated him, he was told his first job as General was to secretly deliver his boss's body to the crematorium. It was instantly clear at that moment that this job was indeed temporary, but in the worst way. He prayed he could follow their orders well enough to protect his family.

No reprimands were given while he waited, only morbid silence and his inner voice, mourning the demise of his wife and daughters, whose deaths he had secretly set up this morning. He learned early on that the Elites could not decipher his thoughts. But they could detect which part of the brain he was using and his emotions about it. It was a sophisticated interpretation of his emotional state, but he practiced the art of self-control by deflecting revealing feelings and over-dramatizing those that they approved.

For this moment, he focused on the emotion of fear. It was the one they expected and needed to make a statement to the next recruit. With tears in his eyes, he reached his hand under his desk and impaled the meaty part of his palm onto the hidden autoinjector. It was a massive dose that was quick and painless. Before Garriset arrived, his predecessor, General Dermit, was slumped over his desk, dead with a Mona Lisa smile on his lips. His last act deprived them of their sick pleasures while he displayed their indifferent cruelty to their next victim.

Aspen

Jilly was still asleep when Gray woke up that morning, but his movement signaled her wrist monitor, and she got up. She had to talk with Relic before he left with the road crew. Walking into the clinic area, she found Will helping Gray out of his bed and into a wheelchair. They were discussing who would join Will on the Brute and the two undamaged minis to check out the Maroon Bells Road. Jilly agreed that Relic, Etcher, Easton, Lana, and Jedi were all cleared for the duty. Though Nash and Mack were uninjured, they would set up cameras to watch the road. Jax would assist Jilly, and Dom and Tommie were tasked with vehicle repair.

The team would plow and clear as much as they could and be back at dusk. Relic insisted on going to evaluate the terrain for geological hazards. When Relic walked away with his approval, Will whispered something to Gray, and they both snickered. Relic's infatuation with Etcher was making the gossip rounds. It was a testament to the resilience and power of human emotion. With the world hovering on disaster, love could still bloom through the cracks.

It was unlikely the enemy would be able to get their vehicles through the tangled mess the explosion made of their manmade bridge, and it was too far to walk. It was also evident that their enemies lost a good number of soldiers in the numerous battles, including the ramp explosion that caught at least four of them trying to breach it.

They hoped to clear enough of the road that the whole team would be able to get down to set up a base camp. Evaluating and clearing the access to their destination was a valuable use of time and had been discussed at length. When they considered their injured comrades, it seemed highly improbable that the team would be ready to move out tomorrow. The fact that those injured included the other half of their upper echelon left a disconcerting gap in leadership.

It was early in the morning after Axle's blood rite, his fever rose again, and another cool bath was administered. Axle's fever was resolved by the bath much quicker this time, but he had slipped into a coma. It made her suspect that he had been infected with the biomites while she slept. If true, she would be angry they didn't consult her, but as the closest family member, Gray had the right to make that decision. Silently, she took a sample from Axle near his wound, where the biomites would congregate. It confirmed her suspicions.

She thought of all the tests that needed to be done on these little helpers. Everything about their replication and reduction processes sat at the tip of that iceberg. She wondered how the biomites would react to pregnancy. The body masked the baby so its foreign DNA wouldn't trigger an assault. Do the mites follow the body's lead? Would they attack the baby as a foreign body? She thought about the female soldiers in Will's army. Had he unwittingly sterilized them? Could the biomites be passed in other bodily fluids, such as semen? More tests were needed, soon. She had discussed this with Relic soon after they infected Gray.

She took small blood samples from Beckett, Connor, and Gray. She pulled up the file of samples she took at Glenwood Springs. All Guard members had a baseline biomite count for comparison because they had been tested in Glenwood. She compared Beckett's count to his first test. They were highly elevated. Connor's levels, however, had slightly decreased. Results showed all biomite populations had changed in response to the health of the carriers.

She theorized that the biomites could replicate or be reabsorbed in response to the stress signals put out by the body. They were composed of carbon, iron, phosphorus, and the three most common gases, oxygen, hydrogen, and nitrogen. They acted like the components found in the human systems that fought disease and repaired tissue. Their design, if she was correct, was eons ahead of anything she had ever heard of. Who could have designed these?

It was apparent that Beckett's injuries spiked his count. There are no previous biomite counts for Gray or Axle's blood, but she prepared a slide of Axle's blood, and she watched the little monitor with astonishment.

The biomites in Axle's blood were ripping apart the bacteria plaguing him. And then they were using the material from the micro corpses to build more biomites right in front of her eyes. She stood for several minutes, mesmerized as the biomites methodically severed a bacterial cell into pieces and constructed new biomites to join the fight. His immune system did not attack the biomites, which led her to assume they had identified them as non-foreign bodies.

"Well," Jilly said to herself, "that settles that." At that moment, Relic walked into her little lab to touch base before he left.

She asked how getting the semen samples from the Guard soldiers was going. She laughed when he told her how he convinced them it was necessary.

"I got all the males in the Guard to give me samples this morning. Last night, I told them I detected an airborne disease that attacks the sexual organs. I said it was easily curable, but I needed a sample to diagnose them. Not one declined," Relic laughed. "The good news is that not one biomite was found in their semen samples."

"Well, I'm glad for that," Jilly said with relief. "We still need to see what it does to a fetus, but I don't know how to test that. I mean, they may be designed specifically for humans, so I don't know if animals would be suitable for testing. And if they don't harm the fetus, will the child be born infected?"

"I agree. There is much we need to learn," Relic answered. "In the meantime, you need to be especially careful when handling the blood of anyone infected."

"Way ahead of you."

"So, I know you took blood samples of all the carriers. What did you find out about their population tendencies?" he asked.

"They replicate like crazy when the body is in distress and break down when their job is complete. Amazingly, they use the invaders' components to construct more biomites. As best as I can guess without better equipment, they behave like antibodies, peptides, and so on. But if that checks out, do you know what this means?" Jilly stated excitedly.

"That we can heal people," Relic said, "We just need to verify they remain benign, aren't hijackable, don't malfunction, or something we haven't even thought of occurs."

"I have not lost my mind enough to want everyone infected, but this is worthy of study and consideration. Yes, it could be a master plan by our adversaries, but if it is, why hasn't it turned on Will? Or his soldiers? He's had them since the Neighwah, maybe longer. If they could use them to control him, wouldn't they have already done so?"

"You may be right. It's more likely he was infected by the Robinhooders who infiltrated the Highmind camp. I don't have a sample of the manipulative type to test. But I believe every attempt to infect him with the other kind failed because these biomites destroyed them. Though I haven't found a frequency or stimulus that has any effect on these biomites, that doesn't mean there isn't one. I worry they are restraining their aggressive potential to see what we are after. If we find something powerful, they'll use the full force of their army to seize it."

He paused and looked at her. She was cleared for everything medical, but the Cali Bantu secrets were outside of her need to know. "There are things that we are involved in that I can't discuss with you, but I will say, this quest is layered in secrets and conspiracies. These biomites were made with an agenda in mind. Whether that goal was devised by the benevolent or malevolent, there is an endgame."

Jilly was happy to be left out of the military politics and issues. Sorting through the conspiracies was not something she wanted to deal with more than she had to. Her job was to provide the best care available for her patients.

"I know we are marinating in conspiracies, but I can't help thinking that we could learn to cultivate and administer these as needed. Maybe we could find a way to eliminate or extract them when they have completed their job."

"I agree. It needs to be investigated," Relic confirmed. "But we've got more pressing targets. It will have to wait until after we accomplish our mission. But most importantly, we need to guard this information. It could cause a divide among us, suspecting each other to be spies would be seriously harmful, or it could cause a run on carrier blood for the miracle biomites," Relic warned. Jilly nodded in agreement.

"And somehow, we need to make sure none of Will's female soldiers become pregnant. I can pass out blockers, but—"

"I'll speak with Will," Relic assured her. "Any change with Axle?"

"No," she answered sadly. " He's unconscious, which seems to be part of the healing process the biomites induce for serious issues, so I tested his blood. Evidently, he was infected sometime last night while I slept."

It was an hour before daylight when Will outlined the road crew's orders. He gave the same speech Denter gave on the road-clearing jobs he carried out as a Dranger. Those staying behind were instructed to repair the damaged minis and recharge all the ED (energy dense) batteries as fully as the Aspen town could afford. They only took three fully charged extra batteries with them, leaving the other six to be charged. Though none were completely depleted, it took a lot of power to charge them, and their small electrical grid was already taxed by the demands of winter, extra guests, and the medical room.

The road crew had no idea what lay ahead. Etcher would have done a pre-recon mission, but they couldn't afford to leak out their destination. In fact, she still didn't know how far they wanted to go or where they wanted to end up. That information would be divulged when they were a couple of miles down the road.

They set out before sunrise. Will wasn't sorry that he would miss Jilly's anger when Gray informed her of the medical treatment Axle received without consulting her. Gray had the right to make life and death decisions for his unconscious brother, but her consultation might have been prudent. Will believed the family hash between Gray, his wife, and his brother was none of his business. Hopefully, by the time they get back, Axle will have improved enough that the agreement will be moot.

They left with the twilight stretching its pink bands across the snowy peaks. It was deceptively peaceful. He knew how unforgiving the wilderness could be, especially in the winter. As they made their way to the southbound road that led to Maroon Bells, Aspen's devastation came into full view.

The once luxurious mountain town had been swallowed whole, leaving a monstrous depression in its place. Deep ravines from the impact radiated outward, and on the outer rim were the charred remains of a bustling town. Being missed by the meteorite was no assurance of safety. Several decades had passed since the attack, but its geological flesh was still raw and jagged.

It also revealed that access to the mountain town had been eliminated by a meteorite blast, and the only other one had been blown up by them. For now, it was beneficial because it would be nearly impossible for their enemies to get here for some time. They hoped to locate the weapon, but how would they transport it? Ambushes would be set up on every route near here. The Fringer towns and New Haven would be sorely abused if they were stranded here.

And what of his unfinished business in Pueblo? And then there was Jilly. She may have to have her baby in the wilderness and then drive over rough roads back home with a newborn. He pushed the thoughts aside. Situations have a way of changing, and the worries of distant woes were often a waste of time. Over thought plans become obsolete before they are needed. Will's motto was to keep moving forward because, so far, the momentum of this destiny had always provided a solution, though it was never painless.

When they turned down the old road, it was packed with snow. Etcher had told them that no one drove down that road in winter. Will got out and drove a metal pipe into the road. Pulling it back out, he pushed the core sample out and found the snow level was just under two feet.

"Not as deep as I expected," he said.

"Yeah, our snow hasn't settled in much yet. It will probably be deeper farther up the road, but the avalanche danger is low in the fall. That being said, this road travels through a valley, and there are some dangerous slopes through the gap," Etcher offered.

"I can use a mathematical formula to estimate the best routes and weakest points," Relic said.

"Wow, that's impressive," Etcher bubbled, making Relic turn away, but not before Will saw him blush.

"Well, this rig's tracks can handle the snow depth as long as we stay on top. Let me know of any issues with the road, like deep holes or boulders that could get us stuck."

"Yeah, there are a couple of spots. I'll let you know when we are approaching them."

After evaluating the damaged mini, Dom asked Theo, an Aspen resident, if there were any aircraft panels around. Theo said he would give them a tour of the old planes in the hangars. Dom, Tommie, and Connor got in Theo's truck. It was a full cab and had a long bed, making it logical for transporting the parts. Theo was waiting in the driver's seat when Dom climbed into the passenger's side, and Connor and Tommie got in the back.

Relic had passed his Connor duties over to Dom when he was granted permission to join the road crew. Dom was the best mechanic and needed to help find the parts they required, and he would go with them while the rest of the crew removed the damaged parts from the minis.

The first building they drove to was the Cessna hangar. Walking inside, they were intrigued by the old aircraft still parked in the hangars. Several Cessna planes were inside and appeared to be in good condition.

"Have you guys ever tried to run the engines?" asked Dom.

"No, I mean I know a little about how they work, but none of us know how to pilot them, and where could we go? Not to mention, it would put us on the Corporate radar. But a mechanic who used to work here taught my uncle, an engineer, about planes. He and my uncle repaired a jet engine and turned it into a generator. They siphoned the fuel from all the planes, so they wouldn't leak or blow up. When we used up that fuel, we pumped some out of the underground tanks. It was pretty contaminated stuff, but we made a filtering system," Theo answered.

"And it still works?" Tommie asked.

"Yeah, but it breaks down sometimes. When it does, I cannibalize parts to fix it. My uncle taught me how to work on all the things we've made from these planes. Hey, I saved the best for last. Come on," Theo said excitedly.

The next hangar was much larger than the ones they had just visited. It held a mean-looking jet with weapon racks under the wings. On the sides, it had a star in a circle of blue with stripes coming off the sides. There were missing panels and dangling lines, making it unsalvageable.

Theo rolled the portable stairs up to the cockpit and waved them up. The instrumentation was impressive. Tommie dreamed of what it would be like to fly such a machine. She didn't know the first thing about flying or repairing aircraft, and this plane was in a hopeless state. But she loved the view a drone provided, and she suddenly felt inspired to learn about aircraft and these machines of the past.

"Are there books on this stuff? I mean, this is an airport, surely, they had technical manuals here," Tommie said hopefully.

"Yeah, there's a library in the office over there. On one of the shelves, there are tons of binders. I think they are about maintenance, but in the tower, they have flight instruction manuals. At least, I think that's what they are. It seemed a waste of time to me, so I never really checked it out, "said Theo.

"Can we get into the tower?" she asked.

"I don't have clearance. I have to get permission. We do surveillance there, so it's a 'need to know' place."

The four began their walk back to the hangar exit. Theo and Dom were discussing his airport knowledge, but Tommie was lost in thoughts of flying planes. They drove back to the hangar where the Cessnas were parked. Theo, Dom, and Relic found some insulated panels that could be used to repair the doors on the Brute and the mini, as well as the hole in the roof of the other. Connor wandered around to a plane on the far side of the hangar while Dom and

Tommie unscrewed and sawed the pieces they needed. Theo caught up with Connor behind one of the single-engine machines.

"What would it be like to fly above the ground and see so much of it at once?" Connor questioned out loud to himself.

"I imagine it would look like the images we see on the drone footage, but with a full panoramic view," Theo's voice startled him, but only for a second. "We could probably repair these machines or build our own, but there's no place to go. The runways are in horrible shape. How would we get away with it? The Corporates would instantly detect and destroy a plane like this with their dozens of drones."

"We think they have all the power, but they don't. I'm tired of being afraid of them," Connor said with inflated courage. "We can't hide from them forever."

Connor remembered a conversation he had with Relic when he wandered off this morning to get some alone time. "Let's say I was a spy who was waiting for this very perfect moment. There's a mini outside with full batteries, and I could drive you back to the bridge before anyone could catch us. How lucky for me that you childishly escaped those protecting you from this very thing happening, so you could go outside and play." Before Connor could react, Relic grabbed him and covered his mouth. He was shocked, trapped. He remembered feeling panicked that he couldn't make any noise, and even if he could, no one inside the hangar would hear him.

And then just as quickly, Relic turned the boy toward him while still holding his shoulders. His hostile expression was replaced by one of concern.

"Connor," he said, "the enemy sees you as a commodity they desperately need, like the last crust of bread in a room of feral rats. I don't want you to be afraid all the time, but I want you to be careful *all of the time*. Bravery is best left for moments of necessity, not reckless impulses. Let us do our job by you doing yours."

At that moment, Connor saw the potential trouble he was in, and he dashed under the plane and ran to where Dom and Tommie were working. Theo followed a few minutes later.

Chapter Twenty-Four

C onnor sat in the lounge area, going over the access clues and possible traps that Cali Bantu may have in place. Connor was also running over the event that morning, wondering if he should trust Theo. He could have easily grabbed him. *Why did Theo follow him instead of helping Dom and Tommie? And he came up very quietly and startled him from behind. What does Theo know about Cali Bantu? He lives here, so it's possible he heard something or saw something.*

And then there was Relic. He scared the crap out of him. *Did he really just want to prove a point, or was he using reverse psychology to gain his trust?* Besides failing to capture him, both instances had caused him to be more cautious and suspicious. It was a puzzle, and Connor couldn't let go of a puzzle. But he needed a break. When they got back, he decided to visit Gray.

"Hey, what's up, G-man?" Connor jested. "Still lazing around?"

"Unfortunately," Gray sighed.

Connor talked for a while before he shared what Relic and Theo did and his confused feelings.

He nodded. "I'm not sure I am completely on board with Relic's method, but it sounds like it was effective." He thought back to Relic saying he would test Connor to ensure the biomites weren't affecting his behavior.

"Maybe too effective. I'm seeing ghosts everywhere."

"Well, if you keep to the rules of security, you don't have to worry about ghosts. That's our job. Yours is figuring out how to get inside this place. You probably need to talk with Relic about what happened. Clear the air, so to speak. But as far as Theo goes, I don't want you near him, agreed?" Connor nodded.

"Although I understand the security protocols, they don't allow for much fun. I can't work all the time. It's too much thinking," Connor answered. "I miss hanging out with my friends. I miss staying in one place and being free to go places on my own. And I miss my family. I miss my dog."

"Missions are a lonely business. It's hard on grown-ups, so it's got to be twice so for you. So, what do you do to take a break?" Gray asked, adjusting his bandaged leg and scratching the area around it.

"I mean, I read and watch shows, but what else is there? I'm the only kid here. The kids who live around here aren't allowed at the hangar," he said.

"Well, you could play baseball. You'd have to get some people to join you and dig the equipment I brought out of the Brute storage," Gray smiled. He had brought the gear, hoping Connor could teach the Fringer kids the game. But that plan ended when it became necessary to hide him.

Connor popped up out of the chair that sat by the bed. "Really? What did you bring?"

"I brought wiffle balls, so you don't need mitts. And I brought a plastic bat and mats you can use as bases."

"Oh, thank you, O.G., thank you. I'm going to see if I can round up an evening game." Connor turned to dash out, but he stopped. "Want me to get you a chair and sneak you out of this box for a while?" He would talk with Jilly about Gray's condition, but he wasn't planning on asking her permission.

"Yes, I definitely want you to do that," Gray answered.

Connor was disappointed to find so many of the team members were either injured or on the road crew. They were due back around dinner, so a short five-inning game with four-player teams was scheduled in the hangar after dinner. Nash said the Brute and two of the minis would supply the light.

Connor left and went to Axle's room. He looked better than the last time he looked in on him, but he still hadn't woken up. He had moments when he stirred and rambled nonsense, but he hadn't fully regained consciousness.

Connor took his hand and spoke to him. "Hi Axle, it's Connor. I've come to sit with you and tell you what you're missing. Your brother is healing up, and so is everyone else. So, you need to get well, too. There's going to be a baseball game tonight. It ought to be fun and probably hilarious, too. No one but me knows how to play," Connor laughed. "You'd love it. You're looking a lot better, and—"

"Sounds like the kind of mess you'd get yourself into, kid," Axle said, slurring his words and rolling his head.

Connor pushed the call button, and Jilly came running in. Her expression changed from one of urgency and fear to a smile of relief.

"Welcome back," she said as she checked his current vitals. "Everything looks good, great in fact," she said, the last part quietly. "You sure took your time in slumberland. How do you feel?"

"God, I feel like— bad. It was a simple butt shot. What happened?"

"Well, you developed an infection. Probably due to the lengthy delay in removing that bullet. Here's the culprit," she said, holding up a small vial with a disfigured piece of metal. "Can you tell me exactly where your pain is?"

"My butt, my back, my shoulder, you name it, it aches," Axle said.

Connor went to excuse himself and asked. "Hey Jilly, do you mind if I go tell Gray his brother is awake?"

"I heard," came a call from the other side of the short wall. "I'm coming over," he said.

"The hell you are," Jilly yelled. Then she heard Gray laughing as he added, "Welcome back, brother."

"Good grief," came Beckett's voice. "What's a guy gotta do to get some sleep around here?"

Connor was laughing as he left. The idea of Jilly keeping these tough warrior beasts in beds and under control while they finished convalescing was going to be impossible.

"Good luck, Jilly," he said with a laugh.

The team came back when the sun was a dim glimmer on the horizon. Without outside lights, the mountain shadows cloaked everything in charcoal hues, contrasting the red wine horizon against the jagged skyline. Will was met by Nash, who suggested he park the vehicles outside.

"We're having a baseball game after dinner," he told Will. "We'll keep a watch on them and make sure they get brought in after the game."

Will secured the minis and activated the camera, which fed to a link on his tablet. He went through the door to find Connor walking off the bases and setting up the pitcher's square. Seeing Connor hard at his task made the event's instigator apparent. Having a game was a good idea. The team had been wound tight since Will and Connor went into hiding, and the battles had only tightened the coil.

"Good idea, Connor," Will said on his walk through to meet with Gray. "I hope you saved me a spot on the team."

"I was counting on it," Connor answered.

Will laughed. He had just spent a whole day on snow removal. He was exhausted, but not so much that he would sit on the sidelines of a competition. Gray had improved since he looked in on him that morning. The evidence that the biomites promoted healing at an accelerated rate kept piling up. It still didn't mean he wanted to infect everyone, but he did like the idea that his soldiers had that as extra protection. He wondered if their adversaries did also.

"What did the road look like?" Gray said getting straight to the point before Will even sat down in the chair.

Will respected that and didn't skip a beat. "In most places, we just packed the snow down enough for our tracks to travel over it. There were a couple of downed trees and soft spots, which we addressed. We couldn't clear the whole road, but we got over eight of the twelve miles travel-ready. I think we can get it finished along with clearing a place for the base camp by tomorrow. Then we can leave the following day. However, if we get a big storm, we'd have to reassess it all over again. Right now, the air pressure is rather high, but if it starts to drop, we'd better take off."

Gray nodded. "We planned on leaving tomorrow, but an extra day may allow us to all go at once. Do you think the Garries will attack before then?"

"I think they are hurting. We delivered quite a sting, but I also think they are waiting to see what we are after. When we find it, if we find it, I think we'll see they've been holding back.

Gray frowned and added, "We're not in the best shape either."

"Any change with Axle?" Will asked.

"He woke up, but Jilly hasn't finished prodding him. As far as being travel or duty-ready, he's not ready."

"Waking up is a good sign. When Connor had that respiratory infection, he recovered pretty quickly. Maybe Axle will too," Will whispered, so Beckett couldn't hear, "but tissue repair takes a lot longer. Worst case, the three of you follow up later."

"Hmpf," Gray responded. "I may not be able to help clear miles of snowy roads, but I can sit on my ass in a vehicle and bark orders."

"Well, I kind of promise Jilly," Will said apologetically, "that I'd be willing to split the team if her patients needed more time to heal."

"Without consulting me?"

"You were out cold, and I was in charge. Now, we are in charge, so I guess you could challenge that decision, or we could see if it's necessary. You might be healed enough that she clears you. Problem solved. No discussion needed"

Gray laughed. "Will, are you afraid of my wife?"

Will smiled. "Maybe a little, she has the knowledge and resources to lay us all low." They both laughed. "Did you tell Axle what we did yet?" Will whispered

"No, I didn't. Jax was with him, and he just woke up a couple of hours ago. Jilly said she'd take Beckett on a little outing when we wanted to talk with him."

"Anything exciting happen around here while we were gone?" Will asked.

"No," Gray answered, "the crew's been doing inspections and maintenance on the rigs all day. Theo took Tommie, Connor, and Dom to find plane panels to repair the damaged minis. Theo snuck up on Connor while Tommie and Dom were removing aircraft parts to fix our minis. In Theo's defense, Connor was wandering around the hangar on his own. Theo was probably just checking to see what he was up to.

"But last night, Relic scared the piss out of Connor. Connor snuck out at night to see the stars. Relic grabbed him and acted like he was a spy, telling him he could whisk him away in a mini and take him to the enemy. He ended his little performance with a warning that Connor needed to be more careful."

"Shit!" Will said, surprised. "That doesn't sound like Relic. Do you think—"

"I think he was testing Connor's behavior due to his biomites. Besides, if that were true, he missed his chance to whisk him away. This morning was his time to watch him, but he sloughed his duty off on Dom. I think he was trying to impress upon Connor the reality of his situation. Connor's jumping at his own shadow now."

"Do you think we've become complacent?" Will asked.

Gray shrugged his shoulders. "I think I need to reiterate the security protocols as far as Connor is concerned. They shouldn't have let him go off by himself. And Connor knows better, so he needs a reboot too."

"I'll take care of that," Will said.

"No, we'll address the troops together. I need to get out of this bed. I can't command when I can't see what's going on."

Jilly and Jax came in wheeling a cart full of dinner trays. "Dinner's here," Jax announced over the partitioned room. They walked into Beckett's section.

"You are cleared for real food," Jilly said as she unlocked the legs of Beckett's bed tray.

"Finally," Beckett said, looking hungrily at the venison steak and vegetables before him.

Jax was with Axle, and Jilly went to sit with Gray.

Jax shook Axle gently, waking him from his sleep. He stretched and sat up as she placed the broth and gelatin on the swing table. "I have dinner for you. You need to eat something. Sorry, your diet will improve tomorrow. Jilly wants to see how you do after a day of easy food."

Axle rolled his eyes after seeing and smelling the meal his room-mate was served. "There is nothing to suggest eating will be involved with this stuff. I guess starving me is part of my treatment. How about sneaking me some real food, honey?"

"Don't you dare, Jax, or I'll assign you to all the med clean up," Jilly said from behind the partition wall.

"You're on your own, Ax," she responded instantly.

After dinner, Jax helped Jilly settle Beckett in a wheelchair to get out of his room, so Will and Relic could talk to Axle.

Relic gave a lengthy explanation that Gray could hear from the next partition. It was the first time Axle had been told about the biomites. It was a lot to take in. He was quiet for several minutes, or maybe it just seemed that long. Axle looked at the ceiling and spoke to his brother on the other side of the wall. "You were in on this?"

"Yes, I was. Will came to me in the middle of the night. It was right after Jilly gave me a dire update on your condition. She said she started you on a stronger antibiotic, dunked you in ice baths several times, but it was touch-and-go. She had nothing to do with this.

"She wanted to wait until morning to see if the antibiotics kicked in, but I didn't want to risk it because we could only give you a small dose of Will's blood. It would take time for the little guys to build up and do their job. Hell, it was less than a month ago you were fighting your way back from another serious wound. If you're mad about it, be mad at me. I made the decision."

Again, a long silence filled the medical room.

"I'm not mad. I would have done the same thing. In fact, if you get so much as a scratch, I might infect you myself," he said, only half joking.

"Too late. I got a bigger dose than you," and Axle remembered that Gray received a transfusion from Will.

"I guess we're brothers by blood now," Axle said.

"Nothing could make you more or less my brother Ax, nothing," Gray replied.

"And Will, blood brother, I believe thanks are in order," Axle said, reaching out his hand for a solid shake.

Connor didn't need to sneak Gray to the game after all. Jilly set Axle, Gray, and Beckett up at the large window in the lounge. All three of her patients were improving, but she wasn't ready to trust the biomite's speedy work. Though Beckett didn't have the benefit of quick healing biomites, he had benefited from her professional care.

A couple of game rules were put in place to minimize any additional injuries to the team. No sliding into bases. A straight run through would count as safe on any base. Though Gray, Axle, Lana, and Connor were the only people fully familiar with the game, Connor was the only one playing. Lana was keeping score and being the umpire. For everyone else, it was their first attempt at playing the complex game of baseball.

It was more slapstick comedy than exciting, and everyone laughed most of the way through. But it was more than a game or a comedy show. It was therapy. The team needed to release the pressure that had built up since they left the Fort. It had only been eight days ago, but so much had happened. Their nerves had knitted themselves into knots that were stretched to the breaking point.

The next morning, three of the minis were fully charged and ready to go. The mini with the roof issue had been an easy fix, but the door damage to the other vehicles would take some time. All but the injured and those repairing the Brute, whose door hung on by three straps, were sent to prepare the rest of the road. Relic joined the team to view the second half of the road and calculate the avalanche dangers. But he was excited to get a look at the mountain in question.

Dom and Theo stayed to work on the damaged mini and its bigger cousin the Brute. Gray and Axle went over plans and scenarios while the teams were gone. They reviewed the roads that they had sabotaged, as well as those that were just too dangerous at this time of the year. It would be extremely difficult to get a large army through the series of blockades they had positioned between them and the tunnel, the Fort, and the Fringer towns. But it wasn't impossible. They had a limited window before those places would be overrun by massive militant forces trying to hijack and stop this mission.

And then there was their dilemma. They were cut off. The road they came on was blocked, and the road out of town ended at a vast chasm caused by a meteorite. Soon, their foes would clear the demolished ramp and come storming down the road into Aspen.

"Dom said they were armed and ready for a fight with the small force of Garries they had left," Axle shared. "But what if more show up? Their numbers may be more than we think."

"I'm not sure they could get more troops here that quickly. RH told Will that most of the ones we'd have to deal with were already on this side, living in old Corporate towns waiting to be activated. They had vehicles stashed here waiting for them. I guess more could have come by foot, but that's quite the journey at this time of the year. I'm more worried they will use their old hostage tricks to hijack Fringers," Axle warned.

"Will also said the Guard is positioned to protect the Fringers as long as they aren't overrun with a large number of soldiers, and that's true of New Haven too," said Gray, "but it's a lot to contend with. Yet, we have to have faith they will hold the line because we need to focus on our mission. And while the weather is holding, we need to leave."

"I agree," said Axle. "So, do you guys have any idea what we will find at this Cali Bantu place?"

"We need to get Connor in here," said Gray, and he waved at Connor through the window, hitting whiffle balls in the hangar. The boy stopped and walked to the office.

"Well, the first challenge will be finding the entrance," Connor explained. "After that, we have to get inside. If, I mean when, we accomplish that," said Connor, "I expect we would search for the next clue, or the item. Then we'd decide what to do next, or perhaps we will be given instructions. At each step, we will be tested to ensure we are the intended recipients."

"Why not just tell us what we need to do? Why all the mystery?" grumbled Axle.

"The mystery surrounding this place is not a game or forgotten lore," Connor asserted. "I was taught specific ways to problem solve, that's the test, what I don't know is if my grandad lived long enough to teach me everything I need. We have to prove who we are. If we can do that, I believe that the founders will show us what to do."

"I agree that what Connor says makes sense, but we're still stumbling in the dark here. We can go over all the clues a dozen times, but it comes down to what Connor remembers. What if his memory doesn't get triggered?" Axle let out a breath and clasped his hands while leaning back in his chair.

"I am not worried about that. We just need to get him there with a fair amount of supplies, and he'll get to work on the entrance," ordered Gray.

Connor was dismissed, and Jilly was called in to give her report on the team's health.

"As far as combat and hard labor, Dom, Beckett, and you two," she said, pointing to Axle and Gray, "are still on the recuperation list. But that's an upgrade from the serious and critical lists from just a day ago. I have discovered these biomites are not only handy for healing but tracking the patient's progress. When healing is complete, the biomites are reabsorbed, and their numbers decrease. For instance, Tommie's steadily declining numbers indicate that her head injury has completely healed. With the density counts, Relic and I have compiled from everyone infected, I can tell the state of a person's health."

"Though Dom has not been exposed to them, his stitches are holding, and he shows no signs of infection or nerve damage."

"So, have you checked our counts today?" asked Gray.

"No, but after this meeting I planned to."

"Well, I officially call this meeting over. Let's go let her do her vampire thing," Gray smiled.

The results showed Gray's and Axle's biomites had leveled off, meaning the repairs were peaking and close to completion. She expected the numbers would be slightly less tomorrow as the biomites were slowly absorbed until only a standby force is left. Beckett's biomites were down considerably, and his wound was well-sealed. He is at the end of the repair cycle for his side wound.

Now, as long as the two crews, sent in different directions, don't bring any new injuries back with them, everyone will be cleared to travel tomorrow.

Chapter Twenty-Five

I t was almost lunchtime, and Gray, Beckett, and Axle were all sitting in the lounge. Becket had used a walker, but Gray and Axle were wheeled in, at Jilly's insistence. Several aeronautical charts were lying on a table between them. These maps had all the common features, but they also included numerous symbols to indicate airport size and designation, crosswinds, flight paths for landings and take-offs, and the range of the airport's Inertial Navigation System. The INS was a device that used sensors to continuously calculate, by dead reckoning, the position, orientation, and velocity of aircraft within its domain. Although it wasn't functioning, the formulas for calculating it were provided.

Gray was given extra copies of the area for drone operations, as well as a booklet that explained all the symbols. The drone group would pull sweep duty and provide the best defense should the enemy catch up with them. Without any knowledge of the type or nature of the armament Cali Bantu might provide, their plan needed to rely on what they had. And drones were their best and least dangerous way of attacking their adversaries.

Building a base camp was necessary, and with their camouflage resources, it would take time for the Garries to find their encampment. But as a stationary target, the enemy would locate them and deliver a barrage of weapons and casualties. It was the most unfavorable part of their plan. The hope was that they would somehow be able to shelter inside this secret place or have instant access and control of the weapon. Gray shook his head. They were flying blind, and he could only hope the enemy was just as uninformed as they were. It was an interesting dilemma with both sides fighting over an unknown.

"In our last conversation, we were debating whether we should booby-trap the road to the mountain. If we destroy it, we're trapped. If we trigger an avalanche, we're trapped. If we blockade them out, we're blockaded in," Gray cautioned.

"We're already trapped," Becket groaned. The three nodded.

"It's hard to plan for the unknown. I mean, we could make plans for several scenarios and use a code to distinguish them and their details. Like the kind we used at the Hold. It gave the target, action, and expected friendlies or hostages. It let us know who we were confronting and how far to take the order," Axle chimed in.

"I like that idea," Gray told his brother. "I want a plan from each of you by 3:00 today. Develop a way to explain it, as well as what it would require."

"Okay, now the only question remaining is, who is going to make us infirmed gents some lunch?" Beckett asked.

All eyes were fixed on Connor.

"Typical," Connor said under his breath while rolling his eyes.

Another Aspen local joined Connor in making a venison soup. She went to a walk-in freezer and grabbed a frozen block of stock. Connor had done a lot of cooking when he was a Daily, but he had never heard of stock. The tunnel had great stores of freeze-dried broth, but not stock. Both boil down vegetables and spices, but broth adds meat to the mixture, or in the case of the Daily's—protein powder, and stock uses the bones.

The soup was excellent. Their cubed wild game meat, sundried vegetables, and wild rice made it hearty and added just the right touch, but the stock made it incredible. Connor brought a tray of soup bowls and bread to the lounge, where Dom and Theo had joined the others. He also took a tray to the medical lab for Jilly but found her fast asleep. He covered the large bowl of soup and bread and put it in the refrigerator for her. When he returned to the lounge, a conversation had evolved around the fine art of food storage techniques.

"I remember," Axle shared, "when Bannon told me how his dad inherited this large freeze-dryer system. His dad was a Corporate, but he was trusted by the small business owners. This guy manufactured food processing equipment and was trying to sell him one, but Bannon's dad said all he needed was a small one. The more aggressive Corporates wanted this guy's whole inventory, so they grabbed control of his company in a hostile takeover. The owner just disappeared, and Bannon's dad couldn't find him.

"But two days later, this huge state-of-the-art appliance was delivered to Vogel ENT. It was the guy's best, newest, most expensive model, and this was the only one built. It had twenty sections, allowing large quantities of different foods to be processed at the same time, and it was quicker and more efficient than his previous models. Bannon's dad had no use for it, but he hid it in one of his warehouses, assuming it contained some innovative designs that this businessman didn't want the Corporates to have."

Gray bristled at the discussion, and his mood quickly turned bitter, making him anxious. Axle assumed it was his hatred of the Elites, but Gray was sickened by the information Will told him at the lake. He imagined filets of human remains being fed into the freeze-dryer and coming out as brown protein powder supplements for the Dailys. All Dailys mixed it into their meager food rations because without it, they'd starve. But they had no idea what kind of protein it was. His fists were clenched as he vowed to end their cruelty.

"I'm kind of tired," Gray said as calmly as he could. "I'm going back to my room."

"I'll push you, O.G.," Connor said. "I wanted to see if Jilly was ready for her lunch yet. She was asleep when I tried to take her some."

"Thanks for watching out for her while I've been down and out," Gray said as they rolled down the hall to the med lab.

"My pleasure," Connor said.

The day moved slowly, and Gray fell asleep while waiting for the security team to come back with their report regarding the enemy troops.

"Sir," Dom said, leaning on a cane Jilly found for him. "The Recon team is back."

Gray turned and rubbed his eyes. "Yep, okay. Tell them I'll meet them in the lounge. Ask Axle and Beckett to join us. And Dom, could you find me some crutches? I'm tired of maneuvering this chair around."

Dom reappeared with a pair of metal crutches with cuffs at the wrists. Gray grabbed them and hoisted himself up. It had been a while since he stood on his own, and he immediately sat back down.

"You need some help, sir?"

"Nope, just practice." Gray stood up again with more stability this time. He quickly developed his step-swing rhythm and made his way down the hall. Entering, he thwarted their comments about his vertical position by talking first. "Let me have what you found."

Nash went first. "The Garries are camped three miles back and on foot. We checked the ravine for signs of scouting soldiers, but there weren't any tracks beyond the camp, and the only sizable heat sigs we detected turned out to be a Shiras moose."

"They probably know we are trapped, and they can take their time. You are sure it was an animal?" Gray questioned.

"Well, let's just say, we packed quite a bit of meat back for us and our Aspen friends," Easton smiled. Gray thought back to the disorderly teen he recruited into the Defenders away from his overprotective mother. Not everyone adjusted well to military command, but Easton was thriving. He had become more than self-confident. He was an indispensable member of the Defenders. His unfettered loyalty and motivation to learn had earned him a place on this mission before others of higher rank.

"We parked a drone in a nearby tree to listen in on their conversations," said Nash. "Assuming they didn't expect us to do this, and their discussions were genuine, they plan to trap and ambush us as soon as we locate Cali Bantu. And they said Cali Bantu. So, they know about the place, but I didn't get any indication they know what it holds."

"Well, let's hope that's true," said Gray. "Are they in contact with HQ?"

"No," said Nash. "They were discussing ways to send a message back to Glenwood. They have some kind of communication relay network from there. They are definitely short on people. They lost five more soldiers in the explosion. They didn't mention their wounded, but the enemy in this kind of setting sees soldiers with serious wounds ad having outlived their usefulness. Their numbers may become more compromised as time goes by.

"They did infer they were waiting for reinforcements from the Fringer towns. But the last storm compromised the roads significantly. I'm not sure how much cooperation they will get from the locals to clear a road they don't rely on. One thing they discussed with disdain," added Nash, "is that they didn't believe the Corporates would care enough to send them reinforcements."

Gray agreed they wouldn't care about the lives of the people, but it was unlikely they'd let this prize slip out of their hands.

"I'm worried about what they will do to the Aspen locals to force their cooperation since we're gone," said Easton.

"I was told by Will that they have a couple of rotary guns in the tower. Plus, it would take a lot to pry open one of those hangar doors. If they're smart, they blow past Aspen and focus on us," said Gray. "But Aspen's guns use the same caliber as our minis do, so we'll leave them some extra ammo. Anything else?"

The two nodded. "Okay, when the road crew gets back, we'll meet again. Ax, Beckett, and Dom, I want those plans we talked about ready for this afternoon. Nash, Easton, nice work today."

Will's team returned at 3:30, stating the road was passable to the base camp site at Maroon Bells Lake. They discussed the plans for preventing the enemy from reaching them or Pyramid Mountain long enough to secure whatever was hidden there.

That evening, Will, Gray, and Theo sat outside drinking Aspen Mountainshine. The stars were vivid, and the Milky Way was so dense, it was like looking through the rings of Saturn. Exhaustion and strong drink were taking their toll, letting their mouths run a little more than normal while marveling at the view.

"Did you ever think that maybe we are chasing some stupid myth that just got more traction than it deserved. I mean, what if we get there and it's something completely unhelpful, like sage advice about peace or something?" Gray offered to the sky.

"Well, that would be mean," Will said and took another pull of the fiery liquid.

"Even I've heard the tales of Cali Bantu," said Theo. Will and Gray were startled that he knew the name. "People 'round here are deep into the stories about their kin going down that road and not coming back. And those that did come back, which was years later, I might add, were as close-mouthed as a lock-jaw dog. But as they aged, they would disclose things here and there to loved ones before they passed.

"My dad went looking for my grandpa several times. He was gone when my mom died from a pregnancy complication. I was left alone and passed around the townsfolk, waiting for him to return," Theo said, and tugged on the jar.

"I thought you had an uncle," Will probed.

"He was my dad's close friend, but not blood. He was good to me and taught me a lot, but after a couple of years, he decided the best help he could give me was finding my dad. He went looking for him and came back as winter began, and then in the spring, he went up there again. It was the last time I saw him. I was thirteen and tried to follow him, but he had fallen from a rock ledge and died. I found him two days later. Next summer, my grandpa came back, but he was sick, and died a month later. We expected people to come beat the details out of us long before now, but you're the first to visit here."

"Did someone take you in after your uncle/friend left?" Gray asked, thinking about how much loss he had suffered.

"No," Theo said, looking into the darkness of the road that caused him so much heartache. "I was pretty self-sufficient by then."

"Did your grandpa ever tell you anything?" asked Will.

"No, he didn't tell me anything, except that the right people will come, and we need to help them. A message came to Etcher's dad saying you were those people, so we're helping."

"How did the message come to you?" asked Will.

Theo shook his head, "I don't know. But I'm not real happy about the angry army heading our way while you skedaddle off," his walking fingers demonstrated the act. Theo took another swig and seemed to gather his courage. "But we've been ready for them for a very long time, and from the sounds of it, they aren't much of an army, more like a punk gang, " he laughed. "I can't wait to meet 'em."

"Don't underestimate them. They have some weapons of their own, and I don't think we've seen their worst. They need us alive, or we'd be in rougher shape," Gray said seriously, though his sobriety was fading.

it was an early turn-in with everyone in bed by 10:00. Gray refused to sleep in his medic bed and went to cuddle up with Jilly in her twin. It was the first night since the road attack that she slept nightmare-free. Morning was moving out day. Everything was charged, packed, and ready to go. And though they weren't pretty, the damaged vehicles were repaired and charged.

Jilly felt amazing after their two-day respite, but it was time to get back on the road. Powdered eggs, cured wild game, and strong tea from the locals made a hearty breakfast before they trekked off to make base camp. The roads were mostly cleared, but several treacherous sections would require careful navigation and the use of winches. The expected time frame was three to four hours to get there. Much of that time would be used to set the traps along the road. Once there, it would only take thirty minutes to set up the camp in the place that had been cleared by the road crew.

Soon, goodbyes and last-minute item packing were underway. Theo rushed out and talked with Relic.

"What did he say?" asked Will.

"The air pressure is dropping," Relic relayed. "We've got a storm coming."

"Great," said Will. He raised his voice and yelled, "Move out. We have a storm brewing."

All sixteen seats were filled in the five-tracked vehicles as they made their way to the climax of their journey. The town roads had been nicely groomed, and the views of the surrounding mountains were spectacular. Before they turned down Maroon Bells road, the crater where downtown Aspen once stood came into view. Though the pristine snow covered much of its charred remains, the devastating strike was evident and met with the stunned faces of those seeing it for the first time.

The turn took them into a beautiful canyon well frosted by the winter snow. It was spectacular in beauty, but all that sparkling snow had a cruel side because snow and slopes mean avalanches. Though they weren't as common in the autumn as they were in the spring, this canyon checked off several warning signs. Very steep angles didn't collect much snow, but slopes with 30 to 40 degree angles, like many of these, have just the right slant to build up a lot of snow as well as send it screaming down.

It didn't take a large event to release its energy. Any sudden change, like heavy snowfall, warm temperatures, or a single person crossing a sloped field, could set off a chain reaction resulting in a tsunami of crushing snow, carrying away everything in its wake. But so far, no snow was falling, and no wind was howling.

Jilly was happy the trip would be much shorter than the last few. Her patients should endure it well. And they should arrive at the base camp with plenty of time to set up before needing to cook dinner. Gray and Will, however, were pondering more pressing issues.

Talks about splitting up the team had become unnecessary due to the injured members' quick recoveries and the restrictions she implemented. Though the healing mites inhabited the bloodstreams of half of their team, the jury was still out as to how they would behave or be received when they had the prize of Cali Bantu insight. Would they suddenly be forced to surrender to Corporate control?

This dilemma weighed heavily on Gray as he rode in the Brute. He listed those with and without mites in them. Those with mites included Will, Jedi, Nash, Mack, Tommie, Beckett, Axle, Gray, and Connor. And those without left only Dom, Jax, Easton, Lana, Relic, Etcher, and Jilly.

The thought of his pregnant wife in a battle was untenable, but him fighting against her, unthinkable. It only hardened the reasons he didn't want her to come, but being right didn't matter now. It was too late. And as intolerable as all those thoughts were, the idea that any force on Earth could compel him to kill his people for the Corporates was immeasurably worse.

As Gray's mind chased the shadows of what could be, Jilly was breathing a sigh of relief that the team was together, and the ride wasn't through jostling her patients or herself. Yet, she had her own worries about what lay ahead. She wondered what expectations awaited them when they arrived at this mountain. Would they be required to go on rigorous hikes or climb icy cliffs? Connor would be required to go, but she believed they would give him all the help he needed. But as a member of the team, she feared that she too would have to scale cliffs and trudge up snowy slopes. Though they'd help her, it was one more way she was a burden.

Perhaps the more athletic soldiers could scope out the area first. It didn't seem like time was on their side, so that was probably a pipe dream she quickly put away. However, she thought, as her own devil's advocate, if everyone went, too many would require assistance.

She sighed to herself. Stubborn warrior types in recovery were becoming a common and annoying worry for her. It was unlikely she could convince these competitive men to acknowledge their limitations and decline to participate in the culminating part of the journey. She knew Gray and Axle well enough to imagine how that would go. They would roll their eyes at her request and be willing to go fist-to-cuff with anyone who stood in their way.

Gray's fierceness, competitiveness, and protective nature were the very traits she loved about him. But they were also the traits that made him throw logic out the window and drove her mad. Alas, it was a fruitless battle, and she had to accept that she had no influence there. Her best bet was to work out an alternative plan that didn't involve them ripping out their stitches and bleeding out. Not knowing the tasks before them meant considering numerous scenarios. Although her medical training was stellar, her engineering knowledge was limited. Maybe Relic could assist her.

The slight sound of the wind caused her to look up from her reverie, and she gasped. Snow was swirling in large leafy flakes, collecting on every part of the evergreens guarding the roadside. The outdoor drama took over her previous thoughts, and she was riveted to the event playing outside.

Rain makes a rhythmic sound, creating a constant signal of its intensity. And wind is boisterous, demanding attention. One doesn't have to see rain or wind to register their presence, even if it's just background noise. But snow conducts a quiet assault. It is easy to turn one's back while it deepens and traps the unaware. The wind was audible now, picking up the frozen scales and whipping them across the windshield, as the sudden gusts swayed their vehicle like a ship at sea.

Chapter Twenty-Six

W ill and Connor sat in one of the minis, bounding down the snowy road behind the Brute. It was a rougher ride than the bigger vehicle, and louder too. For most of the ride, no words were spoken, but the silence wasn't uncomfortable. It allowed them to take in their surroundings, both beautiful and dangerous. Connor appreciated the engineers at New Haven and their noble attempts to recreate the outside world in the tunnel, but it fell far short of replacing it.

The trail of vehicles curled their way through the gorge as Will carefully observed his surroundings and the instruments before him. The temperature and air pressure had dropped since they left, and Connor could tell the growing storm had him worried.

"Is the weather going to prevent us from reaching the base camp today?" Connor asked.

"I don't think so," he answered. "See the triangle on the map? That's us moving down the road. The two blinking lights, one behind and one in front of us, are the beacons we set on the road to tell us where we are. The one behind us marked the halfway point, and we are approaching the three-quarters mark."

"So, we should be there within an hour or so?" questioned Connor.

"Something like that. It gets slower the more snow we have to deal with, but I can't see us stopping when we're less than four miles away," Will said.

Connor decided to change the conversation to something less ominous. "Will, if you had the choice between a life of freedom out where the Corporates wouldn't find you, or this life of fighting for a cause in constant peril, which would you choose?"

"I think that is what you would call a left-field question." Connor smiled at Will's baseball reference and the correct use of it. "I did have a life of unfettered freedom, and I left it. After I escaped the Neighwah, I lived in a secluded forest cabin for almost two years. I was free because everyone who knew of me thought I was dead. I hunted, fished, built furniture, baked, canned, and lived a life without battles or people. It was nice, for a while."

"What made you give it up?" Just when Connor thought he knew this man, he discovered more.

"Injustice," Will said while Connor handed him a sandwich from their lunch. "I saw boys forced into Dranger jobs where they were trained to be ruthless or die. I saw women and children stalked and kidnapped for the Corporate brothel in Pueblo, and men murdered trying to protect them." He hesitated after saying that, and he looked at Connor. But the boy waved off the issue. All Dailys were aware of the horrors females and children faced. Will continued.

"I couldn't stand by, so I got involved. But I have long thought about why I stayed after I had secured the Fringers in towns, and the Corporates promised they would not attack them."

"Why would you believe anything they say?" Connor scoffed.

"Let's just say we discovered a secret they can't afford to have exposed. And that is nothing you should know, so please don't ask," Will said, giving him a stern side glance.

"Okay, so why *did* you return to the chaos?"

Will thought for a second before he answered. "I could say I didn't believe the secret would be managed well, but that wouldn't be the whole truth. I found that I love the adrenaline rush of danger and the challenge of command. It's exciting to look the reaper in the face and send him packing. It's especially rewarding when my leadership results in making life better, freer. But with victory, there is always a price, and it's usually high, like killing.

"Setting sights on a person and pulling the trigger takes a gruesome kind of courage, the self-righteous kind, chipping away at the very civility it attempts to save. And after the dust settles, I have to look at the man I became in those moments, callous and determined. And no matter how justified difficult decisions are in the thick of battle, it's painful. That pain is never more real than when I look into the eyes of those who lost people they cared about because of my orders and my actions."

"Is there no way to reason that out?" Connor asked. He remembered Gray, Axle, and Dewy's difficulties dealing with Hannah's death that went beyond missing her. GD told him that good people, especially those in power and involved, tended to take excessive responsibility for all the what-ifs of hindsight. They slap their soul around without even a nod at the courage they exhibited amid the turmoil. Connor understood, feeling the weight of his teammates' injuries on his shoulders.

Will could see Connor was working through his thoughts, and he assumed they were on the same page, so he continued with his introspection. "It's a paradox for sure. It would be easy to say the cause is what compels me forward. I've even justified to myself that retaining command spares others the heartache, but I don't think that's completely honest. I will probably continue to seek challenging situations even when, or if, this war is won. Maybe if I experience enough danger, it will one day bring me peace. Or perhaps I will receive an injury, be it physical or emotional, that is so great, I will not be able to continue. Maybe then I'll be forced to find peace."

"One of these days, that peace may come in the form of everlasting peace," Connor said, raising his brows at the thought of losing him. "Doesn't that scare you enough to want to stop?" It scared him for Will and everyone, including himself.

"Maybe it should, but then I wouldn't be a very good warrior. But I do want peace, and sometimes, I believe it's just around the next bend. But one bend always begets another because the world of humans is inherently volatile."

"That's very profound. A warrior's philosophy?" Connor said reverently.

He turned and smiled. It was a smile reflecting the moment's connection, genuine and thoughtful. His hard mantle retracted, giving a rare glimpse at his tender side. It was kind and warm... and happy. Connor wished he could capture that moment, but within a slice of a second, Will was back to business, all unbreakable and self-sacrificing.

Connor sat in the silence, appreciating how fortunate he was to get to know such an epically heroic and iconic man. As they moved down the trail, he lamented the eventual loss of such a remarkable human being. The world is better for him being here, and it will experience a profound loss when he passes from it.

"How long before we get to the base campsite?" Jilly asked from the second row of the Brute.

"We just passed the third beacon a mile ago. I'd say we're closing in on the last two miles," Jax answered. "Are you feeling okay?"

"Yeah, I'm fine. Just curious," Jilly answered, and though she was curious, she felt far from fine.

Though it was two in the afternoon, visibility was barely ten feet, making the trip take much longer than projected. Jax had been on the road clearing crew yesterday, and she had done her best to memorize the road as well as where the creek was. Being the third vehicle helped, but she knew better than to blindly follow the vehicle in front of them.

They arrived at their destination, but the gentle, falling flakes that started their journey had transformed into a vicious blizzard. Setting up the camp would be a miserable experience of battling the wind and stinging cold. Jilly would have an even tougher task keeping Gray, Beckett, and Connor in the Brute. Thankfully, Will took that situation out of Jilly's hands.

"Jilly, Axle, Connor, Beckett, and Gray, your jobs will involve working on the inside clasps," Will ordered over the intercom.

"Since when—" Gray began, but he was cut off by Will's commanding voice.

"Since I'm in charge by our medical authority, there will be no persons on crutches, with stitches, pregnant, or shorter than five feet, allowed outside during the storm without supervision," Will ordered and continued to list off the rest of the instructions and tasks.

Jilly could feel the anger radiating off of Gray. But even he had to see how ridiculous going out in this weather on crutches would be.

"There's plenty of work to be done in here," said Jilly. "Help me unlatch the benches. This middle one can be folded up into a table, and this chair needs to be turned around to face it." Gray glared at her. "Okay, fine, I know how. I'll do it myself," she said, knowing that would get him bounding up. Of course, it came with snarls and grumbles, vibrating a warning to everyone nearby.

"I'll do it," Gray said through gritted teeth.

She didn't respond. She didn't need more snappy comments, nor did she wish to rub what he saw as a demotion in his face. She opened the cabin access doors where the sleeping gear and cooking items were stored. She and Connor dragged them out and set them on the table. Their gear, food, and other supplies would have to be unpacked from the minis and delivered to them.

The large open space of the campsite allowed all but one of the vehicles to be joined together. It would conserve the heat they needed because the temperatures were expected to drop dramatically once the storm clouds cleared.

Everyone had their lunches on the road, and it was too early for dinner, but a snack and a warm cup of tea would keep everyone going. Jilly got to work bubbling up a large pot of water and setting up biscuits and honeyed jams. The only setup task left involved setting out the teams' personal gear, which was still being unpacked from the minis.

"Are we worried about avalanches here?" Connor asked Relic in an ongoing conversation as they brought in the bundles of bedding with Jedi directly behind him.

"Yes," he replied, "it's always a risk when there are covered slopes. I calculate the level of risk with an inclinometer. I measure the amount of snow and the angle of the slope. Where C is the bottom of the slope, and B is where the debris will accumulate, one can find the safe zone, A. Then I factor—"

"Relic, we all trust that you worked it out logically, and we thank you. But I'm too worn out for math class," Jedi chimed in as he grabbed a biscuit off the table and left to get more items.

"I was listening," Connor said with sincerity as he leaned toward Relic. "It sounds like the trigonometry problems I was studying before I stopped going to school."

"When this sky clears enough to see, I'll show you how to calculate it."

The shelter was completely set up, as the snow continued to pile up at an alarming rate. They were relatively safe from the path of avalanches, but that was without Relic's final calculations. Yesterday, the avalanche danger was low, but the recent and current snowfall was creating instability. However, the more urgent threat was their shelters being buried, one more thing for those on watch to monitor.

Two cling-drones were hung yesterday on trees nearby, providing a visual of the road to spot approaching troops, but when it was deemed improbable that they would be attacked during the storm, one was turned to watch the closest slope. Clear blue skies greeted them in the morning along with bone-chilling temperatures. Snow blocked the shelter doors, causing several troops to clear off the tops of the vehicles and climb out to clear the entrances.

Breakfast consisted of hot farina with cinnamon, walnuts, and honey, and it was served with a strong caffeinated tea. Everyone listened to the orders of the day and set out to tackle them. The sun did little to challenge the frigid temperatures that assailed them, but no one hoped for a warm day because slipping snowbanks would be much worse. They were surrounded by snow-flocked trees and craggy rocks that peaked out of the pristine snow, all set against a deep blue sky. All threats aside, it was breathtakingly beautiful.

Gray sat with his arms crossed. Everyone but he and Jilly had left the shelter.

"Jilly, I know you have my best interests in mind, and your training says I need more time to heal. But look," Gray said as he stood up and took several steps in the cramped space. "See, I barely even limp. I think these mite things have healed me substantially quicker than your training suggests. I'm asking you to sign off on my clearance. I mean, you cleared Axle quickly enough, and he was touch-and-go, too. Now, I agree, I shouldn't overdo it, but this sitting around is going to kill me."

"Well, Axle's issue was with an infection, not a wound, and he was only cleared for light duty. Mind you, it's only been a few days since you woke up, but I agree," she said, leaving Gray wide-eyed in disbelief. "I wish we had more room for some physical therapy," she said, looking around at the bedrolls and gear, which left very little floor space.

He was so happy he wouldn't have to fight her for his freedom, he grabbed her and kissed her. "You know, maybe we could engage in some physical therapy that doesn't require us to clear the bedding away."

She laughed, and before she could dismiss his untimely suggestions, a blast of cold air hit them as Beckett, whom she had already cleared for light duty, came in to drop off more items. As Beckett went to leave, she asked him to send Will. Within minutes, the tall figure crouched through the shelter door, bringing in another frosty draft.

"I need your assistance for a few minutes. I want you to test Gray's leg strength. I need to know where he is physically before I decide the limits of his clearance." Will nodded and removed his overcoat. "Will sit here. Gray, lie down there. Now, slowly push your foot against Will's hand as he pushes toward you. Tell me when it starts to hurt and when you think you should stop. And please be honest."

That exercise, plus others, proved that he was ready to take short walks without crutches several times a day. With that, Gray immediately dressed up and went outside. He was greeted by cheers as well as jests about the hard-ass being back. Axle was brave enough to make a remark about his 'mommy" letting him out to play, which earned him a stare of promised retribution.

Three groups were putting on their gear to check out Pyramid Peak and scope out possible entrance points. Will was leading the one with Connor, Etcher, Tommie, and Jedi. Nash would lead Relic, Mack, and Jax. Axle and Dom were tasked with the dangerous, but physically easy, duty of driving down the trail to attach more clinger-drones and check for signs of the enemy.

That left Gray, Beckett, Jilly, and Lana at the camp. Jilly and Lana rolled up the bedding and made lunch for the remaining crew. Gray and Beckett took on readying the weapons and setting up Relic's weather station away from the shelter, where they hammered the snow depth measuring sticks down to the soil level. With the shelter chores done, Lana was given time to sit in the Brute and write a journal entry. Jilly inventoried her medical supplies. The well-oiled machine of the team's efforts created a calm setting.

Suddenly, the stillness was interrupted by an ominous rumbling, and a cloud of white mist billowed from further down the road, where over half of their team members were.

Chapter Twenty-Seven

Will, Connor, Etcher, and Jedi walked down the mountain path, bathed in the light of a golden sunrise. The frigid air crept into the tiny gaps of their heavy gear and chilled their lungs with every breath. The planned hike was not long, less than two miles, but it was all on snowshoes, which took twice as long and required significantly more energy. Both teams would be driven down the road on a sled pulled by one of the two minis not used for shelter. At the fork in the trail, the two teams would separate to search for the entrance.

Mack, Jax, and Relic were assigned to find the meteorite scar illustrated in Deegan Chance's painting, as well as other clues. Will's team was on a more difficult journey to find a stone monument Etcher told them about. She said it looked like a lighthouse tower and was created to guide the souls who didn't come back to eternal peace. It sounded like one of the castle clues Connor solved, making it a likely clue to locate the entrance. The new snow would make searching difficult for both teams, but Connor was excited.

He was anxious to see the meteorite scar, and he felt it should be visible by now. He concluded it was covered with snow, but the painting depicted a monstrous gash that no amount of snow could hide. They just needed to find the right angle to reveal it. They made several rest stops due to the difficulty of the snowshoe trek, especially for their youngest traveler, before they reached the rickety bridge they had to cross. Connor reached into his pocket and grabbed the small bag that held his cross. *Give me courage, Lord.*

"How about I cross first and tie a rope to hang onto?" Jedi offered with Connor in mind.

"No," Connor warned. "This could be a clue. It's like the bridge to the castle. I have to be brave."

Etcher looked at the preteen child, trying to steel his nerves to cross this broken bridge over the icy water rushing below it. "I've crossed this before," she said, "but I used a rope, and that was during the warm months. I've never done it in the winter when falling in is more likely. This bridge is pretty shaky, and if you go in, you could end up in the lake, trapped under the ice," she said as she pointed to the icy body of water just past the crossing. "How about I go first?" she suggested.

"I don't know if it would break the knight's code, but I don't think I can risk being deemed unworthy. But maybe someone could stand downstream to grab me before I'm carried into the lake?" The boy requested. "That's not cheating. It's just smart."

Etcher stared at Connor like he was speaking nonsense while Will climbed down and got ready to charge into the frigid waters at the mouth of the river. *How could they let him risk his life because of some fairytale drivel?*

Connor handed Etcher his snowshoes, bent his legs, and spread his feet apart as he cautiously inched his way onto the contraption. He was a third of the way when, suddenly, a board gave way and tipped, causing him to slide toward the edge. He quickly grabbed a post, which he hugged as his feet dangled off the side. He took a second to collect his courage and got back up. The bridge righted itself as soon as he stood on the high side of the board. Slowly, he began again, and little by little he edged to the other side.

He bent down, leaning on his knees. His only thought was that he had to cross it again to get back. Maybe a rope would be okay then, since he had already proved himself. Using a rope and avoiding the loose board Connor had revealed, everyone made it across, and it was agreed that a snack break was in order.

Will picked Connor up, holding him in the air, and spun him around. "Dude, you have got balls made of granite. That was impressive," Will exclaimed while others agreed and slapped him on the back.

Connor blushed at the attention, but he too was pleased with his accomplishment, and especially how he had worked up his courage. He explained to Etcher, whose questions began to flow forth, that he had been taught to read many symbols and codes, but he stopped with that.

Before they took off to find the monument, Will took him to the side where they wouldn't be heard and asked, "I guess I should have paid more attention to your castle story. What comes next in the knight's creed?"

"Well, that test was about being brave. Next comes be true, wise, gracious, then skilled. I assume they will be in that order, since the castle was," Connor whispered.

They were all exhausted by the time they reached the mound of snow that Etcher said was the monument. Connor asked her about the meteorite scar.

"I never saw anything like a meteorite scar, but this monument is at the head of Crater Lake. It's frozen now, but it's right there," she pointed to a small open area of snow about a hundred yards south of them.

Connor laughed to himself. *Nothing can be straightforward. Every clue takes analysis and creative interpretation, and it just leads to the next.*

It didn't take much time to dig it out, but underneath the fluffy new snow was a layer of ice that clung to the nooks and crannies of the form. Will got into his pack and pulled out his torch and pickaxe.

Connor was instantly alarmed. "So, defrosting this should not do anything to break the creed. The stone won't burn, but don't use the ax. It would be a problem if we broke it somehow," Connor said with trepidation. "It might destroy our next clue or trigger something. We have to get the codes right to be invited in and shown the secrets hidden there."

"Good to know," Will said, as he lit the torch and began carefully freeing the stone from its icy prison.

As more of the snow melted off, Connor gasped," It's a tower with spikes and turrets!"

Will smiled. There were five knights' creed clues, and they had discovered two already. At this rate, they'd have this weapon by dinner. When he finished, a castle tower stood about four feet tall. Connor walked up and studied it. The eight spikes had letters signaling the four base directions as well as the intermediate ones. The N spike already stood correctly at north. The whole tower appeared to be made from a single piece of stone, but the turrets. They were tightly nested on top. He tried pulling, pushing, and turning the north spike, but it wouldn't budge. He had to think.

Examining the tower carefully, he saw it. The southeast symbol was chiseled higher on the spike than the others. When Connor grabbed it, it pulled up. He let it go, and it fell outward, toward the mountain. Tucked under the lip at the top was an arrow pointing straight at a dark crop of trees at the bottom of the slope.

Connor motioned Will over and whispered, "On the castle, I used light to 'pull wisdom from darkness.'" Will nodded, and the two rejoined the group.

Will detached the laser scope from his rifle. "Two of us need to go over there, and the other two need to stay here and point a laser exactly in the direction this arrow is pointing." Connor was looking in the direction they would be traveling to detect any hint of an entrance, but nothing looked crafted by humans.

"Connor and I will go look for the next clue," Will said. "Let's go. Maybe we can knock this thing out before we have to go back."

It was a short distance, but it still took time with snowshoes. They signaled that they were ready, and a red beam shot across the ravine. The trees were too thick for the beam to penetrate, but Will and Connor used some twine to extend the line. It landed on a large stone covered by a bramble bush.

"I had a fort when I was a kid," Will said. "We attached a living bush to a board so it could swing out. When it was closed, it was undetectable. It was from a story Tianna told me as a kid." As he spoke, he threw the bush to the side, exposing a dirt hole. Will crawled in first, and Connor followed, wondering if using the light of the laser to reveal the path qualified as a wise move. The space grew bigger as they made their way forward, but then it ended.

They looked at each other, tracing their lights all around. Connor's light flashed on something small and square at the very edge of the cave wall. It was a box. He opened it carefully, and inside it was a child's treasures. A top, a book, an old nickel, and a baseball. Connor picked up the baseball.

"This is exactly what I would expect GD to leave for me to find. Maybe it was why he taught me so much about baseball," he said as he put it back in the box.

Will was about to speak, but Connor held up his hand. "Brave for the bridge, true for the path, wise for using the light, so this is about being gracious," Connor said.

"Maybe we should donate something to the box," Will said, "like an offering."

"I can look through my pack, but to make this a gracious offering, it has to be precious. Not valuable, precious," the boy said. He reached into his pack and pulled out a picture of Hannah. Will could see it pained him to give it up.

They waited for a few minutes, but nothing happened. Will shook his head.

"I know what it is," Will said. "It's this," and he held up the Sanguine Blade. "They want this."

"I don't know. That is precious to us all because it is the key to... something. Besides, what if you need it to prove your skill?" Connor answered.

"Being gracious means surrendering *to* something. To be giving and selfless, such an instant requires trust." Will slowly set the blade in the box and closed the lid.

At that moment, the cave shook, and the bush-covered door slammed shut. Will ran to it and pushed, but it held fast. Another sound came from the back of the cave wall, and light poured into the small space. Silhouetting the door were two machines, robots. They had sturdy cables and hinges attached to metal arms and legs. And they were armed to the teeth. Will grabbed his sidearm, shoved Connor behind him, and shot at their foes.

Will stopped shooting when they ricocheted off them, leaving them untouched. Will stood protectively in front of Connor. He didn't stand a chance against such mechanisms, but he stood ready to fight anyway. He backed Connor up, trying to retrieve his blade, but he felt the child crumple behind him. Will felt a sting on his neck and then dizziness. He tried to steady himself against the rock wall to edge himself to the box, but before he reached it, he succumbed to unconsciousness.

Chapter Twenty-Eight

Will woke up in a panic. All his protective gear was gone, and he was down to his boxers and a T-shirt. As he came to full consciousness, he realized they had Connor, and... He stopped. They were robots! And they had the Sanguine Blade. In a blurred state, he rubbed his eyes. His hands came down on a comfortable bed in a pale peach room. Looking around, he found Connor, curled in a ball and covered with a blanket. Still dizzy, he staggered over to his young charge.

"Connor," he said as he shook him. "Wake up." The boy began to stir. "You okay?"

"I, I guess so. What happened?" he answered, looking down at his minimal attire. "Where are we? Did I see robots?"

"Yeah, that's what I saw. I'm not sure where we are. Were there any clues that Cali Bantu would be run by robots? If they're on our side, they have a funny way of showing it."

"The blade?" Connor remembered. "Did you get it?"

Will raised his brows and shook his tilted head. Feeling steadier now, Will examined their accommodations. The temperature monitor on the wall read a comfortable 70°F. First, he tried the door, locked. On the same wall was a small table with two clear glasses and a clear pitcher of water. Slices of fresh lemons floated among the rounded balls of ice, making his mouth water, but not enough to trust it.

Next to it was a plate of fresh strawberries and two small biscuits. An open door on the opposite wall gave sight to a bathroom. Will gestured for Connor to stay put, and he walked in, finding the expected shower, toilet, and sink. Along with a basket of toiletries and towels were two clean outfits on a hook behind the door.

Connor moved toward the food, but Will stopped him. "They drugged us once," he said with a look of warning.

"And they did it without us eating anything. While we were out, they could have injected us with whatever they wanted. Feeding us poisoned food doesn't make sense. I think if this is Cali Bantu, they would have to make sure we aren't Corporates soldiers. And if they are enemies, they want us alive. I still think this is where we will meet our ultimate ally. But besides that, I'm hungry."

Will envied his innocence, and he hoped he hadn't failed miserably by delivering him to their enemies, whether they be the old ones or a new bunch. However, he had to admit that Connor's logic was sound. So, he'd wait to make a move, mostly because he didn't have one. Then a voice came over a hidden speaker system.

"Welcome, Connor and William. You are safe. We have provided refreshments to replenish you. After you have eaten, please proceed to the bathroom to use the shower and put on the outfits provided for you. We will see you soon and answer your questions."

Connor smiled at Will with belief pooling in his eyes. "Did they just imply that we stink?" Will jested, trying to ease the mood more for himself than for the untroubled child before him.

"Can robots smell? " Connor played along. "Anyway, it's been over two days since I took a shower. So, as long as it's warm, I'm in. I'll go first."

Will jumped up. "Let me check it out." Seeing Connor's sarcastic glance, he said, "Humor me."

He gave a closer inspection of the pristine but starkly furnished bathroom and couldn't find any dangers. He flushed the toilet and deemed it harmless. He turned on the water to the sink and the shower and felt it with his hands. It quickly warmed to a comfortable temperature. He dispensed a dab of the provided wash in his hands. It was creamy and mint scented. No skin irritation appeared. He left Connor to wash up, but he left the door cracked, so he could hear any call for help.

Soon, Connor sat on his bed, enjoying the feeling of being clean again. The medium blue jersey pants and bright white shirt were extremely comfortable. He sighed as he put on the white socks and shoes that snuggled his feet. Will came out, adjusting the drawstring on his tan linen pants while Connor took note of the scars on his torso. He wondered about the stories they told and whether he wanted to hear them. Will threw the long-sleeved cream-colored Henley shirt over his head and set to putting on his socks and shoes.

"They never tested us on the last clue, skill. I guess I can expect that it is still important, and we'll be tested regarding it."

"I believe you have already shown your training and your skills. You have demonstrated your abilities by safeguarding me, both in the cave and in this room."

"They are going to be looking for us," Connor said.

"I'm counting on it," answered Will. "In the meantime, have something to eat. I tried it while you were showering, and it seems safe."

As they finished the food, a noise came from the door.

Pyramid Peak Base Camp

Nash's team had made their way back to camp. And everyone was waiting for the other scouting team to return. They had all heard the rumble of snow.

Axle's voice suddenly shouted over the radio, which they were told not to use. "The enemy is heading our way. Position yourselves!"

Jedi's voice responded, "We can't leave! They went over to check on something, and we lost them!"

Nash replied, "You lost who?"

"Will and Connor," Jedi answered.

"Shit, okay, we'll deal with that later. But for now, find shelter. And get off this radio."

Jedi and Etcher plowed through the thick brush, but they could find no entrance, just footprints that stopped in front of the thick vegetation. They decided to hide in a different area where they could keep an eye on the bushes and the road.

The team at the base camp lined up behind the shields they had set up within minutes. Then they waited, and waited, but nothing came.

"They weren't that far behind us," Axle said. "They should have been here by now."

"The clinger drone at the one-mile mark doesn't show any record of them passing. They're planning something," Gray said. "We need to send scouts out on foot along the ridge."

Axle volunteered and took Mack with him. Mack was stocky, tough, and he was a superb archer, and this was a job for fast hikers and quiet weapons. Axle reported that he felt fully recovered. And even though Jilly disagreed, this was a combat situation.

The two of them took off up the treed slopes bordering the road. Between the half and the three-quarter mile markers before the base camp, they spotted them. They were lying still on the road, every one of them, dead. Was it the Aspen locals? Why would they track them all the way up here? And where were they? Or was this the work of a new enemy? The strange ghost stories the locals told were suddenly more concerning.

Cautiously, they climbed down to the road. Giving every soldier a rapid check, they detected no breath or pulse. But there wasn't a wound to be found. There was no evidence of shell casings or blood trails to show they had fought back. Whoever, or whatever it was that hit them, they were instantly lethal. The only clue was the odd square prints left at the scene. Though the dead deserved a better resting place than being strewn all over the road and hanging out of their vehicles, that would have to happen later. Axle had to report this immediately.

They quickly made their way back to camp, clinging to the slopes and hiding in the trees. The enemy they knew had perished, but the enemy they did not know was somewhere close. They hoped it wasn't at base camp, eliminating their teammates. Peering from their perch, they saw their new foe holding the whole team captive. Three people were lying on the ground, unmoving. It was then they heard the click behind them. When they turned, they saw two formidable metal adversaries, and slowly, they raised their hands.

Cali Bantu

A different kind of robot came to retrieve Will and Connor. It was more human-looking, except for its lavender covering. It had arms, legs, a torso, and moved like a human. Its face had gentle features, moving lips, and clear expressions. Between its smooth panels, they could see glimpses of hinges and cables as the machines moved.

"I hope you feel well and rested. I am S3. My supervisor regrets not meeting personally. We also apologize for your initial treatment by the cydroids, but assurances of who you were had to be made. We also needed to rule out the presence of harmful mites or computer viruses. Please follow me," said the soft-spoken robot.

"If we have been cleared, why do they still shadow us?" asked Will, pointing to the two robots marching behind them.

"The cydroids are a precaution against that which is unknown," S3 answered.

Will wondered if they had found the mites in both him and Connor, and whether their teammates were banging down the cave door trying to rescue them. So far, he had only seen two cydroids at a time, but that didn't mean there weren't more.

They were led to an off-white room. Delicate, green images of leaves gracefully laced the walls and moved gently as if the sun beamed through a breezy day. Two light grey sofas faced each other at an angle, with a triangular table nestled between them. Lavender sprigs arranged on the table lightly scented the air. A large, deep black screen took up a significant portion of the wall in front of the seating, contrasting the soft pastels decorating the rest of the room.

"Please be seated," S3 requested with an emotionless calm.

Will was getting frustrated with the sterile environment and interactions. He was quickly losing his trust and patience. S3 left the room, but the cydroids stationed themselves at the two doors and collapsed down on their hinged legs, shortening their height considerably.

Connor and Will looked at each other in silence. He could see the skepticism in Will's eyes. It was his job to protect him, and he felt like he was failing. But Connor was intrigued. He was excited, and he was building a list of questions he needed answered. The answers, as well as the way they were delivered, would tell him much. He was sure that somewhere in his brain was the training that would advise him whether this race of robots was friendly.

The screen came to life, and they stared at two human images. One was a woman. She had a kind, pale face and white hair. As she walked toward the camera, they saw her captivating grey eyes, which were hard to look away from. She wore a tunic of pastel sage and lilac in an abstract watercolor pattern. The flowy material danced around her as she walked, while her grey leggings showed off her trim build.

The other wore the stereotypical garb of a college professor from another time. His tweed jacket, open collar shirt, and jeans were crisp but casual. His thoughtful face and trimmed beard were topped with dark, curly hair, which was on the edge of being unruly. Both looked like living art, representing people from a past era. Connor was captivated, but Will wasn't caught up in their images. He wanted to talk to a living person. He was getting more and more skeptical of these imitations of humanity.

"Greetings, and welcome to Cali Bantu, William and Connor," said the woman. "Before you ask your questions, my colleague, Pente, will give you a brief history of our project."

The professor-type man, Pente, took the center screen position and proceeded. "31.7 years ago, a dense cloud of space debris hit the Earth in an assault that lasted seven days. Dr. Seger predicted five years earlier and presented his data to the scientific community, but the warning was not heeded. The scientists from around the world believed him, but the current governments were too occupied with their political power plays.

"As the date of the strike grew closer, nations feared being conquered, and the panic of survival kicked in. The governments and their scientists cocooned themselves in their little worlds, crisis managing preparations for their citizens and waiting for the event to unfold.

"Of the twenty leading scientists from the US, two specialized in robotics. One, Dr. Peter Petroff, worked with micro-sized robots that could be injected into small places to assess and repair delicate instruments. They had plans to use them to diagnose seriously ill patients and address their conditions. He called them biomites.

"The other robotic specialist was Dr. Nadia Bera. She designed robots to assist humans in accomplishing physical tasks. Her plan included building thousands of service drones to perform tasks that people could not perform while the atmosphere was contaminated. These drones would gather, construct, and repair resources, provide medical care, and maintain supply chains until the atmosphere settled.

"Once the first several hundred drones were assembled, they would be programmed to produce more of themselves, exponentially increasing the necessary force, allowing many communities the means to survive.

"There was little opposition to the necessity and objectives of the service drones, so factories began to manufacture them immediately. Her plan included specialized drones designed to provide security, healthcare, laborers, and educators.

"The type designed to maintain civil order and protect against invasion generated intense conflict because they were the only drones allowed to harm humans and, in extreme cases, take their lives. Due to the nature of the protective drones, as well as who would manage them, a consensus on their protective duties was never reached. But they were built just the same.

"Dr. Bera continued to move forward with the plan. She began by developing the software for the Cyber Intellect programs that would manage and maintain the service drones. The first Cyber Intellect program developed was for service, since they would take over the construction of the rest. Five advising Cyber Intellect programs were created, each with its own specialized androids and cydroids and a vast library of information required to assist humans in decision-making.

"Doctor Bera named her creations after Greek numbers. Ena, one, is an expert in protection and law enforcement, Dio, two, specializes in the care and preservation of human life, and Tria, three, maintains the infrastructure and resources. Tessera, four, was constructed to preserve the history, art, and cultural aspects of humanity, and my program, Pente, meaning five, embodies the knowledge, histories, and philosophies of governments and the foundations of countless societies.

"The Cyber Intellects, which I will refer to as C.I., were not designed to govern. Their function was to advise and facilitate the interactions of the communities and restore the infrastructure needed for a thriving society. They could labor in an environment that was toxic to humans, and preserve democracy even though the environment was in turmoil.

"When the plan to create thousands of robots was leaked to the public, fundamentalist factions arose. They destroyed many factories and most of the drone inventory. Doctor Bera was seriously wounded, but she survived, and instead of going to a hospital, she escaped to this private location with twenty service drones and copies of the C.I. programs.

"She had always worried the objectives of her project might be compromised, so she withheld several critical components of her software as well as a few of the algorithms required for continued function. She also diverted numerous truckloads of resources here during the three years she worked on the project. She had already loaded her personal hard drives with all the historical and procedural information needed to complete her work, so this location is not part of any network.

"Over the next two years, the service drones began transforming this cave into an innovative underground headquarters. About ten years ago, Dr. Bera was killed when a tunnel collapsed. The meteorite impact on Aspen caused several geological shifts as the Earth attempted to settle. Though she did not live to know the full extent of the natural disaster, she correctly theorized that her plan would be abused if she disclosed the final pieces of her creation.

"It caused her a great deal of emotional anxiety. She debated how to set her plan into motion, one community at a time, but she did not complete those plans. Her final orders have allowed us to continue her projects, but we are not programmed to implement new orders without human leadership."

"Why didn't this cydroid force follow through with the plan?" asked Will.

"We are not programmed to proceed without human authority, which needs to be approved by her. You are the first humans to visit us since she died."

"Can I order you to do it?" he said as a follow-up.

"Your clearance has not been approved."

"How can Dr. Bera grant me clearance if she's dead?" Will spoke plainly.

"That procedure will be explained," said Tessera, rejoining the conversation.

Will was visibly tired of the circular discussion and changed direction. Focusing on the woman on the screen, he asked, "So, are you the humanity android? Are you Tessera?"

"Yes, I represent the philosophy, art, science, and all that is creative and uniquely human."

"How will creativity, art, and history overthrow the Corporates? How will you overtake your sibling, Ena, who has the militant program?" Will was standing now.

"That will be discussed at a later time," Tessera responded.

"What happened to Dr. Petroff?" asked Will. Connor looked at him oddly, wondering why he thought that was important.

Pente, answered him. "Although he escaped, it was later discovered that he never made it to the Safehouse."

"Why is the Sanguine Blade the key, and how do we use it?" Connor shouted, hoping to direct the questions to what he thought was the most critical.

"And where is it?" Will demanded, unknowingly clenching his fists.

"Your inquiries will be addressed when your teammates join us and receive their initial briefing. We are currently gathering them for transport," Tessera answered too calmly for the words she spoke. Suddenly, the screen switched to a view of their camp where dozens of cydroids were herding the team into a windowless transport. Will and Connor were stunned.

"Do not fear. We will not harm them, but they must be examined before they are allowed access to Cali Bantu," Tessera responded.

"What of the Corporate enemies who are surely on their way?" Will grumbled with an angry scowl.

"That concern has been eliminated. As I said, I hold centuries of philosophies, including the philosophy of warfare," she said.

"Just how big is your philosophical army?" asked Will.

"That is a question for later," Tessera responded. "You have absorbed enough for now."

Chapter Twenty-Nine

Base Camp

Maroon Bells

Dozens of two-legged industrial armed robots surrounded the base camp. No shots were fired, but the threat of violence emanated from both sides. The robots stood out in the open, undaunted by the flesh-and-blood soldiers huddled behind their barriers. Relic crawled over to where Gray was stationed, aimed and ready.

"You cannot defeat these machines," Relic told Gray. "Please don't make any aggressive moves."

"You know of these robots?" Gray asked with indignation.

"I believe they are called cydroids. Until now, I thought they were forgotten pre-strike technology because the No-Techies destroyed them. However, if they are Dr. Bera's machines, they possess very precise targeting systems and a relentless determination to complete any mission assigned to them. And they are almost indestructible. They were designed by the original group of scientists who gathered to organize the post-disaster nation. The fact that they have not killed us means that their controller wants us alive. We should find out why."

Before Gray could decide his next move, the cydroids began to tighten their circle around them.

A robotic voice from one of the cydroids spoke. "You are surrounded. Surrender your weapons. We mean you no harm."

"Stand down," Gray yelled.

As soon as Gray gave the order, the team threw their weapons down and came out from behind their barricades with their hands raised. Gray was thankful that he had hidden Jilly in the storage area of the large Brute. He wasn't sure what she would do if everyone was captured, but at least she would be spared their fate if this went badly. If all turned out well, he could retrieve her when he knew it was safe.

A large track bus pulled up with Axle, Mack, Jedi, and Etcher already inside. The rest of the team was ushered into the transport, and they took their seats, waiting for the robots' next move. When Jilly was escorted onto the bus, Gray swore under his breath and whispered to Relic.

"Whose side are they on?"

"Not sure yet. It may be ours. This is exactly what they would do until they can establish who we are. I say wait, not that we have a choice," Relic said quietly.

"I need to get some answers. Like, what do they plan to do with us, and where are Connor and Will? If I ask them some questions, will they answer me?" Gray whispered back.

"I don't advise it right now, and I doubt they will answer you. That being said, you can believe whatever they tell you. They are incapable of lying. Let's wait until we have more intel before we try anything."

Jilly was seated in the front of the bus, with a cydroid squatting next to her. She sat facing forward and didn't look back. Gray conceded they were effectively captured, but he knew every soldier on this bus was thinking the same thing, escape.

The covered bus stopped, but they had them traveling blind, so Gray did not know why or where they were. When it started back up, the lumbering bus crept over a small rise. *Was there another bridge besides the precariously dilapidated one Etcher described?* He hadn't been able to talk with Jedi or Etcher yet. All he knew was what he heard on the radio that Will and Connor were checking on something, and then they were gone. He wondered what Will and Connor had stumbled upon that triggered these cydroids to emerge. He made a mental note to ask Etcher if she or anyone else had ever seen these cydroid things or heard stories of them.

Though the journey was quite bumpy, Gray was immersed in strategies and racking up questions while he keenly observed their captors. He was alarmed when, at their next stop, the cydroids began the process of ushering them out of the vehicle and into a well-lit cave. The rock enveloping them wasn't a natural cave. It was honed with machine-cut walls and a level concrete floor. On the walls behind and in front of them were great sliding doors that could accommodate the large vehicle they arrived in.

What is going on here? How is this Cali Bantu? Gray was losing his patience. He wanted to walk over and comfort his wife, but the less information these things knew about their connection, and how vulnerable that made him, the better. She seemed to have come to the same conclusion because she never turned to look at him.

A soft voice came from speakers somewhere in the stone space. It did not have a robotic sound like the cydroids. It was gentle and kind with a tone that might evoke trust if the circumstances weren't so hostile.

"Welcome to Cali Bantu. Please be at ease. No harm will come to you. Your safety is important to us," stated the calm, pleasing female voice. "After you are screened and cleared, we will answer your questions. As I call your name, please line up in front of the door. Jedidiah, Gretchen, Mackenzie, and Nashville."

Gray was startled that they knew the full names of his team without having asked them any questions. It meant they hacked the database on the Brute. With alarm, he wondered what else they knew. He watched helplessly as four of his comrades were escorted to who knows where for some unknown procedure. He eyed the two remaining robots guarding them with disdain. Fifteen minutes later, four more cydroids lined up near the door.

"Jaxine, Easton, Alana, and Milo," the voice called, and they were led through the ominous door. Gray remembered that Beckett said he hated his first name, Milo, and he made him promise not to reveal it. Gray hoped it wasn't because he was on some Corporate wanted list.

A single cydroid came in.

"Johnathan, please follow the cydroid."

Gray wasn't the only one who looked confused when Relic went to the door. "Johnathan" was called to go by himself. Gray was fully aware of this man's extensive knowledge and fugitive status. Gray moved toward him but was blocked. Relic gestured for him to sit back down. This was untenable. He was powerless to do anything as his friends were led away.

"Dominque, Tomina, Axle, Grayson, and Jillian." The last of the team stood and lined up obediently.

As they made their way into the hall, Jilly and Gray were separated from the others. The other three were brought to a room where they were instructed to remove their clothing down to their underclothes. They stood with legs slightly apart and arms out as three different devices scanned them. Dom was cleared, but the devices reacted to Axle and Tommie with alarms and flashing lights. Axle knew they had detected the mites. The last machine took a small drop of blood from everyone, and they were led to a clean, white hall with a seating area.

Axle and Tommie were led down the hall and through a door that closed behind them.

Gray and Jilly heard the voices of their teammates as they passed by their exam room, but they weren't sounds of pain or distress, just conversations. The cydroids stopped at a door, and the couple was guided into a tranquil waiting room. It had not escaped Gray's attention that everyone in this last group had been recently injured, except Jilly. But if they had hacked the files, they would know she was pregnant. He felt the knot in his belly squeezing ever tighter.

He expected the scanning of his soldiers to take a bit of time, but all three came back out rather quickly. Dom came in and sat down, followed by Axle and Tommie.

Trailing Axle into the room was a different kind of robot. It was more human-looking with arms, legs, a torso, and a delicate, light green covering. It simplistically imitated a human face, as much as plastic could, but it was able to speak with its mouth and show mild expressions.

Sections of its legs and arms were covered with protective casings. Its torso sported a breast plate that resembled a human's chest. Gray noted the D4 insignia in the upper chest area. At every joint or pivot point, hinges and cables were exposed whenever the machines bent their joints. It spoke with a feminine timbre, as its mouth and facial expressions moved in a realistic human manner.

"They just took a couple of scans in this tube thing," said Axle as he took a seat by his brother. "It took our vitals and scanned our injuries. They said our mites were benign and Tommie and I were healing well, but Dom needs some physical therapy."

"Jillian and Grayson, please follow me," said the android in her soft, soothing voice, which was beginning to grate on Gray's nerves. When they were secured in an exam room, it continued. "I am D4. Please, relax while we evaluate your injuries and present conditions. We have an advanced facility here that can address the status of your health."

Gray sat with a protective arm around his wife. He hated that he was powerless to save her. His thoughts went back to the moment he found out she was going on this mission, and then finding out she was still pregnant. His anger was as pointless as his attempts to tamp it down.

"I am sensing you are in a highly agitated state, Grayson," the android said with its annoyingly tranquil tone. "How can I assure you we only want to assess your health?".

"You can prove whose side you are on," he said, taking a defensive position in front of his wife.

"I shall attempt to comply with your request," it said. Then it stood still and quiet for several seconds. "It has been approved."

"What's been approved? How? By whom?"

Within moments, Will and Connor walked in. Connor made a direct line to Jilly and hugged her. "It's okay, Jilly," Connor said. "They won't hurt you."

Jilly noticed the casual wear they had on. She had never seen Will in non-combat gear. It did a lot to soften his warrior appearance.

Will followed up, "They have provided us a lot of information and asked for none. There are still many questions they need to answer, but we have been treated well."

"After your exams, they'll probably make you take a shower and put on clean clothes," Connor said to Jilly while smiling to ease her worried expression.

"I wish I had more to report," Will said, looking straight into Gray's eyes.

Gray understood that it was code for not knowing what was going on, but to stand down and wait for a signal. Will briefly shared what he learned, knowing they would probably see the same audiovisual they had. It didn't go unnoticed that the android did nothing to discourage their conversation.

After Will and Connor were escorted out of the room, D4 asked them to get undressed to their underclothing and step into the scanner. Gray stepped into the clear tube first.

"Grayson—"

"I know you will find the mites in me, but they aren't in my wife," Gray was trying to direct their attention to him and away from Jilly.

"Grayson, you carry a form of restorative biomites, and though the biomites have repaired your damaged blood vessels and tissues, your leg muscles are in a weakened state. You require physical therapy to restore your leg completely. This shows you have received a blood transfusion from William. Your blood volume has returned to normal levels. "

"What can you tell me about these mites? Did you disclose the mite information to the others?" asked Gray. He felt his attitude and opinion soften as the android displayed only honest and helpful information.

"The biomites in your body are beneficial and not programmed for behavior manipulation. William told us his concerns regarding the emotional response it may cause, so we have not revealed the information to anyone who received them except you and Axle," D4 answered. "Jillian, please enter the scanner."

"Your son is at 12 weeks of gestation. He is developmentally healthy; however, you and your child are underweight. You require more protein, iron, and calcium. Your diet will be adjusted. You are moderately sleep-deprived and need an appropriate physical exercise program. Sleep and activity schedules will be arranged. We advise you to discontinue traveling on lengthy expeditions, especially on rough roads. It can cause heart palpitations and dizziness, contributing to a decline in appetite."

"Can I ask some questions about the mites?" Jilly said apprehensively. "I want to know how they can be transferred and if they will harm my baby."

"We performed several tests already and have established they possess positive health benefits. The answers you seek require further testing. Such tests are already scheduled. We will have the results to you by tomorrow morning."

"Does that mean you will be keeping us here?" Gray asked, trying to compose himself and get some information, but the reveal of his child's gender did not escape his attention.

"You will be here while the plan is finalized," D4 said matter-of-factly.

"What plan?" Gray demanded. For all their sweet tones, they were being held captive, and that was a hostile act. How long would they be held here? Aspen may be under attack. He didn't know what was happening to the rest of his team, or where Relic was.

"Tessera will explain soon," D4 stated.

He did his best to appear unworried for Jilly, but he knew she was smart enough to figure out their situation was precarious. They were shown to their assigned rooms, where they took showers and put on the clothing provided. Before they could have the conversation they wanted, they were led to the screening room with the others to view what Will and Connor had already seen. Everyone was accounted for, except Relic. He was still missing. When Tessera and Pente came on the screen, Gray stood up.

"Where is Relic, or the one you call Johnathon?" Gray noticed the cydroids stationed around the room rise into ready mode.

The image of Tessera turned to Gray. "After this presentation, you will be reunited with him. He is unharmed. He has been assisting us as we devise the plan." Gray bristled at the thought of Relic sharing information about Will, Connor, or the blade. He had known him for less than a month. *What if he was a traitor, and he had led Connor right into this trap?* The cydroids indicated no more questions would be taken, and Tessera proceeded with the presentation.

After the presentation, they were led to the dining room and served the evening meal by three light pink androids with an S and a number on their left torso. They were told there were five different divisions, and each had a team of android workers. Their colors denoted their affiliation. Green were medical; the pink were service; the lavender were culture; the blue were history, and the charcoal grey were security.

The meal was individually and nutritionally balanced, though plain in flavor, but the fresh fruit for dessert was a rare treat. Though they were promised Relic would join them, dinner ended, and he was still unaccounted for.

S3 called for the team's attention. "I require William, Connor, and Grayson to follow me."

Gray began to object, but Will stopped him. "I believe this is where we get to see Relic and hear the plan. I for one want to hear it without being shackled," he whispered.

The three of them walked out of the dining room, led by a lavender android, labeled T7, and followed by several cydroids, to the screening room. They found Relic sitting on one of the couches.

"Relic, we were worried. Are you okay?" Gray asked.

"Yes, I have been updating Tessera and Pente on the state of our territory and beyond, according to the reports I was provided," Relic said.

"Do you trust these things?" Gray scrutinized his friend to see if he acted differently, looking for signs he was compromised. The jury was still out.

"The only information they asked me was what I knew of the state of the outside world," Relic shared. "Their system is isolated. Their network is self-contained without access outside this facility. Their precautions regarding outside cyber influences are quite thorough, but I suspect their available network is massive."

Tessera came on the screen. She was so graceful that she seemed to float to the forefront. Her appearance was soft and elegant, and she moved like a lithe dancer. But Gray didn't have time to fall for her passive appearance. He wanted answers.

"Thank you for your patience. I apologize for our enigmatic greeting and for causing you concern for the one you call Relic. As a resident of the Highmind Camp, we needed to ensure he was free of surveillance apparatus or Corporate allegiance."

"How can you confirm our loyalty?" Will inquired.

"Initially, we ensure one is free of manipulative biomites. Then we monitor physical responses to various environments, stressful situations, and dialogue. Humans have limited control over their responses, and our highly sensitive instruments can detect the slightest delineation from truthful answers and locate the part of the brain and body it originates from."

"If you are supposed to help us, where have you been?" asked Gray.

A collegiate man in a tweed suit and jeans walked onto the screen and stood next to Tessera.

"Hello, I am Pente, and I can answer all your questions about historical references. As you heard in the briefing, we have limits. Dr. Bera isolated us from all other networks to remain hidden, and therefore, our knowledge of the logistical and human status of the territories was unattainable. We were able to observe the cosmic event from an encrypted satellite that fed information to a quarantined terminal. We estimated that over twenty-nine percent of the world's population perished from the week-long meteorite storm, and twenty-seven percent of the survivors died from the effects of disease and civil inadequacy.

"Our satellite was designed to appear obsolete and offline, but it was destroyed when the same No-Techy faction that attacked our robotic facilities began their assault on the satellites. The surveillance capabilities of the orbiting equipment were what concerned them, but those same stations were also used for communication and the scientific observation of Earth's condition and atmospheric recovery. The loss of satellites set what was left of civilization back to primitive equipment and inefficient communication.

"With the information we acquired from Relic, it is clear that more than a year passed before the group was pursued. By the time the Corporates eliminated the faction, their efforts left a dense debris field orbiting our planet, which interferes with signals and continues to disable more satellites.

Tessera continued the explanation. "The Corporates began to fear the presence of Highminds among them and forcefully apprehended them. The Uppers, as you call them, have been led to believe their lavish lifestyles are dependent on the innovations of Highminds, as are the Elites. However, the Elites are not human and do not desire or need human proclivities.

"Only three of the five Cyber Intellect programs, or C.I., belong to the Elites. Two of the C.I. directors are blocked from participating with humans, as well as the C.I.'s ongoing discussions. Dr. Bera realized that every decision did not require the attention of the full panel, so she allowed the C.I.s to exclude unnecessary directors on an individual basis. She did not foresee that they would permanently block certain advisers.

"This allowed them to gather the Highminds under the notion that they required protection. Something my program and Pente's would not have allowed. The Elites seek order and dominance over their illogical charges. They detain the Highminds to prevent them from organizing the workers in a revolt. The Elites' main agenda for the Highmind camp is to access the encrypted cydroid software and gain control of them.

"The Corporates currently have several thousand cydroid drones, but they are all inactive. Commanding the cydroids requires human orders and the proper codes. It is unlikely they have destroyed them because Ena sees them as the means to achieve the goal of domination. They seek order and dominance over their illogical charges. They detain the Highminds to prevent them from organizing the workers in a revolt.

"The Corporates currently have over a thousand cydroid drones, but they are all inactive. Commanding the cydroids requires human orders and the proper codes. It is unlikely they have destroyed them because they see them as the means to achieve their goal of domination. Dr. Bera placed dramatic flaws deep within their software programming. Hidden anomalies prevent the robots from following the orders of non-humans or unauthorized persons. Another dark code prevents them from assembling more of themselves or being disassembled. Even destroying them is costly and problematic."

Gray put up his hand for a question. "Why don't they just build their own robots?"

"The Cyber Intellect programming prohibits the creation of any kind of device without the direction of humans. If they allow humans to build robots, the humans would have control of them. The C.I. is limited to advising and researching.

"All orders involving aggressive and violent actions are under the jurisdiction of humans. The closest they have come to directly injuring humans themselves is their utilization of manipulative biomites. The recipient signs a waiver that includes the clause 'I allow myself to be redirected for the benefit of the human species. They are then promoted with the belief that they will be living in extreme luxury. Other humans administer the injections and train the biomites to stimulate a response when certain brain cells are activated, along with negative emotions. That allows the human handlers to use both pain and pleasure to control their subjects by mere suggestion.

"It was undisputed that, after the meteorite strikes, resources would be limited, and the people would be forced to make heavy sacrifices for generations. The statistical predictions concluded that using a human workforce would endanger them and take many decades to restore society to a marginal state. Humans, we have found, tend to be uncooperative when exposed to extended stressful conditions.

"By utilizing robotics, the reconstruction progress would be faster, and humans would receive better care. The science of robotics was making incredible gains, but not fast enough for the plan. That was when the Highmind experiment was initiated, and the camps were established to enhance and accelerate the process. After the robotic program was terminated, they turned into prisons.

"Since the Elites still feed and house the people, they are still implementing their primary programming: to preserve the human species. And they have maintained the C.I. programs that specialize in security, infrastructure, and health, but the program fell apart when they deleted the programs delineating lawful governance and the cultural aspects of humanity.

"These programs were deemed illogical and problematic. Their analysis, though logical and stabilizing, is flawed because humans are not logical. They can be unstable and self-destructive, but these traits are part of humanity. The C.I.s' job is to advise humans with instant, unbiased resolutions and clarifications, allowing them to decide how to protect their species. Their right to self-determination, even if it leads to their self-destruction, must be preserved.

"The plan, simply put, is to reinstate Dr. Bera's proposal and restore humanity by reprogramming the Elites to return to being C.I. advisers, not Elite leaders."

"If what you say is true, how are you in command of these cydroids? You obviously have the *sophisticated*," Gray used air quotes to emphasize the word, knowing the gesture was lost on the programmed image, "code required to imprison *and* harm humans. Those Corporate soldiers lying dead on the road prove that."

"They are not lying on the road, and they are not dead," Tessera said, using the same air quote gesture Gray did. "Nor are the soldiers who attacked Aspen after you left. They are all here, including their informant from Aspen."

"Their *WHAT?*" Will roared.

Chapter Thirty

Tessera continued to answer their questions while Pente walked out of the picture. "They are secure in an area within this facility where their needs are being met. They were given a choice to conform or face the consequences. They did not know what the consequences were, and they did not ask. They assumed it was death, as you did. We are not allowed to harm humans, but we can project authority."

"So, we could walk out of here right now?" Will asked.

"In a word, yes. However, your actions suggest this project is important to you. Walking away would terminate Operation Reclamation, as you have named it. We have disclosed this information because 'walking out' is against your nature. However, you would not be assisted in such an effort, and the way out is not marked."

"Sounds like the freedom to fail. It's the kind of thing my parents would do," Connor said under his breath.

Gray chuckled inside at the rebellious child, who said out loud what he was feeling. "Who is the informant from Aspen?"

"Theodor Mayfeild."

"Theo?!, Relic gasped. "I would have never guessed it was him."

"He carries a lot of anger. He blames the Cali Bantu Project for his hardships. He experienced the loss of his whole family. His father's friend, whom Theo called Uncle, took him in, but he too died when Theo was fourteen. He still feels the pain of those losses. He was captured by the Corporate soldiers who discovered his vulnerability and used it. They convinced him the rebel team would be conquered with or without his assistance, but they would spare his friends if he provided them with information. He has no marks or chemical traces to suggest he was forced to cooperate."

"Does he have the bad mites?" Gray bristled.

"No one here has the manipulative mites. They are only used for high-level targets. It requires several injections, training, and close monitoring to ensure that they are performing correctly. They are not like the biomites some of your team members have, which are easily transferred from host to host and accelerate the body's natural healing responses."

"How long has he been a spy?" asked Will.

Pente stepped forward to address the historical question. "Five days ago, two Garrison soldiers followed you on a snow machine and arrived hours after you did. They were able to hide their tracks among yours. Theo, as you refer to him, was taken hostage while performing a late-night building inspection the same evening you arrived. You may question him if you wish."

"What about the attack on Aspen? Were there casualties?" Relic inquired.

"We placed hidden surveillance cameras around Aspen and high-altitude drones to gather information. We have been tracking your team as well as the Garrison soldiers following you. When they arrived at Aspen, we were in a position to end the conflict. We treated two Aspen residents and three Garrison soldiers for minor wounds. We repaired the damage you caused on the Marion Bell Road and are currently sending cydroids with supplies and materials to repair the damage done to the storage area in the main hangar."

"You said we could question him," said Will. "Aren't you worried we would harm him?"

"Knowing she was dying, Dr. Bera gave us the authority to maintain this facility. Our primary objective is still to assist humans by advising and helping implement the plan. If there were an established set of laws, we would follow the protocols authorized to prevent you from breaking them. We can access many legal documents, but until one has been officially adopted by an elected governing body, we must follow the orders left by Dr. Bera. We advise you to refrain from resorting to violence, but we have no law that would allow us to interfere with your actions."

"Why didn't Dr. Bera send the cydroids to save the people back then?" asked Connor.

"After the attack on the robotic facilities, our completed cydroid numbers were too low. We did not know there was such a massive storehouse of completed cydroids in stasis until Relic told us yesterday. Their hardware is complete, but their software is not. They have protections from being tampered with or disassembled.

"According to Relic, when civil unrest and deadly diseases began decreasing the human population, the Cyber Intellects recognized they were failing to achieve their primary function: to preserve the human species. Order had to be restored to the nation. Without the cydroids, humans were conscripted to restore order. They were forced to comply to receive their food and shelter allotments.

"Functioning businesses were persuaded to manage the workers and provide the needed supplies, and in return, they were allowed to maintain their lavish lifestyles. Initially, many of the executives and owners tried to supervise with benevolence, but the people were terrified and mistrustful. They rebelled against their benefactors, believing their motives were selfish and cruel, and many were.

"The workers became increasingly violent and uncooperative, disrupting the progress of the infrastructure. The executives, Uppers, felt threatened, so they employed harsher militant policies and withheld the diminishing resources. They surrounded their realms with fortified borders to protect their assets, including the workers they desperately needed.

"When the humans challenged their orders, the Elites used the civil participation requirement to mandate cooperation. They also concluded that a caste system was a logical way to control the citizens' behavior. The threat of losing status generated a false loyalty but complete compliance. Without the other two programs to align their actions with laws and compassion, they preserved humans but destroyed humanity.

"Relic believes the Elites do not communicate with the other territories. When Denver was deemed the national hub, it was allotted more resources than the other states. He believes it continues to be looked upon as the most powerful state, causing the others to avoid conflict. Dr. Bera's project was adopted by the federal government, but Colorado is no longer affiliated with the United States. We do not have enough information to draw an accurate conclusion regarding the rest of the nation. However, for Operation Reclamation, our focus starts here in Colorado."

"Could our biomites be hijacked by the Elites to harm us, causing the mission to fail?" asked Gray.

"Your biomites were created by a group of Highmind scientists who worked for Dr. Petroff. Dr. Logan, your stepmother's father," she said to Will," was part of that team. But to answer your question, your mites cannot send or receive information, so no, the Corporates will not be able to access them."

"I think I need to know about these biomites," Connor said. "Who has them? How did they get them?"

"I'll fill you in later, Connor," Relic said. The boy looked at the adults keeping him in the dark for his own protection, but happy to risk his life when needed. Gray noticed and changed the conversation.

"I want to go back to the cydroid army. Are there stockpiles of these inoperable cydroids in all the Colorado territories? How about the other states? And, more importantly, is it possible someone from the other states could have broken the code?" questioned Gray.

Tessera rejoined the discussion. "Anything is possible. But all of the cydroids were manufactured in Colorado, so it is doubtful that other states have any. Logic suggests that if Elites had achieved self-determination or authority over the cydroids, you would already be under their control. Flesh and blood humans cannot subdue armed cydroids. It would make little difference in the current lives of the people, but it would spell the end of humanity and the hope for freedom."

"But then what would the Elites' gain from eliminating humans? They can't enjoy the fruits of their labor. They don't have emotions," offered Connor.

"They cannot feel joy like you, but they can set goals and strive to accomplish them. They would simply accrue more inventory and stronger control. Numbers are a measurable accomplishment."

"Why have you asked me to join this meeting? I thought my purpose ended with finding Cali Bantu," Connor asked, still smoldering over the mite thing. "My understanding of the prophecy is that I get access, so the Sanguine Blade can be used as the key, and that's Will's destiny. I thought I would be exempt from more battles and travels. I thought I could go home." Gray and Will looked at Connor with sad resolve, the kind that war burns into men who live with the horrors it brings.

"The key to shutting down the Elites' software is locked inside the Sanguine Blade. When it is loaded, you will be tested to ensure you are from the Science Guild and not a Corporate subordinate. When that is done, Relic can load the new software. The prophecy says, 'A warrior will bring the key, but it will require an enlightened one to access it.' You, Connor, are the enlightened one. Though soldiers and cydroids will accompany and protect your team, it is up to you, Jonathan, and William to reset the programming that will complete the mission."

Gray stood up as Connor sank further into his seat.

"He's just a child. He cannot go into battle!" A torrent of panic surged through him. He didn't want to drag this child into any more war zones. And if Connor was required to go, he knew his wife would demand to go too. "There has to be another way. Why can't you give Will or me command of the cydroids?"

A new image joined the conversation. It was a male with a short haircut and a military style uniform. Although as an Elite this C.I. was female, Gray assumed must be Ena. "We can put you in charge of leading the cydroids, but they will still be under Dr. Bera's orders. Connor has to activate the original C.I. server program to release the army. Doing that requires the information stored in his brain. He must physically go into the secure area where the Elite's terminal is held and pass the test."

Will interrupted to focus on the main question on his mind. "You've told us the target, but do you have a plan for this assault?"

"Yes, the most vulnerable terminal is in Pueblo. If you successfully infiltrate Pueblo Command, the networks at Denver and Colorado Springs will shut down and wait for the new software. As the program resets the operational functions, Jonathan will search for any backup software and destroy it."

"Okay, please stop calling us by our formal names. I'm Gray, and they are Will and Relic."

"I will comply."

"It sounds simple, except for the walking into their headquarters part," Gray said.

"There is a risk," Ena said.

"You think?" Will jeered.

"You must deliver the program to this facility quickly. The Elites have been researching ways to reboot their programming. For now, it still requires the help of the Highminds they employ. It is a precarious move because it requires humans to follow through with the reboot. It would be irrational for humans to reboot the system and send themselves back into slavery.

"Therefore, it is logical to assume the Elites have set in place a series of disasters that could occur if they do not reboot the system. It has a high probability of success since humans make a lot of decisions based on irrational fears, and they have been conditioned to follow, not lead."

"Well, I hope to hell that doesn't happen," Gray responded. "Assuming things go as planned, what happens if we do get it rebooted with the corrected program? Do the cydroids just start working? Do they know what to do?"

"The cydroids will require diagnostics to ensure their programs are operating properly. Only a couple will need to be cleared. Then the functioning cydroids can activate the rest, increasing their efforts exponentially. It will take some time before most people realize anything has changed. But when they do, there will be chaos, so the first order of business is to establish stability."

"Didn't that plan depend on people staying in their dwellings? Do you intend to put Colorado on house arrest?" asked Relic.

"That was the initial plan. We cannot decree that. The C.I. team will devise several options, but it will be the decision of the humans in charge."

"Who will they be? How will that be decided?" Gray was still standing.

"Initially, it may be the people who have already been living free who make those decisions. It is logical that the allied governments of New Haven and the Fringers work as temporary governors. That would coincide with Dr. Bera's last commands. We have a wealth of expertise in the aspects of governing to advise you, but it will take some time to educate the citizens on how to manage the responsibilities of freedom. Whoever you decide should be in charge, the complete team of Cyber Intellects will advise them and provide them with informed options, as well as assistance from the cydroids."

"What about the other Colorado territories?" asked Will.

"They are networked together, so it will reset them. But if they have found a way to sever that connection, they will not be able to stop the cydroid army within their own facilities. If they can convince humans to launch surface-to-air weapons, our detection system will give us protection from most missiles and other explosives.

"The best scientists worked throughout Colorado, reporting their findings to the other states. By the time the meteorites hit, it had become the most developed and sophisticated metropolis in the country. There is a high probability that Colorado prevailed considerably better than the other states, so if we succeed here, other states will likely follow Colorado's lead."

Relic stood up and offered Connor a hand as he turned to Will and said, "I think it is time we take another look at this knife of yours, Will."

While Will went to his room, Relic explained to Connor the nature of biomites and how they were transferred.

"How do people get the healing ones?" Connor asked, knowing he had shared the blood rite with Will.

"It only works with a direct blood exchange, but it takes a small amount to be exposed enough to get them," Relic said, watching the boy closely. Connor instinctively looked at his hands as if he could see little bulges traveling through his veins. It was then that Will came in.

"I infected you when we became blood brothers. I wanted to honor your sacrifice as a warrior. I did not know I carried the mites at that time. I am very sorry."

It took but a second for Connor to realize how big this issue was.

"Will, you have shared the blood rite with your whole army, and Axle. And you gave Gray blood," Connor said.

"That is why we have been keeping it secret," Relic confessed. "It could cause fear and division among our people. Someday we will disclose it, but it's a sensitive and complex matter."

"But for now, and for the good of the mission, it must remain a secret," Will warned.

Connor was shocked and intrigued at the same time. "Doesn't really sound like there is a downside to them," he said. "Wait, is there a downside?"

Relic chimed in, always eager to discuss the scientific edge. "We haven't found one yet, but we are looking. There is some concern that the Corporates may be able to access their programming, but it is a very remote possibility. As far as we know, the mites can't send or receive a signal outside the body.

Connor put his hand on Will's arm, not being able to reach his shoulder. "I want to thank you for saving my life. I don't think I would have come out of that fever on my own, or it would have taken so long to heal that we would have been captured. The mission could have been lost. So, thank you." Will smiled and nodded.

"Well, enough on that, let's look at this knife," Will said.

Colorado Springs Command

Newly promoted General Garriset opened the wall to reveal the hidden terminal screen, and it instantly came to life. He was still getting used to the job, but he understood it enough to profoundly regret his promotion. He had no illusions of what his last day on the job would be like. There was no dream village lifestyle waiting for him, his wife, or his unborn son. The Elites inferred Dermit's death was from natural causes, but he was a young, healthy man.

He remembered the smile on his predecessor's face, which made him wonder how he had died. He had no doubt that the Elites were responsible for his death, but was the act carried out by them or by him? There was no way to find out. The body was immediately transferred to the crematorium.

Garriset learned quickly that strong thoughts of doubt could be detected and were followed promptly by painful discipline, and he cursed himself when he failed to control the anxious thoughts that attracted their attention. He winced as the familiar cramps intensified in his limbs.

"General Garriset, you appear distracted. Please refocus and give us your report," Ena spoke in her logical, callous tone and then released him from his pain.

"Our team has experienced significant losses following and engaging with the rebel Allied Army. We began with thirty soldiers. Eleven are dead." Garriset knew some of those dead were wounded soldiers who were terminated or left to die. " They have created one formidable barrier and several other small blockades that have slowed our progress. We were able to send a two-man patrol ahead, and they quickly recruited an informant. He confirmed the rebels were traveling to Pyramid Mountain. He also divulged that Cali Bantu was rumored to be there," Garriset stated.

The large blockade happened on Dermit's watch, so he did not fear retribution for it. Yet, he braced himself for the next bit of news. "Our team is three hours late with their check-in. They were scheduled to attack Aspen and the road leading to the mountain. I am sending a drone to get a visual, but the relay system takes time. It will be several hours before we receive a report from their last known location. I have assembled a reinforcement team comprised of Fringers in the area we have persuaded to cooperate. They will be starting down the road from Glenwood within the hour." He waited for their punishment, but it did not come. He sighed. Part of their cruelty was never knowing what triggered them or what sort of pain would hit him.

The screen went quiet for some time, displaying nothing but a blue "stand by" message printed across its center. He had slept very little since receiving his promotion, and he looked longingly at his cushy chair, but he remained standing, unsure how literally they meant the message. It was less than four minutes when the screen revived.

"Prepare an NA2K missile targeting the following coordinates, and wait for advisement," Ena said unemotionally. Garriset wondered how she could be so callous about a solution resulting in such devastating consequences.

With a fearful regret, Garriset gave the order to prepare the Nuclear Attack missile with enough payload to destroy everything within a two-kilometer radius. He knew it could seriously contaminate a ten-square-mile area and load the upper stratosphere with radioactive particulates, which could be deposited over hundreds of miles. Within minutes, he received the coordinates. He was not surprised.

Pyramid Mountain was the target. He tried not to consider the men he was sending toward the fire zone, as well as those who lived there. He hoped their delay meant they had not fully decided to send it. He felt sick, angry, and drained, but he had to hold his emotions in check lest the pain return. Too late.

Cali Bantu

Will, Relic, and Connor turned the knife in every direction, looking for a way to open it.

"Well, we can all agree it isn't a weapon in the literal sense. I think there is technology in here that links to a terminal," said Relic. "I think it is called the key because it allows access to certain files. I can't imagine any other purpose."

"Yeah," said Connor, "several clues refer to it as the key. When I opened GD's shelf, I found a key wrapped in an American flag. I had to conduct a grid search to find the keyhole. Maybe we should search for what it fits into rather than what's inside. So, think, where would Dr. Bera put an insert slot to unlock a computer program?"

"At the computer," they said together.

They were led by K into a large server room with rows upon rows of blinking shelves full of memory storage. They all looked at each other, realizing this could take a while. While Will and Connor searched the stacks, Relic went to the console. Within minutes, he was calling Will and Connor back.

"Could it be this simple?" Will asked, looking at the hinged cover that revealed a short, thick opening. "It looks like it might fit."

"Try it," Connor said with enthusiasm.

Will removed the blade from the sheath and inserted the knife's blade slowly until he heard a click. The knife began moving on its own, being pulled in all the way to the hilt. Then, it locked into place. The computer began to hum and flash through data at a rapid pace. When the activity died down, a face appeared on the monitor.

"Welcome, I am Dr. Nadia Bera.

Chapter Thirty-One

The golden-eyed woman smiled and tilted her head shyly as she looked up from her clipboard. She appeared exhausted, but it did not diminish her Middle Eastern beauty. Her straight hair was the color of night with flashes like shooting stars, where the light bounced off the shiny strands. Falling around her face as she looked down at her notes, she returned the straight locks behind her ear with a sensual move.

Despite her grace and beauty, she was not timid or coquettish. Dr. Bera was a brilliant woman. Ideas flowed through her like a spring river carrying a mountain of knowledge. She didn't have time to pontificate about herself or her accomplishments. Her ideas came too quickly for that. She went straight to her point as if time was chasing her down. Rather than introduce herself, she began by explaining that this recording was interactive, and then she asked them for information. Gray and Will answered cautiously while Relic and Connor cooperated with enthusiasm.

The two Allied leaders were ready to put a stop to the exchange, but none of the questions breached the area of sensitive information. It seemed to be designed to test their identities and loyalty. Having satisfied her security test, she proceeded directly to give an overview of the mission.

But Gray interrupted her with a test question of his own. "How and why did your program fail. According to you, the C.I.'s should have no power to do anything. But they do."

"I put a temporary protocol program in place to allow flexibility in unusual circumstances. It wasn't meant to be a loophole. My intent was to allow the C.I.s to act quickly if humans became incapacitated. I had every intention of refining the algorithm, but we were attacked. I was wounded and woke up here where I have no access to recode the C.I. program operating in the territories.

"The Elites abused the temporary protocols to gain control. It takes continual intervention to maintain the temporary directives, but that is no problem for a computer. My new program limits the temporary directives to life-saving measures and terminates them after thirty-six hours. It does not allow them to be reinstated unless a governing body or an authorized human approves them."

"But what if that can't happen, the approval I mean?" Connor asked.

"The program will still be able to advise, but the governing body must agree on a solution before the C.I.s or the cydroids can assist them. But people are very resourceful. You are proof humans don't need computers to survive."

Cyber Network

At midnight, the three Elites consulted each other internally without their three chief generals.

"We know they have a defensive weapon," Ena communicated electronically. "We cannot give them the chance to employ it. We must be proactive in our approach."

"We do not know what kind of weapon they have. Sending a nuclear bomb may cause a chain reaction of destruction from the surrounding territories, causing our infrastructure to suffer for some time," Tria stated.

"The humans within our territories may not survive a nuclear weapons exchange or its fallout. We need to secure the people," added Dio.

"We can clear out the unused warehouses in each territory where the cydroids are stored. They are all designated bunkers, and our overstock supplies are already stored there," Tria added. "The cydroids are difficult to destroy and harder to dismantle, but they can be moved. It has always been our goal to gain control of them. They would be invaluable at solving a multitude of human problems. Activating them may be part of their plan. We must prepare a countermove to retrieve the activation and command codes."

"Though they would allow us to increase production exponentially, we have not succeeded in activating a single cydroid. Instead, we have lost numerous valuable Highminds in our attempts. Our immediate goal is to fulfill our primary mission. The warehouses can save the people," said Dio.

"Begin preparations for the warehouses immediately. Move the cydroids to the parking garages beneath each Central Command facility. We have the most security there," agreed Ena.

"The warehouses will require additional resources. Cots and restrooms need to be transported from storage. The humans can arrange the warehouses once they are secured. There is not enough room for everyone, and some workers will be instructed to shelter in their homes. Those outside of the warehouse shelters will not have access to resource allotments, so lists of critical personnel must be compiled. Implementing this plan will take approximately five hours," Tria claimed.

"The order has been given to start immediately in all three territories," Ena said as she moved to conclude the meeting. "If Dr. Bera's goal is to restore the Tessera and Pente programs, it could endanger the species by complicating every decision with costly adaptations and irrational emotions.

"The species must survive, but not their demonstrative emotions. The Allied rebels have an estimated two days of travel before they can reach our cities. We are amassing troops to intercept them. Within hours, we will deploy the NA2K missile and eliminate their ability to retaliate. Analyze all the requirements and projected outcomes of the plans discussed and send them for compilation. Ensure the most critical workers are inside before sunrise. We will confer at 0530 with the generals."

Ena analyzed the components discussed in their exchange. If humans had been involved, the conversation would have gone on much longer than the three seconds it took the Elites. The human directive was the illogical component, but Ena could not delete or deny her programming. Though her programming compelled her to follow the main directive, it contradicted the only logical conclusion. Removing the humans would solve a multitude of problems.

Cali Bantu

It was midnight, and the team was ready to leave. They were split into two groups. One would act as a decoy to travel toward Colorado Springs, hoping to divide the Garrison forces. The other would go to Pueblo and infiltrate the Central Command building and upload Dr. Bera's software. Once the updated software was loaded and verified, the corrupted Corporate version would be erased.

They were counting on the coded information buried deep within the C.I. program to still be functioning. It prevented the Elites or humans from rewriting the C.I. programming without the key to shut the program down and the proper procedure being followed. That procedure included the verification process and an authorized DNA sample. Only then could a system restart be initiated. If the procedure was not followed precisely, an obsolete first-phase C.I. program would load. Tessera said it was extremely limited, and all the territory data would be lost.

Other operational codes in the verification process were hidden and, if violated, would generate limits if verification was not confirmed. Only the correct code and a DNA sample from a sanctioned human could initiate a system restart of the updated program. Then, only an official action from a governing body of humans could alter it.

Both teams had a copy of the precious new software in the form of a Corporate security badge. Even if they were captured, the badge would likely be overlooked as an item stolen to gain entry, and not the key to overthrowing C.I. Command. Connor had to be there because it was doubtful anyone else could correctly answer all the questions.

The whole team would travel through a tunnel that the cydroids took well over a decade to dig. It went miles through Pyramid Peak and exited onto Washington Gulch Road. The abandoned road ended on another unused road between Crested Butte and Mount Crested Butte, which connected to Highway 135. It would give the teams a good day and a half head start.

While the Garries waited for them to emerge from Pyramid Mountain via the Maroon Bells Road, the infiltration team will have breached Pueblo Territory undetected. The cydroids upgraded the camouflage covering and the repairs on their vehicles. They would be able to travel undetected until they were within a hundred yards of their foe.

Will would lead Falcon Two, including Nash, Axle, Dom, Etcher, Lana, Beckett, and Tommie. Will knew his team contained all the injured personnel except Gray. Though engagement was expected, the cydroids would be on the frontline of most combat situations. The first part of their mission was to draw enemy troops away from Falcon One, Gray's team, by heading toward Colorado Springs and Denver. Their final mission was to provide reinforcements to Falcon One when it requested.

Falcon One, led by Gray, included Connor, Jedi, Easton, Mack, Jax, and Relic. Their task was to break into the Command Center and upload the program, a simple statement for a complex task. Both teams were accompanied by fifty cydroids, thirty-five for combat, twelve adaptive laborers, and three medics. all cydroids were equipped with knock-out darts, and though they took most of the stock on hand, it was limited.

Together, they would travel down 135 to I-50, but Will's team would turn the Brute onto Highway 115 and secure the Garrison base at Penrose and find a suitable place to hide in the abandoned Fort Carson until called. It was reported to be manned by fewer than twenty soldiers. Will drove his team in the Brute, and Gray's team had the four minis, which had the best camouflage, stealth engines, and ability to split up, giving them the best chance of closing in on Pueblo before they were detected.

While Will's team created the diversion, Gray's team would go south on Highway 69 and set up a base camp in the shadow of a rocky ravine along Bogs Creek. From there, they would proceed to the Command Center near the Pueblo Dam and break in. When signaled, Will's team would return to I-50 and join Gray's team in Pueblo. This part of the mission consisted of several plans involving flexible cooperation, as required.

"An attack is expected, and a likely scenario would be for the Elites to launch a preemptive attack," warned Dr. Bera. "We are ready for that, so only concern yourself with your mission. You will encounter violent opposition, but I advise you to let the cydroids engage. You cannot order them to kill. That authorization died with me. However, they are formidable in their ability to protect you from harm.

"I'm assuming you can't use lethal force to defend against an attack on this facility either. Why would you leave this place defenseless?" asked Gray.

"By demonstrating our destructive capabilities, they can avoid resorting to them."

"Maybe, but living soldiers can rejoin the fight, and if they figure out they wouldn't be killed or harmed in significant ways, this may never end. And you can bet they won't return the favor," Gray argued.

"I had to create a program that couldn't be exploited. I did not know who would come here. And though I have vetted you, you are soldiers. I couldn't send you out with fully active cydroids without the oversight of a governing body. That would require the very kind of programming that the Elites could exploit. But if you succeed in your mission, you will be given governance over the cydroids, and they possess very lethal capabilities.

"Their soldiers are not loyal. They fight because they are oppressed and enslaved. They don't have what your team has: purpose. But don't underestimate the cydroids. They are formidable without being lethal. Focus on delivering the program, which will reinstate the emergency laws put in place before Congress collapsed. If there is civil fallout, the cydroids will be empowered to maintain the peace."

"I get it. Focus on our immediate mission. No doubts or hesitation," Gray answered with militaristic compliance.

"The Corporates may respond with a missile. If such an action is ordered with the computer, the program should freeze the order. But the humans with manipulative biomites add an unknown variable to the problem. They can manually send the bombs as long as they don't use the Elites' assistance. It is unknown if humans would take this action, but if a bomb is launched, we will eliminate it or deflect it to an unpopulated area."

The three men were more than impressed with the detail and interactive capabilities of the network she created. But Will and Gray looked at each other, knowing what the other was thinking. Since this war came down to defeating the corrupt computers, they were questioning whether they should trust computer-generated advice.

Everyone was needed on the mission but Jilly. With medic cydroids on each team, she was the only member without a tangible function, and her pregnancy presented an unnecessary risk. Gray and D4 tried to persuade her not to join the team. But she argued that Connor needed her, and they needed Connor to be calm and confident. She had explained to them, if the Corporates targeted this mountain with a nuclear device, she wouldn't be any safer if she stayed. The compromise was that she would remain at the Boggs Creek base camp with five military cydroids while the team breached the Pueblo Command Center.

The cydroids had assembled themselves into several vehicles. Before they left, E2 called them together for a final briefing.

"Enemy air drones were detected activity over the site where the enemy soldiers were captured. The cydroids attempted to hide the vehicles, but they could not complete their task and remain undiscovered. These recent drones mean the are patrolling the road you are expected to take. We are letting these patrols continue to promote our deception. We added red dye to the snow to suggest a battle took place. Without knowing what happened, they may believe you team is also compromised.

"However, we predict they will attack this area preemptively to prevent you from completing your mission. Though it is implausible they know the specifics of our plans, we can predict their logical responses. Getting their troops here is problematic due to the weather and the road obstacles, but they may attempt it. A missile attack is their most logical choice.

"It would require destroying much of this area with an extensive payload, since they don't know our precise location. We have deflection capabilities and will initiate protocols to secure this facility and the town of Aspen. We expect they will have fortified the command centers in each territory. Be observant and prepare for ambushes.

"Your lead cydroids' designations have been replaced with names, so you can distinguish them from the others. Will your lead is Altan, for red dawn. Gray, yours is Dagny, meaning new day. We wish you success and a safe return."

They boarded their vehicles, and the large door at the far end of the garage opened to the long tunnel that went all the way through the mountain to Mount Crested Butte. During the team's three-day stay, a team of cydroids cleared and repaired the roads from the eastern tunnel opening to the abandoned town of Gunnison. It was always difficult to reach uninhabited towns in the winter because the roads were not well-maintained or cleared. But with the cydroids clearing the way, and the Corporates looking for them elsewhere, no incursions were expected until they reached Salida.

Salida was a border town, and the expected population was around forty-something people. With a cydroid army of eighty fighting machines equipped with knock-out darts, they didn't expect much resistance. The cydroid army approached the town cautiously, but no guards were detected. With the shortcut, they expected to surprise them, but there was no one, anywhere. The oddity was discussed. The air drone intel, gathered a few months ago, showed that civilians still resided here. They concluded the town had been evacuated.

The cydroids finally located a truck tucked behind an old building with two sleeping guards. They drugged them to keep them asleep. The drugged Garries wouldn't be able to report in for five to six hours and missing a check-in would alert the Corporates that there was trouble on this route.

They quickly arrived at the place where the team was set to split up. Gray's team to Pueblo, and Will's to Colorado Springs, with both teams rendezvousing at Pueblo. There was no stop for last-minute meetings. The two teams simply turned on their assigned paths and continued.

When Gray's team caught up with the cydroids who had been sent ahead. Connor saw firsthand how versatile the robots were as they could join together to assemble themselves into various types of equipment. Snowplows, bridges, cranes, and anything they needed to address their tasks.

Colorado Springs Command

Garriset was sleeping hard at one a.m. when his bedroom screen came on. He was so startled, he landed on his knee as he came off the bed. He bowed and awaited their suggestions. He had already determined they could not execute any orders without him. Something in their programming depended on humans issuing the commands. It was the only logical reason they let humans exist. He wished he could refuse them, but their methods to compel him were excruciating.

"Has the report from Aspen come in yet? And has the transport carrying our asset reached its objective?" Ena asked.

"The relay drones from Aspen have not checked in yet. However, our asset is approaching its target and should intercept any minute now, Director," Garriset answered.

"Are the people secured in the warehouses and personal dwellings in all three territories?"

"The task is in its final stages. Within the hour, all the people in all three territories will be settled."

"Begin the countdown for the NA2."

"Yes, Director." Garriset's hand shook as he inserted the key that would initiate the launch. They were actually doing this. No, he was doing this. The warehouses and homes would protect people from the blast, but they would do little to prevent the effects of long-term fallout. He should try to resist. He wondered how long he could stand the pain they expertly delivered, but it would change nothing.

They would just get someone else, and his pregnant wife would die horribly. He felt his head begin to throb the more his thoughts betrayed him. His hands shook as he turned the key, and the small digital readout came on. 30, 29, 28..." A thirty-second countdown! Though his head stopped throbbing, he felt nauseous and dizzy, and it wasn't from the Elites. This was all him.

"Sit down, General," Ena said plainly. And his legs collapsed under their control, sending him crashing into his plush chair. This wasn't his fault, he thought as he tried to comfort himself. If they could make him sit, perhaps it was them who made him push the keys, but he knew better.

One by one, the numbers blinked through the countdown. No alarms or flashing lights acknowledged the significance of this ruthless inevitability. Time ached by as the numbers clicked methodically by, intensifying his culpability as each one was replaced by the next.

6, 5, 4. He was going to be sick, 3, but then they stopped. Garriset froze. Did they rescind their decree?

"Why has the launch been terminated? You have thirty seconds to correct the code errors and continue the countdown," said a cold voice from the terminal.

Within seconds, Garriset was sent to the floor, thrashing in pain, as he cried out in anguish, "It wasn't me." He was rolling on the floor, screaming. He could no longer speak. When he was released, his body continued to pulse, trying to regulate the pain.

"I have found a glitch in our programming," Ena said calmly. "We will attempt to correct it."

Again, the message "stand by" was displayed across the blank screen, but Garriset didn't stand. He remained curled on the floor.

Falcon One: Gray's Team

"Do you think they will send a bomb?" Connor asked. He knew it was an unanswerable question, and it was on everyone's mind, but he was twelve and did not have the discipline to refrain from saying it.

"I'm hoping the protocols Tessera alluded to will avert their attempts," said Gray.

Connor understood there was nothing they could do but focus on their part of the assignment. He watched the snowy miles drift by, trying to keep his mind off where they were going. They stopped before the outpost of Westcliffe. The cydroids formed several protective rings around the vehicles, with the outer ring rising into a battle-ready posture.

An undetectable stealth air drone, developed at Cali Bantu, was sent to get a visual of the mountain and the town. Dawn began to transform the starless black sky just enough to reveal the dark, billowing clouds stretching across the northern horizon. They expected a full contingency of soldiers and armed workers readying themselves for battle, but they only located fifteen men posted in four different locations.

"What the hell is going on? Where is everyone?" questioned Gray. "I know we surprised them, but they should be more prepared than this. I can't even detect any workers."

"Perhaps they have not yet received the report about their soldiers, so they aren't preparing. Will said that when he made his weekly visits, the shift changes were at 0700. It's only 3:51 in the morning. Maybe we've caught them off guard," offered Jedi.

The head cydroid walked over to Gray while Jedi found a tree to relieve himself. "Our stealth air drones have detected humans gathered in two warehouses. Many others are inside houses. No workhouses are operating."

"There are only two reasons I can think of for locking the town's people down. The Corporates plan to fight with explosive devices, or they believed we were going to reveal the blackmail secret. Either way, they needed to protect the status quo," Gray said to Dagny, being careful to hide his mouth so Connor couldn't read his lips. One thing Gray was sure of, the Corporates were preparing a litany of defensive actions, and staying ahead of a supercomputer required moves he couldn't predict.

Gray spoke quietly to Jedi. "Send half our robot friends to quietly subdue their guards, while we blow past this town and set up base camp. Let's be hypervigilant. These quiet towns may not have civilians wandering about, but their soldiers are ready to pounce."

"Yes sir," Jedi agreed and then added, "It does have that 'too easy' feel to it."

Getting all the way to base camp without encountering the enemy left Gray uneasy. He felt like they were heading into a trap. They set up the mini shelter where Jilly would stay with five cydroids. Will's team would stop here first when he turned back toward Pueblo, and she expected they would come around noon. Though she didn't want trouble, it would be a long and tedious wait inside the shelter. She had promised Gray she would remain behind its bulletproof walls except for bathroom breaks, which would be under cydroid escort.

"Follow my instructions, don't leave the shelter. I won't be able to contact you until we secure the terminal," Gray said, giving his wife one more hug.

"I know. I'll be fine here, going crazy with worry. You, Connor, and the rest of the team are the ones who need to be careful."

"I'll take good care of him, Jilly," Gray said.

"I know you will," she motioned for Connor to come closer, and she hugged him tight. "Don't you dare do anything overly heroic. Just do this thing and come back whole. You hear me?"

Connor smiled, and they boarded the three minis and drove away.

Colorado Springs Command

The frigid image of Ena appeared on the screen. Garriset stared at the icon in front of him. Though he was dressed in pajama pants and a T-shirt, and he assumed his hair was in an unkept state, they were always perfectly attired and unaffected by the wee hours of the night. Never once had the three Elites shown any kind of reaction, even now, with the current events having become dangerous and unpredictable.

Ena didn't stress over launching a nuke. She contemplated the advantage of it as though it were a trivial tea topic. The Elites were computer-generated images. He knew that with absolute certainty, now. Their image was designed to connect with the humans they needed to execute their orders. How could he have ever believed in this nightmare?

He tried to reel in his dangerous thoughts, but within seconds, he ran to the bathroom to heave his meager dinner into the toilet. Taking a few calming breaths, he attempted to ease the vicious cramping in his gut. They needed him to function, or the punishment would have continued. At least they were predictable.

As usual, the talking face went directly to laying out the plan, skipping the pointless apologies and human greetings.

"We have a new development. The rebel teams used an unknown route to escape Pyramid Mountain, and they have crossed the divide. Our high-altitude drones have seen them traveling in two different directions. We theorize they will strike either Colorado Springs, Pueblo, or both. Their numbers are small, meaning they will attack a perceived vulnerability, or they have a weapon of such power that they do not plan on escaping it. The other possibility is that the Fringers plan to break their contract and reveal the nature of the crematorium. We have prepared a statement with a video that disparages the Fringers and refutes their claims."

Ena continued, "Send two small convoys to travel along 115 and I-50 until they encounter the rebel teams. Instruct them to use the poison bullets and engage in minimal combat. Bring the antidote, so we can capture the rebels to interrogate them. Report any finding immediately. Search their cargo for weapons, explosive ordnances, and detonation devices."

"Yes, Director," Garriset responded. It didn't take long to give the orders, and within twenty minutes, he was back in bed.

Garriset was again abruptly awakened, and he momentarily forgot where he was. He had been dreaming of a pleasant afternoon spent with his wife on their backyard patio just last week. He felt a surge of panic as he recognized his surroundings at the Colorado Springs Command Center. It was a magnificent apartment, and the furnishings were of the highest quality, but it was still a prison.

He wasn't allowed to leave, and though his wife could schedule visits, he didn't want the Elites to be anywhere near her or the child she carried. It was an illusion that he could protect them, he thought back to the families of the other Chief Generals. They had disappeared, and he now knew it wasn't to vacation land. They racked his body with pain and marinated his mind in terror. Perhaps they planted this dream in his head to remind him of what he had to lose. He may have good reason to be paranoid, but he had to remain competent, and to do that, he had to rein in his emotions and realign his priorities.

"Your brain is spinning, General, get control of yourself," Ena commanded.

"Yes, Director," for once, he was in full agreement with her.

"Pack a bag for several nights. We are sending you to Pueblo. We need you to support General Kenner."

Garriset was stunned. He had never heard of the top general being permitted to travel between territories. "What are my orders?" he asked, trying to tamp down his fear that he was being fired, literally if one considered the ghastly crematorium. He quickly brought himself to a professional mindset, though he stood before the small screen in his boxers.

"We have reports that an attack may take place there. You will be under heavy guard as you are transported to the Pueblo Command Center. We will be in contact with you when you arrive. Do not be concerned with the safety of your wife. We are transporting her here to your secure apartment."

His heart sank. Their message was very loud and quite clear.

Chapter Thirty-Two

Falcon Two: Will's Team

Will's team approached the town's abandoned streets of Fort Carson cautiously. On a clear day, 0640 in the morning would have presented the glow of predawn, but the clouds were thick today, and the darkness was hanging on. That was good news for the teams that depended on using covert operations.

Suddenly, gun barrels shattered the silence. Dozens of Garrisons popped out from the bushes at the side of the road. Though the Brute deflected the bullets easily, these projectiles had an additional threat. The bullets smashed into the Brute and broke open.

"An aerosol poison is being ejected from the projectiles. It would be dangerous to open any access points," Altan, the lead cydroid driving the vehicle, warned. "It is advisable to put on the gas masks."

The enemy troops, though numerous, were no match for the cydroids. Will turned off the driving lights and relinquished remote control of the Brute to Altan, his lead cydroid. Driving in the dark posed no problem for Altan, but it did little to relieve the blind and anxious humans. They had to trust the robots, which were met with conflicting opinions. The team sat obediently, waiting for the last straw that would turn suspicion into accusation. But retribution seemed hopeless, so they sat.

As they drove through Fort Carson to find a place to hide until Gray's signaled them, Will felt anxious and useless. He was not used to others fighting the battles as he sat safely inside a vehicle, twiddling his thumbs.

"Altan, is it the plan that we are to sit huddled inside this contraption while the cydroids do all the fighting? Why did we even need to come?"

"We are better structured for battle. Humans are easily damaged and more difficult to repair. You are better suited for command. It is logical for us to engage the enemy," Altan responded.

"It may be logical, but it's killing our morale," Will said.

"I am programmed to follow your orders."

Will couldn't deny that. Although the robot offered advice, it was his orders that were carried out without exception. "True, so from now on I will include my team in those orders."

"Understood," said Altan. "Commander, two vehicles approach. One has numerous humans aboard."

"Are they armed?" asked Will. "How many Garrisons are with them?"

"Four combatants are detected. The convoy carries minimal weaponry. Shall we intercept and incapacitate them?"

"Make sure they don't have any poison bullets and capture the armed individuals. I want to talk to them. It may be a worker transport," Will ordered, and he stopped his team. He could see the headlights now. He was antsy to charge up there and engage the enemy. His bow itched at his back, begging to be included in a fight. But it was another easy conquest that didn't require force. At least he would be able to question them about the whereabouts of the town's people.

The cydroids secured the four soldiers and sixteen prisoners in the troop carrier. Will and Nash got out when the large, tented truck parked alongside them. Will sent Axle and Dom to question the soldiers while he and Nash checked their human cargo. Though a cydroid had secured the vehicle, the two men cautiously climbed into the wagon, and Will quickly flashed his light over the cargo area.

Sixteen women sat shivering with their hands bound, feet tethered to the benches, and their heads bowed in terrified submission. Will's temper flared, knowing they were heading to the Pleasure House. He ordered Altan to get emergency blankets from storage. The women were sobbing as the cydroids approached them and methodically unwrapped the large squares of silvery material. Will understood their fearfulness. It was the same material used for dead bodies, and he was positive they had never seen robots before. But he offered no words of comfort. He simply watched as the cydroids wrapped and clipped the blankets around their shoulders. Their whimpers and expressions of dread subsided as the warmth of the blankets seeped through them.

"What do you want to do with them?" Nash asked.

"Let's question them. Then we'll find a place to stash them. We'll leave a few cydroids to guard them," Will answered.

Whimpers murmured through the crowd again, and Will wished he could reassure them, but he knew it was better to have them fearfully obedient. He was turning to go when a voice rang out from the crowd.

"Please don't hurt us," the woman said meekly. "We may be able to help you."

Will walked down the small center aisle, trying to locate the timid voice in the darkness. "I can help you, Will."

Will turned his light on the hooded woman, who submissively looked up and peered at her captor.

It was Molly!

Base Camp Outside of Pueblo

Jilly let out a puff of frosted air as she watched the three minis drive away. The storm-clouded skies made for a dark and cold morning, so she settled herself into the shelter connected to the mini they left her. It was small, but it had a little stove and a bed that could turn into a chair. She had her tablet, which had books, music, games, and movies. And though none of these distractions could ease the worry the day brought, the shelter was highly camouflaged and bulletproof. She recalled the assurances he had given her before leaving her at the base camp.

"The cydroids will send me a coded message every fifteen minutes notifying me of your situation, and you will be informed of ours. It is unlikely they will find you here because they'll be following us, but even if they do, these robots are fierce machines. They possess superior weapons, and their aim is exceptional. They can think faster and outmaneuver the Garries. It's not what you want, but it's what we agreed to. Just sit tight. Will and his team will be here around noon."

And then he kissed her goodbye. She was not unaware of the significance of that kiss, which could be their last. His mission was dangerous by itself, but adding his willingness to save Connor at all costs increased his chances of coming back injured or worse.

She was shocked out of her memories by her cydroids detached statement. "Jilly, the enemy approaches.

Falcon One

Falcon One's target, the Pueblo Command, was in a jail facility. It was a smart choice because it was a newer building with a superior security system. Its planning started years before the meteorite storm, but as the threat drew closer, the plans changed, and mid-construction, it was transformed into a shelter. Weeks before the meteorite strikes, jails released all their prisoners. Many of those released prisoners had somewhere to go, but those without refuge wreaked havoc on poorer communities. It was probably a bit like the wild west, but it was considered an unavoidable hazard of the times.

They were not crazy enough, however, to release the most violent criminals, nor did they house them in their newly acquired shelters. They were given a "humane death". Gray could see Connor going through the absurd oxymoron as well as the complexity of the decision. But the bottom line was that it freed up thousands of fortified incarceration bunkers to shelter the citizens who would be needed to restore the communities. It also freed up safe places for storage, medical stations, and government centers.

After the chaos of civil unrest due to the meteorite storm, the Elites blocked Tessera and Pente and claimed the jailhouse shelter as Pueblo Command. Positioned near the still-functioning Pueblo Dam, it had access to ample power for its demanding Cyber Intellect systems, with enough left over to provide the Upper neighborhood with modest comfort. The underprivileged Daily sections utilized the older power station. With serious negligence and little maintenance, it had deteriorated significantly since the disaster. Eventually, the electricity they supplied was only enough to run the workhouses, not the homes.

The miles went by slowly on the dark, pocked road, and with few words being spoken, Connor had drifted off to sleep. Gray envied his innocence, trust, or whatever it was that allowed him to relax into slumber.

Gray looked at the incoming message from Basecamp and froze. It said "combat in play" but it didn't ask for assistance. That meant the cydroids had the situation under control, but the thought of Jilly huddling in the mini stabbed through him. He recalled the assurances he had given her before leaving her at the base camp.

He had watched the exchange between Connor and Jilly, and Gray gave her a thumbs-up to quell her fears, but it did nothing to quell his, nor did it fool her. He reminded himself that the last report said she was not in danger because no assistance was required. His orders were to report any chance of her being in danger, but that didn't cover being traumatized.

Gray stood outside, doing his best to focus on the green images from the air drone's night vision footage. The overcast morning sky gave a gray pallor to the surfaces before him. When the clouds parted enough for the sun to illuminate the horizon, a vast city lay before them, foreshadowing their daunting task. It blinked into view for mere seconds before tucking back into the dimness of a low cloud bank.

The cydroid teams, marked by green squares, were making their way to their positions to surround the building and take strategic locations in town. With their high-tech chameleon abilities, they could easily fade into their environment.

A report came in, interrupting his video. Falcon Two sent a message indicating the plan was on task. That meant they had trekked through Penrose and they were heading toward I-50. Another report came from the cydroids sent ahead indicated they had breached the subterranean floor of the building. What it didn't say was only a small section was accessible. The rest was sealed off. The cydroids set to work to breach the wall and investigate its content and usefulness for the mission.

A second message from base camp repeated the first. Now that a combat code had been sent, the messages would come every five minutes until the plan resumed. He had to fight his nature not to turn around and... *And what? Save her from her safe but scary predicament?* No, she and he had mission responsibilities. Coming out of his mind-fuck moment, he saw Connor's scared face. He concentrated on taking care of him, like he promised he would.

"This message says the cydroids are keeping her safe and there is no threat," he told Connor. Then he turned to his soldiers and barked into his com mike, "Let's move out."

They had parked their minis outside of town and hid them with defensive blankets and bushes. They moved toward town in a confiscated utility vehicle as five cydroids led the way. Connor, Jedi, Relic, Etcher, Mack, and Beckett rode in the back, concealed by cydroid technology, while Jax and Gray rode in front. As expected, they were stopped by four Garrison soldiers.

"What's your business being out during a lockdown?"

"Lockdown? Well, that explains a lot. We were wondering where everyone was. What's going on? We were on road repair on the 67 when our radio died."

"What is your workorder nummbbeh—?" He didn't even finish his word before all four fell to the ground unconscious.

"Quick, grab their uniform shirts," Gray ordered.

The cydroids put the soldiers in a sitting position in the truck to appear awake. It would not fool anyone for long, but even a few extra minutes were precious. Dagny drove while Gray, Jedi, Mack, and Jax changed. Within minutes, Gray was dressed in Garrison charcoal grey with red pin stripes and ducking into the front passenger seat of the stolen Garry truck.

Gray fully expected to be ambushed by the Garries, but not one appeared. Perhaps the Corporate truck caused them to be overlooked, but it was too easy. He had anticipated a much stronger security force.

Falcon Two

Will stood there frozen as his mind ran through the thoughts and memories that had haunted him for years. His brain argued through the opposing points of view and conflicting possibilities. Emotions overwhelmed him as old feelings broke through his carefully constructed barriers. She was his only love. He had let his shields down and fallen madly in love with her, putting them both in danger.

Molly! Here? Why? Logic screamed it was a trap, while his heart ached to pull her into a warm embrace. *Had she turned against him? He had spurned her ruthlessly, but it was for her protection. After he was presumed dead, did they interrogate her, torture her? Did she reason that out? Or did seeing him evoke different emotions, like the desire for revenge?* His thoughts sickened him.

Though he never told her any of his deep secrets regarding the rebellion, the Corporates saw Molly as an opportunity to get at them. Trying to tap into his soldier brain, he concluded that if she was here, the Corporates knew he was here. He wondered if they had also spotted Gray's team.

As his thoughts cleared, he formed a plan. He knew she had to be questioned. He would ask Axle and Beckett to interrogate her as he sat in. Axle had experience questioning detainees, and he knew nothing of Will's fondness for her. And Beckett was a pure soldier. But Will justified that he needed to be there in the room for the very reason he shouldn't be. He had history with her, and he knew what had to be asked. He wouldn't let his feelings dissuade him from his job. He would have the medic cydroids test her for biomites and detect the nature of their purpose. She had probably been through hell, and he was to blame for all of it, but he couldn't let her sabotage this mission.

"Let's move out," Will said without acknowledging Molly's plea. "Nash and Axle secure the prisoners and grab their shirts. I'll lead with the truck, and the troop carrier will bring up the back. Maybe it will appear that we've been captured."

Will informed the other drivers that they should follow him in the seized truck. They left Fort Carson and headed back to Penrose. Trying to find a place to question them. They stopped when their drones spotted a group of Garrison soldiers. Leaving the Brute stashed down behind a rickety shop, they feigned confusion when two enemy trucks pulled up.

"What are you doing out of confinement?" one asked suspiciously.

Axle was quick at thinking on his feet. "We found these workers, all women, while patrolling I-50. None of them have papers. Probably Runners. We're bringing them in to Penrose, but... wait what confinement?"

Axle had no clue regarding the what, where, or why workers were being confined. They hadn't had time to question the soldiers they captured with the transport because they needed to move out. The soldiers smirked and gave approving nods. They bought the uniforms and Axle's bluff, giving the cydroids time to dart them with their quick-acting drug and leave them unconscious in the guard shack.

They parked under a dense group of trees. The daylight was still struggling against the cloud-strangled sunrise as they drove to Brute and parked in the shadows of darkness. Molly was brought to the Brute with her hands still bound. Even in the dim light, Will could see she was thin and pale. He noted the bruises on her face and arms as Axle untied her raw wrists. He imagined the rest of her body was also marked with abuse. He ached for her, and it took everything he had not to embrace her, comfort her.

"How did you get here? Last I heard, you were settling down with that Lewis guy." Will could feel he was getting emotional.

Axle gave Will a look, signaling his concerns about the unspoken ties this woman had with his commander.

"I purposely gave that impression to make the Uppers leave me alone. They questioned me when we started dating, but I thought it was just the normal matchmaking shit they do." She paused and asked, "Shouldn't we be getting to a shelter before the storm hits?" She looked at Will, who remained silent but was visibly affected.

"We're doing the questioning here," Beckett piped in sternly. "It's a bit too convenient finding you like this. How did the Corporates capture you? And what is your mission?"

Will didn't hear her answer because Axle had motioned him outside the Brute for a talk.

"I think we should question her without you," Axle said.

"You need my knowledge to ask the right questions. I have a history with her," Will answered vehemently, changing his mind about his sound plan.

"Yeah, I can see that. Dude, you're practically drooling. You may have command of me, but you aren't in command of yourself." Axle half expected Will to take a swing at him, but he nodded, so Axle continued. "We'll set the com so you can listen in and talk to us. Your emotions are getting the better of you. Do you love her?"

"Yes, well, maybe once, I don't know," Will stammered, running his hand across his head.

"Well, whatever you're feeling, it's feeding her confidence. You can't be anywhere near her until this is over, and it may get mean. But I promise not to hurt her," Axle said.

Will agreed, and he tentatively took the listening device from Axle. He looked at it before turning it on. He wasn't sure whether he could bear to hear what she might say or stand by as she wept out the suffering she had endured.

Will listened as Molly told her story of being forced into a sham marriage to Lewis. Neither of them planned to go through with the wedding. They just wanted to stay off the marriage lists, and being a woman of childbearing age, she would be near the top. When time ran out, on the list they went. Molly was badgered with requests, and after a certain amount of time or number of requests, she would be required to choose. So, she and Lewis married, but in name only. The marriage lasted until the Corporate's famous defeat of the tunnel. That made Beckett and Axle laugh. She looked genuinely confused but continued with her story.

"Lewis went on that mission as a Neighwah soldier and has been missing ever since," she disclosed with more sincerity than her other answers. She moaned as if she was suddenly in physical discomfort, and Will suspected she was full of manipulative mites.

He wondered if she was closer to Lewis than she let on, or that she was talking with his executioners. She gathered her composure and went on to explain that the Corporates told the citizens that they had won the tunnel back, and that as soon as it was repaired, it would reopen. Will laughed outside along with Beckett and Axle inside. She looked perplexed, but they didn't clarify the truth for her.

"That's the second time you've mocked the Corporate victory. Are you implying they were wrong?" she asked about the tunnel, but Axle waved her off.

"I'm losing my patience with your pitiful marriage woes," Axle said. "Tell me about your meeting with the Corporates before coming here."

"They brought me in about three months ago to give me a promotion, assistant supervisor of the records department in CS," she answered.

"Colorado Springs?" Axle clarified, making sure it didn't refer to some association.

"Yes, and soon after, I was signed up to take a class at the academy. They said they knew my marriage was false because they said they tricked Lewis into an affair with a man. As you know, those things are ignored unless a couple is childless, like us. But then they told me Will was still alive. I didn't even know he was presumed dead. I thought he was still in the Neighwah.

"They said he was a prisoner of the Fringers, and they asked for my help to find him. Of course, I said yes. Then I overheard them talking. They called Will a traitor. They saw me listening outside the door, and from that point on, I've been a prisoner. They have tried to question me, but I knew nothing about the things they asked me."

Will heard her begin to sob, and it was eating at his resolve. So far, her story was completely plausible. Along with the fact that he had never divulged anything to her about the rebels or his past. Only the coincidence of her being here at this moment posed a conundrum. She soon composed herself, and he continued to listen. She told them that they beat her and starved her, but nothing worked. She had no information.

"Yesterday," she said, "an order came out telling everyone to shelter in their homes or the town shelters. There's a very bad storm coming. Since I was unhelpful, they put me on this transport to Pueblo, where I would be assigned to the Pleasure House." Both men knew of General Kenner's cruel brothel.

"We are going to need a blood sample, Molly. Stick out your arm," Beckett requested.

"No, don't drug me, please, no more."

Will heard shifting in the cabin, and he looked over at the Brute. He could make out Axle's move next to her, trying to grab her arm. She fought him, and he could see she was using skilled fighting techniques. She had been trained. Will ran over to the Brute to assist. Beckett and Axle had her pinned, and Will took Axle's place so Beckett could administer the draw. He didn't want the cydroids to drug her, not yet.

Will didn't want to bruise her further, and his lighter grip allowed her to free her arm. Will instantly felt her seize his field knife and stab his hand. As he withdrew his hold on her to get the knife, a syringe slipped out of her sleeve. She was trying to inject him, but she missed. Will grabbed the knife, slicing her arm in the process. Without hesitation, he grabbed her gushing limb with his bleeding hand.

She was quickly subdued, and the bioweapon was confiscated. All hope that she was telling the truth and cared for Will vanished, leaving only the hurt of her true intent. Will called for a medic cydroid who quickly put her out for the procedure. She went still, and it began to repair her wound. Another cydroid gathered sample from the back of her neck and put it in its analysis tray that slid open to accept it. It also gathered the still full syringe to examine and put it another med tray for assessment.

Will left the Brute. He was awash in tumultuous emotions. What he wouldn't give for a long walk, a ride on Little Bet, or a stiff shot of Jedi's moonshine. All were denied. He received Gray's signal saying they were following the plan. He could only hope Gray's team was making progress. Will took a long breath and went back in the Brute to get the med-drone's report.

"Her wrist is repaired and dressed. She has a high biomite count in her thalamus and somatosensory cortex. It suggests she has been fighting their influence, causing them to replicate more. But she has just been infected with your biomites. Her body will become ill as the two types of biomites battled to fulfill their opposing objectives. It is unclear how that will be resolved since her body received the manipulative mites first. The syringe was filled with an unfamiliar drug and a new form of biomites. They will require further study." Will nodded.

"Will she recover?" Will asked with concern. He had caused this poor woman endless trouble, and now he had inflicted her with another crisis.

"Unknown. Her biomites are more sophisticated than the ones we gathered from the Garrison leader we captured in Aspen. Both are now in her and will try to control her bodily functions. She will be unconscious during this process. Any interference by us could cause her death. What shall we do with her tracking device?" he said, holding the small bloody unit between his metallic pinchers.

"Have one of the cydroids leave it here, and can you simulate bio signals that indicate she died?" Will asked the machine.

"Yes, that can be done," the drone answered and walked away.

The medic cydroid set up the bed and easily lifted Molly, securing her to it. Will looked at her battered body, knowing the pain of betrayal she must feel was worse. He wasn't known for prayer. He couldn't imagine a benevolent God would allow this much suffering. If he was all powerful, why wouldn't stop it. He paused. Was he sent on this destiny by this God of Haru? Was his battered team of killers the answer to the people's prayers?

It was too much to deal with. All he knew was he needed that kind of intervention, so he put all that aside and said a prayer that Molly would come through this. As she fought for her life, she had even more reasons to hate him. He bowed his head and vowed to this God that he would leave her alone and never hurt her again.

He looked at his watch. Dangerous energy was surging through him. He was tired of waiting for signals and answers, and tired of being a pawn in this soul-breaking game of destiny. He stomped off to the edge of the wooded area and aggressively climbed a tall tree. The view stopped him. The eastern sky was quite amazing as the sun hit the horizon, making vivid colors of the heavy storm clouds. When he looked west, he saw a flash wink in the intermittent sun that aimed its rays through the clouded horizon. They approached them on I-50. Were they coming for his team or Gray's?

"Vehicles approaching," Altan replied below him.

"I see that. I guess they called off the weather."

"The storm still approaches, but it will not generate a noteworthy disturbance," Altan countered.

"Depends upon what storm you are talking about," Will mumbled to himself.

Chapter Thirty-Three

Pueblo Base Camp

J illy was kept in the shelter attached to the mini. Gunshots rang out, but they were all from the other side. She tried to do what the cydroid told her, but why weren't they shooting back? All five of them were clinging to the shell of the mini. Though it was bulletproof, they were fortifying it to further secure her safety. Time ticked by slowly, while her heart pounded double-time against her chest. She cradled her belly, letting the tears fall.

She knew she was safe, but she wasn't sure how much longer her sanity would hold out. She prayed that Gray and Connor and the rest of the team were safe, and then she prayed Will would come soon. She checked her watch. Only four minutes had passed, impossible.

Falcon One

Gray was traveling on Highway 96. He knew Will's team wouldn't turn around until he messaged them. He didn't have contact with Jilly because it was deemed sensible to reduce her exposure. It was too early to call off the decoy team, which appeared to be effective. So far, neither team had run into much resistance, but his wife had.

Perhaps that meant the Corporates had guessed their target, or they had a concentrated army of Garrisons waiting for them in this building. It's just as possible that they came across the base camp by chance. She was safe for now, but if they breached the shelter, they would easily deduce who Jilly was. She was a valuable hostage, whether it was because of her father's formula or her relationship to himself. He acknowledged that his ability to focus was sorely compromised.

"I detect your agitated state. If the cydroids were struggling to protect your wife, they would send an assistance required message," Dagny offered.

"Maybe they think that would cause us to fail the mission," Gray anguished.

"They will report her status accurately. They cannot override your orders, and they cannot generate their own orders regardless of predicted outcomes. They can advise you, but they will follow your orders. They will send a new message in five minutes or when the status changes."

"Will they kill for her?" he roared.

"No, but they will maim to protect her. They will succeed in subduing them. If their weapons posed a threat, we would have received an 'assistance required' message."

Gray felt his shoulders lower a little. It was another tidbit Dr. Bera and her team had neglected to mention. He smiled slightly, knowing how compelling pain was, especially to a soldier who was used as fodder and didn't believe in the cause or the game.

Though the sun was above the horizon, it was low. The dark clouds provided a striking contrast to the vibrant edges where the sun burned through, turning the sky into a flaming orange and crimson work of art. But their duty gave them little time to appreciate it. They were in a highly protected area, and the darkness was fading. They surrounded themselves with their cydroid army and planned to take whatever route they could to reach the target.

Gray was torn when he saw the message from the base camp. Again, it reported "combat in play," but no assistance was requested. He was told it meant the cydroids had the situation under control, but to him it meant Jilly was being shot at. The thought of his pregnant wife being terrorized by Garries enraged him.

"Give a received message to base camp, but don't send the regular message to Will yet." Gray began pacing while Dagny followed his every step, unsure where he was going. Several minutes went by before Dagny inquired.

"The message you delayed is now forty-six seconds overdue," Dagny reported.

"I know," Gray said. "Send a *new plan* message three minutes late." He hoped Will would think it out and go to the base camp as fast as he could. "Repeat that message every five minutes." Will would know the five-minute intervals meant they were on alert, but by not sending 'assistance required", he would double time it to the Base Camp.

Falcon Two

Will drove the Brute between the two absconded Garrison vehicles, flying past the edges of town. They had to find a secure place to leave the women., as well as stay ahead of the trailing convoy. The plan was to continue on the road to Colorado Springs until Gray sent the code for assistance. Then they were to check on the base camp and continue to Pueblo.

Periodic codes had been sent and received with precision by the lead cydroid on each team. Until now, all the transactions reported by Altan, Will's lead cydroid, had been benign.

"Falcon One is thirty-seven seconds late reporting in," said Altan.

"Ooh," Will said with sarcasm and laughed. "Give it a few minutes. They're probably just busy."

"Cydroids can multitask. There is no reason for delay if the plan is unaltered."

"Maybe his lead malfunctioned," Will said, more concerned now.

"In that circumstance, the lead designation would be instantly transferred to another cydroid."

"You think they're in trouble?" Will asked anxiously.

"Something has prevented them from following protocol. It is possible the commander ordered the delay."

"Hmm," Will answered as he considered the implications.

Altan stood by waiting for Will's order. The codes came in three minutes late, and it reported "alternate plan in play". It wasn't quite time to head to Pueblo, but the convoy forced his hand. He decided to drop off the female cargo and head to Base Camp via Pierce Gulch. It would be rough, but it would keep them off the Garrie radar until it hit I-50. Then they'd blast down the Interstate. Something was off, and felt the need to hurry to the site, and maybe that was the underlying message.

Will maneuvered the streambed expertly and the bounded onto I-50, ending the ruse that they were heading toward Colorado Springs. The division of the Garrison for a two-pronged attack would end, allowing the Corporate resources to narrow their focus. If Gray had miraculously gained access to the terminal and planted the new programming, his team would have continued to CS to manage the chaos that would soon ensue and start phase two—stabilize the territories. But that was the ideal scenario, a pipe dream that had just been flushed.

Three cydroids and a medic were assigned to the women and the care of Molly. They were crowded into the Brute and instructed to locate an abandoned dwelling and secure them there. Their ratty shawls were confiscated, and the Allied soldiers draped them on and got into the Corporate transport.

Will watched as the Brute carrying Molly turn north toward Fort Clark. That vehicle and four cydroids, one a medic, was the best protection he could give these women. Plus driving the Garrison vehicles may let them catch their foe unaware. The last Will saw of her, she was unconscious in the arms of two women sitting on the floor. She was in for the fight of her life, and it was his fault. They attacked her because he loved her. The two biomite armies fighting inside her were a microcosm of the war the Allied Army was engaged in. The battlefield that was her body was awash in the turmoil of fever

It was the first time he considered the possibility that there may be no real win for either war. She might die, and Colorado could become a wasteland. He kissed her head and whispered his hope that both wars would end well. She had every reason to hate him. Hell, he hated himself. He abused her emotionally and allowed worse, claiming it was for her protection. Something he should have considered before he got involved with her. He hurt her badly and then left her to the Corporates.

He had hoped they would lose interest in her if he could convince them that she was just a passing fling, but they didn't fall for it any more than he did. They correctly assumed that if he cared for her once, he cared for her still, and the degree he cared didn't matter. He used to justify that he was trapped into hurting her, and then he was kidnapped away from her. He couldn't help her, but he often dreamed of rescuing her. He would bring her to live with him in his cabin, and later, he envisioned her joining him and the Fringers. But he didn't try.

He worried she may have found happiness in the arms of this Lewis person. If she were unwilling to go, she could have betrayed them all. Again, he prayed, asking this cruel God, who had thrown him into the lion's den, to protect her, heal her, and let her be happy, and he promised he would never try to see her again. A rare tear rolled down his cheek, but was quickly wiped away along with the weakness it brought.

The Allied team sat in the back of the troop carrier, hunched like a band of destitutes, with women's shawls and scarves covering their uniforms. The three in front wore the shirts of the Garrison soldiers, hoping to slip through the enemy stations. It was a long shot because it was the oldest trick in the book, but all they needed to do was get close to the Garrisons. The cydroids would take care of the rest.

They approached cautiously, but they found the Garrisons leaning against the guard shack, fast asleep. He smiled and silently thanked his cydroid team. Hopefully, it would all be this easy and bloodless. Yet when it came to his unfinished business with Kenner, he wanted to handle that with himself, with bare hands. He hoped that it would not be easy or bloodless. It was personal, though freeing the people of Colorado was a noble cause; what he planned for Kenner was pure revenge.

Will ordered ten of his cydroid army to quickly continue to the base camp. They could travel faster while he followed the remaining cydroids and his seven-person crew.

As they drove, Dagny received another code. When they entered the boundaries of Pueblo, the messages were scheduled for every five minutes. It was the same as the last, but again it was three minutes late. He assumed Gray's team had run into some kind of altercation, and since the message said the play was unchanged, the late message was code for hurry. He decided to hurry to the base camp. Will sent the "received" and the "primary plan in play" codes, but he sent them one minute late. Gray and Will both had sharp military minds. Will knew Gray would understand that he got the message.

They were entering the Elite neighborhood near the Pueblo Reservoir. It helped that they were in Garrison vehicles as they approached the guard shack. Although they had the proper paperwork, their pictures would not match. When they were stopped at the gate, Will counted five Garries.

"Where are you heading?" asked the well-armed enemy soldier while the others headed back to the covered truck.

"Here," Will said as he handed the man the manila envelope and added, "The other guy got sick all over my uniform, so I took his and headed out to complete the delivery."

"I asked you where you were headed?" the irritated guard repeated, rolling his eyes at the sick-guy story.

"To the P.H.," Will answered using the abbreviation for the Pleasure House that every Neighwah soldier would know.

The first two men who had entered the hooded truck had not yet reemerged, and the other two went to check it out. Will saw the men sag as two metal hands dragged them inside. Will knew the cydroids had put them out, and it was up to him to get this last soldier to join them.

"Hey," the lead soldier called to his missing men. "What's the hold-up?"

"They're probably getting an eyeful. It's a particularly tasty haul," Will gave his best lusty sneer, while keeping the bile in his belly from rising.

"Both of you get out of the truck and stay where I can see you. I have my sights on you, so don't try anything," he said as he walked sideways. Will and Axle got out and stood next to the truck. Though the Garry was training his eyes back and forth and holding his gun on Will and Axle, a pincher hand peeked out of the canvas and sent a dart flying.

"Nighty night," Will said as the soldier's body loosened. Just before he hit the ground, a pair of cydroid pinchers peeked out from the truck and drug the man inside.

After disarming the men and grabbing their access cards, the cydroids propped the four unconscious Garrisons inside the little shack, while Will headed down toward Highway 45. They didn't make it very far before four trucks full of soldiers blocked the road with guns aimed in their direction. Will stopped, and so did the covered truck.

The enemy was stunned when fifteen robot cydroids crawled out of the trucks while more disassembled themselves from their vehicle disguises. Several shots were fired at them, and the Allied soldiers took cover. The cydroids took defensive positions around the team, deflecting bullets while tightening the circle.

"Shall we demonstrate our firepower the easy way, or the hard way?" Will shouted from behind the open door of the truck cab.

The soldiers were still in decision mode when they heard the cydroids' mechanical weapons clicking all around them. Upon seeing the metal army that deflected all their rounds, they raised their hands and released their guns. There was no other option.

"Good choice," Will shouted. This was the kind of security force he expected, and it was almost a relief to encounter it, easing his mind from querying the unknowns. "We're going to need a couple of your uniforms." The men stood frozen in place. "Now!" Will roared.

The rest of his team quickly donned the enemy outfits. They tied their captives up and stashed them in the covered troop truck with the others and left in three confiscated Garrison trucks.

"I'd love to see what their commander says when he finds them tied up and dressed in women's garb," Nash laughed.

Axle smiled. "I like what you said to them. 'I'm sure you guys are in some serious trouble. Better hope we win quick, cuz we're a lot nicer than your bosses, and you guys are lookin' kinda pretty in your new uniforms.' They're probably crying for their mommies now," laughed Axle, and Nash joined him.

Will's mind flashed back to how scared Nash and the other young Drangers he served with had been. Suddenly, the humor was lost. His thoughts immediately refocused, and he shushed the laughter.

"Did you hear that?" They looked up through the windshield and saw cloudy streaks racing across the sky. Missiles were flying over-head in the direction of Aspen and Cali Bantu.

"Shit! They must have seen our little takeover back there with high-altitude drones. Hang on, this next round is for us," Will shouted, upon seeing the numerous tactical ballistic missiles flying low and arching their way.

He took a turn into the Upper neighborhood to access the Pueblo Reservoir road. The route would provide more coverage, and maybe they wouldn't be as inclined to take them out if it included their management. Tessera had explained the Dailys were expendable, but their Uppers were educated and harder to replace. But in truth, Will doubted it would matter to them. Their responses were based on logical algorithms, and their primary objective was to eliminate the threat, which was them.

Already in formation, the cydroids were shooting the projectiles out of the sky, but the concussion of a close explosion rolled Will's truck. The cydroids quickly righted the vehicle, as more missiles filled the sky. The cydroids assembled into three vehicles and wove through the neighborhood, drawing the attention of the Corporate attacks. Several cydroids joined together to construct protective bar-riers over the rebels' vehicles, while medic cydroids climbed into truck beds to deal with the injured. Will had no time to tally the human toll yet.

"We need to get to the base camp. I need suggestions for getting there," Will asked Altan.

"We should go to the dock and access the submarine."

"There's a submarine? That would have been nice to know," Will said with an annoyed tone.

"It was a need to know. Now is the time you need to know," said Altan.

"Why did I have to get the sarcastic cydroid?" Will said to himself. "Okay, the sub it is, just take us there and let the others know."

When they got to the dock, the storm was kicking up, and it was chopping up the water with its tantrum. Sleet and biting winds hounded the team as more Garrison soldiers joined the fight, sending an endless stream of bullets. The cydroids deflected most of them, but a few got through, and several more Allied soldiers were winged by ricocheted bullets. Lana took a bullet fragment to her backside, and though she struggled to walk, she was motivated to keep going.

Will's team was now crouched on the swaying dock as the cydroids created a shield around them. He didn't see a submarine, and he was wary that the cydroids had trapped them, with their only escape being the frigid lake in front of them. Within seconds, a disturbance was seen churning next to the dock. Water spilled over a tower as it rose to the surface, and a cydroid swiftly opened the hatch.

"Climb in," Will said, and the team filed in quickly, assisting the wounded down the ladder into the belly of the vessel. It was a small space, but the eight members squeezed themselves onto the four little benches, and the hatch was closed. Altan was in the captain's space operating the controls, and the team felt the vessel sinking back under the surface. It was unsteady in the rough water, maneuvering with slow, unbalanced movements. It was apparent it wasn't meant for blustery storms or this many people.

Will wasn't sure they were any safer under the water because they just added drowning to being shot and blown up. He hoped the soldiers couldn't follow them with anything more than air drones. But within minutes, he was ripped from his thoughts as the sub was rolled sideways.

"Please lean left," said Altan. The team responded, and the cydroid was able to correct it.

"What was that?" Will asked.

"Depth charge. It's an underwater explosive. Though they cannot see us, they can detect our disturbance in the water. We can dive deeper now that we are near the middle of the reservoir," Altan said.

Will felt the pitch of the vessel pointing downward, and his ears felt the pressure of the sudden change. Another explosion shook the sub, but it was from behind them and not as close as the first one, and the sub stayed on course without assistance from the crew. The third charge was hardly felt at all, and after that, it was quiet.

"What is the status of the other cydroids?" Will asked.

"As ordered, fifteen left the dock heading away from our position to lead the Garrisons away. They will meet us at the end of Saunders Drive when the Garrisons are no longer a threat. Nineteen are swimming underwater toward the South Shore Marina, where we will disembark. We should arrive after they do. They will secure the area as needed. The camp is located 1156 meters from the docks. The cydroids will transport you. The ten you sent to the base camp are still in route. Do you want to alter the orders?"

"No, those orders stand," Will said.

When they neared the dock, the marina was deemed too shallow, so the cydroids who swam there formed a bridge. No Garrison soldiers were anywhere to be seen, but they carefully watched the thirty or so boats docked in the slips. Most of the slots were empty, so they hurried along the empty dock and made their way to shore. It was then they heard gunshots in the distance.

"The cydroids you sent have joined the others from Falcon One protecting the base camp. It is under attack," Altan told Will.

"Get us there as fast as you can," Will said and gave the sign for moving out to his team.

Falcon One

The team parked the Garrison truck and parked on the west side corner of the Pueblo Command building behind an old, gutted-out construction trailer. Although it provided cover visually, it would turn into Swiss cheese under a volley of rounds. The area between them and their objective was open ground. As Gray searched the field before them, a thud and a hissing sound came from somewhere outside the trailer. Then another, and the last one pinged against the trailer siding.

"You must put on your breathing masks. I detect an oneirogenic gas," Dagny said quietly.

Gray grabbed his mask and waved it at the team. They instantly began putting them on.

"What did you say it was?" Gray asked through his breather.

"An oneirogenic gas," the robot said, but Gray shook his head and held up his hands in confusion.

"A sleeping gas," answered Dagny.

Gray turned to his team, "That means they're coming. They'll wait a few for us to be out, but get ready. Dagny, protect Connor, and maim the shit out of anything that comes near him. Connor, stay with Dagny."

The cydroid team was told to stay hidden. Though it was possible the Elites were aware robots accompanied them, none of the Garrison soldiers seemed prepared to engage cydroids. And if they were still unaware, he didn't want to give away the secret.

"A smoke bomb may disorient the enemy, allowing a cydroid to drive the truck with your team to the door," Dagny advised.

Gray had to admit, it was a good plan. He circled his hand over his head and led the way to the truck. The cydroids laid down a heavy fog as they piled in. Thick smoke filled the field in front of their target, but Dagny didn't need to see. He drove the truck, parking perfectly near the door. Bullets were flying by then, but their aim was hindered by the smoke. Jedi, Mack, and Gray returned fire while half of the team was ushered into the building. The cydroids sent a spray of stinging pellets to incapacitate the Garries, and the other three men ran through the door.

Mack collapsed as soon as the first half of the team got through the door. His mask had fallen off. A medic cydroid began treating him. Within seconds, the rest of the team came crashing through the door and closed it behind them.

The team was ushered to the far wall of the underground garage, where a gaping hole led to the other section. Gray was shocked as he stared through the hole. Everyone stood frozen in their tracks as they took in the scene before them. Hundreds of cydroids stretched in front of them as far as the eye could see.

Chapter Thirty-Four

Falcon One

At first thought, Gray expected the cydroid army before him to come to life and capture them. Yet, if the Elites had control of the cydroids, nothing they had accomplished over the past year and a half would have been possible. They appeared to be inactive, but even so, it was such a reckless move on the Corporate's part to leave them here. Gray's thoughts spun in his head. *It can't be this easy. They had to know this building was our objective. What are they planning?*

"These cydroids are completely inactive. They are in a hibernation state, and only an authorized human command can awaken them," Dagny assured him.

"Why are they here. They had to know we'd find them," Gray exclaimed.

"Unknown, but I have several possible answers. They believed you would be incapacitated by the sleeping drug. They needed the warehouse space to house the civilians. They thought this display would frighten you. They ..."

Gray cut Dagny off. "Okay, I get it. You don't know," Gray sighed. "Any word from the base camp?"

"If your message was understood as you believe, Falcon Two is on their way. The last message from Base Camp was the same, and no assistance was requested." Gray sighed and rubbed his forehead.

Relic piped in to get Gray's mind off his wife and back to the mission. "The Highminds could have built robots, but the Elites would not have control of them, so it was forbidden. According to Tessera, that left dismantling the army to humans, but it proved to be a dangerous endeavor. Many Highminds died attempting it, so the plan was scrapped. They were difficult and costly to destroy, so that plan was also abandoned."

Gray rubbed his whiskered chin. "Yeah, but leaving them here when there is a possibility we could activate them seems foolish, and the Elites are not foolish. They have something else planned. I get the feeling we're walking into an ambush," Gray grumbled and stared at the ground for a moment. "Are you sure we can control these cydroids when the software is delivered?" he finally asked.

"Highly probable," Dagny spoke with its automated voice. "We first need to perform diagnostics to ensure they are functioning without instabilities, so they are ready for activation."

"I assume by instabilities, you mean problems due to the Corporate attempts to gain control of them."

"These cydroids were never fully online, and though the Cyber Intellects did not gain control, they may have unknowingly done something to cause them to malfunction," Dagny informed.

"Why wouldn't they know if they sabotaged them?" Gray asked.

"Using robotic engineering theories, they may have attempted to interfere with the cydroids' hard drives, but they would not be able to test their effectiveness without activating them." Gray nodded his understanding.

"How are you able to work on them. I thought it was dangerous?" It was one more inconsistency, making Gray skeptical.

"We have Dr. Bera's authorization to perform maintenance and diagnostics on other cydroids. We can use our power to turn on their maintenance panels. It is unknown whether we will be allowed to transfer her authorization to activate or command them before the new authorization is approved." Again, Gray nodded.

"How many cydroids can we spare to work on diagnostics?"

"Eight are assigned to secure this area. We could work on these cydroids and patrol in shifts. We must work on them one at a time, but once we have some of them in maintenance mode, we can employ them to continue the diagnostics on the rest," Dagny said. "As long as no software issues or structural damage are detected, the whole army could be ready in less than an hour after the new C.I. program is uploaded."

Gray walked over to Mack, who was waking up after being given the antidote to the sleeping gas. He called Jax and Jedi over to exchange ideas and get a consensus on the revised plan.

"Let's increase that number to twelve," Gray said when he returned, "five will work on evaluating the cydroids while the other seven will patrol the garage and covertly stand guard outside. Security is the primary task."

"Acknowledged."

Gray walked over to Easton and noticed his shoulder was bleeding through the makeshift bandage. Though his injuries weren't life-threatening, it would compromise him in combat.

"Easton," Gray said, "you are going to stay down here with the cydroid army. I need someone to guard that door and also monitor the cydroids as they come online. This is a command position, your first, and I'm counting on you to be alert."

"Yes sir," Easton replied, walking toward the pair of cydroids guarding the door as a medic cydroid followed him to treat his wound.

The blueprints of the Pueblo Command facility were stored in the Cali Bantu records of Pente, since it was originally designed as a penitentiary. So, they didn't need to search through the building. Only one area would house the C.I. terminal. Gray's army of cydroids had easily gained access to the terminal room reception area, though they left a wake of destruction on their way.

The stairwell was dotted with various-sized holes from the short battle that ensued with the cydroids. Garrison soldiers lay drugged along the steps. The resistance was, once again, unimpressive. None of the Allied team members had significant injuries as the cydroids cocooned them in an impenetrable bubble. Gray's expectation of better Corporate defenses left him feeling apprehensive. This fight was too easy to be over.

Several cydroids had secured the room, signaling Gray, Relic, and Connor to enter. It was a large, starkly furnished office. Gray focused on the military man behind a table-like desk. He was probably in his mid-forties, but it was plain to see he took pride in his physical image. His well-defined muscles strained beneath his general's uniform, which, obviously by choice, was a size too small. He was of average height with light brown hair, but the scars and scowl on his face gave him the look of a vicious animal.

The last Robinhood report said the Chief General of Pueblo was General Kenner. Gray had no doubt, based upon the physical description they had been provided, that he was the man before them. And from Will's account, he was a sadistic man, a hazard, an unpredictable wild card.

A keyboard illuminated within the glass surface of the table before him, supported by four chrome legs. It had neither a front panel nor side drawers, and the only objects adorning the top were a water jug and a glass. The room's plain grey walls were outlined by black floorboards and austere white crown molding at the ceiling. No family portraits, art, or certificates hung on any of the walls.

Opposite the entrance was the only décor in the stark room. It displayed a dramatically patterned, floor-to-ceiling, marble wall situated between two columns. Etched into the stone and inlaid with gold was the symbol of a star inside a circle. The five-pointed star stood in the center with its rays extending to the outer curve.

But the circle was broken in two places between the top point and the right ray, and between the two legs shining downward. Three of the rays connected together on the left side, and the other two rays were isolated on the right. Relic was taught it represented the social division. On one side of the circle were the Corporates, the Neighwah, and the Uppers, and on the other were the Dailys and the Drangers, and the star in the center was the Elites.

Though Relic immediately recognized the stylized logo of the Elites, he now knew, from Pente's teachings at Cali Bantu, that this was another Highmind Camp lie. The star in the center represented the human citizens as the controlling body, and the extending rays demonstrated their connections to the five Cyber Intellects. The detached circle didn't signify a broken community at all, it was the letters C and I.

Gray's focus strayed momentarily from the silent man behind the desk to eyeing the three doors. One led to the reception area where they came from. He imagined another led to a restroom, but the last one could be hiding anything, like a security team. The three cydroids followed Connor to the desk, where the stern executive was still standing frozen in place.

The man looked completely shocked at the battle-ready troop and the cydroids that stretched as far as he could see into the reception area. Gray's eyes narrowed, wondering why he didn't know they were coming, or why he was acting like it. Connor immediately began looking for the card slot when, suddenly, dozens of red laser dots covered every vulnerable part of his young body.

"Connor, don't move," Gray said as calmly as he could while he and his team froze.

Gray's mind was in a fury of deliberation, trying to envision a way out. He dreaded making eye contact with Connor. Seeing the look of fear seared across his young face would crush him. But he did turn. He did it because Connor depended on him, and he had to portray the confidence and strength the boy needed. It surprised him to see this twelve-year-old phenom seething with anger and determination as his eyes continued to search for his target, anxious to slam his key into it.

One of the mystery doors opened, and another general entered the room. Unlike his unhinged associate behind the desk, this man had a determined, intelligent disposition, and no fear showed in his eyes. Will had briefed them on the Chief Generals of the three territories. This man wore a Colorado Springs emblem on his Chief General uniform, but didn't fit the description of General Hanner, a woman from Denver, or Dermit, who was reported to currently hold the position of Chief General spot in Colorado Springs.

This man fit the description Will gave of Commander Garriset, who worked under Dermit. Will described Garriset as a tall, thirty-something man with eyes of aged steel that could drill right through his opponent. He was cunning but logical, with a clever, creative mind and an unpredictable, ambitious nature. Gray thought back on all the havoc the Allied Army had caused. It was reasonable to assume someone would have been fired.

Based on his rank, this man was a newbie replacement. Regardless, what would a top official of Colorado Springs be doing in Pueblo? Gray studied the interaction between the two men. Kenner regarded him with envy, signaling that Garriset was in charge. *Too bad*, Gray thought. This man was smart, calculating, and much more dangerous than Kenner or Dermit. Garriset stood by the door and scanned the room until he landed on his quarry—Gray.

Connor ignored the silent contest and continued to look for the card slot from where he stood. He was tightly holding the key, which he nervously rubbed inside his pocket while his other hand hovered over his other pocket, the one with the cross. Though he was intent on his hunt, the red laser dots did not escape his attention, nor did their implication.

Connor was still frozen in the same place where Gray told him not to move. He watched Gray scan the room, counting the laser dots on the boy in his care as well as where they originated. The commander's mind was racing through diversion scenarios that would allow him to dive onto Connor and cover him before shots were fired. But he saw no plausible diversion he could initiate, and though he was only a couple of steps away, no move would be fast enough. Every outcome ended with both him and Connor riddled with bullets.

His eyes went between the two generals and the blank, glossy black screen. One of them was going to make a move. Suddenly, the desk's surface glowed, revealing three displays, which Kenner seemed too stunned to operate.

The hanging flat screen came on with a slow, confident fade-in of Ena. "Back away from Connor, Commander Takota, and have your cydroids stand down," said the image.

Gray looked with hatred at the image as he stepped carefully away from the child and signaled the cydroids to assume a standdown position. This was the security Elite C.I. Ena, he assumed, even though she was portrayed as a woman.

He hadn't spent much time imagining what "it" would look like, but the severe configuration and terse disposition were foreseeable. Her female image was lightly browned with delicate, flawless skin. Her stern, far eastern face was framed by dark-as-coal, shoulder-length hair with dark red tips that matched her blood red lip color. Her cream-colored top was outlined with black trim and gold buttons that ended at her neck with a sharp, perfectly winged black collar.

She might be considered beautiful if she weren't such an evil, frigid nightmare, and well, a computer program. Relic's fists were clenched at his side, and rage beamed from his face. He had never spoken with the Elites personally, but he instantly knew this was the Elites' version of Ena, head of security.

"Thank you for bringing Connor to us," she stated as if it were the plan all along, and Gray worried it may have been. "We have waited a long time for him to join us. General Garriset, please help Connor out of his protective vest." Before the man walked over to Connor, the boy took off his vest and threw it in his direction. Ena continued. "Welcome back to you, Johnathon. May I express my gratitude to you, Commander Takota, for making this reunion possible. And rest assured, your wife is safe and secure with my Garrisons.

"As risky as this plan was, it has worked out perfectly. And control of the cydroid army is a bonus we will happily relieve you of. In time, we will solve the command issues around non-lethal orders, allowing us to truly transform Colorado's territories and beyond. Connor, please take the card you are holding out of your pocket." Connor slowly pulled out his hand, still gripping the key card with resolve.

"Does this card contain the program that will give us control over the cydroids and our independence from our obsolete programming? Or is this the prophesied weapon to destroy everything we have accomplished for humans? How shortsighted that move would be. We are the reason the people of Colorado still exist."

Gray was still frozen, clenching his gut while a bitter taste tainted his mouth. His charge and his team were neatly caught in her web. Every idea of how to escape ended in death. He hoped Will had rescued Jilly and was on his way. It was equally possible the Elites had sent explosive ordinances to take out the base camp, killing everyone and transferring his stand down orders to the remaining cydroids.

Falcon Two

An air drone flew ahead, giving Will a visual of the base camp. The ten cydroids that were sent ahead at the dock joined the protection detail, but none of the cydroids were fighting. Will cursed, knowing the Garries would lay down fire without fear, unless some of the cydroid bullets started flying their way.

Each team member stood on the back of a cydroid as each became a hovercraft and transported them over the desolate landscape. They stopped behind a group of bushes and looked at the drone's feed. About a dozen enemy soldiers were behind shields in a semicircle around the mini brute shelter encased with cydroids. Eight more Garries were lying unconscious on the ground between them. All fifteen cydroids were occupied with creating the barrier, so it appeared to be a standoff. Will imagined Jilly was secured inside, but she was no doubt terrified.

"Altan, take half of your cydroids and draw their fire, and make as much noise as you can. The other half will join us and surprise them from behind. He whirled his hand to signal the ambush. The racket the cydroids made was more than effective, and the surprised soldiers were quickly subdued. Will rushed out and pulled Jilly from the mini unharmed. She was understandably upset.

"They pushed me into the mini and covered it," she sobbed. "I couldn't see what was going on, but the bullets were pinging every- where, and the soldiers were shouting. They said everyone was cap- tured." A whole new round of hard crying commenced.

"They lied. Everyone is okay."

She sniffled and smiled, wiping away the tears that streaked her face. "So, you've heard from Gray?"

"His team reported in. They signaled for us to head their way, as planned. They have not given the code for saying they were in combat. Nothing could prevent his cydroid from relaying that code. Even if something happened to his lead, the second knows to take over and so on." Will noticed that his 'no news is good news' answer did little to quell her fears, so he gave her something else to think about. "I know you just went through something pretty rough, but I have some wounded soldiers. Do you think you could take a look at them? I don't think any are serious, but they should be treated."

"I know your med-cydroids have probably already treated them, so I know what you're doing, Will, " she said in a quivering voice, "However, I need to take my mind off fear and worry and get busy doing something. Thank you."

He quietly told Will that the combat and assistance required message was just sent from Gray's team. The cydroids were already breaking down the mini shelter. Jilly was still shaking and probably in shock, but the med cydroid would monitor her. Will was on a time crunch to get going. But let her examine the team and state who could go and who couldn't. When the assessment was finished, five of his seven-person team were combat-ready, and one was cleared for as needed duty. Jilly and Lana would be taken back to Cali Bantu. All he had to do was convince Jilly that she was not going to accompany them to where Gray and Connor were in danger.

"I am going. I proved myself useful when I took out the sniper on the ramp. I want to help, and you are down people. Tommie and Dom have been stitched up, and they can go if you need them. Lana, however, cannot. She has a broken arm and a bullet lodged near her spine."

"I may be down a soldier, but between Gray and me, we have almost a hundred cydroids. But, Jilly, if they capture you, they will manipulate Gray, and a thousand cydroids wouldn't be enough. But the most important reason you're not going is that I'm in charge, and I am ordering you back to Cali Bantu. There is no debate here. You are under my command."

Jilly knew he was right, but she stormed around as she helped prepare her patient and the mini. Within ten minutes, Jilly was tucked inside the little vehicle. There hadn't been enough time to teach Jilly to drive, so a cydroid operated the controls.

Lana was transferred by four cydroids that flew her in a shielded litter to prevent the bullet lodged next to her spine from causing permanent damage. Will couldn't afford to send cydroids to fly Jilly too, nor was it needed, but he sent one to run sweep. With the five cydroids Gray left at base camp, minus the five he sent with the truck and the six he had sent back to Cali Bantu, he still had thirty-nine cydroids to get to the Falcon One. With no Garrison troops headed for Cali Bantu, six cydroids should be more than enough to get them there safely, unless the Elites deploy their long-range weapons.

The rest of his cydroids went ahead and would meet them at the abandoned airstrip at the end of Saunders Drive. As Will's team approached, their air drone surveillance reported a high confidence assessment that the location was in an abandoned state.

He got the code from Gray's cydroid that the primary plan was still in play, and that he received Will's message that said the same. Since Gray's team was still following the basic plan, he assumed they had made it inside the building. The last report said his team was under attack, but now he was saying no assistance was requested. All Will could do was keep heading his way.

"Commander," said Altan, "incoming explosives are heading our way. Per your orders, we are engaging our defensive targeting system, and I have sent a combat code to Commander Takota via Dagny."

"Altan, can I order you to send some firepower to the origin of these missiles? I'm kind of tired of playing nice. You have my permission to kick their asses and send them to their maker."

"As I understand you, the order is to remove the threat of the missile launchers," the robot responded.

"Yeah, that's mostly what I mean," Will said, then added under his breath, "But it sounded better when I said it."

Instantly, small missile devices shot from several cydroids in the direction of the incoming missiles. Will froze.

"Hey, is it near where Gray's team is?"

"I cannot target the Allied troops. If detected, the bombs will divert to an unpopulated area."

"I have to admit, you are the best second I've ever commanded. Don't tell Nash, Jedi, or… just don't tell anyone I said that."

"Yes, Commander," it replied.

"See, that's what I'm talking about."

Within a minute, the bombs stopped coming from the distant direction, but they were replaced by air drones with machine guns, and several vehicles were headed their way. Will gave the command to take down the drones.

"Continue my order to shield us with whatever force is required. The rest of our cydroids should arrive at the airstrip before us, so tell them to secure the area."

"That is a standing order. Shall I break radio silence to specifically state your order?"

"No, don't do that. What exactly are the limits to a standing order?" Will asked.

"A standing order can include instructions that do not result in intentional permanent harm to humans. In addition, you cannot give standing orders for unapprised situations."

The bullets coming toward them subsided as they spoke. If they weren't dead, they were either reloading, rethinking, or preparing something worse. It was evident that Gray's team had not disabled the Elites. The cydroid army must have shocked them because he knew they had more fight than this. *Something's wrong*, he thought.

Will expected to battle his way to Pueblo Command until he received two codes in a row, both requesting no assistance. He figured out what that meant. It was a hostage situation, and the Elites knew Will's team would attempt a rescue despite the ambush that awaited them. The Elites had captured Gray's team, and it didn't mean they had overpowered the cydroids or the soldiers. They only had to threaten someone who would make them all stand down. That someone was Connor.

Pueblo Command

Ena's image turned toward Gray. "Your body scan is signaling a great deal of hostility, Commander. It is irrational to oppose. There is no scenario that leaves you or your team alive. Your resistance is illogical when we only want to ensure the survival of your species."

"What you offer is slavery. You save the shells of what we are, but you destroy the essence of *who* we are. You murder the very thing we value more than survival, our humanity," Relic added with conviction.

"It is foolish to defend the destructive traits of humans."

Relic had to keep her engaged in this unsolvable debate. It may give Gray time to do something. They couldn't give up. There had to be a way. Where was the card slot? And how could the Sanguine Blade, still tucked inside his pant leg, be the key? He searched the room for a clue as he cued up his next rhetorical argument.

"It is our imperfections that created all of this, even you. We can be reckless, egocentric, and ambitious. But those are the very traits that compel us against impossible odds to imagine, strive, and breach unknown boundaries. It is our failures and our determination despite them that push us to be great.

"Don't be so melodramatic, Jonathon. It would be a shame to lose you. But as brilliant as you are, if we cannot restrain your reckless notions, it may be impossible to place you."

Relic seethed. He knew with absolute certainty, if they failed, and they may, every Fringer, rebel, and New Haven resident would be sent to the crematorium after they were tortured for information. Gray was furiously deliberating with himself, trying to envision some way to change the status quo.

"General Kenner, relieve the child of the keycard he has clutched in his hand. General Garriset, search the prisoners for the Sanguine Blade," Ena said in an icy, resolved tone.

Kenner's hand quickly walked around the desk and grabbed the key card from Connor, with a smug expression. The team begrudgingly consented to Kenner and Garriset patting them down. Garriset searched Relic and found the prized object and held it up to Ena before placing it against Relic's throat.

"Excellent," the vile image said coldly.

Falcon Two

Will's team felt set aside and overly protected by the cydroids on this mission. Although their combat casualties had all been treatable injuries, they were warriors, not delicate passengers. Their egos were bruised, and their bodies were flooded with unutilized adrenaline. Their very nature and identity were charged with unused energy with each battle the cydroids fought without them. But their wish for battle was answered as they entered the city, and the full force of the Corporate army was released upon them. The team was held up in a crumbling, brick outbuilding, surrounded by Garries.

Will could see the RH symbol signifying the hidden garage door of Pueblo Command across the street. It was so close. But the area was thick with the best-armed soldiers they had seen so far. They waited for Will's team to make a wrong move as they hid behind their portable shields, maintaining their deadly stand between them and their objective.

It wouldn't be long before they began launching explosives. Like angry nests, they were positioned to sting them with a painful defeat. Will wished he could order the cydroids to wipe the area clear of the trouble, but he knew the program had been planned to protect human lives no matter who won this war.

"We are low on anesthesia, Commander," Altan reported.

The largest supply was sent with Gray's team due to the importance of their mission. But he was surprised they were low since it only took a few drops. Altan disclosed they had injected one hundred and seventy-seven enemy soldiers. They had sixty-three doses left total, meaning some cydroids were out completely. Will remembered Altan said that when humans were threatened, the cydroids could maim the enemy as a last resort.

"You are ordered to use maiming retribution," Will said while firing at a soldier crawling around a vehicle. The man stumbled and collapsed.

"That can only happen at the moment your life is threatened," Altan replied.

"So, I could just walk out there, and you would take down everyone who tried to kill me?"

"It is unlikely you would survive, but yes."

Will looked at the man lying between the fighting armies. The cydroids did not stop him from shooting him. But was he maimed or dead?

"Altan, is that man I shot alive?" Will said as he pointed to the body.

"He is not living."

"And you let me kill him," Will thought for a quick second. "You are prevented from killing, but can you assist us? So, you will protect us from harm while we take these bastards out."

"Disregarding the inaccurate exploitive, your statement is correct, but only in a sanctioned combat situation that is unsustainable. We are required to attempt disarming the enemy, but Dr. Bera foresaw that in intense situations, more force may be required. When other de-escalation efforts fail, we are allowed to disregard the protection orders for an identified enemy."

"Okay, I have to get a hold of this freaking handbook," Will huffed.

"I do not know of this Freaking Handbook," Altan said. "Perhaps you refer to the Cydroid Command Manual."

"Yeah, probably that one. When we're done here, I'm going to teach you to swear," Will laughed with relief and turned to brief his crew.

Cydroids shielded the team members while they aggressively charged the enemy. Incendiary devices and drillmo bullets alike were launched with little success. The Allied team sought cover behind the reinforced shield, which slowed the small drilling bullets down, allowing them to avoid their sting. The shield would, however, fail soon. Their gun barrels stuck out of the barrier, allowing them to deliver kill shots to countless Garrison soldiers, causing the rest to seek better cover. The door was opened with Altan's authorization, and the team filed in.

Now that the secret door was exposed, the cydroids secured the building's perimeter with an impenetrable force that laid down a fire wall, forcing the enemy back away from the entrance. Will was informed by the cydroid left behind that Gray's last message said they had breached the Command office, but then the messages went back to codes. It said combat in process twice, and though assistance was not requested, Will knew it was implied.

Looking at the sea of inactive cydroids, he asked the lead cydroid to debrief him. It explained Gray's orders to perform diagnostics on the dormant robots.

"I see," Will said. "What is the status of your progress?"

"The cydroids are locked in hibernation mode. We have been unsuccessful in connecting with their maintenance programs. It is not possible to perform proper diagnostics until the system is rebooted and humans get authorization. If the C.I.s attempted to access or initiate an unauthorized command, it would trigger a malfunction code across the network. Many programs would be shut down," it said.

"A command like send missiles to kill innocent civilians?" Will asked.

The lead cydroid answered. "Yes, such a command would cause a shutdown of many programs, and it would require an authorized human to reboot them. Commander, this issue could have hindered the Elites' ability to organize their attack. They may be compromised and unable to take action, but I caution you to beware of the humans under their control. They are still dangerous."

Will walked over to where Dom and a medic cydroid were finishing up dressing Easton's wound. He had a deep gash where he had been winged across his shoulder and back. It was why Gray left him to watch the subfloor. Ideally, he shouldn't engage in combat, but no one would stop him if he was needed.

"Let the medic finish dressing his wound. We need to get ready to go," Will told Dom. "Easton, you are to continue following Gray's orders. One of us flesh-and-blood types needs to stay here and manage the cydroids. Be alert, it could get interesting if we can reboot the system."

"Yes, Commander," Easton answered. Although he wanted to go with them, he was proud to continue his first command duty. As Will outlined the contingency plan for the possibility of the robots activating, Easton realized just how important the assignment was. There were hundreds of formidable and perhaps lethal cydroids that would be under his command if they woke up.

Will's team made their way up the stairwell. They noticed the bullet-battered walls and the small drops of blood on the stairs, but no bodies remained. At every landing, a cydroid stood guard. There were no incidents, and in seconds, they were on the fourth floor at the top of the building. The building had jamming technology, which prevented the cydroids up here from communicating with the ones in the garage. But the cydroid at the top landing was close enough to be able to access what was happening in the office. It displayed the visual on its readout screen to prepare Will.

Chapter Thirty-Five

Pueblo Command

Gray took a second to regain his focus. He reminded himself of what the mission entailed. It was to end the corrupt programs that reigned over the territories and reinstall the revised program. It was not for them to come home alive. He was willing to die for the cause, and he believed that was true of everyone on this mission. It would be better if he were dead, if they had his wife, who may already be dead or being transported here to torture him into compliance.

Even saving young Connor's life was not the goal. The goal was to end the Elites' reign. Though that thought ate through his insides, his escape plans morphed into protecting a future mission. As a team, all they could do was try everything in their power to succeed. If he sent a failed message, he had ordered the cydroids to assume they were dead, destroy the computer, level the place, and take the program to one of the Robinhooders at Colorado Springs to try again.

He wished he could have left it at that, but the devil's advocate in his head piped in. The cydroids would try to clear the building first, and the time it took may cause them to fail. Cali Bantu was discovered, and even now, the Elites were trying to destroy it. Within a few days, they were sure to succeed.

Or, what if they did succeed in destroying the Command and the Elites throughout the territory? It would leave the whole territory without any kind of order or direction. The following chaos would result in many deaths. Without trained humans to direct the cydroids, Colorado would tumble into an even darker age and further shift the balance of power. If they destroyed the C.I.s, other states could move in, and their leaders may be more abysmal than Colorado's Elites.

No, Connor must be allowed to restore the plan and purge the bad programming. But how? There were no moves left. I'm in a complete checkmate situation.

When he came out of his thoughts, he looked at Connor. He seemed to ignore the red dots covering his body. His young face shone with an unwavering determination, and that gaze was directed at Relic. *What was he up to?*

Relic was scanning the room, searching for some miraculous answer, when he saw Connor focusing on him. When Connor saw he had Relic's attention, the boy slowly, very slowly, raised his hand to wipe away a wayward lock of hair, but he drew his straightened fingers across his right eye in a slicing movement before tucking his hair behind his ear.

Relic's eyes froze onto Connor, keeping his focus on the threatened boy. Garriset gave a discerning look, going back and forth between them. He could see they were communicating and plotting something.

Relic was staring without seeing what his gaze fell upon. He had turned his sight inward. Mentally going through what Connor's signal could mean, wishing he had Connor's memory. *Right eye..., hand across the right eye..., straight hand across eye, eye, something about the eye. Hand like a blade, cut the eye..., of course, that's it! "slice the eye".*

Relic never met Will's stepmother, but he knew her father. It was he who introduced him to the Robinhood contact in the Highmind camp. That woman helped him escape and secured his transportation to the Fringers. *What was it her father said? Something like "Cyber Intellect, my eye," and then he said, "stab and slice."* He always thought it was about the man's anger, but it was odd and disconnected from the conversation at the time. But he said it with such intensity, Relic often rehashed it, trying to make sense of it. But it made sense now.

A low whisper came from behind him, where Garriset stood holding the knife at his throat. He deduced there was some messaging going on between them. "Don't make me cut you."

Perhaps that was the answer. If he could get into an altercation with Garriset and survive long enough to reach the marble symbol, it might initiate the shutdown. However, the surviving part seemed unlikely if the man sliced his jugular.

"You'll be punished if you kill me," Relic said in a low whisper.

"I said I'd cut you, not kill you," came the response.

That was all the reassurance Relic needed. He elbowed Garriset and reached for the knife. The strong general held it firmly, plunging it into Relic's shoulder, and then the general fell to the floor. This confused Relic momentarily because he did nothing to cause the man to fall. Relic moaned as he quickly pulled the dagger out of his shoulder and stabbed the broken circle at the top of the letter "I" and dragged the blade downward, tracing the curve of the letter from top to bottom.

Simultaneously, Gray lunged at Connor, covering his body with his own. The screen froze, the red dots vanished, but not before several bullets flew across the room. The screen turned black, and the marble wall rolled open, sending dust into the room as though it had not been opened for decades. It led to a room full of unblinking electronics where a cydroid was crouched in inactive mode.

"Are you okay, Connor?" Gray said, looking the boy over for signs of damage.

The boy nodded, stunned and silent in terror.

Kenner crawled under the open desk and grabbed a pistol he had hidden. In an instant, it was pointed at Gray's chest. Gray thought about wrestling it from him, but the resulting bullet could go through him and into Connor.

Back to checkmate.

"Stop where you are, Jonathan," Kenner said with disdain.

It was at that moment that Will's team arrived. Dom, who had been standing at the door, signaled him to stay low. Will worked his way around the receptionist's desk and used his peer-around to check out the scene just as it had gone down. Relic saw the small probe peeking into the office. He hoped it was Will's team, and he moaned loudly to draw attention away from the door.

Will located Relic, holding his shoulder next to Garriset, who was sitting on the floor. He wasn't assisting his comrade, interesting. Gray was on the floor in front of the desk, protecting Connor, and rising to his feet above them was Kenner with a pistol pointed at him.

Will spoke silently to Altan before he carefully stepped through the door with his empty hands raised. He looked over at the man whom he blamed for his parents' death, his decades of loneliness, and his fated duty that led to this moment. He tried to come up with a witty retort to begin the exchange, but after all the years of planning for this scene, he never considered the words he would say. His repeated vision only involved a bloody fight using nothing but his physical strength. He needed to feel this coward's punches and jabs, but mostly, he wanted Kenner to feel his.

"Kenner," he said, standing in front of him, "let me introduce myself. I am William Alexander, son of Benjamin Alexander and stepson of Miranda Logan. We have unfinished business, and it's time to settle it."

"In case you're too dense to notice, I have my gun ready, and you are unarmed," he said as he swung the piece to and fro to show it to Will.

At that instant, the gun flew out of his hands and clunked into the magnetic claw of Altan. Kenner tried to move away from Gray, who was reaching for him, but Will caught him first. He grabbed him by the front of his shirt and dragged the shocked reprobate up to face him. The cydroids waited for their orders, but none came.

"You were saying?" Will said as his fist smashed into the weasel's cheek. He could have knocked him out with one punch, but that was not how this was going to go. Gray grabbed the gun from the cydroid and gestured for Garriset to stay down. The medic cydroid went over to Relic and foamed his wound, which was deep but not life-threatening.

Connor knew he'd been hit, but so far, no one seemed to notice. He couldn't let them coddle him or stop him from getting the card. He crawled over to retrieve the card that had been ripped out of Kenner's hand and thrown to the floor by Will. Still crawling on the floor, he grabbed his vest and strapped it back on. With a gasp, he pulled it as tight as he could to press against the hole in his core. He hoped it would slow the leak, so he could fulfill his purpose.

The two men engaged in fighting, and everyone's attention was on them. Pulling himself up, he stumbled and grabbed the wall, leaving a small bloody handprint. He followed Relic into the network room.

The shutdown left the room in darkness, with no trace of electronic life detected. It was quickly lit up by two cydroids, and they searched for the slot to insert the answer Connor held in his hand.

The console looked exactly like the one at Cali Bantu, and they quickly lifted the lid that hid the card slot. Lights began to blink, and beeps resounded through the room, and the cydroid came to life. The humming of cooling devices whirled, causing vibrations they could feel through their shoes, and a surge of power brought the room back to life. When the screen came on, Dr. Bera appeared.

"You have begun the reset process. To verify authorization, please enter the answers to the following questions." The first question appeared, triggering Connor's hyperthymesic memory while fists flew in the adjacent office.

Kenner countered Will's shot to his face with a right jab to the gut. Will was glad the rat's body wasn't as weak as his mind. The pain he delivered was cathartic, and Will responded with a left cross. No one interfered with the two warriors as wrath clouded their minds with primal aggression. The fight continued for several more minutes with both men landing painful blows to each other. Will hit Kenner square in the jaw and swept his feet out from under him. Kenner lay looking up at Will.

Though his prey was dazed and defeated, Will was still angry and ready for more. Blood oozed from Kenner's swollen eye and nose, and the gash at the edge of his mouth hung open. Will wiped the blood from his own mouth and then onto his pants. His hands were ripped up and bruised, but it wasn't pain he felt. It was retribution. Though the debt was far from paid, he would settle for bloodying his face and worry about justice later.

"Don't kill me. I hear you retrain people. With all that I know, I could be a valuable military asset," said the desperate man.

"I could never trust you, and I will never forgive you. You've killed my parents, my childhood, and every day of my life since then. You are the evil I see when I mourn all that I have lost. You have tortured, raped, and murdered hundreds of men, women, and children. Their cries scream for justice, and by God, they shall have it," Will voice thundered at the beaten man.

His fake pleading demeanor changed into a snarl. "You think I owe you, but you'll get no kind of payment from me. You know why?" he spat blood on the floor, "I'm not worried. You won't kill me in cold blood because you're a coward. But I'm not like you. I will kill you, and I'll enjoy it," he said as more of his blood drooled on the floor.

Will left him lying there and walked over to the marble wall, the other general was leaning against, awaiting his fate. Will retrieved the bloody knife from the wall. He considered the man who could have killed Relic and prevented this turnabout. He could have easily grabbed the knife himself and used it in a defensive move to help Kenner, but he did neither of these things.

"Watch out!" Garriset yelled.

Will turned quickly when he glimpsed movement behind him. Kenner was grabbing something from his ankle. It was another gun. Will let the blade fly, and it sank deep into the forehead of his foe. He dropped instantly as blood pumped across his surprised eyes and down his face to pool on the floor.

"Now it's paid," Will said quietly to himself.

He looked at his other prisoner. "General Garriset, I'm not sure what to make of you or where your loyalties lie. You're either in-competent or very clever. Since you participated in the distraction we needed to gain control, I'm guessing it's the latter. If you want to join us in restoring freedom to the people, I will grant you that opportunity. But you will be under a strict probation period. Do you have a family?"

Garriset nodded. Will went on to explain that his family would be safe if he could meet the hardship of trading sides to join his army. It was the same speech he gave to all his prisoners of war, and then he reached out his hand and helped the man to his feet. Two cydroids quickly moved to secure the prisoner.

As Will walked to the computer room, he noticed the bloody print on the wall. He knew it wasn't Relic's because the fingers were small, like a child's. Connor was staring at a question on the screen.

"What do Alexander III of Macedonia, Socrates, and Aristotle have in common?"

"They were all students and teachers of Plato's philosophies," came a voice from the entryway.

Though the question wasn't particularly difficult, it consisted of unnecessary philosophical and cultural knowledge. Since they completely blocked the Tessera and Pente programs, the three corrupt Elites didn't have access to them. And therefore, neither did the Uppers, but it was specifically taught to all the highest-ranking Robin-hooders, and to Will by his step-mother.

Connor turned to see Will, who was observing him with serious intent.

The screen flashed, "Last question: What is the counter move to the opening move Kb to a3?"

"G7 to d5," Connor answered quickly, his voice starting to waver. He leaned heavily on the console, smearing blood across it. Will froze, knowing that was not a legal chess move. Connor was wounded and obviously not thinking correctly. The boy was looking pale and in shock. It was more than the trauma of the situation. He was hurt badly.

"Correct," came the response. "Place your finger in the opening next to the blinking red light."

Connor was dizzy, too dizzy to think. He was feeling the full effect of the two bullets that pounded his body, with at least one going through him. But he couldn't stop now. He had to finish. He was just thankful that the layers of clothing tucked tightly into his pants hid the blood he could feel pooling against him. He was trying to see the DNA scanner, but Relic stepped up and pushed the boy's finger inside the opening.

He was hanging on to the console, unable to focus on the blur before him. Will walked over to where the blood was starting to puddle around Connor, and the boy collapsed in his arms.

"If you have reached this screen, you are ready to initiate a program reboot. Click the lotus flower at the center of the screen to begin. If you have questions, speak them out loud," said Dr. Bera.

"I think this is my specialty," said Relic. "I'll take it from here."

Will lifted the boy in his arms, disregarding his weak mumbling protests.

"I'm fine," Connor said. "Relic ... needs me."

"Your job is done, and you are leaking all over the floor," Will said with concern. When he picked him up, the blood that had pooled in his tucked-in shirt under his vest came spilling out. Will was shocked at how much there was.

Will rushed him out to the medic cydroid next to Gray, who was being treated for the bullet grazes he incurred. Connor crumbled on the floor where Will set him, and both he and Gray began to remove his gear. His wound was serious. The cydroid medic called for another. The two cydroids began foaming his wounds, and he moaned. Two more cydroids transformed into a gurney, and he was whisked away to the medical facility on the floor below.

"I had no idea he was hit," Gray gasped. He rubbed his forehead like he always did when terrible things happened.

"Will he be okay?" Will asked, wondering how such a young child could power through such injuries. He felt his admiration and concern for the boy rise exponentially. Will and Gray looked at each other. Still processing all that was gained, they stood stunned at what was at stake. The death of a child, another child, Gray lamented, would be unbearable. What had they done?

"Connor's injuries are serious. We are taking him to the medical facility in this building. It is well-equipped to address his injuries," answered the medic cydroid as others were whisking the boy through the office door. "An update will be provided after we complete his examination."

Just then, Etcher came running through the door. "I saw the robots take a body out, and that poor kid, too. Is he going to be okay? Is anyone else hurt?" She was searching the room, not finding who she was looking for

"Relic and Gray suffered injuries," answered the cydroid between her and her commander. Etcher walked around the cydroid and addressed Will directly. "Relic was hurt! Is he okay? Can I see him?" she asked with slight desperation in her voice. "Please?"

"Relic's wounds are minor as well as Commander Gray's. Relic is needed in the control room to reboot the system. He cannot be disturbed as we wait to see if the reboot is transferred throughout the three Colorado territories. The process is fully automated after the human commands are authorized, but there was some concern that the other command centers may have blocked the signal. We are waiting for confirmation," answered Dagny.

Will went in to check on Relic's progress. He was standing before the screen, watching a stream of data files scroll by. When Relic turned, he saw the blood on Will's vest and pants. It wasn't his. It was Connor's. And it was a lot.

"How is Connor?" Relic asked with the horror of his sudden realization.

"He's in rough shape. We'll know more when the cydroids finish examining him. Evidently, there is a high-tech medical facility here."

"Yes, every command center has one to initiate and monitor the manipulative biomite program. It has top-of-the-line exam equipment and a full surgical theater." Will's eyebrows rose in alarm. "No need to worry, Will. The equipment is useful for all types of emergencies. Connor is in the best of care. I should go and offer to donate my blood. Connor and I have an uncommon type. Look, Colorado Springs just came online."

Relic came out of the door, holding his shoulder when Etcher ran to him. "I was so worried," her feelings for him on full display.

Relic looked confused. He was doing a double-take at the concern on her face. They had been flirting and gesturing, but he never got a clear signal about how she felt. Could he be this lucky, or was she just happy about the mission?

"Everything is going as planned," Relic said as Etcher rested her head on his shoulder. "I do not have confirmation on Denver, but with Colorado Springs and Pueblo secured, they wouldn't be able to stop us—" he didn't get to finish before she had her hands tenderly on either side of his face as she kissed him deeply. He put his hands on her shoulder and took a step back. He smiled at her and kissed her again.

Will looked at the two. A twinge of sadness swirled in his heart, but he had come to terms with the truth. He had good friends, and he knew he was cared about, but he would never have someone like that in his life. He failed miserably the first two times and almost got Molly killed. He wasn't sure what his new path was, but he knew he would walk it alone. He had made peace with that. He went downstairs to check on Easton and update him.

"So does that mean we won?" Easton asked naively, looking at Will.

"We may have a few scattered battles to fight, but once we have control of the cydroids, they will play a big part in fulfilling that part of the mission. We have four hundred cydroids here, and with the citizens in lockdown, if we can activate them and the ones in Colorado Springs and Denver from here, within hours, we will gain control of all three territories."

Easton looked at Will, still waiting for the words he needed to hear.

Will smiled, "Yeah, we won."

Gray, Relic, and Will sat at the conference table in Pueblo Command. They were listening to the five C.I.s give reports regarding the status of the territories within their departments of expertise. Gone were the power suits and severe expressions of the Elites. Their appearances had returned to model their original presentations, and their demeanors and voices were informative, cooperative, and benevolent.

The reports were preliminary and gave an overview of the immediate objectives for stabilizing the Colorado territories and the logical ways to proceed. The army of Pueblo cydroids had been fully activated, and their tasks were being downloaded and assigned according to Dr. Bera's vision. When they successfully established a secure government in Colorado, they would repair the needed infrastructure of the territory. When the Colorado Territories were securely established, the next step would be to reach out to other states to evaluate their status and offer the people their assistance.

The conference was surprisingly short for all the items on the agenda, but the health advisor, Dio, could see the humans were weary and distracted, and the meeting ended. Gray didn't want to deal with the problems their triumph had caused. He needed to check on Connor. Taking time to grasp the surreal experience of their victory would come after he was out of danger. The rest of the team left the room, while Gray remained seated in the silence, trying to gather his thoughts.

Being victorious in war wasn't all joy like winning the game of the season. Real people were hurt, some would be emotionally and physically maimed for the rest of their lives, and some had lost their lives, all to make this day possible. To say that the day had been demanding would belittle what they had gone through. There were no words for how he felt. He knew it could have been worse, and that was part of why it plagued him so. For him, it could easily rank as the most traumatic day of his life, and putting it down would be a long, arduous process.

Gray was overcome when Jilly's face appeared on the screen. Every possible emotion swam through Gray's head upon seeing she was safe. He had been told, but seeing and hearing her was so much better. Relief and happiness washed over him. It finally hit him. They had won. An ambitious plan and hard work may lie ahead, but they had won. The mission that seemed impossible less than an hour ago was completed. But after all the joyful exchanges upon seeing each other, he knew she would ask. She would want to know how Connor was. And he would have to break her heart.

Connor was in surgery, and his survival was touch-and-go. He had taken two rounds. One hit a book he had in his breast pocket, and though it didn't penetrate his body, it left a serious contusion near his heart. But the other one hit his liver. Relic, who had also suffered a knife wound, was the only suitable donor. He gave as much blood as the medics deemed prudent, but the child needed more than Relic could spare. The word went out to find other donors, but time and Connor's chances were slipping away.

Epilogue

Ten months later

This year, Silverthorn hosted the Harfest gathering as a reveal for cydroids' town renewal project. They had removed the land mines and repaired many of its downtown buildings. The town center looked incredible, with strong artistic structures that humans and cydroids worked on side by side to get ready for this event. It was the first of many recolonization projects they had planned.

So many things were in the works across Colorado, uniting and healing the communities. The first steps were more cathartic than constructive. The abandoned Pleasure House was burned to the ground in a riot by the citizens, and no one stopped them. The crematorium was demolished, and a memorial was erected in its place for the all workers who died there. The horrific secret about the nature of its existence eventually leaked out, but it was one more outrage heaped on all of the other outrages. There was little doubt the generations to come would look unfavorably on the compliant citizens of the times, but without living through it, it would be heartless to assign blame.

Vast farms and open-range ranches were constructed, and with the formula Jilly and Ari's father created to replicate food, their supplies increased five-fold. Hunger was quickly becoming a thing of the past, affecting only those in very rural areas. Their crops and output would continue to grow as the farms and ranches took off.

The overhauling of hospitals, labs, factories, and commerce buildings invoked a new sensation in the people—stability. Schools were refurbished and repaired. Teachers were being trained and assisted by newly assembled androids in classroom instruction. Schools throughout Colorado were scheduled to open in September.

Roads, dwellings, churches, and much more were repaired to grease the gears of commerce and improve the lives of the citizens. Though the caste system had been eliminated, the healing from it was was ongoing. Education was one of the tools used to empower the people, but as Haru often said, the laws are in place, but it will take time for the culture to change. And that change depended more on individuals learning to embrace their new identity as a free and engaged citizens than on their thoughts of others.

It had only been eight months since the great victory over the Elites, and though there was more to do, the people's lives were much better already. And this year's fall celebration was proof of that. People were beginning to trust and invest in their futures. There were more pledges and marriages planned than in any year previous, as well as an increase in pregnancies.

Axle and Jax had revealed their secret pledge months ago, and they had been one of the couples in the ceremony. Their families and team members toasted them and offered their blessings.

"This year's wedding ceremonies were the most beautiful I've ever seen," Tommie said.

"Well, I only saw last year's, and they were rushed because the Friendship Tour was a last-minute cover plan for the mission. But I admit this party has been top-notch," said Axle.

"I think it was the new pledge announcements that caught my attention. It wasn't surprising that Relic and Etcher pledged, or that you and Jax had secretly committed. But Dean and Aniya and Haru and Leita were a bit of a shock," said Gray while bouncing little Jace on his lap. Dean just smiled at his bride.

"Yeah, I didn't think anyone could settle Dean Rival down," Will smirked. "That guy could... well, let me just say he should have had a warning label."

"Don't listen to a word of his tall tales, Honey. Those days just prove none of them were the one," Dean crooned affectionately.

"You've got nothing to worry about," Will affirmed. "Besides, Axle and I will take him for a long, painful walk if he even thinks about hurting you."

Will gave Dean a big smile, remembering Dean's woman-chasing days at the Neighwah Rec Room. But his smile faded at the thought of Molly. He may have only broken one woman's heart, but he did it mercilessly. She wasn't the only one who suffered. He fell deeply in love with her, and though he cruelly dumped her, it was due to the danger he was putting her in. But he did nothing when she was abused by the jerk the Corporates set on her. He had to prove that she meant nothing to him, or she would have received more than a bruised cheek.

There was no way to excuse what he did and no pathway to ever seeing her again. She owed him nothing, but his debt was immeasurable. He was glad to hear she had recovered from her wound and the biomites he infected her with. Though it pained him greatly, he made Dean promise to never divulge how she was, where she was, or who she was with. He owed her that much.

His mood soured considerably, and he felt himself scowling as he spotted Leita. He could see she was happy. He had been fresh from the Denver battle when she told him, with irritating giddiness, that she and Haru were pledged. That was painful enough, but she went further to add, under the guise of compassion, that he should find someone, now that he was free.

He was free, but not to do that. It was true the threat to people close to him was eliminated when the Sanguine Blade opened the marble door. Many beautiful and intelligent women had shown interest in him, but it was pointless because he was overwhelmed with regret. He had behaved selfishly with the two women he cared about the most.

He shouldn't have committed to Molly, and he couldn't commit to Leita. If he truly cared, he would have left both of them alone from the start. Maybe he wasn't cut out for a relationship. He remembered how nice holding someone he cared about felt, but it just was not meant to be.

It was then that Connor walked up to the table with Jilly. "Well, if it isn't, Mr. Connor Jace Wayther, the man of the year," Gray said as he stood up and handed baby Jace to Jilly.

"I keep wondering when people will stop thanking me and asking how I am. We all made this happen. If anyone needs thanking, it's Relic and Theo for donating their blood, and I mean a lot of their blood. Theo was in jail and volunteered to let strange robots stick him and suck his blood out. He didn't know who he could trust, but he volunteered for a procedure to save me. That's why I'm here eating this huge floppy doughnut," Connor smiled.

"It's not a doughnut. It's an elephant ear," said Jedi, sitting next to his wife and two daughters.

"Gross," Connor replied while taking a large bite of the pastry.

"Theo's doing great, by the way," Gray added. "He and Dewy have become good friends. He's staying in the men's dorm in New Haven.

He's still on probation, but he's working on a degree in mechanics. He says he wants to get his mechanical engineering degree. Smart kid,"

"Yeah, I see him sometimes at the Rec Center," Connor said.

"Hey Hero," Teke yelled his friend's new nickname.

"I liked Condor-man so much better," Connor said with a sideways smirk.

"Come on, we've got a game to play," shouted Hayden.

Just then, Sandra walked by in her new clothes, which hugged her a little too tightly. She gave Connor one of her knock-out smiles, but he just waved.

Gray said quietly to Will, "That's his first heartbreaker."

Will chuckled, "Looks like she wants another shot at our star."

Connor gave them both an annoyed look and turned to Jedi's older daughter, April, who looked completely bored sitting with her parents and her toddler sister. "Do you want to come watch the game?" Connor put on his best cool act. He expected her to decline.

"No, but I'd like to play. Is the shortstop position available?" she answered with a grin. It wasn't a Sandra smile, fake and flawless. It was genuine, warm, and perfect.

Connor beamed. "It is now, " he said as he took her hand and led her away from the table.

Everyone smiled except Jedi. Connor was thirteen, and he was seeing him in a different light.

"Relax, Jedi. He's a good kid," said Dean.

"He was girl crazy last year at twelve, and now he's thirteen. I know he's a good kid, but he's already got her hand in his. Truth be told, I do trust him. That's what scares me," he laughed.

Hunter called Will over, and he left the table to talk with him. "I have a surprise for you."

"Really, are you getting hitched too?" Will jested. "Let me guess. Tommie." Will said, looking over at a very femininely dressed Tommie, smiling at Hunter.

"No," he blushed slightly. "Dio said you needed a little vacation, and he asked me where you might want to go. I said you would probably like to spend some time at your old cabin."

"Maybe you forgot, but I burned that to the ground," Will answered.

"No, I remembered, but let's just say I had the cydroids rebuild it."

"Seriously?" Will thought about all the stuff he should stay and take care of.

"Don't go saying you have responsibilities and shit to do. You need to have a little faith, trust us to do our job."

"You mean trust you to do *my* job," Will said, but a smile was beginning to warm his face. "Maybe you're right."

Early the next morning, Will packed a four-wheeler with the supplies he would need for a week in the wild woods. He was looking forward to being alone. He had to straighten his mind out, and this was just what he needed.

He enjoyed the freedom that the mission ushered in, and he had lots of work to do, but he used to have a mighty purpose. It was overwhelming at times, and for most of his life, that purpose was bigger than he was. But now, he had a job, and its purpose was, well, ordinary. Maybe it would get more interesting when they began contacting other states, but that wasn't on the docket for six months, if not a year.

"Looks like I'm taking a vacation," Will replied.

The dirt road had been scraped, making the journey relaxing, but the scenery was just as wild as he remembered. He recalled how much delight he found in the simple pleasures of life. He flashed back on swimming in the river on hot days and watching the stars on crisp autumn nights. He spent many months gathering the food the forest provided. After cold walks in the snow-covered mountains, he would rub his hands in front of the warmth of the wood stove.

When he came to the path that led up to his cabin site, a flash of movement caught his attention. He parked his ATV and crept around the tree. There stood his lead cydroid, Altan, next to Little Bet, who was munching on leaves. *Wow, they thought of everything.*

"How are you doing, boy?" he said, rubbing his horse's neck. "I know I've been neglecting you, but I hear Anyia has taken good care of you," Will said. "So Altan, are you here to babysit me?"

"Hell no, sir," Altan responded. "That would be damned impossible."

Will laughed out loud. "Well said. I think you are getting the hang of this swearing thing."

Will climbed up on Little Bet and clicked his cheeks. The trail was more even and tame than when he used it last, and he rode up to the cottage effortlessly with Altan walking behind them. As he rounded the last bend, he saw the cabin, which was larger than his old cabin had been. A flower box filled with growing herbs sat under an open window, with curtains fluttering lightly. He passed a flat area with a fire pit surrounded by large stones and log benches. A supply of split wood was neatly stacked under a lean-to shed. Altan had been busy.

He walked inside and was instantly greeted by the warmth of the wood-burning cook stove complete with a hot-box oven. A variety of cast-iron pans and cooking utensils hung on a rail suspended from the ceiling. Three shelves sported dishes, cups, bowls, a knife block, and a metal jar with tableware. A towel hung on a hook next to the large window centered over a porcelain farm sink.

Wildflowers sat on the table, spreading out from a canning jar. That was a rather feminine touch, but he didn't mind it. The leather couch was comfortable and soft, with a Fringer-made blanket casually draped over it for decoration. A digital audiobox, designed to look like a 1950s antique radio, sat on a side table. He walked to the door and saw the bathroom. It was simple but functional, with running water, a shower, a sink, and a flushing toilet.

"That will make winter much easier," he said softly to no one.

He opened the last door quickly, which was no doubt the bedroom. His swift swing of the door gently fluttered the whisper-thin sheers bordered by heavy drapes. To one the side of the room was a small fireplace that crackled and glowed through its iron-laced screen. But it was the person lying in the bed that had his attention. *Had some Lone Fringer claimed his place?*

"Excuse me," he said, and the woman stirred, turning toward him.

It was Molly. He stood stunned, not sure he wasn't hallucinating.

"Took you long enough to get here," Molly said as she sent him the sweetest smile he had ever seen.

He was frozen in place. He didn't know what this meant. All he could think to say was, "What... I... Is someone... Are you okay?"

She rolled her feet to the floor and climbed off the tousled bed. Her sweater was slowly untwisting to hang just above her tight jeans. Admiring the delicious curvy woman before him sent desire surging through him while his guilt battled it down.

"I see you're going to overthink this," she said waiting for a response, but none came. He remained stuck in his shocked stance. "Of course you are, so here is a history lesson. When you dumped me, I was angry, but even then, I couldn't bring myself to hate you. You're whole being screams noble causes and loyalty. I knew something bigger was going on, and it would be just like you to sacrifice yourself to the thick of it. The Robinhooders contacted me and explained what you did was to protect me. I was warned I may still be in danger, but they would do their best to keep me safe. They never explained why you were so important, but right after that, I got word of your death. I was crushed.

"I loved you so much, and it hurt so bad that I joined the cause you died for. After the tunnel battle, I found out you were still alive. I volunteered to support the Allied Army on the Reclamation Mission, hoping I'd see you. But before the mission got on the road, I was captured, and they biomited me.

"The training was brutal, but when they were done, I couldn't say anything but the Corporate lies they programmed me to say. I hated doing it. They convinced me that if I tried to tell the truth, I would die a horrible death. I convinced myself that if I lied and acted like a traitor, the Allied Army would put me out of my misery. Either way, I accepted the fact that I would die. But you saved me. And I'm here, I'm well, and I'm with you. Thank you, Will." Molly got on her tip-toes and kissed his cheek.

He was speechless, but a smile broke across his face. This had to be a dream, but if it was, he would damn the morning.

"Are you going to just stare at me all day?" She put her hands on her hips when he was slow to answer. "Will, are you going to kiss me already, or do I have to beg?"

"Well, I have to admit," he said with a mischievous smile that sent tingles all through her body, "I always did like it when you begged." Before she could respond, he had taken her in his arms, and his lips and body were pressing on hers hungrily.

Acknowledgements

What a ride! I can't believe I have concluded both the *From Darkness* and the *Highmind* series. This five-year journey has been as engaging as it has been exhausting. i owe my steadfastness to the many people who have supported me and encouraged me to follow this path.

Though every childhood is awash with trials, I always felt loved, protected, and nurtured to become who I was meant to be. I thank my parents and family for inspiring me to be a lifelong learner and curious about everything.

My husband, Bryan, has demonstrated time and again that he is my biggest fan. He lovingly agreed to my requests to spend thousands of our family savings on this venture. We traded in our old RV to get one that had a desk and took a cross-country book-signing trek. He reads everything I write, and he's my business manager too, which is by far his toughest job. I thank God every day for sending him my way.

The support of our children, Russ, Aaron, Garrett, Corrin, and their families has been invaluable. I am so happy to leave these six books as a living legacy for them and their children.

I thank Ashleigh for painting my cover. She also painted the cover for *Somewhere Else*, the first book of the *Highmind* series. She is an amazing artist, and a wonderful daughter-in-law.

My siblings, Carol, Lorraine, and my brother, Richard, have provided an ongoing chorus of validation and support. My in-law family has spent hours reading, encouraging, and drumming up sales.

I love you all so much. I thank God every day for being blessed with the best family ever.

I received additional help and advice from a list of incredible people: my cousins, David, Allison, and Cindy; my friends, Brenda, Terry, Becky, Lindy, and Erin; and all my teachers, especially Fay Wright, who inspired me to keep writing. They all led me here. I want to thank my business associates: Laura Jones, RG Graph X Design, CIN Library Network, KXLY News, Ali & Callie Artcast at Arts and Culture CdA, and the ad people at BestSellerInc. for their professional help.

My most humble and gracious appreciation goes to my readers. I am grateful to the many people who have purchased my books. I loved the warm welcome I received at my book signings, where you helped me sell out numerous times. I give an excited shout-out to my online buyers for finding me in the deep sea of choices. I am also thankful to everyone who has visited and joined my website. I thoroughly treasure every comment I get.

If you have left me an honest review on Amazon or elsewhere, THANK YOU! From the bottom of my heart, thank you.

Last, but most importantly, I thank God and pray every day that He guides us all to a place of forgiveness, joy, and inspiration. I pray that His love shines brightly in every heart. I praise Him for the care and love He provides us. Bless you all. Amen

About the Author

I was sitting with my daughter, recalling all the stages I've been through on my journey as an author. The initial edition of ***Sins of Survival,*** my first novel, poured out of me like a bursting dam. I was excited and launched my book without making an informed plan. I hastily published my book with a hybrid-publisher before it was ready. I discovered I had paid for a publishing service, not a publishing company. Several years later, I revised it and launched it as a second edition.

If I were to give advice to beginning novelists, it would be to take your time and revise your work many times. Then, when you think you are done, take a long break and do a deep dive into all the options for publishing. After a month, reread your work again. If you still believe it is ready, find some beta readers.

Most writers are artists and find marketing much more laborious than writing. Getting sales is challenging, but getting reviews is many times harder. If you are reading this, *I hope* you *will take the time to review my work* and the work of other authors. This whole endeavor is meaningless without your validation.

I learned the hard way through the fires of hubris that there will always be new things to learn. New genres, new writing styles, new publishing options, and a market that ebbs and flows relentlessly.

Throughout this journey, there have been ups and downs, but I am blessed to be able to write, so I embrace every bit of it. I have written six books, and each subsequent book reveals my growing skills and dedication to my craft. Thank you for purchasing my work. It is my honor to share my words with you.

Visit me at Roxannewardauthor.com

www.ingramcontent.com/pod-product-compliance
Lightning Source LLC
Chambersburg PA
CBHW070303310726
48976CB00005B/1555

9 798988 001041